Mr. Scarborough's Family
Vol. I

Mr. Scarborough's Family
Vol. I

by

Anthony Trollope

CAMBRIDGE
SCHOLARS
PUBLISHING

classic texts

Mr. Scarborough's Family vol. I, by Anthony Trollope

This book in its current typographical format first published 2008 by

Cambridge Scholars Publishing

12 Back Chapman Street, Newcastle upon Tyne, NE6 2XX, UK

British Library Cataloguing in Publication Data
A catalogue record for this book is available from the British Library

ISBN (10): 1-84718-713-7, ISBN (13): 9781847187130

CONTENTS

CHAPTER I. MR. SCARBOROUGH

It will be necessary, for the purpose of my story, that I shall go back more than once from the point at which it begins, so that I may explain with the least amount of awkwardness the things as they occurred, which led up to the incidents that I am about to tell; and I may as well say that these first four chapters of the book—though they may be thought to be the most interesting of them all by those who look to incidents for their interest in a tale—are in this way only preliminary.

The world has not yet forgotten the intensity of the feeling which existed when old Mr. Scarborough declared that his well-known eldest son was not legitimate. Mr. Scarborough himself had not been well known in early life. He had been the only son of a squire in Staffordshire over whose grounds a town had been built and pottery-works established. In this way a property which had not originally been extensive had been greatly increased in value, and Mr. Scarborough, when he came into possession, had found himself to be a rich man. He had then gone abroad, and had there married an English lady. After the lapse of some years he had returned to Tretton Park, as his place was named, and there had lost his wife. He had come back with two sons, Mountjoy and Augustus, and there, at Tretton, he had lived, spending, however, a considerable portion of each year in chambers in the Albany. He was a man who, through many years, had had his own circle of friends, but, as I have said before, he was not much known in the world. He was luxurious and self-indulgent, and altogether indifferent to the opinion of those around him. But he was affectionate to his children, and anxious above all things for their welfare, or rather happiness. Some marvellous stories were told as to his income, which arose chiefly from the Tretton delf-works and from the town of Tretton, which had been built chiefly on his very park, in consequence of the nature of the clay and the quality of the water. As a fact, the original four thousand a year, to which his father had been born, had grown to twenty thousand by nature of the operations which had taken place. But the whole of this, whether four thousand or twenty thousand, was strictly entailed, and Mr. Scarborough had been very anxious, since his second son was born, to create for him also something which might amount to opulence. But they who knew him best knew that of all things he hated most the entail.

The boys were both educated at Eton, and the elder went into the Guards, having been allowed an intermediate year in order to learn languages on the Continent. He had then become a cornet in the Coldstreams, and had, from that time, lived a life of reckless expenditure. His brother Augustus had in the mean time gone to Cambridge and become a barrister. He had been called but two years when the story was made known of his father's singular assertion. As from that time it became unnecessary for him to practise his profession, no more was heard of him as a lawyer. But they who had known the young man in the chambers of that great luminary, Mr. Rugby, declared that a very eminent advocate was now spoiled by a freak of fortune.

Of his brother Mountjoy,—or Captain Scarborough, as he came to be known at an early period of his life,—the stories which were told in the world at large were much too remarkable to be altogether true. But it was only too true that he lived as though the wealth at his command were without limit. For some few years his father bore with him patiently, doubling his allowance, and paying his bills for him again and again. He made up his mind,—with many regrets,—that enough had been done for his younger son, who would surely by his intellect be able to do much for himself. But then it became necessary to encroach on the funds already put by, and at last there came the final blow, when he discovered that Captain Scarborough had raised large sums on post-obits from the Jews. The Jews simply requested the father to pay the money or some portion of it, which if at once paid would satisfy them, explaining to him that otherwise the whole property would at his death fall into their hands. It need not here be explained how, through one sad year, these negotiations were prolonged; but at last there came a time in which Mr. Scarborough, sitting in his chambers in the Albany, boldly declared his purpose. He sent for his own lawyer, Mr. Grey, and greatly astonished that gentleman by declaring to him that Captain Scarborough was illegitimate.

At first Mr. Grey refused altogether to believe the assertion made to him. He had been very conversant with the affairs of the family, and had even dealt with marriage settlements on behalf of the lady in question. He knew Mr. Scarborough well,—or rather had not known him, but had heard much of him,—and therefore suspected him. Mr. Grey was a thoroughly respectable man, and Mr. Scarborough, though upright and honorable in many dealings, had not been thoroughly respectable. He had lived with his wife off and on, as people say. Though he had saved much of his money for the purpose above described, he had also spent much of it in a manner which did not approve itself to Mr. Grey. Mr. Grey had thoroughly disliked the eldest son, and had, in fact, been afraid of him. The captain, in the few interviews that had been necessary between them, had attempted to domineer over the lawyer, till there had at last sprung up a quarrel, in which, to tell the truth, the father took the part of the son. Mr. Grey had for a while been so offended as to find it necessary to desire Mr. Scarborough to employ another lawyer. He had not, however, done so, and the breach had never become absolute. In these circumstances Mr. Scarborough had sent for Mr. Grey to come to him at the Albany, and had there, from his bed, declared that his eldest son was illegitimate. Mr. Grey had at first refused to accept the assertion as being worth anything, and had by no means confined himself to polite language in expressing his belief. "I would much rather have nothing to do with it," he had said when Mr. Scarborough insisted on the truth of his statement.

"But the evidence is all here," said Mr. Scarborough, laying his hand on a small bundle of papers. "The difficulty would have been, and the danger, in causing Mountjoy to have been accepted in his brother's place. There can be no doubt that I was not married till after Mountjoy was born."

Mr. Grey's curiosity was roused, and he began to ask questions. Why, in the first place, had Mr. Scarborough behaved so dishonestly? Why had he originally not married his wife? And then, why had he married her? If, as he said, the proofs were so easy, how had he dared to act so directly in opposition to the laws of his country? Why, indeed, had he been through the whole of his life so bad a man,—so bad to the woman who had borne his name, so bad to the son whom he called illegitimate, and so bad also to the other son whom he now intended to restore to his position, solely with the view of defrauding the captain's creditors?

In answer to this Mr. Scarborough, though he was suffering much at the time,—so much as to be considered near to his death,—had replied with the most perfect good-humor.

He had done very well, he thought, by his wife, whom he had married after she had consented to live with him on other terms. He had done very well by his elder son, for whom he had intended the entire property. He had done well by his second son, for whom he had saved his money. It was now his first duty to save the property. He regarded himself as being altogether unselfish and virtuous from his point of view.

When Mr. Grey had spoken about the laws of his country he had simply smiled, though he was expecting a grievous operation on the following day. As for marriage, he had no great respect for it, except as a mode of enabling men and women to live together comfortably. As for the "outraged laws of his country," of which Mr. Grey spoke much, he did not care a straw for such outrages—nor, indeed, for the expressed opinion of mankind as to his conduct. He was very soon about to leave the world, and meant to do the best he could for his son Augustus. The other son was past all hope. He was hardly angry with his eldest son, who had undoubtedly given him cause for just anger. His apparent motives in telling the truth about him at last were rather those of defrauding the Jews, who had expressed themselves to him with brutal audacity, than that of punishing the one son or doing justice to the other; but even of them he spoke with a cynical good-humor, triumphing in his idea of thoroughly getting the better of them.

"I am consoled, Mr. Grey," he said, "when I think how probably it might all have been discovered after my death. I should have destroyed all these," and he laid his hands upon the papers, "but still there might have been discovery."

Mr. Grey could not but think that during the last twenty-four years,—the period which had elapsed since the birth of the younger son,—no idea of such a truth had occurred to himself.

He did at last consent to take the papers in his hands, and to read them through with care. He took them away with that promise, and with an assurance that he would bring them back on the day but one following—should Mr. Scarborough then be alive.

Mr. Scarborough, who seemed at that moment to have much life in him, insisted on this proviso:—

"The surgeon is to be here to-morrow, you know, and his coming may mean a great deal. You will have the papers, which are quite clear, and will know what to do. I shall see Mountjoy myself this evening. I suppose he will have the grace to come, as he does not know what he is coming for."

Then the father smiled again, and the lawyer went.

Mr. Scarborough, though he was very strong of heart, did have some misgivings as the time came at which he was to see his son. The communication which he had to make was certainly one of vital importance. His son had some time since instigated him to come to terms with the "family creditors," as the captain boldly called them.

"Seeing that I never owed a shilling in my life, or my father before me, it is odd that I should have family creditors," the father had answered.

"The property has, then, at any rate," the son had said, with a scowl.

But that was now twelve months since, before mankind and the Jews among them had heard of Mr. Scarborough's illness. Now, there could be no question of dealing on favorable terms with these gentlemen. Mr. Scarborough was, therefore, aware that the evil thing which he was about to say to his son would have lost its extreme bitterness. It did not occur to him that, in making such a revelation as to his son's mother he would inflict any great grief on his son's heart. To be illegitimate would be, he thought, nothing unless illegitimacy carried with it loss of property. He hardly gave weight enough to the feeling that the eldest son was the eldest son, and too little to the triumph which was present to his own mind in saving the property for one of the family. Augustus was but the captain's brother, but he was the old squire's son. The two brothers had hitherto lived together on fairly good terms, for the younger had been able to lend money to the elder, and the elder had found his brother neither severe or exacting. How it might be between them when their relations with each other should be altogether changed, Mr. Scarborough did not trouble himself to inquire. The captain by his own reckless folly had lost his money, had lost all that fortune would have given him as his father's eldest son. After having done so, what could it matter to him whether he were legitimate or illegitimate? His brother, as possessor of Tretton Park, would be able to do much more for him than could be expected from a professional man working for his bread.

Mr. Scarborough had looked at the matter all round for the space of two years, and during the latter year had slowly resolved on his line of action. He had had no scruple in passing off his eldest-born as legitimate, and now would have none in declaring the truth to the world. What scruple need he have, seeing that he was so soon about to leave the world?

As to what took place at that interview between the father and the son very much was said among the clubs, and in societies to which Captain Mountjoy Scarborough was well known; but very little of absolute truth was ever revealed. It was known that Captain Scarborough left the room under the combined authority of apothecaries and servants, and that the old man had fainted from the effects of the interview. He had undoubtedly told the son of the simple facts as he had declared them to Mr. Grey, but had thought it to be unnecessary to confirm his statement by any proof. Indeed, the proofs, such as they were,—the written testimony, that is,—were at that moment in the hands of Mr. Grey, and to Mr. Grey the father had at last referred the son. But the son had absolutely refused to believe for a moment in the story, and had declared that his father and Mr. Grey had conspired together to rob him of his inheritance and good name. The interview was at last over, and Mr. Scarborough, at one moment fainting, and in the next suffering the extremest agony, was left alone with his thoughts.

Captain Scarborough, when he left his father's rooms, and found himself going out from the Albany into Piccadilly, was an infuriated but at the same time a most wretched man. He did believe that a conspiracy had been hatched, and he was resolved to do his best to defeat it, let the effect be what it might on the property; but yet there was a strong feeling in his breast that the fraud would be successful. No man could possibly be environed by worse circumstances as to his own condition. He owed he knew not what amount of money to several creditors; but then he owed, which troubled him more, gambling debts, which he could only pay by his brother's assistance. And now, as he thought of it, he felt convinced that his brother must be joined with his father and the lawyer in this conspiracy. He felt, also, that he could meet neither Mr. Grey nor his brother without personally attacking them. All the world might perish, but he, with his last breath, would declare himself to be Captain Mountjoy Scarborough, of Tretton Park; and though he knew at the moment that he must perish,—as regarded social life among his comrades,—unless he could raise five hundred pounds from his brother, yet he felt that, were he to meet his brother, he could not but fly at his throat and accuse him of the basest villany.

At that moment, at the corner of Bond Street, he did meet his brother.

"What is this?" said he, fiercely.

"What is what?" said Augustus, without any fierceness. "What is up now?"

"I have just come from my father."

"And how is the governor? If I were he I should be in a most awful funk. I should hardly be able to think of anything but that man who is to come to-morrow with his knives. But he takes it all as cool as a cucumber."

There was something in this which at once shook, though it did not remove, the captain's belief, and he said something as to the property. Then there came questions and answers, in which the captain did not reveal the story which had been told to him, but the barrister did assert that he had as yet heard nothing as to anything of importance. As to Tretton, the captain believed his brother's manner rather than his words. In fact, the barrister had heard nothing as yet of what was to be done on his behalf.

The interview ended in the two men going and dining at a club, where the captain told the whole story of his father's imagined iniquity.

Augustus received the tale almost in silence. In reply to his brother's authoritative, domineering speeches he said nothing. To him it was all new, but to him, also, it seemed certainly to be untrue. He did not at all bring himself to believe that Mr. Grey was in the conspiracy, but he had no scruple of paternal regard to make him feel that this father would not concoct such a scheme simply because he was his father. It would be a saving of the spoil from the Amalekites, and of this idea he did give a hardly-expressed hint to his brother.

"By George," said the captain, "nothing of the kind shall be done with my consent."

"Why, no," the barrister had answered, "I suppose that neither your consent nor mine is to be asked; and it seems as though it were a farce ordered to be played over the poor governor's grave. He has prepared a romance, as to the truth or falsehood of which neither you nor I can possibly be called as witnesses."

It was clear to the captain that his brother had thought that the plot had been prepared by their father in anticipation of his own death. Nevertheless, by the younger brother's assistance, the much-needed sum of money was found for the supply of the elder's immediate wants.

The next day was the day of terror, and nothing more was heard, either then or for the following week, of the old gentleman's scheme. In two days it was understood that his death might be hourly expected, but on the third it was thought that he might "pull through," as his younger son filially expressed himself. He was constantly with his father, but not a word passed his lips as to the property. The elder son kept himself gloomily apart, and indeed, during a part of the next week was out of London. Augustus Scarborough did call on Mr. Grey, but only learned from him that it was, at any rate, true that the story had been told by his father. Mr. Grey refused to make any farther communication, simply saying that he would as yet express no opinion.

"For myself," said Augustus, as he left the attorney's chambers, "I can only profess myself so much astonished as to have no opinion. I suppose I must simply wait and see what Fortune intends to do with me."

At the end of a fortnight Mr. Scarborough had so far recovered his strength as to be able to be moved down to Tretton, and thither he went. It was not many days after that "the world" was first informed that Captain Scarborough was not his father's heir. "The world" received the information with a great deal of expressed surprise and inward satisfaction,—satisfaction that the money-lenders should be done out of their money; that a professed gambler like Captain Scarborough should suddenly become an illegitimate nobody; and, more interesting still, that a very wealthy and well-conditioned, if not actually respectable, squire should have proved himself to be a most brazen-faced rascal. All of these were matters which gave extreme delight to the world at large. At first there came little paragraphs without any name, and then, some hours afterward, the names became known to the quidnuncs, and in a short space of time were in possession of the very gentry who found themselves defrauded in this singular manner.

It is not necessary here that I should recapitulate all the circumstances of the original fraud, for a gross fraud had been perpetrated. After the perpetration of that fraud papers had been prepared by Mr. Scarborough himself with a great deal of ingenuity, and the matter had been so arranged that,—but for his own declaration,—his eldest son would undoubtedly have inherited the property. Now there was no measure to the clamor and the uproar raised by the money-lenders. Mr. Grey's outer office was besieged, but his clerk simply stated that the facts would be proved on Mr. Scarborough's death as clearly as it might be possible to prove them. The curses uttered against the old squire were bitter and deep, but during this time he was still supposed to be lying at death's door, and did not, in truth, himself expect to live many days. The creditors, of course, believed that the story was a fiction. None of them were enabled to see Captain Scarborough, who, after a short period, disappeared altogether from the scene. But they were, one and all, convinced that the matter had been arranged between him and his father.

There was one from whom better things were expected than to advance money on post-obits to a gambler at a rate by which he was to be repaid one hundred pounds for every forty pounds, on the death of a gentleman who was then supposed to be dying. For it was proved afterward that this Mr. Tyrrwhit had made most minute inquiries among the old squire's servants as to the state of their master's health. He had supplied forty thousand pounds, for which he was to receive one hundred thousand pounds when the squire died, alleging that he should have difficulty in recovering the money. But he had collected the sum so advanced on better terms among his friends, and had become conspicuously odious in the matter.

In about a month's time it was generally believed that Mr. Scarborough had so managed matters that his scheme would be successful. A struggle was made to bring the matter at once into the law courts, but the attempt for the moment failed. It was said that the squire down at Tretton was too ill, but that proceedings would be taken as soon as he was able to bear them. Rumors were afloat that he would be taken into custody, and it was even asserted that two policemen were in the house at Tretton. But it was soon known that no policemen were there, and that the squire was free to go whither he would, or rather whither he could. In fact, though the will to punish him, and even to arrest him, was there, no one had the power to do him an injury.

It was then declared that he had in no sense broken the law,—that no evil act of his could be proved,—that though he had wished his eldest son to inherit the property wrongfully, he had only wished it; and that he had now simply put his wishes into unison with the law, and had undone the evil which he had hitherto only contemplated. Indeed, the world at large rather sympathized with the squire when Mr. Tyrrwhit's dealings became known, for it was supposed by many that Mr. Tyrrwhit was to have become the sole owner of Tretton.

But the creditors were still loud, and still envenomed. They and their emissaries hung about Tretton and demanded to know where was the captain. Of the captain's whereabouts his father knew nothing, not even whether he was still alive; for the captain had actually disappeared from the world, and his creditors could obtain no tidings respecting him. At this period, and for long afterward, they imagined that he and his father were in league together, and were determined to try at law the question as to the legitimacy of his birth as soon as the old squire should be dead. But the old squire did not die. Though his life was supposed to be most precarious he still continued to live, and became even stronger. But he remained shut up at Tretton, and utterly refused to see any emissary of any creditor. To give Mr. Tyrrwhit his due, it must be acknowledged that he personally sent no emissaries, having contented himself with putting the business into the hands of a very sharp attorney. But there were emissaries from others, who after a while were excluded altogether from the park.

Here Mr. Scarborough continued to live, coming out on to the lawn in his easy-chair, and there smoking his cigar and reading his French novel through the hot July days. To tell the truth, he cared very little for the emissaries, excepting so far as they had been allowed to interfere with his own personal comfort. In these days he had down with him two or three friends from London, who were good enough to make up for him a whist-table in the country; but he found the chief interest in his life in the occasional visits of his younger son.

"I look upon Mountjoy as utterly gone," he said.

"But he has utterly gone," his other son replied.

"As to that I care nothing. I do not believe that a man can be murdered without leaving a trace of his murder. A man cannot even throw himself overboard without being missed. I know nothing of his whereabouts,— nothing at all. But I must say that his absence is a relief to me. The only comfort left to me in this world is in your presence, and in those material good things which I am still able to enjoy."

This assertion as to his ignorance about his eldest son the squire repeated again and again to his chosen heir, feeling it was only probable that Augustus might participate in the belief which he knew to be only too common. There was, no doubt, an idea prevalent that the squire and the captain were in league together to cheat the creditors, and that the squire, who in these days received much undeserved credit for Machiavellian astuteness, knew more than any one else respecting his eldest son's affairs. But, in truth, he at first knew nothing, and in making these assurances to his younger son was altogether wasting his breath, for his younger son knew everything.

CHAPTER II. FLORENCE MOUNTJOY

Mr. Scarborough had a niece, one Florence Mountjoy, to whom it had been intended that Captain Scarborough should be married. There had been no considerations of money when the intention had been first formed, for the lady was possessed of no more than ten thousand pounds, which would have been as nothing to the prospects of the captain when the idea was first entertained. But Mr. Scarborough was fond of people who belonged to him. In this way he had been much attached to his late brother-in-law, General Mountjoy, and had perceived that his niece was beautiful and graceful, and was in every way desirable, as one who might be made in part thus to belong to himself. Florence herself, when the idea of the marriage was first suggested to her by her mother, was only eighteen, and received it with awe rather than with pleasure or abhorrence. To her her cousin Mountjoy had always been a most magnificent personage. He was only seven years her senior, but he had early in life assumed the manners, as he had also done the vices, of mature age, and loomed large in the girl's eyes as a man of undoubted wealth and fashion. At that period, three years antecedent to his father's declaration, he had no doubt been much in debt, but his debts had not been generally known, and his father had still thought that a marriage with his cousin might serve to settle him—to use the phrase which was common with himself. From that day to this the courtship had gone on, and the squire had taught himself to believe that the two cousins were all but engaged to each other. He had so considered it, at any rate, for two years, till during the last final year he had resolved to throw the captain overboard. And even during this year there had been periods of hope, for he had not finally made up his mind till but a short time before he had put it in practice. No doubt he was fond of his niece in accordance with his own capability for fondness. He would caress her and stroke her hair, and took delight in having her near to him. And of true love for such a girl his heart was quite capable. He was a good-natured, fearless, but not a selfish man, to whom the fate in life of this poor girl was a matter of real concern.

And his eldest son, who was by no means good-natured, had something of the same nature. He did love truly,—after his own fashion of loving. He would have married his cousin at any moment, with or without her ten thousand pounds,—for of all human beings he was the most reckless. And yet in his breast was present a feeling of honor of which his father knew nothing. When it was explained to him that his mother's fair name was to be aspersed,—a mother whom he could but faintly remember,—the threat did bring with it its own peculiar agony. But of this the squire neither felt or knew anything. The lady had long been dead, and could be none the better or the worse for aught that could be said of her. To the captain it was not so, and it was preferable to him to believe his father to be dishonest than his mother. He, at any rate, was in truth in love with his cousin Florence, and when the story was told to him one of its first effects was the bearing which it would have upon her mind.

It has been said that within two or three days after the communication he had left London. He had done so in order that he might at once go down to Cheltenham and see his cousin. There Miss Mountjoy lived, with her mother.

The time had been when Florence Mountjoy had been proud of her cousin, and, to tell the truth of her feelings, though she had never loved him, she had almost done so. Rumors had made their way through even to her condition of life, and she in her innocence had gradually been taught to believe that Captain Scarborough was not a man whom she could be safe in loving. And there had, perhaps, come another as to whom her feelings were different. She had, no doubt, at first thought that she would be willing to become her cousin's wife, but she had never said as much herself. And now both her heart and mind were set against him.

Captain Scarborough, as he went down to Cheltenham, turned the matter over in his mind, thinking within himself how best he might carry out his project. His intention was to obtain from his cousin an assurance of her love, and a promise that it should not be shaken by any stories which his father might tell respecting him. For this purpose he he must make known to her the story his father had told him, and his own absolute disbelief in it. Much else must be confided to her. He must acknowledge in part his own debts, and must explain that his father had taken this course in order to defraud the creditors. All this would be very difficult; but he must trust in her innocence and generosity. He thought that the condition of his affairs might be so represented that the story should tend rather to win her heart toward him than to turn it away. Her mother had hitherto always been in his favor, and he had, in fact, been received almost as an Apollo in the house at Cheltenham.

"Florence," he said, "I must see you alone for a few minutes. I know that your mother will trust you with me." This was spoken immediately on his arrival, and Mrs. Mountjoy at once left the room. She had been taught to believe that it was her daughter's duty to marry her cousin; and though she knew that the captain had done much to embarrass the property, she thought that this would be the surest way to settle him. The heir of Tretton Park was, in her estimation, so great a man that very much was to be endured at his hands.

The meeting between the two cousins was very long, and when Mrs. Mountjoy at last returned unannounced to the room she found her daughter in tears.

"Oh, Florence, what is the matter?" asked her mother.

The poor girl said nothing, but still continued to weep, while the captain stood by looking as black as a thunder-cloud.

"What is it, Mountjoy?" said Mrs. Mountjoy, turning to him.

"I have told Florence some of my troubles," said he, "and they seemed to have changed her mind toward me."

There was something in this which was detestable to Florence,—an unfairness, a dishonesty in putting off upon his trouble that absence of love which she had at last been driven by his vows to confess. She knew that it was not because of his present trouble, which she understood to be terrible, but which she could not in truth comprehend. He had blurted it all out roughly,—the story as told by his father of his mother's dishonor, of his own insignificance in the world, of the threatened loss of the property, of the heaviness of his debts,—and added his conviction that his father had invented it all, and was, in fact, a thorough rascal. The full story of his debts he kept back, not with any predetermined falseness, but because it is so difficult for a man to own that he has absolutely ruined himself by his own folly. It was not wonderful that the girl should not have understood such a story as had then been told her. Why was he defending his mother? Why was he accusing his father? The accusations against her uncle, whom she did know, were more fearful to her than these mysterious charges against her aunt, whom she did not know, from which her son defended her. But then he had spoken passionately of his own love, and she had understood that. He had besought her to confess that she loved him, and then she had at once become stubborn. There was something in the word "confess" which grated against her feelings. It seemed to imply a conviction on his part that she did love him. She had never told him so, and was now sure that it was not so. When he had pressed her she could only weep. But in her weeping she never for a moment yielded. She never uttered a single word on which he could be enabled to build a hope. Then he had become blacker and still blacker, fiercer and still fiercer, more and more earnest in his purpose, till at last he asked her whom it was that she loved—as she could not love him. He knew well whom it was that he suspected;—and she knew also. But he had no right to demand any statement from her on that head. She did not think that the man loved her; nor did she know what to say or to think of her own feelings. Were he, the other man, to come to her, she would only bid him go away; but why she should so bid him she had hardly known. But now this dark frowning captain, with his big mustache and his military look, and his general aspect of invincible power, threatened the other man.

"He came to Tretton as my friend," he said, "and by Heaven if he stands in my way, if he dare to cross between you and me, he shall answer it with his life!"

The name had not been mentioned; but this had been very terrible to Florence, and she could only weep.

He went away, refusing to stay to dinner, but said that on the following afternoon he would again return. In the street of the town he met one of his creditors, who had discovered his journey to Cheltenham, and had followed him.

"Oh, Captain Mountjoy, what is all dis that they are talking about in London?"

"What are they talking about?"

"De inheritance!" said the man, who was a veritable Jew, looking up anxiously in his face.

The man had his acceptance for a very large sum of money, with an assurance that it should be paid on his father's death, for which he had given him about two thousand pounds in cash.

"You must ask my father."

"But is it true?"

"You must ask my father. Upon my word, I can tell you nothing else. He has concocted a tale of which I for one do not believe a word. I never heard of the story till he condescended to tell it me the other day. Whether it be true or whether it be false, you and I, Mr. Hart, are in the same boat."

"But you have had de money."

"And you have got the bill. You can't do anything by coming after me. My father seems to have contrived a very clever plan by which he can rob you; but he will rob me at the same time. You may believe me or not as you please; but that you will find to be the truth."

Then Mr. Hart left him, but certainly did not believe a word the captain had said to him.

To her mother Florence would only disclose her persistent intention of not marrying her cousin. Mrs. Mountjoy, over whose spirit the glamour of the captain's prestige was still potent, said much in his favor. Everybody had always intended the marriage, and it would be the setting right of everything. The captain, no doubt, owed a large sum of money, but that would be paid by Florence's fortune. So little did the poor lady know of the captain's condition. When she had been told that there had been a great quarrel between the captain and his father, she declared that the marriage would set that all right.

"But, mamma, Captain Scarborough is not to have the property at all."

Then Mrs. Mountjoy, believing thoroughly in entails, had declared that all Heaven could not prevent it.

"But that makes no difference," said the daughter; "if I—I—I loved him I would marry him so much the more, if he had nothing."

Then Mrs. Mountjoy declared that she could not understand it at all.

On the next day Captain Scarborough came, according to his promise, but nothing that he could say would induce Florence to come into his presence. Her mother declared that she was so ill that it would be wicked to disturb her.

CHAPTER III. HARRY ANNESLEY

Together with Augustus Scarborough at Cambridge had been one Harry Annesley, and he it was to whom the captain in his wrath had sworn to put an end if he should come between him and his love. Harry Annesley had been introduced to the captain by his brother, and an intimacy had grown up between them. He had brought him to Tretton Park when Florence was there, and Harry had since made his own way to Cheltenham, and had endeavored to plead his own cause after his own fashion. This he had done after the good old English plan, which is said to be somewhat loutish, but is not without its efficacy. He had looked at her, and danced with her, and done the best with his gloves and his cravat, and had let her see by twenty unmistakable signs that in order to be perfectly happy he must be near her. Her gloves, and her flowers, and her other little properties were sweeter to him than any scents, and were more valuable in his eyes than precious stones. But he had never as yet actually asked her to love him. But she was so quick a linguist that she had understood down to the last letter what all these tokens had meant. Her cousin, Captain Scarborough, was to her magnificent, powerful, but terrible withal. She had asked herself a thousand times whether it would be possible for her to love him and to become his wife. She had never quite given even to herself an answer to this question till she had suddenly found herself enabled to do so by his over-confidence in asking her to confess that she loved him. She had never acknowledged anything, even to herself, as to Harry Annesley. She had never told herself that it would be possible that he should ask her any such question. She had a wild, dreamy, fearful feeling that, although it would be possible to her to refuse her cousin, it would be impossible that she should marry any other while he should still be desirous of making her his wife. And now Captain Scarborough had threatened Harry Annesley, not indeed by name, but still clearly enough. Any dream of her own in that direction must be a vain dream.

As Harry Annesley is going to be what is generally called the hero of this story, it is necessary that something should be said of the particulars of his life and existence up to this period. There will be found to be nothing very heroic about him. He is a young man with more than a fair allowance of a young man's folly;—it may also be said of a young man's weakness. But I myself am inclined to think that there was but little of a young man's selfishness, with nothing of falseness or dishonesty; and I am therefore tempted to tell his story.

He was the son of a clergyman, and the eldest of a large family of children. But as he was the acknowledged heir to his mother's brother, who was the squire of the parish of which his father was rector, it was not thought necessary that he should follow any profession. This uncle was the Squire of Buston, and was, after all, not a rich man himself. His whole property did not exceed two thousand a year, an income which fifty years since was supposed to be sufficient for the moderate wants of a moderate country gentleman; but though Buston be not very far removed from the centre of everything, being in Hertfordshire and not more than forty miles from London, Mr. Prosper lived so retired a life, and was so far removed from the ways of men, that he apparently did not know but that his heir was as completely entitled to lead an idle life as though he were the son of a duke or a brewer. It must not, however, be imagined that Mr. Prosper was especially attached to his nephew. When the boy left the Charter-house, where his uncle had paid his school-bills, he was sent to Cambridge, with an allowance of two hundred and fifty pounds a year, and that allowance was still continued to him, with an assurance that under no circumstances could it ever be increased. At college he had been successful, and left Cambridge with a college fellowship. He therefore left it with one hundred and seventy-five pounds added to his income, and was considered by all those at Buston Rectory to be a rich young man.

But Harry did not find that his combined income amounted to riches amid a world of idleness. At Buston he was constantly told by his uncle of the necessity of economy. Indeed, Mr. Prosper, who was a sickly little man about fifty years of age, always spoke of himself as though he intended to live for another half-century. He rarely walked across the park to the rectory, and once a week, on Sundays, entertained the rectory family. A sad occasion it generally was to the elder of the rectory children, who were thus doomed to abandon the loud pleasantries of their own home for the sober Sunday solemnities of the Hall. It was not that the Squire of Buston was peculiarly a religious man, or that the rector was the reverse: but the parson was joyous, whereas the other was solemn. The squire,—who never went to church, because he was supposed to be ill,—made up for the deficiency by his devotional tendencies when the children were at the Hall. He read through a sermon after dinner, unintelligibly and even inaudibly. At this his brother-in-law, who had an evening service in his own church, of course never was present; but Mrs. Annesley and the girls were there, and the younger children. But Harry Annesley had absolutely declined; and his uncle having found out that he never attended the church service, although he always left the Hall with his father, made this a ground for a quarrel. It at last came to pass that Mr. Prosper, who was jealous and irritable, would hardly speak to his nephew; but the two hundred and fifty pounds went on, with many bickerings on the subject between the parson and the squire. Once, when the squire spoke of discontinuing it, Harry's father reminded him that the young man had been brought up in absolute idleness, in conformity with his uncle's desire. This the squire denied in strong language; but Harry had not hitherto run loudly in debt, nor kicked over the traces very outrageously; and as he absolutely must be the heir, the allowance was permitted to go on.

There was one lady who conceived all manner of bad things as to Harry Annesley, because, as she alleged, of the want of a profession and of any fixed income. Mrs. Mountjoy, Florence's mother, was this lady. Florence herself had read every word in Harry's language, not knowing, indeed, that she had read anything, but still never having missed a single letter. Mrs. Mountjoy also had read a good deal, though not all, and dreaded the appearance of Harry as a declared lover. In her eyes Captain Scarborough was a very handsome, very powerful, and very grand personage; but she feared that Florence was being induced to refuse her allegiance to this sovereign by the interference of her other very indifferent suitor. What would be Buston and two thousand a year, as compared with all the glories and limitless income of the great Tretton property? Captain Scarborough, with his mustaches and magnificence, was just the man who would be sure to become a peer. She had always heard the income fixed at thirty thousand a year. What would a few debts signify to thirty thousand a year? Such had been her thoughts up to the period of Captain Scarborough's late visit, when he had come to Cheltenham, and had renewed his demand for Florence's hand somewhat roughly. He had spoken ambiguous words, dreadful words, declaring that an internecine quarrel had taken place between him and his father; but these words, though they had been very dreadful, had been altogether misunderstood by Mrs. Mountjoy. The property she knew to be entailed, and she knew that when a property was entailed the present owner of it had nothing to do with its future disposition. Captain Scarborough, at any rate, was anxious for the marriage, and Mrs. Mountjoy was inclined to accept him, encumbered as he now was with his father's wrath, in preference to poor Harry Annesley.

In June Harry came up to London, and there learned at his club the singular story in regard to old Mr. Scarborough and his son. Mr. Scarborough had declared his son illegitimate, and all the world knew now that he was utterly penniless and hopelessly in debt. That he had been greatly embarrassed Harry had known for many months, and added to that was now the fact, very generally believed, that he was not and never had been the heir to Tretton Park. All that still increasing property about Tretton, on which so many hopes had been founded, would belong to his brother. Harry, as he heard the tale, immediately connected it with Florence. He had, of course, known the captain was a suitor to the girl's hand, and there had been a time when he thought that his own hopes were consequently vain. Gradually the conviction dawned upon him that Florence did not love the grand warrior, that she was afraid of him rather and awe-struck. It would be terrible now were she brought to marry him by this feeling of awe. Then he learned that the warrior had gone down to Cheltenham, and in the restlessness of his spirit he pursued him. When he reached Cheltenham the warrior had already gone.

"The property is certainly entailed," said Mrs. Mountjoy. He had called at once at the house and saw the mother, but Florence was discreetly sent away to her own room when the dangerous young man was admitted.

"He is not Mr. Scarborough's eldest son at all," said Harry; "that is, in the eye of the law." Then he had to undertake that task, very difficult for a young man, of explaining to her all the circumstances of the case.

But there was something in them so dreadful to the lady's imagination that he failed for a long time to make her comprehend it. "Do you mean to say that Mr. Scarborough was not married to his own wife?"

"Not at first."

"And that he knew it?"

"No doubt he knew it. He confesses as much himself."

"What a very wicked man he must be!" said Mrs. Mountjoy. Harry could only shrug his shoulder. "And he meant to rob Augustus all through?" Harry again shrugged his shoulder. "Is it not much more probable that if he could be so very wicked he would be willing to deny his eldest son in order to save paying the debts?"

Harry could only declare that the facts were as he told them, or at least that all London believed them to be so, that at any rate Captain Mountjoy had gambled so recklessly as to put himself for ever and ever out of reach of a shilling of the property, and that it was clearly the duty of Mrs. Mountjoy, as Florence's mother, not to accept him as a suitor.

It was only by slow degrees that the conversation had arrived at this pass. Harry had never as yet declared his own love either to the mother or daughter, and now appeared simply as a narrator of this terrible story. But at this point it did appear to him that he must introduce himself in another guise.

"The fact is, Mrs. Mountjoy," he said, starting to his feet, "that I am in love with your daughter myself."

"And therefore you have come here to vilify Captain Scarborough."

"I have come," said he, "at any rate to tell the truth. If it be as I say, you cannot think it right that he should marry your daughter. I say nothing of myself, but that, at any rate, cannot be."

"It is no business of yours, Mr. Annesley."

"Except that I would fain think that her business should be mine."

But he could not prevail with Mrs. Mountjoy either on this day or the next to allow him to see Florence, and at last was obliged to leave Cheltenham without having done so.

CHAPTER IV. CAPTAIN SCARBOROUGH'S DISAPPEARANCE

A few days after the visits to Cheltenham, described in the last chapters, Harry Annesley, coming down a passage by the side of the Junior United Service Club into Charles Street, suddenly met Captain Scarborough at two o'clock in the morning. Where Harry had been at that hour need not now be explained, but it may be presumed that he had not been drinking tea with any of his female relatives.

Captain Scarborough had just come out of some neighboring club, where he had certainly been playing, and where, to all appearances, he had been drinking also. That there should have been no policemen in the street was not remarkable, but there was no one else there present to give any account of what took place during the five minutes in which the two men remained together. Harry, who was at the moment surprised by the encounter, would have passed the captain by without notice, had he been allowed to do so; but this the captain perceived, and stopped him suddenly, taking him roughly by the collar of his coat. This Harry naturally resented, and before a word of intelligible explanation had been given the two young men had quarrelled.

Captain Scarborough had received a long letter from Mrs. Mountjoy, praying for explanation of circumstances which could not be explained, and stating over and over again that all her information had come from Harry Annesley.

The captain now called him an interfering, meddlesome idiot, and shook him violently while holding him in his grasp. This was a usage which Harry was not the man to endure, and there soon arose a scuffle, in which blows had passed between them. The captain stuck to his prey, shaking him again and again in his drunken wrath, till Harry, roused to a passion almost equal to that of his opponent, flung him at last against the corner of the club railings, and there left his foe sprawling upon the ground, having struck his head violently against the ground as he fell. Harry passed on to his own bed, indifferent, as it was afterwards said, to the fate of his antagonist. All this occupied probably five minutes in the doing, but was seen by no human eye.

As the occurrence of that night was subsequently made the ground for heavy accusation against Harry Annesley, it has been told here with sufficient minuteness to show what might be said in justification or in condemnation of his conduct,—to show what might be said if the truth were spoken. For, indeed, in the discussions which arose on the subject, much was said which was not true. When he had retired from the scuffle on that night, Harry had certainly not dreamed that any serious damage had been done to the man who had certainly been altogether to blame in his provocation of the quarrel. Had he kept his temper and feelings completely under control, and knocked down Captain Scarborough only in self-defence; had he not allowed himself to be roused to wrath by treatment which could not but give rise to wrath in a young man's bosom, no doubt, when his foe lay at his feet, he would have stooped to pick him up, and have tended his wounds. But such was not Harry's character,—nor that of any of the young men with whom I have been acquainted. Such, however, was the conduct apparently expected from him by many, when the circumstances of those five minutes were brought to the light. But, on the other hand, had passion not completely got the better of him, had he not at the moment considered the attack made upon him to amount to misconduct so gross as to supersede all necessity for gentle usage on his own part, he would hardly have left the man to live or die as chance would have it. Boiling with passion, he went his way, and did leave the man on the pavement, not caring much, or rather, not thinking much, whether his victim might live or die.

On the next day Harry Annesley left London and went down to Buston, having heard no word farther about the captain. He did not start till late in the afternoon, and during the day took some trouble to make himself conspicuous about the town; but he heard nothing of Captain Scarborough. Twice he walked along Charles Street, and looked at the spot on which he had stood on the night before in what might have been deadly conflict. Then he told himself that he had not been in the least wounded, that the ferocious maddened man had attempted to do no more than shake him, that his coat had suffered and not himself, and that in return he had certainly struck the captain with all his violence. There were probably some regrets, but he said not a word on the subject to any one, and so he left London.

For three or four days nothing was heard of the captain, nor was anything said about him. He had lodgings in town, at which he was no doubt missed, but he also had quarters at the barracks, at which he did not often sleep, but to which it was thought possible on the next morning that he might have betaken himself. Before the evening of that day had come he had no doubt been missed, but in the world at large no special mention was made of his absence for some time. Then, among the haunts which he was known to frequent, questions began to be asked as to his whereabouts, and to be answered by doubtful assertions that nothing had been seen or heard of him for the last sixty or seventy hours.

It must be remembered that at this time Captain Scarborough was still the subject of universal remark, because of the story told as to his birth. His father had declared him to be illegitimate, and had thereby robbed all his creditors. Captain Scarborough was a man quite remarkable enough to insure universal attention for such a tale as this; but now, added to his illegitimacy was his disappearance. There was at first no idea that he had been murdered. It became quickly known to all the world that he had, on the night in question, lost a large sum of money at a whist-club which he frequented, and, in accordance with the custom of the club, had not paid the money on the spot.

The fatal Monday had come round, and the money undoubtedly was not paid. Then he was declared a defaulter, and in due process of time his name was struck off the club books, with some serious increase of the ignominy hitherto sustained.

During the last fortnight or more Captain Scarborough's name had been subjected to many remarks and to much disgrace. But this non-payment of the money lost at whist was considered to be the turning-point. A man might be declared illegitimate, and might in consequence of that or any other circumstance defraud all his creditors. A man might conspire with his father with the object of doing this fraudulently, as Captain Scarborough was no doubt thought to have done by most of his acquaintances. All this he might do and not become so degraded but that his friends would talk to him and play cards with him. But to have sat down to a whist-table and not be able to pay the stakes was held to be so foul a disgrace that men did not wonder that he should have disappeared.

Such was the cause alleged for the captain's disappearance among his intimate friends; but by degrees more than his intimate friends came to talk of it. In a short time his name was in all the newspapers, and there was not a constable in London whose mind was not greatly exercised on the matter. All Scotland Yard and the police-officers were busy. Mr. Grey, in Lincoln's Inn, was much troubled on the matter. By degrees facts had made themselves clear to his mind, and he had become aware that the captain had been born before his client's marriage. He was ineffably shocked at the old squire's villany in the matter, but declared to all to whom he spoke openly on the subject that he did not see how the sinner could be punished. He never thought that the father and son were in a conspiracy together. Nor had he believed that they had arranged the young man's disappearance in order the more thoroughly to defraud the creditors. They could not, at any rate, harm a man of whose whereabouts they were unaware and who, for all they knew, might be dead. But the reader is already aware that this surmise on the part of Mr. Grey was unfounded.

The captain had been absent for three weeks when Augustus Scarborough went down for a second time to Tretton Park, in order to discuss the matter with his father.

Augustus had, with much equanimity and a steady, fixed purpose, settled himself down to the position as elder son. He pretended no anger to his father for the injury intended, and was only anxious that his own rights should be confirmed. In this he found that no great difficulty stood in his way. The creditors would contest his rights when his father should die; but for such contest he would be prepared. He had no doubt as to his own position, but thought that it would be safer,—and that it would also probably be cheaper,—to purchase the acquiescence of all claimants than to encounter the expense of a prolonged trial, to which there might be more than one appeal, and of which the end after all would be doubtful.

No very great sum of money would probably be required. No very great sum would, at any rate, be offered. But such an arrangement would certainly be easier if his brother were not present to be confronted with the men whom he had duped.

The squire was still ill down at Tretton, but not so ill but that he had his wits about him in all their clearness. Some said that he was not ill at all, but that in the present state of affairs the retirement suited him. But the nature of the operation which he had undergone was known to many who would not have him harassed in his present condition. In truth, he had only to refuse admission to all visitors and to take care that his commands were carried out in order to avoid disagreeable intrusions.

"Do you mean to say that a man can do such a thing as this and that no one can touch him for it?" This was an exclamation made by Mr. Tyrrwhit to his lawyer, in a tone of aggrieved disgust.

"He hasn't done anything," said the lawyer. "He only thought of doing something, and has since repented. You cannot arrest a man because he had contemplated the picking of your pocket, especially when he has shown that he is resolved not to pick it."

"As far as I can learn, nothing has been heard about him as yet," said the son to the father.

"Those limbs weren't his that were picked out of the Thames near Blackfriars Bridge?"

"They belonged to a poor cripple who was murdered two months since."

"And that body that was found down among the Yorkshire Hills?"

"He was a peddler. There is nothing to induce a belief that Mountjoy has killed himself or been killed. In the former case his dead body would be found or his live body would be missing. For the second there is no imaginable cause for suspicion."

"Then where the devil is he?" said the anxious father.

"Ah, that's the difficulty. But I can imagine no position in which a man might be more tempted to hide himself. He is disgraced on every side, and could hardly show his face in London after the money he has lost. You would not have paid his gambling debts?"

"Certainly not," said the father. "There must be an end to all things."

"Nor could I. Within the last month past he has drawn from me every shilling that I have had at my immediate command."

"Why did you give 'em to him?"

"It would be difficult to explain all the reasons. He was then my elder brother, and it suited me to have him somewhat under my hand. At any rate I did do so, and am unable for the present to do more. Looking round about, I do not see where it was possible for him to raise a sovereign as soon as it was once known that he was nobody."

"What will become of him?" said the father. "I don't like the idea of his being starved. He can't live without something to live upon."

"God tempers the wind to the shorn lamb," said the son. "For lambs such as he there always seems to be pasture provided of one sort or another."

"You would not like to have to trust to such pastures," said the father.

"Nor should I like to be hanged; but I should have to be hanged if I had committed murder. Think of the chances which he has had, and the way in which he has misused them. Although illegitimate, he was to have had the whole property,—of which not a shilling belongs to him; and he has not lost it because it was not his own, but has simply gambled it away among the Jews. What can happen to a man in such a condition better than to turn up as a hunter among the Rocky Mountains or as a gold-digger in Australia? In this last adventure he seems to have plunged horribly, and to have lost over three thousand pounds. You wouldn't have paid that for him?"

"Not again;—certainly not again."

"Then what could he do better than disappear? I suppose I shall have to make him an allowance some of these days, and if he can live and keep himself dark I will do so."

There was in this a tacit allusion to his father's speedy death which was grim enough; but the father passed it by without any expression of displeasure. He certainly owed much to his younger son, and was willing to pay it by quiescence. Let them both forbear. Such was the language which he held to himself in thinking of his younger son. Augustus was certainly behaving well to him. Not a word of rebuke had passed his lips as to the infamous attempt at spoliation which had been made. The old squire felt grateful for his younger son's conduct, but yet in his heart of hearts he preferred the elder.

"He has denuded me of every penny," said Augustus, "and I must ask you to refund me something of what has gone."

"He has kept me very bare. A man with so great a propensity for getting rid of money I think no father ever before had to endure."

"You have had the last of it."

"I do not know that. If I live, and he lets me know his whereabouts, I cannot leave him penniless. I do feel that a great injustice has been done him."

"I don't exactly see it," said Augustus.

"Because you're too hard-hearted to put yourself in another man's place. He was my eldest son."

"He thought that he was."

"And should have remained so had there been a hope for him," said the squire, roused to temporary anger. Augustus only shrugged his shoulders. "But there is no good talking about it."

"Not the least in the world. Mr. Grey, I suppose, knows the truth at last. I shall have to get three or four thousand pounds from you, or I too must resort to the Jews. I shall do it, at any rate, under better circumstances than my brother."

Some arrangement was at last made which was satisfactory to the son, and which we must presume that the father found to be endurable. Then the son took his leave, and went back to London, with the understood intention of pushing the inquiries as to his brother's existence and whereabouts.

The sudden and complete disappearance of Captain Scarborough struck Mrs. Mountjoy with the deepest awe. It was not at first borne in upon her to believe that Captain Mountjoy Scarborough, an officer in the Coldstreams, and the acknowledged heir to the Tretton property, had vanished away as a stray street-sweeper might do, or some milliner's lowest work-woman. But at last there were advertisements in all the newspapers and placards on all the walls, and Mrs. Mountjoy did understand that the captain was gone. She could as yet hardly believe that he was no longer heir to Tretton: and in such short discussions with Florence as were necessary on the subject she preferred to express no opinion whatever as to his conduct. But she would by no means give way when urged to acknowledge that no marriage between Florence and the captain was any longer to be regarded as possible. While the captain was away the matter should be left as if in abeyance; but this by no means suited the young lady's views. Mrs. Mountjoy was not a reticent woman, and had no doubt been too free in whispering among her friends something of her daughter's position. This Florence had resented; but it had still been done, and in Cheltenham generally she was regarded as an engaged young lady. It had been in vain that she had denied that it was so. Her mother's word on such a subject was supposed to be more credible that her own; and now this man with whom she was believed to be so closely connected had disappeared from the world among the most disreputable circumstances. But when she explained the difficulty to her mother her mother bade her hold her tongue for the present, and seemed to hold out a hope that the captain might at last be restored to his old position.

"Let them restore him ever so much, he would never be anything to me, mamma." Then Mrs. Mountjoy would only shake her head and purse her lips.

On the evening of the day after the fracas in the street Harry Annesley went down to Buston, and there remained for the next two or three days, holding his tongue absolutely as to the adventure of that night. There was no one at Buston to whom he would probably have made known the circumstances. But there was clinging to it a certain flavor of disreputable conduct on his own part which sealed his lips altogether. The louder and more frequent the tidings which reached his ears as to the captain's departure, the more strongly did he feel that duty required him to tell what he knew upon the matter. Many thoughts and many fears encompassed him. At first was the idea that he had killed the man by the violence of his blow, or that his death had been caused by the fall. Then it occurred to him that it was impossible that Scarborough should have been killed and that no account should be given as to the finding of the body. At last he persuaded himself that he could not have killed the man, but he was assured at the same time that the disappearance must in some sort have been occasioned by what then took place. And it could not but be that the captain, if alive, should be aware of the nature of the struggle which had taken place. He heard, chiefly from the newspapers, the full record of the captain's illegitimacy; he heard of his condition with the creditors; he heard of those gambling debts which were left unpaid at the club. He saw it also stated—and repeated—that these were the grounds for the man's disappearance. It was quite credible that the man should disappear, or endeavor to disappear, under such a cloud of difficulties. It did not require that he and his violence should be adduced as an extra cause. Indeed, had the man been minded to vanish before the encounter, he might in all human probability have been deterred by the circumstances of the quarrel. It gave no extra reason for his disappearance, and could in no wise be counted with it were he to tell the whole story, in Scotland Yard. He had been grossly misused on the occasion, and had escaped from such misusage by the only means in his power. But still he felt that, had he told the story, people far and wide would have connected his name with the man's absence, and, worse again, that Florence's name would have become entangled with it also. For the first day or two he had from hour to hour abstained from telling all that he knew, and then when the day or two were passed, and when a week had run by,—when a fortnight had been allowed to go,—it was impossible for him not to hold his tongue.

He became nervous, unhappy, and irritated down at Buston, with his father and mother and sister's, but more especially with his uncle. Previous to this his uncle for a couple of months had declined to see him; now he was sent for to the Hall and interrogated daily on this special subject. Mr. Prosper was aware that his nephew had been intimate with Augustus Scarborough, and that he might, therefore, be presumed to know much about the family. Mr. Prosper took the keenest interest in the illegitimacy and the impecuniosity and final disappearance of the captain, and no doubt did, in his cross-examinations, discover the fact that Harry was unwilling to answer his questions. He found out for the first time that Harry was acquainted with the captain, and also contrived to extract from him the name of Miss Mountjoy. But he could learn nothing else, beyond Harry's absolute unwillingness to talk upon the subject, which was in itself much. It must be understood that Harry was not specially reverential in these communications. Indeed, he gave his uncle to understand that he regarded his questions as impertinent, and at last declared his intention of not coming to the Hall any more for the present. Then Mr. Prosper whispered to his sister that he was quite sure that Harry Annesley knew more than he choose to say as to Captain Scarborough's whereabouts.

"My dear Peter," said Mrs. Annesley, "I really think that you are doing poor Harry an injustice."

Mrs. Annesley was always on her guard to maintain something like an affectionate intercourse between her own family and the squire.

"My dear Anne, you do not see into a millstone as far as I do. You never did."

"But, Peter, you really shouldn't say such things of Harry. When all the police-officers themselves are looking about to catch up anything in their way, they would catch him up at a moment's notice if they heard that a magistrate of the county had expressed such an opinion."

"Why don't he tell me?" said Mr. Prosper.

"There's nothing to tell."

"Ah, that's your opinion—because you can't see into a millstone. I tell you that Harry knows more about this Captain Scarborough than any one else. They were very intimate together."

"Harry only just knew him."

"Well, you'll see. I tell you that Harry's name will become mixed up with Captain Scarborough's, and I hope that it will be in no discreditable manner. I hope so, that's all." Harry in the mean time had returned to London, in order to escape his uncle, and to be on the spot to learn anything that might come in his way as to the now acknowledged mystery respecting the captain.

Such was the state of things at the commencement of the period to which my story refers.

CHAPTER V. AUGUSTUS SCARBOROUGH

Harry Annesley, when he found himself in London, could not for a moment shake off that feeling of nervous anxiety as to the fate of Mountjoy Scarborough which had seized hold of him. In every newspaper which he took in his hand he looked first for the paragraph respecting the fate of the missing man, which the paper was sure to contain in one of its columns. It was his habit during these few days to breakfast at a club, and he could not abstain from speaking to his neighbors about the wonderful Scarborough incident. Every man was at this time willing to speak on the subject, and Harry's interest might not have seemed to be peculiar; but it became known that he had been acquainted with the missing man, and Harry in conversation said much more than it would have been prudent for him to do on the understanding that he wished to remain unconnected with the story. Men asked him questions as though he were likely to know; and he would answer them, asserting that he knew nothing, but still leaving an impression behind that he did know more than he chose to avow. Many inquiries were made daily at this time in Scotland Yard as to the captain. These, no doubt, chiefly came from the creditors and their allies. But Harry Annesley became known among those who asked for information as Henry Annesley, Esq., late of St. John's College, Cambridge; and even the police were taught to think that there was something noticeable in the interest which he displayed.

On the fourth day after his arrival in London, just at that time of the year when everybody was supposed to be leaving town, and when faded members of Parliament, who allowed themselves to be retained for the purpose of final divisions, were cursing their fate amid the heats of August, Harry accepted an invitation to dine with Augustus Scarborough at his chambers in the Temple. He understood when he accepted the invitation that no one else was to be there, and must have been aware that it was the intention of the heir of Tretton to talk to him respecting his brother. He had not seen Scarborough since he had been up in town, and had not been desirous of seeing him; but when the invitation came he had told himself that it would be better that he should accept it, and that he would allow his host to say what he pleased to say on the subject, he himself remaining reticent. But poor Harry little knew the difficulty of reticency when the heart is full. He had intended to be very reticent when he came up to London, and had, in fact, done nothing but talk about the missing man, as to whom he had declared that he would altogether hold his tongue.

The reader must here be pleased to remember that Augustus Scarborough was perfectly well aware of what had befallen his brother, and must, therefore, have known among other things of the quarrel which had taken place in the streets. He knew, therefore, that Harry was concealing his knowledge, and could make a fair guess at the state of the poor fellow's mind.

"He will guess," he had said to himself, "that he did not leave him for dead on the ground, or the body would be there to tell the tale. But he must be ashamed of the part which he took in the street-fight, and be anxious to conceal it. No doubt Mountjoy was the first offender, but something had occurred which Annesley is unwilling should make its way either to his uncle's ears, or to his father's, or to mine, or to the squire's,—or to those of Florence."

It was thus that Augustus Scarborough reasoned with himself when he asked Harry Annesley to dine with him.

It was not supposed by any of his friends that Augustus Scarborough would continue to live in the moderate chambers which he now occupied in the Temple; but he had as yet made no sign of a desire to leave them. They were up two pair of stairs, and were not great in size; but they were comfortable enough, and even luxurious, as a bachelor's abode.

"I've asked you to come alone," said Augustus, "because there is such a crowd of things to be talked of about poor Mountjoy which are not exactly fitted for the common ear."

"Yes, indeed," said Harry, who did not, however, quite understand why it would be necessary that the heir should discuss with him the affairs of his unfortunate brother. There had, no doubt, been a certain degree of intimacy between them, but nothing which made it essential that the captain's difficulties should be exposed to him. The matter which touched him most closely was the love which both the men had borne to Florence Mountjoy; but Harry did not expect that any allusion to Florence would be made on the present occasion.

"Did you ever hear of such a devil of a mess?" said Augustus.

"No, indeed. It is not only that he has disappeared—"

"That is as nothing when compared with all the other incidents of this romantic tale. Indeed, it is the only natural thing in it. Given all the other circumstances, I should have foretold his disappearance as a thing certain to occur. Why shouldn't such a man disappear, if he can?"

"But how has he done it?" replied Harry. "Where has he gone to? At this moment where is he?"

"Ah, if you will answer all those questions, and give your information in Scotland Yard, the creditors, no doubt, will make up a handsome purse for you. Not that they will ever get a shilling from him, though he were to be seen walking down St. James's Street to-morrow. But they are a sanguine gentry, these holders of bills, and I really believe that if they could see him they would embrace him with the warmest affection. In the mean time let us have some dinner, and we will talk about poor Mountjoy when we have got rid of young Pitcher. Young Pitcher is my laundress's son to the use of whose services I have been promoted since I have been known to be the heir of Tretton."

Then they sat down and dined, and Augustus Scarborough made himself agreeable. The small dinner was excellent of its kind, and the wine was all that it ought to be. During dinner not a word was said as to Mountjoy, nor as to the affairs of the estate. Augustus, who was old for his age, and had already practised himself much in London life, knew well how to make himself agreeable. There was plenty to be said while young Pitcher was passing in and out of the room, so that there appeared no awkward vacancies of silence while one course succeeded the other. The weather was very hot, the grouse were very tempting, everybody was very dull, and members of Parliament more stupid than anybody else; but a good time was coming. Would Harry come down to Tretton and see the old governor? There was not much to offer him in the way of recreation, but when September came the partridges would abound. Harry gave a half-promise that he would go to Tretton for a week, and Augustus Scarborough expressed himself as much gratified. Harry at the moment thought of no reason why he should not go to Tretton, and thus committed himself to the promise; but he afterward felt that Tretton was of all places the last which he ought just at present to visit.

At last Pitcher and the cheese were gone, and young Scarborough produced his cigars. "I want to smoke directly I've done eating," he said. "Drinking goes with smoking as well as it does with eating, so there need be no stop for that. Now, tell me, Annesley, what is it that you think about Mountjoy?"

There was an abruptness in the question which for the moment struck Harry dumb. How was he to say what he thought about Mountjoy Scarborough, even though he should have no feeling to prevent him from expressing the truth? He knew, or thought that he knew, Mountjoy Scarborough to be a thorough blackguard; one whom no sense of honesty kept from spending money, and who was now a party to robbing his creditors without the slightest compunction,—for it was in Harry's mind that Mountjoy and his father were in league together to save the property by rescuing it from the hands of the Jews. He would have thought the same as to the old squire,—only that the old squire had not interfered with him in reference to Florence Mountjoy.

And then there was present to his mind the brutal attack which had been made on himself in the street. According to his views Mountjoy Scarborough was certainly a blackguard; but he did not feel inclined quite to say so to the brother, nor was he perfectly certain as to his host's honesty. It might be that the three Scarboroughs were all in a league together; and if so, he had done very wrong, as he then remembered, to say that he would go down to Tretton. When, therefore, he was asked the question he could only hold his tongue.

"I suppose you have some scruple in speaking because he's my brother? You may drop that altogether."

"I think that his career has been what the novel-reader would call romantic; but what I, who am not one of them, should describe as unfortunate."

"Well, yes; taking it altogether it has been unfortunate. I am not a soft-hearted fellow, but I am driven to pity him. The worst of it is that, had not my father been induced at last to tell the truth, from most dishonest causes, he would not have been a bit better off than he is. I doubt whether he could have raised another couple of thousand on the day when he went. If he had done so then, and again more and more, to any amount you choose to think of, it would have been the same with him."

"I suppose so."

"His lust for gambling was a bottomless quicksand, which no possible amount of winning could ever have satiated. Let him enter his club with five thousand pounds at his banker's and no misfortune could touch him. He being such as he is,—or, alas! for aught we know, such as he was,—the escape which the property has had cannot but be regarded as very fortunate. I don't care to talk much of myself in particular, though no wrong can have been done to a man more infinite than that which my father contrived for me."

"I cannot understand your father," said Harry. In truth, there was something in Scarborough's manner in speaking of his father which almost produced belief in Harry's mind. He began to doubt whether Augustus was in the conspiracy.

"No, I should say not. It is hard to understand that an English gentleman should have the courage to conceive such a plot, and the wit to carry it out. If Mountjoy had run only decently straight, or not more than indecently crooked, I should have been a younger brother, practising law in the Temple to the end of my days. The story of Esau and of Jacob is as nothing to it. But that is not the most remarkable circumstance. My father, for purposes of his own, which includes the absolute throwing over of Mountjoy's creditors, changes his plan, and is pleased to restore to me that of which he had resolved to rob me. What father would dare to look in the face of the son whom he had thus resolved to defraud? My father tells me the story with a gentle chuckle, showing almost as much indifference to Mountjoy's ruin as to my recovered prosperity. He has not a blush when he reveals it all. He has not a word to say, or, as far as I can see, a thought as to the world's opinion. No doubt he is supposed to be dying. I do presume that three or four months will see the end of him. In the mean time he takes it all as quietly as though he had simply lent a five-pound note to Mountjoy out of my pocket."

"You, at any rate, will get your property?"

"Oh, yes; and that, no doubt, is his argument when he sees me. He is delighted to have me down at Tretton, and, to tell the truth, I do not feel the slightest animosity toward him. But as I look at him I think him to be the most remarkable old gentleman that the world has ever produced. He is quite unconscious that I have any ground of complaint against him."

"He has probably thought that the circumstances of your brother's birth should not militate against his prospects."

"But the law, my dear fellow," said Scarborough, getting up from his chair and standing with his cigar between his finger and thumb,—"the law thinks otherwise. The making of all right and wrong in this world depends on the law. The half-crown in my pocket is merely mine because of the law. He did choose to marry my mother before I was born, but did not choose to go through that ceremony before my brother's time. That may be a trifle to you, or to my moral feeling may be a trifle; but because of that trifle all Tretton will be my property, and his attempt to rob me of it was just the same as though he should break into a bank and steal what he found there. He knows that just as well as I do, but to suit his own purposes he did it."

There was something in the way in which the young man spoke both of his father and mother which made Harry's flesh creep. He could not but think of his own father and his own mother, and his feelings in regard to them. But here this man was talking of the misdoings of the one parent and the other with the most perfect *sang-froid.* "Of course I understand all that," said Harry.

"There is a manner of doing evil so easy and indifferent as absolutely to quell the general feeling respecting it. A man shall tell you that he has committed a murder in a tone so careless as to make you feel that a murder is nothing. I don't suppose my father can be punished for his attempt to rob me of twenty thousand a year, and therefore he talks to me about it as though it were a good joke. Not only that, but he expects me to receive it in the same way. Upon the whole, he prevails. I find myself not in the least angry with him, and rather obliged to him than otherwise for allowing me to be his eldest son."

"What must Mountjoy's feelings be!" said Harry.

"Exactly; what must be Mountjoy's feelings! There is no need to consider my father's, but poor Mountjoy's! I don't suppose that he can be dead."

"I should think not."

"While a man is alive he can carry himself off, but when a fellow is dead it requires at least one or probably two to carry him. Men do not wish to undertake such a work secretly unless they've been concerned in the murder; and then there will have been a noise which must have been heard, or blood which must have been seen, and the body will at last be forthcoming, or some sign of its destruction. I do not think he be dead."

"I should hope not," said Harry, rather tamely, and feeling that he was guilty of a falsehood by the manner in which he expressed his hope.

"When was it you saw him last?" Scarborough asked the question with an abruptness which was predetermined, but which did not quite take Harry aback.

"About three months since—in London," said Harry, going back in his memory to the last meeting, which had occurred before the squire had declared his purpose.

"Ah;—you haven't seen him, then, since he knew that he was nobody?" This he asked in an indifferent tone, being anxious not to discover his purpose, but in doing so he gave Harry great credit for his readiness of mind.

"I have not seen him since he heard the news which must have astonished him more than any one else."

"I wonder," said Augustus, "how Florence Mountjoy has borne it?"

"Neither have I seen her. I have been at Cheltenham, but was not allowed to see her." This he said with an assertion to himself that though he had lied as to one particular he would not lie as to any other.

"I suppose she must have been much cut up by it all. I have half a mind to declare to myself that she shall still have an opportunity of becoming the mistress of Tretton. She was always afraid of Mountjoy, but I do not know that she ever loved him. She had become so used to the idea of marrying him that she would have given herself up in mere obedience. I too think that she might do as a wife, and I shall certainly make a better husband than Mountjoy would have done."

"Miss Mountjoy will certainly do as a wife for any one who may be lucky enough to get her," said Harry, with a certain tone of magnificence which at the moment he felt to be overstrained and ridiculous.

"Oh yes; one has got to get her, as you call it, of course. You mean to say that you are supposed to be in the running. That is your own lookout. I can only allege, on my own behalf, that it has always been considered to be an old family arrangement that Florence Mountjoy shall marry the heir to Tretton Park. I am in that position now, and I only throw it out as a hint that I may feel disposed to follow out the family arrangement. Of course if other things come in the way there will be an end of it. Come in." This last invitation was given in consequence of a knock at the door. The door was opened, and there entered a policeman in plain clothes named Prodgers, who seemed from his manner to be well acquainted with Augustus Scarborough.

The police for some time past had been very busy on the track of Mountjoy Scarborough, but had not hitherto succeeded in obtaining any information. Such activity as had been displayed cannot be procured without expense, and it had been understood in this case that old Mr. Scarborough had refused to furnish the means. Something he had supplied at first, but had latterly declined even to subscribe to a fund. He was not at all desirous, he said, that his son should be brought back to the world, particularly as he had made it evident by his disappearance that he was anxious to keep out of the way. "Why should I pay the fellows? It's no business of mine," he had said to his son. And from that moment he had declined to do more than make up the first subscription which had been suggested to him. But the police had been kept very busy, and it was known that the funds had been supplied chiefly by Mr. Tyrrwhit. He was a resolute and persistent man, and was determined to "run down" Mountjoy Scarborough, as he called it, if money would enable him to do so. It was he who had appealed to the squire for assistance in this object, and to him the squire had expressed his opinion that, as his son did not seem anxious to be brought back, he should not interfere in the matter.

"Well, Prodgers, what news have you to-day?" asked Augustus.

"There is a man a-wandering about down in Skye, just here and there, with nothing in particular to say for himself."

"What sort of a looking fellow is he?"

"Well, he's light, and don't come up to the captain's marks; but there's no knowing what disguises a fellow will put on. I don't think he's got the captain's legs, and a man can't change his legs."

"Captain Scarborough would not remain loitering about in Skye where he would be known by half the autumn tourists who saw him."

"That's just what I was saying to Wilkinson," said Prodgers. "Wilkinson seems to think that a man may be anybody as long as nobody knows who he is. 'That ain't the captain,' said I."

"I'm afraid he's got out of England," said the captain's brother.

"There's no place where he can be run down like New York, or Paris, or Melbourne, and it's them they mostly go to. We've wired 'em all three, and a dozen other ports of the kind. We catches 'em mostly if they go abroad; but when they remains at home they're uncommon troublesome. There was a man wandering about in County Donegal. We call Ireland at home, because we've so much to do with their police since the Land League came up; but this chap was only an artist who couldn't pay his bill. What do you think about it, Mr. Annesley?" said the policeman, turning short round upon Harry, and addressing him a question. Why should the policeman even have known his name?

"Who? I? I don't think about it at all. I have no means of thinking about it."

"Because you have been so busy down there at the Yard, I thought that, as you was asking so many questions, you was, perhaps, interested in the matter."

"My friend Mr. Annesley," said Augustus, "was acquainted with Captain Scarborough, as he is with me."

"It did seem as though he was more than usually interested, all the same," said the policeman.

"I am more than usually interested," replied Harry; "but I do not know that I am going to give you my reason. As to his present existence I know absolutely nothing."

"I dare say not. If you'd any information as was reliable I dare say as it would be forthcoming. Well, Mr. Scarborough, you may be sure of this: if we can get upon his trail we'll do so, and I think we shall. There isn't a port that hasn't been watched from two days after his disappearance, and there isn't a port as won't be watched as soon as any English steamer touches 'em. We've got our eyes out, and we means to use 'em. Good-night, Mr. Scarborough; good-night, Mr. Annesley," and he bobbed his head to our friend Harry. "You say as there is a reason as is unknown. Perhaps it won't be unknown always. Good-night, gentlemen." Then Constable Prodgers left the room.

Harry had been disconcerted by the policeman's remarks, and showed that it was so as soon as he was alone with Augustus Scarborough. "I'm afraid you think the man intended to be impertinent," said Augustus.

"No doubt he did, but such men are allowed to be impertinent."

"He sees an enemy, of course, in every one who pretends to know more than he knows himself,—or, indeed, in every one who does not. You said something about having a reason of your own, and he at once connected you with Mountjoy's disappearance. Such creatures are necessary, but from the little I've seen of them I do not think that they make the best companions in the world. I shall leave Mr.

Prodgers to carry on his business to the man who employs him,—namely, Mr. Tyrrwhit,—and I advise you to do the same."

Soon after that Harry Annesley took his leave, but he could not divest himself of an opinion that both the policeman and his host had thought that he had some knowledge respecting the missing man. Augustus Scarborough had said no word to that effect, but there had been a something in his manner which had excited suspicion in Harry's mind. And then Augustus had declared his purpose of offering his hand and fortune to Florence Mountjoy. He to be suitor to Florence,—he, so soon after Mountjoy had been banished from the scene! And why should he have been told of it?—he, of whose love for the girl he could not but think that Augustus Scarborough had been aware. Then, much perturbed in his mind, he resolved, as he returned to his lodgings, that he would go down to Cheltenham on the following day.

CHAPTER VI. HARRY ANNESLEY TELLS HIS SECRET

Harry hurried down to Cheltenham, hardly knowing what he was going to do or say when he got there. He went to the hotel and dined alone. "What's all this that's up about Captain Mountjoy?" said a stranger, coming and whispering to him at his table.

The inquirer was almost a stranger, but Harry did know his name. It was Mr. Baskerville, the hunting man. Mr. Baskerville was not rich, and not especially popular, and had no special amusement but that of riding two nags in the winter along the roads of Cheltenham in the direction which the hounds took. It was still summer, and the nags, who had been made to do their work in London, were picking up a little strength in idleness, or, as Mr. Baskerville called it, getting into condition. In the mean time Mr. Baskerville amused himself as well as he could by lying in bed and playing lawn-tennis. He sometimes dined at the hotel, in order that the club might think that he was entertained at friends' houses; but the two places were nearly the same to him, as he could achieve a dinner and half a pint of wine for five or six shillings at each of them. A more empty existence, or, one would be inclined to say, less pleasurable, no one could pass; but he had always a decent coat on his back and a smile on his face, and five shillings in his pocket with which to pay for his dinner. His asking what was up about Scarborough showed, at any rate, that he was very backward in the world's news.

"I believe he has vanished," said Harry.

"Oh yes, of course he's vanished. Everybody knows that—he vanished ever so long ago; but where is he?"

"If you can tell them in Scotland Yard they will be obliged to you."

"I suppose it is true the police are after him? Dear me! Forty thousand a year! This is a very queer story about the property, isn't it?"

"I don't know the story exactly, and therefore can hardly say whether it is queer or not."

"But about the younger son? People say that the father has contrived that the younger son shall have the money. What I hear is that the whole property is to be divided, and that the captain is to have half, on conditions that he keeps out of the way. But I am sure that you know more about it. You used to be intimate with both the brothers. I have seen you down here with the captain. Where is he?" And again he whispered into Harry's ear. But he could not have selected any subject more distasteful, and, therefore, Harry repulsed Mr. Baskerville not in the most courteous manner.

"Hang it! what airs that fellow gives himself," he said to another friend of the same kidney. "That's young Annesley, the son of a twopenny-halfpenny parson down in Hertfordshire. The kind of ways these fellows put on now are unbearable. He hasn't got a horse to ride on, but to hear him talk you'd think he was mounted three days a week."

"He's heir to old Prosper, of Buston Hall."

"How's that? But is he? I never heard that before. What's Buston Hall worth?" Then Mr. Baskerville made up his mind to be doubly civil to Harry Annesley the next time he saw him.

Harry had to consider on that night in what manner he would endeavor to see Florence Mountjoy on the next day. He was thoroughly discontented with himself as he walked about the streets of Cheltenham. He had now not only allowed the disappearance of Scarborough to pass by without stating when and where, and how he had last seen him, but had directly lied on the subject. He had told the man's brother that he had not seen him for some weeks previous, whereas to have concealed his knowledge on such a subject was in itself held to be abominable. He was ashamed of himself, and the more so because there was no one to whom he could talk openly on the matter. And it seemed to him as though all whom he met questioned him as to the man's disappearance, as if they suspected him. What was the man to him, or the man's guilt, or his father, that he should be made miserable? The man's attack upon him had been ferocious in its nature,—so brutal that when he had escaped from Mountjoy Scarborough's clutches there was nothing for him but to leave him lying in the street where, in his drunkenness, he had fallen. And now, in consequence of this, misery had fallen upon himself. Even this empty-headed fellow Baskerville, a man the poverty of whose character Harry perfectly understood, had questioned him about Mountjoy Scarborough. It could not, he thought, be possible that Baskerville could have had any reasons for suspicion, and yet the very sound of the inquiry stuck in his ears.

On the next morning, at eleven o'clock, he knocked at Mrs. Mountjoy's house in Mountpellier Place and asked for the elder lady. Mrs. Mountjoy was out, and Harry at once inquired for Florence. The servant at first seemed to hesitate, but at last showed Harry into the dining-room. There he waited five minutes, which seemed to him to be half an hour, and then Florence came to him. "Your mother is not at home," he said, putting out his hand.

"No, Mr. Annesley, but I think she will be back soon. Will you wait for her?"

"I do not know whether I am not glad that she should be out. Florence, I have something that I must tell you."

"Something that you must tell me!"

He had called her Florence once before, on a happy afternoon which he well remembered, but he was not thinking of that now. Her name, which was always in his mind, had come to him naturally, as though he had no time to pick and choose about names in the importance of the communication which he had to make. "Yes. I don't believe that you were ever really engaged to your cousin Mountjoy."

"No, I never was," she answered, briskly. Harry Annesley was certainly a handsome man, but no young man living ever thought less of his own beauty. He had fair, wavy hair, which he was always submitting to some barber, very much to the unexpressed disgust of poor Florence; because to her eyes the longer the hair grew the more beautiful was the wearer of it. His forehead, and eyes, and nose were all perfect in their form—

> "Hyperion's curls; the front of Jove himself;
> An eye like Mars, to threaten and command."

There was a peculiar brightness in his eye, which would have seemed to denote something absolutely great in his character had it not been for the wavering indecision of his mouth. There was as it were a vacillation in his lips which took away from the manliness of his physiognomy. Florence, who regarded his face as almost divine, was yet conscious of some weakness about his mouth which she did not know how to interpret. But yet, without knowing why it was so, she was accustomed to expect from him doubtful words, half expressed words, which would not declare to her his perfected thoughts—as she would have them declared. He was six feet high, but neither broad nor narrow, nor fat nor thin, but a very Apollo in Florence's eye. To the elders who knew him the quintessence of his beauty lay in the fact that he was altogether unconscious of it. He was a man who counted nothing on his personal appearance for the performance of those deeds which he was most anxious to achieve. The one achievement now essentially necessary to his happiness was the possession of Florence Mountjoy; but it certainly never occurred to him that he was more likely to obtain this because he was six feet high, or because his hair waved becomingly.

"I have supposed so," he said, in answer to her last assertion.

"You ought to have known it for certain. I mean to say that, had I ever been engaged to my cousin, I should have been miserable at such a moment as this. I never should have given him up because of the gross injustice done to him about the property. But his disappearance in this dreadful way would, I think, have killed me. As it is, I can think of nothing else, because he is my cousin."

"It is very dreadful," said Harry. "Have you any idea what can have happened to him?"

"Not in the least. Have you?"

"None at all, but—"

"But what?"

"I was the last person who saw him."

"You saw him last!"

"At least, I know no one who saw him after me."

"Have you told them?"

"I have told no one but you. I have come down here to Cheltenham on purpose to tell you."

"Why me?" she said, as though struck with fear at such an assertion on his part.

"I must tell some one, and I have not known whom else to tell. His father appears not at all anxious about him. His brother I do not altogether trust. Were I to go to these men, who are only looking after their money, I should be communicating with his enemies. Your mother already regards me as his enemy. If I told the police I should simply be brought into a court of justice, where I should be compelled to mention your name."

"Why mine?"

"I must begin the story from the beginning. One night I was coming home in London very late, about two o'clock, when whom should I meet in the street suddenly but Mountjoy Scarborough. It came out afterward that he had then been gambling; but when he encountered me he was intoxicated. He took me suddenly by the collar and shook me violently, and did his best to maltreat me. What words were spoken I cannot remember; but his conduct to me was as that of a savage beast. I struggled with him in the street as a man would struggle who is attacked by a wild dog. I think that he did not explain the cause of his hatred, though, of course, my memory as to what took place at that moment is disturbed and imperfect; but I did know in my heart why it was that he had quarrelled with me."

"Why was it?" Florence asked.

"Because he thought that I had ventured to love you."

"No, no!" shrieked Florence; "he could not have thought that."

"He did think so, and he was right enough. If I have never said so before, I am bound at any rate to say it now." He paused for a moment, but she made him no answer. "In the struggle between us he fell on the pavement against a rail;—and then I left him."

"Well?"

"He has never been heard of since. On the following day, in the afternoon, I left London for Buston; but nothing had been then heard of his disappearance. I neither knew of it nor suspected it. The question is, when others were searching for him, was I bound to go to the police and declare what I had suffered from him that night? Why should I connect his going with the outrage which I had suffered?"

"But why not tell it all?"

"I should have been asked why he had quarrelled with me. Ought I to have said that I did not know? Ought I to have pretended that there was no cause? I did know, and there was a cause. It was because he thought that I might prevail with you, now that he was a beggar, disowned by his own father."

"I would never have given him up for that," said Florence.

"But do you not see that your name would have been brought in,—that I should have had to speak of you as though I thought it possible that you loved me?" Then he paused, and Florence sat silent. But another thought struck him now. It occurred to him that under the plea put forward he would appear to seek shelter from his silence as to her name. He was aware how anxious he was on his own behalf not to mention the occurrence in the street, and it seemed that he was attempting to escape under the pretence of a fear that her name would be dragged in. "But independently of that I do not see why I should be subjected to the annoyance of letting it be known that I was thus attacked in the streets. And the time has now gone by. It did not occur to me when first he was missed that the matter would have been of such importance. Now it is too late."

"I suppose that you ought to have told his father."

"I think that I ought to have done so. But at any rate I have come to explain it all to you. It was necessary that I should tell some one. There seems to be no reason to suspect that the man has been killed."

"Oh, I hope not; I hope not that."

"He has been spirited away—out of the way of his creditors. For myself I think that it has all been done with his father's connivance. Whether his brother be in the secret or not I cannot tell, but I suspect he is. There seems to be no doubt that

Captain Scarborough himself has run so overhead into debt as to make the payment of his creditors impossible by anything short of the immediate surrender of the whole property. Some month or two since they all thought that the squire was dying, and that there would be nothing to do but to sell the property which would then be Mountjoy's, and pay themselves. Against this the dying man has rebelled, and has come, as it were, out of the grave to disinherit the son who has already contrived to disinherit himself. It is all an effort to save Tretton."

"But it is dishonest," said Florence.

"No doubt about it. Looking at it any way it is dishonest, Either the inheritance must belong to Mountjoy still, or it could not have been his when he was allowed to borrow money upon it."

"I cannot understand it. I thought it was entailed upon him. Of course it is nothing to me. It never could have been anything."

"But now the creditors declare that they have been cheated, and assert that Mountjoy is being kept out of the way to aid old Mr. Scarborough in the fraud. I cannot but say that I think it is so. But why he should have attacked me just at the moment of his going, or why, rather, he should have gone immediately after he had attacked me, I cannot say. I have no concern whatever with him or his money, though I hope—I hope that I may always have much with you. Oh, Florence, you surely have known what has been within my heart."

To this appeal she made no response, but sat awhile considering what she would say respecting Mountjoy Scarborough and his affairs.

"Am I to keep all this a secret?" she asked him at last.

"You shall consider that for yourself. I have not exacted from you any silence on the matter. You may tell whom you please, and I shall not consider that I have any ground of complaint against you. Of course for my own sake I do not wish it to be told. A great injury was done me, and I do not desire to be dragged into this, which would be another injury. I suspect that Augustus Scarborough knows more than he pretends, and I do not wish to be brought into the mess by his cunning. Whether you will tell your mother you must judge yourself."

"I shall tell nobody unless you bid me." At that moment the door of the room was opened, and Mrs. Mountjoy entered, with a frown upon her brow. She had not yet given up all hope that Mountjoy might return, and that the affairs of Tretton might be made to straighten themselves.

"Mamma, Mr. Annesley is here."

"So I perceive, my dear."

"I have come to your daughter to tell her how dearly I love her," said Harry, boldly.

"Mr. Annesley, you should have come to me before speaking to my daughter."

"Then I shouldn't have seen her at all."

"You should have left that as it might be. It is not at all a proper thing that a young gentleman should come and address a young lady in this way behind her only parent's back."

"I asked for you, and I did not know that you would not be at home."

"You should have gone away at once—at once. You know how terribly the family is cut up by this great misfortune to our cousin Mountjoy. Mountjoy Scarborough has been long engaged to Florence."

"No, mamma; no, never."

"At any rate, Mr. Annesley knows all about it. And that knowledge ought to have kept him away at the present moment. I must beg him to leave us now."

Then Harry took his hat and departed; but he had great consolation in feeling that Florence had not repudiated his love, which she certainly would have done had she not loved him in return. She had spoken no word of absolute encouragement, but there had much more of encouragement than of repudiation in her manner.

CHAPTER VII. HARRY ANNESLEY GOES TO TRETTON

Harry had promised to go down to Tretton, and when the time came Augustus Scarborough did not allow him to escape from the visit. He explained to him that in his father's state of health there would be no company to entertain him; that there was only a maiden sister of his father's staying in the house, and that he intended to take down into the country with him one Septimus Jones, who occupied chambers on the same floor with him in London, and whom Annesley knew to be young Scarborough's most intimate friend. "There will be a little shooting," he said, "and I have bought two or three horses, which you and Jones can ride. Cannock Chase is one of the prettiest parts of England, and as you care for scenery you can get some amusement out of that. You'll see my father, and hear, no doubt, what he has got to say for himself. He is not in the least reticent in speaking of my brother's affairs." There was a good deal in this which was not agreeable. Miss Scarborough was sister to Mrs. Mountjoy as well as to the squire, and had been one of the family party most anxious to assure the marriage of Florence and the captain. The late General Mountjoy had been supposed to be a great man in his way, but had died before Tretton had become as valuable as it was now. Hence the eldest son had been christened with his name, and much of the Mountjoy prestige still clung to the family. But Harry did not care much about the family except so far as Florence was concerned. And then he had not been on peculiarly friendly terms with Septimus Jones, who had always been submissive to Augustus; and, now that Augustus was a rich man and could afford to buy horses, was likely to be more submissive than ever.

He went down to Tretton alone early in September, and when he reached the house he found that the two young men were out shooting. He asked for his own room, but was instead immediately taken to the old squire, whom he found lying on a couch in a small dressing-room, while his sister, who had been reading to him, was by his side. After the usual greetings Harry made some awkward apology as to his intrusion at the sick man's bedside. "Why, I ordered them to bring you in here," said the squire; "you can't very well call that intrusion. I have no idea of being shut up from the world before they nail me down in my coffin."

"That will be a long time first, we all hope," said his sister.

"Bother! you hope it, but I don't know that any one else does;—I don't for one. And if I did, what's the good of hoping? I have a couple of diseases, either of which is enough to kill a horse." Then he mentioned his special maladies in a manner which made Harry shrink. "What are they talking about in London just at present?" he asked.

"Just the old set of subjects," said Harry.

"I suppose they have got tired of me and my iniquities?" Harry could only smile and shake his head. "There has been such a complication of romances that one expects the story to run a little more than the ordinary nine days."

"Men still do talk about Mountjoy."

"And what are they saying? Augustus declares that you are especially interested on the subject."

"I don't know why I should be," said Harry.

"Nor I either. When a fellow becomes no longer of any service to either man, woman, or beast, I do not know why any should take an interest in him. I suppose you didn't lend him money?"

"I was not likely to do that, sir."

"Then I cannot conceive how it can interest you whether he be in London or Kamtchatka. It does not interest me the least in the world. Were he to turn up here it would be a trouble; and yet they expect me to subscribe largely to a fund for finding him. What good could he do me if he were found?"

"Oh, John, he is your son," said Miss Scarborough.

"And would be just as good a son as Augustus, only that he has turned out uncommonly badly. I have not the slightest feeling in the world as to his birth, and so I think I showed pretty plainly. But nothing could stop him in his course, and therefore I told the truth, that's all." In answer to this, Harry found it quite impossible to say a word, but got away to his bedroom and dressed for dinner as quickly as possible.

While he was still thus employed Augustus came into the room still dressed in his shooting-clothes. "So you've seen my father," he said.

"Yes, I saw him."

"And what did he say to you about Mountjoy?"

"Little or nothing that signifies. He seems to think it unreasonable that he should be asked to pay for finding him, seeing that the creditors expect to get the advantage of his presence when found."

"He is about right there."

"Oh yes; but still he is his father. It may be that it would be expected that he should interest himself in finding him."

"Upon my word I don't agree with you. If a thousand a year could be paid to keep Mountjoy out of the way I think it would be well expended."

"But you were acting with the police."

"Oh, the police! What do the police know about it? Of course I talk it all over with them. They have not the smallest idea where the man is, and do not know how to go to work to discover him. I don't say that my father is judicious in his brazen-faced opposition to all inquiry. He should pretend to be a little anxious—as I do. Not that there would be any use now in pretending to keep up appearances. He has declared himself utterly indifferent to the law, and has defied the world. Never mind, old fellow, we shall eat the more dinner, only I must go and prepare myself for it."

At dinner Harry found only Septimus Jones, Augustus Scarborough, and his aunt. Miss Scarborough said a good deal about her brother, and declared him to be much better. "Of course you know, Augustus, that Sir William Brodrick was down here for two days."

"Only fancy," replied he, "what one has to pay for two days of Sir William Brodrick in the country!"

"What can it matter?" said the generous spinster.

"It matters exactly so many hundred pounds; but no one will begrudge it if he does so many hundred pounds' worth of good."

"It will show, at any rate, that we have had the best advice," said the lady.

"Yes, it will show;—that is exactly what people care about. What did Sir William say?" Then during the first half of dinner a prolonged reference was made to Mr. Scarborough's maladies, and to Sir William's opinion concerning them. Sir William had declared that Mr. Scarborough's constitution was the most wonderful thing that he had ever met in his experience. In spite of the fact that Mr. Scarborough's body was one mass of cuts and bruises and faulty places, and that nothing would keep him going except the wearing of machinery which he was unwilling to wear, yet the facilities for much personal enjoyment were left to him, and Sir William declared that, if he would only do exactly as he were told, he might live for the next five years. "But everybody knows that he won't do anything that he is told," said Augustus, in a tone of voice which by no means expressed extreme sorrow.

From his father he led the conversation to the partridges, and declared his conviction that, with a little trouble and some expense, a very good head of game might be got up at Tretton. "I suppose it wouldn't cost much?" said Jones, who beyond ten shillings to a game-keeper never paid sixpence for whatever shooting came in his way.

"I don't know what you call much," said Augustus, "but I think it may be done for three or four hundred a year. I should like to calculate how many thousand partridges at that rate Sir William has taken back in his pocket."

"What does it matter?" asked Miss Scarborough.

"Only as a speculation. Of course my father, while he lives, is justified in giving his whole income to doctors if he likes it; but one gets into a manner of speaking about him as though he had done a good deal with his money in which he was not justified."

"Don't talk in that way, Augustus."

"My dear aunt, I am not at all inclined to be more open-mouthed than he is. Only reflect what it was that he was disposed to do with me, and the good-humor with which I have borne it!"

"I think I should hold my tongue about it," said Harry Annesley.

"And I think that in my place you would do no such thing. To your nature it would be almost impossible to hold your tongue. Your sense of justice would be so affronted that you would feel yourself compelled to discuss the injury done to you with all your intimate friends. But with your father your quarrel would be eternal. I made nothing of it, and, indeed, if he pertinaciously held his tongue on the subject, so should I."

"But because he talks," said Harry, "why should you?"

"Why should he not?" said Septimus Jones. "Upon my word I don't see the justice of it."

"I am not speaking of justice, but of feeling."

"Upon my word I wish you would hold your tongues about it; at any rate till my back is turned," said the old lady.

Then Augustus finished the conversation. "I am determined to treat it all as though it were a joke, and, as a joke, one to be spoken of lightly. It was a strong measure, certainly, this attempt to rob me of twenty or thirty thousand pounds a year. But it was done in favor of my brother, and therefore let it pass. I am at a loss to conceive what my father has done with his money. He hasn't given Mountjoy, at any rate, more than a half of his income for the last five or six years, and his own personal expenses are very small. Yet he tells me that he has the greatest difficulty in raising a thousand pounds, and positively refuses in his present difficulties to add above five hundred a year to my former allowance. No father who had thoroughly done his duty by his son, could speak in a more fixed and austere manner. And yet he knows that every shilling will be mine as soon as he goes." The servant who was waiting upon them had been in and out of the room while this was said, and must have heard much of it. But to that Augustus seemed to be quite indifferent. And, indeed, the whole family story was known to every servant in the house. It is true that gentlemen and ladies who have servants do not usually wish to talk about their private matters before all the household, even though the private matters may be known; but this household was unlike all others in that respect. There was not a housemaid about the rooms or a groom in the stables who did not know how terrible a reprobate their master had been.

"You will see your father before you go to bed?" Miss Scarborough said to her nephew as she left the room.

"Certainly, if he will send to say that he wishes it."

"He does wish it, most anxiously."

"I believe that to be your imagination. At any rate, I will come—say in an hour's time. He would be just as pleased to see Harry Annesley, for the matter of that, or Mr. Grey, or the inspector of police. Any one whom he could shock, or pretend to shock, by the peculiarity of his opinions, would do as well." By that time, however, Miss Scarborough had left the room.

Then the three men sat and talked, and discussed the affairs of the family generally. New leases had just been granted for adding manufactories to the town of Tretton: and as far as outward marks of prosperity went all was prosperous. "I expect to have a water-mill on the lawn before long," said Augustus. "These mechanics have it all their own way. If they were to come and tell me that they intended to put up a wind-mill in my bedroom to-morrow morning, I could only take off my hat to them. When a man offers you five per cent. where you've only had four, he is instantly your lord and master. It doesn't signify how vulgar he is, or how insolent, or how exacting. Associations of the tenderest kind must all give way to trade. But the shooting which lies to the north and west of us is, I think, safe for the present. I suppose I must go and see what my father wants, or I shall be held to have neglected my duty to my affectionate parent."

"Capital fellow, Augustus Scarborough," said Jones, as soon as their host had left them.

"I was at Cambridge with him, and he was popular there."

"He'll be more popular now that he's the heir to Tretton. I don't know any fellow that I can get along better with than Scarborough. I think you were a little hard upon him about his father, you know."

"In his position he ought to hold his tongue."

"It's the strangest thing that has turned up in the whole course of my experience. You see, if he didn't talk about it people wouldn't quite understand what it was that his father has done. It's only matter of report now, and the creditors, no doubt, do believe that when old Scarborough goes off the hooks they will be able to walk in and take possession. He has got to make the world think that he is the heir, and that will go a long way. You may be sure he doesn't talk as he does without having a reason for it. He's the last man I know to do anything without a reason."

The evening dragged along very slowly while Jones continued to tell all that he knew of his friend's character. But Augustus Scarborough did not return, and soon after ten o'clock, when Harry Annesley could smoke no more cigars, and declared that he had no wish to begin upon brandy-and-water after his wine, he went to his bed.

CHAPTER VIII. ARRY ANNESLEY TAKES A WALK

"There was the devil to pay with my father last night after I went to him," said Scarborough to Harry next morning. "He now and then suffers agonies of pain, and it is the most difficult thing in the world to get him right again. But anything equal to his courage I never before met."

"How is he this morning?"

"Very weak and unable to exert himself. But I cannot say that he is otherwise much the worse. You won't see him this morning; but to-morrow you will, or next day. Don't you be shy about going to him when he sends for you. He likes to show the world that he can bear his sufferings with a light heart, and is ready to die to-morrow without a pang or a regret. Who was the fellow who sent for a fellow to let him see how a Christian could die? I can fancy my father doing the same thing, only there would be nothing about Christianity in the message. He would bid you come and see a pagan depart in peace, and would be very unhappy if he thought that your dinner would be disturbed by the ceremony. Now come down to breakfast, and then we'll go out shooting."

For three days Harry remained at Tretton, and ate and drank, and shot and rode, always in young Scarborough's company. During this time he did not see the old squire, and understood from Miss Scarborough's absence that he was still suffering from his late attack. The visit was to be prolonged for one other day, and he was told that on that day the squire would send for him. "I'm sick of these eternal partridges," said Augustus. "No man should ever shoot partridges two days running. Jones can go out by himself. He won't have to tip the game-keeper any more for an additional day, and so it will be all gain to him. You'll see my father in the afternoon after lunch, and we will go and take a walk now."

Harry started for his walk, and his companion immediately began again about the property. "I'm beginning to think," said he, "that it's nearly all up with the governor. These attacks come upon him worse and worse, and always leave him absolutely prostrate. Then he will do nothing to prevent them. To assure himself a week of life, he will not endure an hour of discomfort. It is plucky, you know."

"He is in all respects as brave a man as I have known."

"He sets God and man at absolute defiance, and always does it with the most profound courtesy. If he goes to the infernal regions he will insist upon being the last of the company to enter the door. And he will be prepared with something good-humored to say as soon as he has been ushered in. He was very much troubled about you yesterday."

"What has he to say of me?"

"Nothing in the least uncivil; but he has an idea in his head which nothing on earth will put out of it, and in which, but for your own word, I should be inclined to agree." Harry, when this was said, stood still on the mountain-side, and looked full into his companion's face. He felt at the moment that the idea had some reference to Mountjoy Scarborough and his disappearance. They were together on the heathy, unenclosed ground of Cannock Chase, and had already walked some ten or twelve miles. "He thinks you know where Mountjoy is."

"Why should I know?"

"Or at any rate that you have seen him since any of us. He professes not to care a straw for Mountjoy or his whereabouts, and declares himself under obligation to those who have contrived his departure. Nevertheless, he is curious."

"What have I to do with Mountjoy Scarborough?"

"That's just the question. What have you to do with him? He suggests that there have been words between you as to Florence, which has caused Mountjoy to vanish. I don't profess to explain anything beyond that,—nor, indeed, do I profess to agree with my father. But the odd thing is that Prodgers, the policeman, has the same thing running in his head."

"Because I have shown some anxiety about your brother in Scotland Yard."

"No doubt; Prodgers says that you've shown more anxiety than was to be expected from a mere acquaintance. I quite acknowledge that Prodgers is as thick-headed an idiot as you shall catch on a summer's day; but that's his opinion. For myself, I know your word too well to doubt it." Harry walked on in silence, thinking, or trying to think, what, on the spur of the moment, he had better do. He was minded to speak out the whole truth, and declare to himself that it was nothing to him what Augustus Scarborough might say or think. And there was present to him a feeling that his companion was dealing unfairly with him, and was endeavoring in some way to trap him and lead him into a difficulty. But he had made up his mind, as it were, not to know anything of Mountjoy Scarborough, and to let those five minutes in the street be as though they had never been. He had been brutally attacked, and had thought it best to say nothing on the subject. He would not allow his secret, such as it was, to be wormed out of him. Scarborough was endeavoring to extort from him that which he had resolved to conceal; and he determined at last that he would not become a puppet in his hands. "I don't see why you should care a straw about it," said Scarborough.

"Nor do I."

"At any rate you repeat your denial. It will be well that I should let my father know that he is mistaken, and also that ass Prodgers. Of course, with my father it is sheer curiosity. Indeed, if he thought that you were keeping Mountjoy under lock and key, he would only admire your dexterity in so preserving him. Any bold line of action that was contrary to the law recommends itself to his approbation. But Prodgers has a lurking idea that he should like to arrest you."

"What for?"

"Simply because he thinks you know something that he doesn't know. As he's a detective, that, in his mind, is quite enough for arresting any man. I may as well give him my assurance, then, that he is mistaken."

"Why should your assurance go for more than mine? Give him nothing of the kind."

"I may give him, at any rate, my assurance that I believe your word."

"If you do believe it, you can do so."

"But you repeat your assertion that you saw nothing of Mountjoy just before his disappearance?"

"This is an amount of cross-questioning which I do not take in good part, and to which I will not submit." Here Scarborough affected to laugh loudly. "I know nothing of your brother, and care almost as little. He has professed to admire a young lady to whom I am not indifferent, and has, I believe, expressed a wish to make her his wife. He is also her cousin, and the lady in question has, no doubt, been much interested about him. It is natural that she should be so."

"Quite natural—seeing that she has been engaged to him for twelve months."

"Of that I know nothing. But my interest about your brother has been because of her. You can explain all this about your brother if you please, or can let it alone. But for myself, I decline to answer any more questions. If Prodgers thinks that he can arrest me, let him come and try."

"The idea of your flying into a passion because I have endeavored to explain it all to you! At any rate I have your absolute denial, and that will enable me to deal both with my father and Prodgers." To this Harry made no answer, and the two young men walked back to Tretton together without many more words between them.

When Harry had been in the house about half an hour, and had already eaten his lunch, somewhat sulkily, a message came to him from Miss Scarborough requiring his presence. He went to her, and was told by her that Mr. Scarborough would now see him. He was aware that Mr. Scarborough never saw Septimus Jones, and that there was something peculiar in the sending of this message to him. Why should the man who was supposed to have but a few weeks to live be so anxious to see one who was comparatively a stranger to him? "I am so glad you have come in before dinner, Mr. Annesley, because my brother is so anxious to see you, and I am afraid you'll go too early in the morning." Then he followed her, and again found Mr. Scarborough on a couch in the same room to which he had been first introduced.

"I've had a sharp bout of it since I saw you before," said the sick man.

"So we heard, sir."

"There is no saying how many or rather how few bouts of this kind it will take to polish me off. But I think I am entitled to some little respite now. The apothecary from Tretton was here this morning, and I believe has done me just as much good as Sir William Brodrick. His charge will be ten shillings, while Sir William demanded three hundred pounds. But it would be mean to go out with no one but the Tretton apothecary to look after one."

"I suppose Sir William's knowledge has been of some service."

"His dexterity with his knife has been of more. So you and Augustus have been quarrelling about Mountjoy?"

"Not that I know of."

"He says so; and I believe his word on such a subject sooner than yours. You are likely to quarrel without knowing it, and he is not. He thinks that you know what has become of Mountjoy."

"Does he? Why should he think so, when I told him that I know nothing? I tell you that I know absolutely nothing. I am ignorant whether he is dead or alive."

"He is not dead," said the father.

"I suppose not; but I know nothing about him. Why your second son—"

"You mean my eldest according to law,—or rather my only son!"

"Why Augustus Scarborough," continued Harry Annesley, "should take upon himself to suspect that I know aught of his brother I cannot say. He has some cock-and-bull story about a policeman whom he professes to believe to be ignorant of his own business. This policeman, he says, is anxious to arrest me."

"To make you give evidence before a magistrate," said his father.

"He did not dare to tell me that he suspected me himself."

"There;—I knew you had quarrelled."

"I deny it altogether. I have not quarrelled with Augustus Scarborough. He is welcome to his suspicions if he chooses to entertain them. I should have liked him better if he had not brought me down to Tretton, so as to extract from me whatever he can. I shall be more guarded in future in speaking of Mountjoy Scarborough; but to you I give my positive assurance, which I do not doubt you will believe, that I know nothing respecting him." An honest indignation gleamed in his eyes as he spoke; but still there were the signs of that vacillation about his mouth which Florence had been able to read, but not to interpret.

"Yes," said the squire, after a pause, "I believe you. You haven't that kind of ingenuity which enables a man to tell a lie and stick to it. I have. It's a very great gift if a man be enabled to restrain his appetite for lying." Harry could only smile when he heard the squire's confession. "Only think how I have lied about Mountjoy; and how successful my lies might have been, but for his own folly!"

"People do judge you a little harshly now," said Harry.

"What's the odd's? I care nothing for their judgment; I endeavored to do justice to my own child, and very nearly did it. I was very nearly successful in rectifying the gross injustice of the world. Why should a little delay in a ceremony in which he had no voice have robbed him of his possessions? I determined that he should have Tretton, and I determined also to make it up to Augustus by denying myself the use of my own wealth. Things have gone wrongly not by my own folly. I could not prevent the mad career which Mountjoy has run; but do you think that I am ashamed because the world knows what I have done? Do you suppose my death-bed will be embittered by the remembrance that I have been a liar? Not in the least. I have done the best I could for my two sons, and in doing it have denied myself many advantages. How many a man would have spent his money on himself, thinking nothing of his boys, and then have gone to his grave with all the dignity of a steady Christian father! Of the two men I prefer myself; but I know that I have been a liar."

What was Harry Annesley to say in answer to such an address as this? There was the man, stretched on his bed before him, haggard, unshaved, pale, and grizzly, with a fire in his eyes, but weakness in his voice,—bold, defiant, self-satisfied, and yet not selfish. He had lived through his life with the one strong resolution of setting the law at defiance in reference to the distribution of his property; but chiefly because he had thought the law to be unjust. Then, when the accident of his eldest son's extravagance had fallen upon him, he had endeavored to save his second son, and had thought, without the slightest remorse, of the loss which was to fall on the creditors. He had done all this in such a manner that, as far as Harry knew, the law could not touch him, though all the world was aware of his iniquity. And now he lay boasting of what he had done. It was necessary that Harry should say something as he rose from his seat, and he lamely expressed a wish that Mr. Scarborough might quickly recover. "No, my dear fellow," said the squire; "men do not recover when they are brought to such straits as I am in. Nor do I wish it. Were I to live, Augustus would feel the second injustice to be quite intolerable. His mind is lost in amazement at what I had contemplated. And he feels that the matter can only be set right between him and fortune by my dying at once. If he were to understand that I were to live ten years longer, I think that he would either commit a murder or lose his senses."

"But there is enough for both of you," said Harry.

"There is no such word in the language as enough. An estate can have but one owner, and Augustus is anxious to be owner here. I do not blame him in the least. Why should he desire to spare a father's rights when that father showed himself so willing to sacrifice his? Good-bye, Annesley; I am sorry you are going, for I like to have some honest fellow to talk to. You are not to suppose that because I have done this thing I am indifferent to what men shall say of me. I wish them to think me good, though I have chosen to run counter to the prejudices of the world."

Then Harry escaped from the room, and spent the remaining evening with Augustus Scarborough and Septimus Jones. The conversation was devoted chiefly to the partridges and horses; and was carried on by Septimus with severity toward Harry, and by Scarborough with an extreme civility which was the more galling of the two.

CHAPTER IX. AUGUSTUS HAS HIS OWN DOUBTS

"That's an impertinent young puppy," said Septimus Jones as soon as the fly which was to carry Harry Annesley to the station had left the hall-door on the following morning. It may be presumed that Mr. Jones would not thus have expressed himself unless his friend Augustus Scarborough had dropped certain words in conversation in regard to Harry to the same effect. And it may be presumed also that Augustus would not have dropped such words without a purpose of letting his friend know that Harry was to be abused. Augustus Scarborough had made up his mind, looking at the matter all round, that more was to be got by abusing Harry than by praising him.

"The young man has a good opinion of himself certainly."

"He thinks himself to be a deal better than anybody else," continued Jones, "whereas I for one don't see it. And he has a way with him of pretending to be quite equal to his companions, let them be who they may, which to me is odious. He was down upon you and down upon your father. Of course your father has made a most fraudulent attempt; but what the devil is it to him?" The other young man made no answer, but only smiled. The opinion expressed by Mr. Jones as to Harry Annesley had only been a reflex of that felt by Augustus Scarborough. But the reflex, as is always the case when the looking-glass is true, was correct.

Scarborough had known Harry Annesley for a long time, as time is counted in early youth, and had by degrees learned to hate him thoroughly. He was a little the elder, and had at first thought to domineer over his friend. But the friend had resisted, and had struggled manfully to achieve what he considered an equality in friendship. "Now, Scarborough, you may as well take it once for all that I am not going to be talked down. If you want to talk a fellow down you can go to Walker, Brown, or Green. Then when you are tired of the occupation you can come back to me." It was thus that Annesley had been wont to address his friend. But his friend had been anxious to talk down this special young man for special purposes, and had been conscious of some weakness in the other's character which he thought entitled him to do so. But the weakness was not of that nature, and he had failed. Then had come the rivalry between Mountjoy and Harry, which had seemed to Augustus to be the extreme of impudence. From of old he had been taught to regard his brother Mountjoy as the first of young men—among commoners; the first in prospects and the first in rank; and to him Florence Mountjoy had been allotted as a bride. How he had himself learned first to envy and then to covet this allotted bride need not here be told. But by degrees it had come to pass that Augustus had determined that his spendthrift brother should fall under his own power, and that the bride should be the reward. How it was that two brothers, so different in character, and yet so alike in their selfishness, should have come to love the same girl with a true intensity of purpose, and that Harry Annesley, whose character was essentially different, and who was in no degree selfish, should have loved her also, must be left to explain itself as the girl's character shall be developed. But Florence Mountjoy had now for many months been the cause of bitter dislike against poor Harry in the mind of Augustus Scarborough. He understood much more clearly than his brother had done who it was that the girl really preferred. He was ever conscious, too, of his own superiority,—falsely conscious,—and did feel that if Harry's character were really known, no girl would in truth prefer him. He could not quite see Harry with Florence's eyes nor could he see himself with any other eyes but his own.

Then had come the meeting between Mountjoy and Harry Annesley in the street, of which he had only such garbled account as Mountjoy himself had given him within half an hour afterward. From that story, told in the words of a drunken man,—a man drunk, and bruised, and bloody, who clearly did not understand in one minute the words spoken in the last,—Augustus did learn that there had been some great row between his brother and Harry Annesley. Then Mountjoy had disappeared,—had disappeared, as the reader will have understood, with his brother's co-operation,—and Harry had not come forward, when inquiries were made, to declare what he knew of the occurrences of that night. Augustus had narrowly watched his conduct, in order at first that he might learn in what condition his brother had been left in the street, but afterward with the purpose of ascertaining why it was that Harry had been so reticent. Then he had allured Harry on to a direct lie, and soon perceived that he could afterward use the secret for his own purpose.

"I think we shall have to see what that young man's about, you know," he said afterward to Septimus Jones.

"Yes, yes, certainly," said Septimus. But Septimus did not quite understand why it was that they should have to see what the young man was about.

"Between you and me, I think he means to interfere with me, and I do not mean to stand his interference."

"I should think not."

"He must go back to Buston, among the Bustonians, or he and I will have a stand-up fight of it. I rather like a stand-up fight."

"Just so. When a fellow's so bumptious as that he ought to be licked."

"He has lied about Mountjoy," said Augustus. Then Jones waited to be told how it was that Harry had lied. He was aware that there was some secret unknown to him, and was anxious to be informed. Was Harry aware of Mountjoy's hiding-place, and if so, how had he learned it? Why was it that Harry should be acquainted with that which was dark to all the world besides? Jones was of opinion that the squire knew all about it, and thought it not improbable that the squire and Augustus had the secret in their joint keeping. But if so, how should Harry Annesley know anything about it? "He has lied like the very devil," continued Augustus, after a pause.

"Has he, now?"

"And I don't mean to spare him."

"I should think not." Then there was a pause, at the end of which Jones found himself driven to ask a question: "How has he lied?" Augustus smiled and shook his head, from which the other man gathered that he was not now to be told the nature of the lie in question. "A fellow that lies like that," said Jones, "is not to be endured."

"I do not mean to endure him. You have heard of a young lady named Miss Mountjoy, a cousin of ours?"

"Mountjoy's Miss Mountjoy?" suggested Jones.

"Yes, Mountjoy's Miss Mountjoy. That, of course, is over. Mountjoy has brought himself to such a pass that he is not entitled to have a Miss Mountjoy any longer. It seems the proper thing that she shall pass, with the rest of the family property, to the true heir."

"You marry her!"

"We need not talk about that just at present. I don't know that I've made up my mind. At any rate, I do not intend that Harry Annesley shall have her."

"I should think not."

"He's a pestilential cur, that has got himself introduced into the family, and the sooner we get quit of him the better. I should think the young lady would hardly fancy him when she knows that he has lied like the very devil, with the object of getting her former lover out of the way."

"By Jove, no, I should think not!"

"And when the world comes to understand that Harry Annesley, in the midst of all these inquiries, knows all about poor Mountjoy,—was the last to see him in

London,—and has never come forward to say a word about him, then I think the world will be a little hard upon the immaculate Harry Annesley. His own uncle has quarrelled with him already."

"What uncle?"

"The gentleman down in Hertfordshire, on the strength of whose acres Master Harry is flaunting it about in idleness. I have my eyes open and can see as well as another. When Harry lectures me about my father and my father about me, one would suppose that there's not a hole in his own coat. I think he'll find that the garment is not altogether water-tight." Then Augustus, finding that he had told as much as was needful to Septimus Jones, left his friend and went about his own family business.

On the next morning Septimus Jones took his departure, and on the day following Augustus followed him. "So you're off?" his father said to him when he came to make his adieux.

"Well, yes; I suppose so. A man has got so many things to look after which he can't attend to down here."

"I don't know what they are, but you understand it all. I'm not going to ask you to stay. Does it ever occur to you that you may never see me again?"

"What a question!"

"It's one that requires an answer, at any rate."

"It does occur to me; but not at all as probable."

"Why not probable?"

"Because there's a telegraph wire from Tretton to London; and because the journey down here is very short. It also occurs to me to think so from what has been said by Sir William Brodrick. Of course any man may die suddenly."

"Especially when the surgeons have been at him."

"You have your sister with you, sir, and she will be of more comfort to you than I can be. Your condition is in some respects an advantage to you. These creditors of Mountjoy can't force their way in upon you."

"You are wrong there."

"They have not done so."

"Nor should they, though I were as strong as you. What are Mountjoy's creditors to me? They have not a scrap of my handwriting in their possession. There is not one who can say that he has even a verbal promise from me. They never came to me when they wanted to lend him money at fifty per cent. Did they ever hear me say that he was my heir?"

"Perhaps not."

"Not one has ever heard it. It was not to them I lied, but to you and to Grey. D— the creditors! What do I care for them, though they be all ruined?"

"Not in the least."

"Why do you talk to me about the creditors? You, at any rate, know the truth." Then Augustus quitted the room, leaving his father in a passion. But, as a fact, he was by no means assured as to the truth. He supposed that he was the heir; but might it not be possible that his father had contrived all this so as to save the property from Mountjoy and that greedy pack of money-lenders? Grey must surely know the truth. But why should not Grey be deceived on the second event as well as the first. There was no limit, Augustus sometimes thought, to his father's cleverness. This idea had occurred to him within the last week, and his mind was tormented with reflecting what might yet be his condition. But of one thing he was sure, that his father and Mountjoy were not in league together. Mountjoy at any rate believed himself to have been disinherited. Mountjoy conceived that his only chance of obtaining money arose from his brother. The circumstances of Mountjoy's absence were, at any rate, unknown to his father.

CHAPTER X. SIR MAGNUS MOUNTJOY

It was the peculiarity of Florence Mountjoy that she did not expect other people to be as good as herself. It was not that she erected for herself a high standard and had then told herself that she had no right to demand from others one so exalted. She had erected nothing. Nor did she know that she attempted to live by grand rules. She had no idea that she was better than anybody else; but it came to her naturally as the result of what had gone before, to be unselfish, generous, trusting, and pure. These may be regarded as feminine virtues, and may be said to be sometimes tarnished, by faults which are equally feminine. Unselfishness may become want of character; generosity essentially unjust; confidence may be weak, and purity insipid. Here it was that the strength of Florence Mountjoy asserted itself. She knew well what was due to herself, though she would not claim it. She could trust to another, but in silence be quite sure of herself. Though pure herself, she was rarely shocked by the ways of others. And she was as true as a man pretends to be.

In figure, form, and face she never demanded immediate homage by the sudden flash of her beauty. But when her spell had once fallen on a man's spirit it was not often that he could escape from it quickly. When she spoke a peculiar melody struck the hearer's ears. Her voice was soft and low and sweet, and full at all times of harmonious words; but when she laughed it was like soft winds playing among countless silver bells. There was something in her touch which to men was almost divine. Of this she was all unconscious, but was as chary with her fingers as though it seemed that she could ill spare her divinity.

In height she was a little above the common, but it was by the grace of her movements that the world was compelled to observe her figure. There are women whose grace is so remarkable as to demand the attention of all. But then it is known of them, and momentarily seen, that their grace is peculiar. They have studied their graces, and the result is there only too evident. But Florence seemed to have studied nothing. The beholder felt that she must have been as graceful when playing with her doll in the nursery. And it was the same with her beauty. There was no peculiarity of chiselled features. Had you taken her face and measured it by certain rules, you would have found that her mouth was too large and her nose irregular. Of her teeth she showed but little, and in her complexion there was none of that pellucid clearness in which men ordinarily delight. But her eyes were more than ordinarily bright, and when she laughed there seemed to stream from them some heavenly delight. When she did laugh it was as though some spring had been opened from which ran for the time a stream of sweetest intimacy. For the time you would then fancy that you had been let into the inner life of this girl, and would be proud of yourself that so much should have been granted you. You would feel that there was something also in yourself in that this should have been permitted. Her hair and eyebrows were dark brown, of the hue most common to men and women, and had in them nothing that was peculiar; but her hair was soft and smooth and ever well dressed, and never redolent of peculiar odors. It was simply Florence Mountjoy's hair, and that made it perfect in the eyes of her male friends generally.

"She's not such a wonderful beauty, after all," once said of her a gentleman to whom it may be presumed that she had not taken the trouble to be peculiarly attractive. "No," said another,—"no. But, by George! I shouldn't like to have the altering of her." It was thus that men generally felt in regard to Florence Mountjoy. When they came to reckon her up they did not see how any change was to be made for the better.

To Florence, as to most other girls, the question of her future life had been a great trouble. Whom should she marry? and whom should she decline to marry? To a girl, when it is proposed to her suddenly to change everything in life, to go altogether away and place herself under the custody of a new master, to find for herself a new home, new pursuits, new aspirations, and a strange companion, the change must be so complete as almost to frighten her by its awfulness. And yet it has to be always thought of, and generally done.

But this change had been presented to Florence in a manner more than ordinarily burdensome. Early in life, when naturally she would not have begun to think seriously of marriage, she had been told rather than asked to give herself to her cousin Mountjoy. She was too firm of character to accede at once—to deliver herself over body and soul to the tender mercies of one, in truth, unknown. But she had been unable to interpose any reason that was valid, and had contented herself by demanding time. Since that there had been moments in which she had almost yielded. Mountjoy Scarborough had been so represented to her that she had considered it to be almost a duty to yield. More than once the word had been all but spoken; but the word had never been spoken. She had been subjected to what might be called cruel pressure. In season and out of season her mother had represented as a duty this marriage with her cousin. Why should she not marry her cousin? It must be understood that these questions had been asked before any of the terrible facts of Captain Scarborough's life had been made known to her. Because, it may be said, she did not love him. But in these days she had loved no man, and was inclined to think so little of herself as to make her want of love no necessary bar to the accomplishment of the wish of others. By degrees she was spoken of among their acquaintance as the promised bride of Mountjoy Scarborough, and though she ever denied the imputation, there came over her girl's heart a feeling,—very sad and very solemn, but still all but accepted,—that so it must be. Then Harry Annesley had crossed her path, and the question had been at last nearly answered, and the doubts nearly decided. She did not quite know at first that she loved Harry Annesley, but was almost sure that it was impossible for her to become the wife of Mountjoy Scarborough.

Then there came nearly twelve months of most painful uncertainty in her life. It is very hard for a young girl to have to be firm with her mother in declining a proposed marriage, when all circumstances of the connection are recommended to her as being peculiarly alluring. And there was nothing in the personal manners of her cousin which seemed to justify her in declaring her abhorrence. He was a dark, handsome, military-looking man, whose chief sin it was in the eyes of his cousin that he seemed to demand from her affection, worship, and obedience. She did not analyse his character, but she felt it. And when it came to pass that tidings of his debts at last reached her, she felt that she was glad of an excuse, though she knew that the excuse would not have prevailed with her had she liked him. Then came his debts, and with the knowledge of them a keener perception of his imperiousness. She could consent to become the wife of the man who had squandered his property and wasted his estate; but not of one who before his marriage demanded of her that submission which, as she thought, should be given by her freely after her marriage. Harry Annesley glided into her heart after a manner very different from this. She knew that he adored her, but yet he did not hasten to tell her so. She knew that she loved him, but she doubted whether a time would ever come in which she could confess it. It was not till he had come to acknowledge the trouble to which Mountjoy had subjected him that he had ever ventured to speak plainly of his own passion, and even then he had not asked for a reply. She was still free, as she thought of all this, but she did at last tell herself that, let her mother say what she would, she certainly never would stand at the altar with her cousin Mountjoy.

Even now, when the captain had been declared not to be his father's heir, and when all the world knew that he had disappeared from the face of the earth, Mrs. Mountjoy did not altogether give him up. She partly disbelieved her brother, and partly thought that circumstances could not be so bad as they were described.

To her feminine mind,—to her, living, not in the world of London, but in the very moderate fashion of Cheltenham,—it seemed to be impossible that an entail should be thus blighted in the bud. Why was an entail called an entail unless it were ineradicable,—a decision of fate rather than of man and of law? And to her eyes Mountjoy Scarborough was so commanding that all things must at last be compelled to go as he would have them. And, to tell the truth, there had lately come to Mrs. Mountjoy a word of comfort, which might be necessary if the world should be absolutely upset in accordance with the wicked skill of her brother, which even in that case might make crooked things smooth. Augustus, whom she had regarded always as quite a Mountjoy, because of his talent, and appearance, and habit of command, had whispered to her a word. Why should not Florence be transferred with the remainder of the property? There was something to Mrs. Mountjoy's feelings base in the idea at the first blush of it. She did not like to be untrue to her gallant nephew. But as she came to turn it in her mind there were certain circumstances which recommended the change to her—should the change be necessary. Florence certainly had expressed an unintelligible objection to the elder brother. Why should the younger not be more successful? Mrs. Mountjoy's heart had begun to droop within her as she had thought that her girl would prove deaf to the voice of the charmer. Another charmer had come, most objectionable in her sight, but to him no word of absolute encouragement had, as she thought, been yet spoken. Augustus had already obtained for himself among his friends the character of an eloquent young lawyer. Let him come and try his eloquence on his cousin,—only let it first be ascertained, as an assured fact, and beyond the possibility of all retrogression, that the squire's villainy was certain.

"I think, my love," she said to her daughter one day, "that, under the immediate circumstances of the family, we should retire for a while into private life." This occurred on the very day on which Septimus Jones had been vaguely informed of the iniquitous falsehood of Harry Annesley.

"Good gracious, mamma, is not our life always private?" She had understood it all,—that the private life was intended altogether to exclude Harry, but was to be made open to the manoeuvres of her cousin, such as they might be.

"Not in the sense in which I mean. Your poor uncle is dying."

"We hear that Sir William says he is better."

"I fear, nevertheless, that he is dying,—though it may, perhaps, take a long time. And then poor Mountjoy has disappeared. I think that we should see no one till the mystery about Mountjoy has been cleared up. And then the story is so very discreditable."

"I do not see that that is an affair of ours," said Florence, who had no desire to be shut up just at the present moment.

"We cannot help ourselves. This making his eldest son out to be—oh, something so very different—is too horrible to be thought of. I am told that nobody knows the truth."

"We at any rate are not implicated in that."

"But we are. He at any rate is my brother, and Mountjoy is my nephew,—or at any rate was. Poor Augustus is thrown into terrible difficulties."

"I am told that he is greatly pleased at finding that Tretton is to belong to him."

"Who tells you that? You have no right to believe anything about such near relatives from any one. Whoever told you so has been very wicked." Mrs. Mountjoy no doubt thought that this wicked communication had been made by Harry Annesley. "Augustus has always proved himself to be affectionate and respectful to his elder brother, that is, to his brother who is—is older than himself," added Mrs. Mountjoy, feeling that there was a difficulty in expressing herself as to the presumed condition of the two Scarboroughs, "Of course he would rather be owner of Tretton than let any one else have it, if you mean that. The honor of the family is very much to him."

"I do not know that the family can have any honor left," said Florence, severely.

"My dear, you have no right to say that. The Scarboroughs have always held their heads very high in Staffordshire, and more so of late than ever. I don't mean quite of late, but since Tretton became of so much importance. Now, I'll tell you what I think we had better do. We'll go and spend six weeks with your uncle at Brussels. He has always been pressing us to come."

"Oh, mamma, he does not want us."

"How can you say that? How do you know?"

"I am sure Sir Magnus will not care for our coming now. Besides, how could that be retiring into private life? Sir Magnus, as ambassador, has his house always full of company."

"My dear, he is not ambassador. He is minister plenipotentiary. It is not quite the same thing. And then he is our nearest relative,—our nearest, at least, since my own brother has made this great separation, of course. We cannot go to him to be out of the way of himself."

"Why do you want to go anywhere, mamma? Why not stay at home?" But Florence pleaded in vain as her mother had already made up her mind. Before that day was over she succeeded in making her daughter understand that she was to be taken to Brussels as soon as an answer could be received from Sir Magnus and the necessary additions were made to their joint wardrobe.

Sir Magnus Mountjoy, the late general's elder brother, had been for the last four or five years the English minister at Brussels. He had been minister somewhere for a very long time, so that the memory of man hardly ran back beyond it, and was said to have gained for himself very extensive popularity. It had always been a point with successive governments to see that poor Sir Magnus got something, and Sir Magnus had never been left altogether in the cold. He was not a man who would have been left out in the cold in silence, and perhaps the feeling that such was the case had been as efficacious on his behalf as his well-attested popularity. At any rate, poor Sir Magnus had always been well placed, and was now working out his last year or two before the blessed achievement of his pursuit should have been reached. Sir Magnus had a wife of whom it was said at home that she was almost as popular as her husband; but the opinion of the world at Brussels on this subject was a good deal divided. There were those who declared that Lady Mountjoy was of all women the most overbearing and impertinent. But they were generally English residents at Brussels, who had come to live there as a place at which education for their children would be cheaper than at home. Of these Lady Mountjoy had been heard to declare that she saw no reason why, because she was the minister's wife, she should be expected to entertain all the second-class world of London. This, of course, must be understood with a good deal of allowance, as the English world at Brussels was much too large to expect to be so received; but there were certain ladies living on the confines of high society who thought that they had a right to be admitted, and who grievously resented their exclusion. It cannot, therefore, be said that Lady Mountjoy was popular; but she was large in figure, and painted well, and wore her diamonds with an air which her peculiar favorites declared to be majestic. You could not see her going along the boulevards in her carriage without being aware that a special personage was passing. Upon the whole, it may be said that she performed well her special role in life. Of Sir Magnus it was hinted that he was afraid of his wife; but in truth he desired it to be understood that all the disagreeable things done at the Embassy were done by Lady Mountjoy, and not by him. He did not refuse leave to the ladies to drop their cards at his hall-door. He could ask a few men to his table without referring the matter to his wife; but every one would understand that the asking of ladies was based on a different footing.

He knew well that as a rule it was not fitting that he should ask a married man without his wife; but there are occasions on which an excuse can be given, and upon the whole the men liked it. He was a stout, tall, portly old gentleman, sixty years of age, but looking somewhat older, whom it was a difficulty to place on horseback, but who, when there, looked remarkably well. He rarely rose to a trot during his two hours of exercise, which to the two attachés who were told off for the duty of accompanying him was the hardest part of their allotted work. But other gentlemen would lay themselves out to meet Sir Magnus and to ride with him, and in this way he achieved that character for popularity which had been a better aid to him in life than all the diplomatic skill which he possessed.

"What do you think?" said he, walking off with Mrs. Mountjoy's letter into his wife's room.

"I don't think anything, my dear."

"You never do." Lady Mountjoy, who had not yet undergone her painting, looked cross and ill-natured. "At any rate, Sarah and her daughter are proposing to come here."

"Good gracious! At once?"

"Yes, at once. Of course, I've asked them over and over again, and something was said about this autumn, when we had come back from Pimperingen."

"Why did you not tell me?"

"Bother! I did tell you. This kind of thing always turns up at last. She's a very good kind of a woman, and the daughter is all that she ought to be."

"Of course she'll be flirting with Anderson." Anderson was one of the two mounted attachés.

"Anderson will know how to look after himself," said Sir Magnus. "At any rate they must come. They have never troubled us before, and we ought to put up with them once."

"But, my dear, what is all this about her brother?"

"She won't bring her brother with her."

"How can you be sure of that?" said the anxious lady.

"He is dying, and can't be moved."

"But that son of his—Mountjoy. It's altogether a most distressing story. He turns out to be nobody after all, and now he has disappeared, and the papers for an entire month were full of him. What would you do if he were to turn up here? The girl was engaged to him, you know, and has only thrown him off since his own father declared that he was not legitimate. There never was such a mess about anything since London first began."

Then Sir Magnus declared that, let Mountjoy Scarborough and his father have misbehaved as they might, Mr. Scarborough's sister must be received at Brussels. There was a little family difficulty. Sir Magnus had borrowed three thousand pounds from the general which had been settled on the general's widow, and the interest was not always paid with extreme punctuality. To give Mrs. Mountjoy her due, it must be said that this had not entered into her consideration when she had written to her brother-in-law; but it was a burden to Sir Magnus, and had always tended to produce from him a reiteration of those invitations, which Mrs. Mountjoy had taken as an expression of brotherly love. Her own income was always sufficient for her wants, and the hundred and fifty pounds coming from Sir Magnus had not troubled her much. "Well, my dear, if it must be it must;—only what I'm to do with her I do not know."

"Take her about in the carriage," said Sir Magnus, who was beginning to be a little angry with this interference.

"And the daughter? Daughters are twice more troublesome than their mothers."

"Pass her over to Miss Abbott. And for goodness' sake don't make so much trouble about things which need not be troublesome." Then Sir Magnus left his wife to ring for her chambermaid and go on with her painting, while he himself undertook the unwonted task of writing an affectionate letter to his sister-in-law. It should be here explained that Sir Magnus had no children of his own, and that Miss Abbott was the lady who was bound to smile and say pretty things on all occasions to Lady Mountjoy for the moderate remuneration of two hundred a year and her maintenance.

The letter which Sir Magnus wrote was as follows:

My Dear Sarah,—Lady Mountjoy bids me say that we shall be delighted to receive you and my niece at the British Ministry on the 1st of October, and hope that you will stay with us till the end of the month.—Believe me, most affectionately yours,

Magnus Mountjoy.

"I have a most kind letter from Sir Magnus," said Mrs. Mountjoy to her daughter.

"What does he say?"

"That he will be delighted to receive us on the 1st of October. I did say that we should be ready to start in about a week's time, because I know that he gets home from his autumn holiday by the middle of September. But I have no doubt he has his house full till the time he has named."

"Do you know her, mamma?" asked Florence.

"I did see her once; but I cannot say that I know her. She used to be a very handsome woman, and looks to be quite good-natured; but Sir Magnus has always lived abroad, and except when he came home about your poor father's death I have seen very little of him."

"I never saw him but that once," said Florence.

And so it was settled that she and her mother were to spend a month at Brussels.

CHAPTER XI. MONTE CARLO

Toward the end of September, while the weather was so hot as to keep away from the south of France all but very determined travellers, an English gentleman, not very beautiful in his outward appearance, was sauntering about the great hall of the gambling-house at Monte Carlo, in the kingdom or principality of Monaco, the only gambling-house now left in Europe in which idle men of a speculative nature may yet solace their hours with some excitement. Nor is the amusement denied to idle ladies, as might be seen by two or three highly-dressed *habituées* who at this moment were depositing their shawls and parasols with the porters. The clock was on the stroke of eleven, when the gambling-room would be open, and the amusement was too rich in its nature to allow of the loss of even a few minutes. But this gentleman was not an *habitué*, nor was he known even by name to any of the small crowd that was then assembled. But it was known to many of them that he had had a great "turn of luck" on the preceding day, and had walked off from the "rouge-et-noir" table with four or five hundred pounds.

The weather was still so hot that but few Englishmen were there, and the play had not as yet begun to run high. There were only two or three,—men who cannot keep their hands from ruin when ruin is open to them. To them heat and cold, the dog-star or twenty degrees below zero, make no difference while the croupier is there, with his rouleaux before him, capable of turning up the card. They know that the chance is against them,—one in twenty, let us say,—and that in the long-run one in twenty is as good as two to one to effect their ruin. For a day they may stand against one in twenty, as this man had done. For two or three days, for a week, they may possibly do so; but they know that the doom must come at last,—as it does come invariably,—and they go on. But our friend, the Englishman who had won the money, was not such a one as these, at any rate in regard to Monaco. Yesterday had been his first appearance, and he had broken ground there with great success. He was an ill-looking person, poorly clad,—what, in common parlance, we should call seedy. He had not a scrap of beard on his face, and though swarthy and dark as to his countenance, was light as to his hair, which hung in quantities down his back. He was dressed from head to foot in a suit of cross-barred, light-colored tweed, of which he wore the coat buttoned tight over his chest, as though to hide some deficiency of linen.

The gentleman was altogether a disreputable-looking personage, and they who had seen him win his money,—Frenchmen and Italians for the most part,—had declared among themselves that his luck had been most miraculous. It was observed that he had a companion with him, who stuck close to his elbow, and it was asserted that this companion continually urged him to leave the room. But as long as the croupier remained at the table he remained, and continued to play through the day with almost invariable luck. It was surmised among the gamblers there that he had not entered the room with above twenty or thirty pieces in his pocket, and that he had taken away with him, when the place was closed, six hundred napoleons. "Look there; he has come again to give it all back to Madame Blanc, with interest," said a Frenchman to an Italian.

"Yes; and he will end by blowing his brains out within a week. He is just the man to do it."

"These Englishmen always rush at their fate like mad bulls," said the Frenchman. "They get less distraction for their money than any one."

"*Che va piano va sano,*" said the Italian, jingling the four napoleons in his pocket, which had been six on yesterday morning. Then they sauntered up to the Englishman, and both of them touched their hats to him. The Englishman just acknowledged the compliment, and walked off with his companion, who was still whispering something into his ear.

"It is a gendarme who is with him, I think," said the Frenchman, "only the man does not walk erect."

Who does not know the outside hall of the magnificent gambling-house at Monte Carlo, with all the golden splendor of its music-room within? Who does not know the lofty roof and lounging seats, with its luxuries of liveried servants, its wealth of newspapers, and every appanage of costly comfort which can be added to it? And its music within,—who does not know that there are to be heard sounds in a greater perfection of orchestral melody than are to be procured by money and trouble combined in the great capitals of Europe? Think of the trouble endured by those unhappy fathers of families who indulge their wives and daughters at the Philharmonic and St. James's Hall! Think of the horrors of our theatres, with their hot gas, and narrow passages, and difficulties of entrance, and almost impossibility of escape! And for all this money has to be paid,—high prices,—and the day has to be fixed long beforehand, so that the tickets may be secured, and the daily feast,—papa's too often solitary enjoyment,—has to be turned into a painful early fast. And when at last the thing has been done, and the torment endured, the sounds heard have not always been good of their kind, for the money has not sufficed to purchase the aid of a crowd of the best musicians. But at Monte Carlo you walk in with your wife in her morning costume, and seating yourself luxuriously in one of those soft stalls which are there prepared for you, you give yourself up with perfect ease to absolute enjoyment. For two hours the concert lasts, and all around is perfection and gilding. There is nothing to annoy the most fastidious taste. You have not heated yourself with fighting your way up crowded stairs; no box-keeper has asked you for a shilling. No link-boy has dunned you because he stood useless for a moment at the door of your carriage. No panic has seized you, and still oppresses you, because of the narrow dimensions in which you have to seat yourself for the next three hours. There are no twenty minutes during which you are doomed to sit in miserable expectation. Exactly at the hour named the music begins, and for two hours it is your own fault if you be not happy. A railway-carriage has brought you to steps leading up to the garden in which these princely halls are built, and when the music is over will again take you home. Nothing can be more perfect than the concert-room at Monte Carlo, and nothing more charming; and for all this there is nothing whatever to pay.

But by whom;—out of whose pocket are all these good things provided? They tell you at Monte Carlo that from time to time are to be seen men walking off in the dark of the night or the gloom of the evening, or, for the matter of that, in the broad light of day, if the stern necessity of the hour require it, with a burden among them, to be deposited where it may not be seen or heard of any more. They are carrying away "all that mortal remains" of one of the gentlemen who have paid for your musical entertainment. He has given his all for the purpose, and has then—blown his brains out. It is one of the disagreeable incidents to which the otherwise extremely pleasant money-making operations of the establishment are liable. Such accidents will happen. A gambling-house, the keeper of which is able to maintain the royal expense of the neighboring court out of his winnings and also to keep open for those who are not ashamed to accept it,—gratis, all for love,—a concert-room brilliant with gold, filled with the best performers whom the world can furnish, and comfortable beyond all opera-houses known to men must be liable to a few such misfortunes. Who is not ashamed to accept, I have said, having lately been there and thoroughly enjoyed myself? But I did not put myself in the way of having to cut my throat, on which account I felt, as I came out, that I had been somewhat shabby. I was ashamed in that I had not put a few napoleons down on the table. Conscience had prevented me, and a wish to keep my money. But should not conscience have kept me away from all that happiness for which I had not paid? I had not thought of it before I went to Monte Carlo, but I am inclined now to advise others to stay away, or else to put down half a napoleon, at any rate, as the price of a ticket. The place is not overcrowded, because the conscience of many is keener than was mine.

We ought to be grateful to the august sovereign of Monaco in that he enabled an enterprising individual to keep open for us in so brilliant a fashion the last public gambling-house in Europe. The principality is but large enough to contain the court of the sovereign which is held in the little town of Monaco, and the establishment of the last of legitimate gamblers which is maintained at Monte Carlo. If the report of the world does not malign the prince, he lives, as does the gambler, out of the spoil taken from the gamblers. He is to be seen in his royal carriage going forth with his royal consort,—and very royal he looks! His little teacup of a kingdom,—or rather a roll of French bread, for it is crusty and picturesque,—is now surrounded by France. There is Nice away to the west, and Mentone to the east, and the whole kingdom lies within the compass of a walk. Mentone, in France, at any rate, is within five miles of the monarch's residence. How happy it is that there should be so blessed a spot left in tranquillity on the earth's surface!

But on the present occasion Monte Carlo was not in all its grandeur, because of the heat of the weather. Another month, and English lords, and English members of Parliament, and English barristers would be there,—all men, for instance, who could afford to be indifferent as to their character for a month,—and the place would be quite alive with music, cards, and dice. At present men of business only flocked to its halls, eagerly intent on making money, though, alas! almost all doomed to lose it. But our one friend with the long light locks was impatient for the fray. The gambling-room had now been opened, and the servants of the table, less impatient than he, were slowly arranging their money and their cards. Our friend had taken his seat, and was already resolving, with his eyes fixed on the table, where he would make his first plunge. In his right hand was a bag of gold, and under his left hand were hidden the twelve napoleons with which he intended to commence. On yesterday he had gone through his day's work by twelve, though on one or two occasions he had plunged deeply. It had seemed to this man as though a new heaven had been opened to him, as of late he had seen little of luck in this world. The surmises made as to the low state of his funds when he entered the room had been partly true; but time had been when he was able to gamble in a more costly fashion even than here, and to play among those who had taken his winnings and losings simply as a matter of course.

And now the game had begun, and the twelve napoleons were duly deposited. Again he won his stake, an omen for the day, and was exultant. A second twelve and a third were put down, and on each occasion he won. In the silly imagination of his heart he declared to himself that the calculation of all chances was as nothing against his run of luck. Here was the spot on which it was destined that he should redeem all the injury which fortune had done him. And in truth this man had been misused by fortune. His companion whispered in his ear, but he heard not a word of it. He increased the twelve to fifteen, and again won. As he looked round there was a halo of triumph which seemed to illuminate his face. He had chained Chance to his chariot-wheel and would persevere now that the good time had come. What did he care for the creature at his elbow? He thought of all the good things which money could again purchase for him as he carefully fingered the gold for the next stake. He had been rich, though he was now poor; though how could a man be accounted poor who had an endless sum of six hundred napoleons in his pocket, a sum which was, in truth, endless, while it could be so rapidly recruited in this fashion? The next stake he also won, but as he raked all the pieces which the croupier pushed toward him his mind had become intent on another sphere and on other persons. Let him win what he might, his old haunts were now closed against him. What good would money do him, living such a life as he must now be compelled to pass? As he thought of this the five-and-twenty napoleons on the table were taken away from him almost without consciousness on his part.

At that moment there came a voice in his ear,—not the voice of his attending friend, but one of which he accurately knew the lisping, fiendish sound: "Ah, Captain Scarborough, I thought it vas posshible you might be here. Dis ish a very nice place." Our friend looked round and glared at the man, and felt that it was impossible that this occupation should be continued under his eyes. "Yesh; it was likely. How do you like Monte Carlo? You have plenty of money—plenty!" The man was small, and oily, and black-haired, and beaky-nosed, with a perpetual smile on his face, unless when on special occasions he would be moved to the expression of deep anger. Of the modern Hebrews a most complete Hebrew; but a man of purpose, who never did things by halves, who could count upon good courage within, and who never allowed himself to be foiled by misadventure. He was one who, beginning with nothing, was determined to die a rich man, and was likely to achieve his purpose. Now there was no gleam of anger on his face, but a look of invincible good-humor, which was not, however, quite good-humor, when you came to examine it closely.

"Oh, that is you, is it, Mr. Hart?"

"Yesh; it is me. I have followed you. Oh, I have had quite a pleasant tour following you. But ven I got my noshe once on to the schent then I was sure it was Monte Carlo. And it ish Monte Carlo; eh, Captain Scarborough?"

"Yes; of course it is Monte Carlo. That is to say, Monte Carlo is the place where we are now. I don't know what you mean by running on in that way." Then he drew back from the table, Mr. Hart following close behind him, and his attendant at a farther distance behind him. As he went he remembered that he had slightly increased the six hundred napoleons of yesterday, and that the money was still in his own possession. Not all the Jews in London could touch the money while he kept it in his pocket.

"Who ish dat man there?" asked Mr. Hart.

"What can that be to you?"

"He seems to follow you pretty close."

"Not so close as you do, by George; and perhaps he has something to get by it, which you haven't."

"Come, come, come! If he have more to get than I he mush be pretty deep. There is Mishter Tyrrwhit. No one have more to get than I, only Mishter Tyrrwhit. Vy, Captain Scarborough, the little game you wash playing there, which wash a very pretty little game, is as nothing to my game wish you. When you see the money down, on the table there, it seems to be mush because the gold glitters, but it is as noting to my little game, where the gold does not glitter, because it is pen and ink. A pen and ink soon writes ten thousand pounds. But you think mush of it when you win two hundred pounds at roulette."

"I think nothing of it," said our friend Captain Scarborough.

"And it goes into your pocket to give champagne to the ladies, instead of paying your debts to the poor fellows who have supplied you for so long with all de money."

All this occurred in the gambling-house at a distance from the table, but within hearing of that attendant who still followed the player. These moments were moments of misery to the captain in spite of the bank-notes for six hundred napoleons which were still in his breast coat-pocket. And they were not made lighter by the fact that all the words spoken by the Jew were overheard by the man who was supposed to be there in the capacity of his servant. But the man, as it seemed, had a mission to fulfil, and was the captain's master as well as servant. "Mr. Hart," said Captain Scarborough, repressing the loudness of his words as far as his rage would admit him, but still speaking so as to attract the attention of some of those round him, "I do not know what good you propose to yourself by following me in this manner. You have my bonds, which are not even payable till my father's death."

"Ah, there you are very much mistaken."

"And are then only payable out of the property to which I believed myself to be heir when the money was borrowed."

"You are still de heir—de heir to Tretton. There is not a shadow of a doubt as to that."

"I hope when the time comes," said the captain, "you'll be able to prove your words."

"Of course we shall prove dem. Why not? Your father and your brother are very clever shentlemen, I think, but they will not be more clever than Mishter Samuel Hart. Mr. Tyrrwhit also is a clever man. Perhaps he understands your father's way of doing business. Perhaps it is all right with Mr. Tyrrwhit. It shall be all right with me too;—I swear it. When will you come back to London, Captain Scarborough?"

Then there came an angry dispute in the gambling-room, during which Mr. Hart by no means strove to repress his voice. Captain Scarborough asserted his rights as a free agent, declaring himself capable, as far as the law was concerned, of going wherever he pleased without reference to Mr. Hart; and told that gentleman that any interference on his part would be regarded as an impertinence. "But my money—my money, which you must pay this minute, if I please to demand it."

"You did not lend me five-and-twenty thousand pounds without security."

"It is forty-five—now, at this moment."

"Take it, get it; go and put it in your pocket. You have a lot of writings; turn then into cash at once. Take them to any other Jew in London and sell them. See if you can get your five-and-twenty thousand pounds for them,—or twenty-five thousand shillings. You certainly cannot get five-and-twenty pence for them here, though you had all the police of this royal kingdom to support you. My father says that the bonds I gave you are not worth the paper on which they were written. If you are cheated, so have I been. If he has robbed you, so has he me. But I have not robbed you, and you can do nothing to me."

"I vill stick to you like beesvax," said Mr. Hart, while the look of good-humor left his countenance for a moment. "Like beesvax! You shall not escape me again."

"You will have to follow me to Constantinople, then."

"I vill follow you to the devil."

"You are likely to go before me there. But for the present I am off to Constantinople, from whence I intend to make an extended tour to Mount Caucasus, and then into Thibet. I shall be very glad of your company, but cannot offer to pay the bill. When you and your companions have settled yourselves comfortably at Tretton, I shall be happy to come and see you there. You will have to settle the matter first with my younger brother, if I may make bold to call that well-born gentleman my brother at all. I wish you a good-morning, Mr. Hart." Upon that he walked out into the hall, and thence down the steps into the garden in front of the establishment, his own attendant following him.

Mr. Hart also followed him, but did not immediately seek to renew the conversation. If he meant to show any sign of keeping his threat and of sticking to the captain like beesvax, he must show his purpose at once. The captain for a time walked round the little enclosure in earnest conversation with the attendant, and Mr. Hart stood on the steps watching them. Play was over, at any rate for that day, as far as the captain was concerned.

"Now, Captain Scarborough, don't you think you've been very rash?" said the attendant.

"I think I've got six hundred and fifty napoleons in my pocket, instead of waiting to get them in driblets from my brother."

"But if he knew that you had come here he would withdraw them altogether. Of course, he will know now. That man will be sure to tell him. He will let all London know. Of course, it would be so when you came to a place of such common resort as Monte Carlo."

"Common resort! Do you believe he came here as to a place of common resort? Do you think that he had not tracked me out, and would not have done so, whether I had gone to Melbourne, or New York, or St. Petersburg? But the wonder is that he should spend his money in such a vain pursuit."

"Ah, captain, you do not know what is vain and what is not. It is your brother's pleasure that you should be kept in the dark for a time."

"Hang my brother's pleasure! Why am I to follow my brother's pleasure?"

"Because he will allow you an income. He will keep a coat on your back and a hat on your head, and supply meat and wine for your needs." Here Captain Scarborough jingled the loose napoleons in his trousers pocket. "Oh, yes, that is all very well but it will not last forever. Indeed, it will not last for a week unless you leave Monte Carlo."

"I shall leave it this afternoon by the train for Genoa."

"And where shall you go then?"

"You heard me suggest to Mr. Hart to the devil,—or else Constantinople, and after that to Thibet. I suppose I shall still enjoy the pleasure of your company?"

"Mr. Augustus wishes that I should remain with you, and, as you yourself say, perhaps it will be best."

CHAPTER XII. HARRY ANNESLEY'S SUCCESS

Harry Annesley, a day or two after he had left Tretton, went down to Cheltenham; for he had received an invitation to a dance there, and with the invitation an intimation that Florence Mountjoy was to be at the dance. If I were to declare that the dance had been given and Florence asked to it merely as an act of friendship to Harry, it would perhaps be thought that modern friendship is seldom carried to so great a length. But it was undoubtedly the fact that Mrs. Armitage, who gave the dance, was a great friend and admirer of Harry's, and that Mr. Armitage was an especial chum. Let not, however, any reader suppose that Florence was in the secret. Mrs. Armitage had thought it best to keep her in the dark as to the person asked to meet her. "As to my going to Montpelier Place," Harry had once said to Mrs. Armitage, "I might as well knock at a prison-door." Mrs. Mountjoy lived in Montpelier Place.

"I think we could perhaps manage that for you," Mrs. Armitage had replied, and she had managed it.

"Is she coming?" Harry said to Mrs. Armitage, in an anxious whisper, as he entered the room.

"She has been here this half-hour,—if you had taken the trouble to leave your cigars and come and meet her."

"She has not gone?" said Harry, almost awe-struck at the idea.

"No; she is sitting like Patience on a monument, smiling at grief, in the room inside. She has got horrible news to tell you."

"Oh, heavens! What news?"

"I suppose she will tell you, though she has not been communicative to me in regard to your royal highness. The news is simply that her mother is going to take her to Brussels, and that she is to live for a while amid the ambassadorial splendors with Sir Magnus and his wife."

By retiring from the world Mrs. Mountjoy had not intended to include such slight social relaxations as Mrs. Armitage's party, for Harry on turning round encountered her talking to another Cheltenham lady. He greeted her with his pleasantest smile, to which Mrs. Mountjoy did not respond quite so sweetly. She had ever greatly feared Harry Annesley, and had to-day heard a story very much, as she thought, to his discredit. "Is your daughter here?" asked Harry, with well-trained hypocrisy. Mrs. Mountjoy could not but acknowledge that Florence was in the room, and then Harry passed on in pursuit of his quarry.

"Oh, Mr. Annesley, when did you come to Cheltenham?"

"As soon as I heard that Mrs. Armitage was going to have a party I began to think of coming immediately." Then an idea for the first time shot through Florence's mind—that her friend Mrs. Armitage was a woman devoted to intrigue. "What dance have you disengaged? I have something that I must tell you to-night. You don't mean to say that you will not give me one dance?" This was merely a lover's anxious doubt on his part, because Florence had not at once replied to him. "I am told that you are going away to Brussels."

"Mamma is going on a visit to her brother-in-law."

"And you with her?"

"Of course I shall go with mamma." All this had been said apart, while a fair-haired, lackadaisical young gentleman was standing twiddling his thumbs waiting to dance with Florence. At last the little book from her waist was brought forth, and Harry's name was duly inscribed. The next dance was a quadrille, and he saw that the space after that was also vacant; so he boldly wrote down his name for both. I almost think that Florence must have suspected that Harry Annesley was to be there that night, or why should the two places have been kept vacant? "And now what is this," he began, "about your going to Brussels?"

"Mamma's brother is minister there, and we are just going on a visit."

"But why now? I am sure there is some especial cause." Florence would not say that there was no especial cause, so she could only repeat her assertion that they certainly were going to Brussels. She herself was well aware that she was to be taken out of Harry's way, and that something was expected to occur during this short month of her absence which might be detrimental to him,—and to her also. But this she could not tell, nor did she like to say that the plea given by her mother was the general state of the Scarborough affairs. She did not wish to declare to this lover that that other lover was as nothing to her. "And how long are you to be away?" asked Harry.

"We shall be a month with Sir Magnus; but mamma is talking of going on afterward to the Italian lakes."

"Good heavens! you will not be back, I suppose, till ever so much after Christmas?"

"I cannot tell. Nothing as yet has been settled. I do not know that I ought to tell you anything about it." Harry at this moment looked up, and caught the eye of Mrs. Mountjoy, as she was standing in the door-way opposite. Mrs. Mountjoy certainly looked as though no special communication as to Florence's future movements ought to be made to Harry Annesley.

Then, however, it came to his turn to dance, and he had a moment allowed to him to collect his thoughts. By nothing that he could do or say could he prevent her going, and he could only use the present moment to the best purpose in his power. He bethought himself then that he had never received from her a word of encouragement, and that such word, if ever to be spoken, should be forthcoming that night. What might not happen to a girl who was passing the balmy Christmas months amid the sweet shadows of an Italian lake? Harry's ideas of an Italian lake were, in truth, at present somewhat vague. But future months were, to his thinking, interminable; the present moment only was his own. The dance was now finished. "Come and take a walk," said Harry.

"I think I will go to mamma." Florence had seen her mother's eye fixed upon her.

"Oh, come, that won't do at all," said Harry, who had already got her hand within his arm. "A fellow is always entitled to five minutes, and then I am down for the next waltz."

"Oh no!"

"But I am, and you can't get out of it now. Oh, Florence, will you answer me a question,—one question? I asked it you before, and you did not vouchsafe me any answer."

"You asked me no question," said Florence, who remembered to the last syllable every word that had been said to her on that occasion.

"Did I not? I am sure you knew what it was that I intended to ask." Florence could not but think that this was quite another thing. "Oh, Florence, can you love me?" Had she given her ears for it she could not have told him the truth then, on the spur of the moment. Her mother's eye was, she knew, watching her through the door-way all the way across from the other room. And yet, had her mother asked her, she would have answered boldly that she did love Harry Annesley, and intended to love him for ever and ever with all her heart. And she would have gone farther if cross-questioned, and have declared that she regarded him already as her lord and master. But now she had not a word to say to him. All she knew was that he had now pledged himself to her, and that she intended to keep him to his pledge. "May I not have one word," he said,—"one word?"

What could he want with a word more? thought Florence. Her silence now was as good as any speech. But as he did want more she would, after her own way, reply to him. So there came upon his arm the slightest possible sense of pressure from those sweet fingers, and Harry Annesley was on a sudden carried up among azure-tinted clouds into the farthest heaven of happiness. After a moment he stood still, and passed his fingers through his hair and waved his head as a god might do it. She had now made to him a solemn promise than which no words could be more binding. "Oh, Florence," he exclaimed, "I must have you alone with me for one moment." For what could he want her alone for any moment? thought Florence. There was her mother still looking at them; but for her Harry did not now care one straw. Nor did he hate those bright Italian lakes with nearly so strong a feeling of abhorrence. "Florence, you are now all my own." There came another slightest pressure, slight, but so eloquent from those fingers.

"I hate dancing. How is a fellow to dance now? I shall run against everybody. I can see no one. I should be sure to make a fool of myself. No, I don't want to dance even with you. No, certainly not!—let you dance with somebody else, and you engaged to me! Well, if I must, of course I must. I declare, Florence, you have not spoken a single word to me, though there is so much that you must have to say. What have you got to say? What a question to ask! You must tell me. Oh, you know what you have got to tell me! The sound of it will be the sweetest music that a man can possibly hear."

"You knew it all, Harry," she whispered.

"But I want to hear it. Oh, Florence, Florence, I do not think you can understand how completely I am beyond myself with joy. I cannot dance again, and will not. Oh, my wife, my wife!"

"Hush!" said Florence, afraid that the very walls might hear the sound of Harry's words.

"What does it signify though all the world knew it?"

"Oh yes."

"That I should have been so fortunate! That is what I cannot understand. Poor Mountjoy! I do feel for him. That he should have had the start of me so long, and have done nothing!"

"Nothing," whispered Florence.

"And I have done everything. I am so proud of myself that I think I must look almost like a hero."

They had now got to the extremity of the room near an open window, and Florence found that she was able to say one word. "You are my hero." The sound of this nearly drove him mad with joy. He forgot all his troubles. Prodgers, the policeman, Augustus Scarborough, and that fellow whom he hated so much, Septimus Jones;—what were they all to him now? He had set his mind upon one thing of value, and he had got it. Florence had promised to be his, and he was sure that she would never break her word to him. But he felt that for the full enjoyment of his triumph he must be alone somewhere with Florence for five minutes. He had not actually explained to himself why, but he knew that he wished to be alone with her. At present there was no prospect of any such five minutes, but he must say something in preparation for some future five minutes at a time to come. Perhaps it might be to-morrow, though he did not at present see how that might be possible, for Mrs. Mountjoy, he knew, would shut her door against him. And Mrs. Mountjoy was already prowling round the room after her daughter. Harry saw her as he got Florence to an opposite door, and there for the moment escaped with her. "And now," he said, "how am I to manage to see you before you go to Brussels?"

"I do not know that you can see me."

"Do you mean that you are to be shut up, and that I am not to be allowed to approach you?"

"I do mean it. Mamma is, of course, attached to her nephew."

"What, after all that has passed?"

"Why not? Is he to blame for what his father has done?" Harry felt that he could not press the case against Captain Scarborough without some want of generosity. And though he had told Florence once about that dreadful midnight meeting, he could say nothing farther on that subject. "Of course mamma thinks that I am foolish."

"But why?" he asked.

"Because she doesn't see with my eyes, Harry. We need not say anything more about it at present. It is so; and therefore I am to go to Brussels. You have made this opportunity for yourself before I start. Perhaps I have been foolish to be taken off my guard."

"Don't say that, Florence."

"I shall think so, unless you can be discreet. Harry, you will have to wait. You will remember that we must wait; but I shall not change."

"Nor I,—nor I."

"I think not, because I trust you. Here is mamma, and now I must leave you. But I shall tell mamma everything before I go to bed." Then Mrs. Mountjoy came up and took Florence away, with a few words of most disdainful greeting to Harry Annesley.

When Florence was gone Harry felt that as the sun and the moon and the stars had all set, and as absolute darkness reigned through the rooms, he might as well escape into the street, where there was no one but the police to watch him, as he threw his hat up into the air in his exultation. But before he did so he had to pass by Mrs. Armitage and thank her for all her kindness; for he was aware how much she had done for him in his present circumstances. "Oh, Mrs. Armitage, I am so obliged to you! no fellow was ever so obliged to a friend before."

"How has it gone off? For Mrs. Mountjoy has taken Florence home."

"Oh yes, she has taken her away. But she hasn't shut the stable-door till the steed has been stolen."

"Oh, the steed has been stolen?"

"Yes, I think so; I do think so."

"And that poor man who has disappeared is nowhere."

"Men who disappear never are anywhere. But I do flatter myself that if he had held his ground and kept his property the result would have been the same."

"I dare say."

"Don't suppose, Mrs. Armitage, that I am taking any pride to myself. Why on earth Florence should have taken a fancy to such a fellow as I am I cannot imagine."

"Oh no; not in the least."

"It's all very well for you to laugh, Mrs. Armitage, but as I have thought of it all I have sometimes been in despair."

"But now you are not in despair."

"No, indeed; just now I am triumphant. I have thought so often that I was a fool to love her, because everything was so much against me."

"I have wondered that you continued. It always seemed to me that there wasn't a ghost of a chance for you. Mr. Armitage bade me give it all up, because he was sure you would never do any good."

"I don't care how much you laugh at me, Mrs. Armitage."

"Let those laugh who win." Then he rushed out into the Paragon, and absolutely did throw his hat up in the air in his triumph.

CHAPTER XIII. MRS. MOUNTJOY'S ANGER

Florence, as she went home in the fly with her mother after the party at which Harry had spoken to her so openly, did not find the little journey very happy. Mrs. Mountjoy was a woman endowed with a strong power of wishing rather than of willing, of desiring rather than of contriving; but she was one who could make herself very unpleasant when she was thwarted. Her daughter was now at last fully determined that if she ever married anybody, that person should be Harry Annesley. Having once pressed his arm in token of assent, she had as it were given herself away to him, so that no reasoning, no expostulations could, she thought, change her purpose; and she had much more power of bringing about her purposed design than had her mother. But her mother could be obstinate and self-willed, and would for the time make herself disagreeable. Florence had assured her lover that everything should be told her mother that night before she went to bed. But Mrs. Mountjoy did not wait to be simply told. No sooner were they seated in the fly together than she began to make her inquiries. "What has that man been saying to you?" she demanded.

Florence was at once offended by hearing her lover so spoken of, and could not simply tell the story of Harry's successful courtship, as she had intended. "Mamma," she said "why do you speak of him like that?"

"Because he is a scamp."

"No, he is no scamp. It is very unkind of you to speak in such terms of one whom you know is very dear to me."

"I do not know it. He ought not to be dear to you at all. You have been for years intended for another purpose." This was intolerable to Florence,—this idea that she should have been considered as capable of being intended for the purposes of other people! And a resolution at once was formed in her mind that she would let her mother know that such intentions were futile. But for the moment she sat silent. A journey home at twelve o'clock at night in a fly was not the time for the expression of her resolution. "I say he is a scamp," said Mrs. Mountjoy. "During all these inquiries that have been made after your cousin he has known all about it."

"He has not known all about it," said Florence.

"You contradict me in a very impertinent manner, and cannot be acquainted with the circumstances. The last person who saw your cousin in London was Mr. Henry

Annesley, and yet he has not said a word about it, while search was being made on all sides. And he saw him under circumstances most suspicious in their nature; so suspicious as to have made the police arrest him if they were aware of them. He had at that moment grossly insulted Captain Scarborough."

"No, mamma; no, it was not so."

"How do you know? how can you tell?"

"I do know; and I can tell. The ill-usage had come from the other side."

"Then you, too, have known the secret, and have said nothing about it? You, too, have been aware of the violence which took place at that midnight meeting? You have been aware of what befell your cousin, the man to whom you were all but engaged. And you have held your tongue at the instigation, no doubt, of Mr. Henry Annesley. Oh, Florence, you also will find yourself in the hands of the policeman!" At this moment the fly drew up at the door of the house in Montpelier Place, and the two ladies had to get out and walk up the steps into the hall, where they were congratulated on their early return from the party by the lady's-maid.

"Mamma, I will go to bed," said Florence, as soon as she reached her mother's room.

"I think you had better, my dear, though Heaven knows what disturbances there may be during the night." By this Mrs. Mountjoy had intended to imply that Prodgers, the policeman, might probably lose not a moment more before he would at once proceed to arrest Miss Mountjoy for the steps she had taken in regard to the disappearance of Captain Scarborough.

She had heard from Harry Annesley the fact that he had been brutally attacked by the captain in the middle of the night in the streets of London; and for this, in accordance with her mother's theory, she was to be dragged out of bed by a constable, and that, probably, before the next morning should have come. There was something in this so ludicrous as regarded the truth of the story, and yet so cruel as coming from her mother, that Florence hardly knew whether to cry or laugh as she laid her head upon the pillow.

But in the morning, as she was thinking that the facts of her own position had still to be explained to her mother,—that it would be necessary that she should declare her purpose and the impossibility of change, now that she had once pledged herself to her lover,—Mrs. Mountjoy came into the room, and stood at her bedside, with that appearance of ghostly displeasure which always belongs to an angry old lady in a night-cap.

"Well, mamma?"

"Florence, there must be an understanding between us."

"I hope so. I thought there always had been. I am sure, mamma, you have known that I have never liked Captain Scarborough so as to become his wife, and I think you have known that I have liked Harry Annesley."

"Likings are all fiddlesticks!"

"No, mamma; or, if you object to the word, I will say love. You have known that I have not loved my cousin, and that I have loved this other man. That is not nonsense; that at any rate is a stern reality, if there be anything real in the world."

"Stern! you may well call it stern."

"I mean unbending, strong, not to be overcome by outside circumstances. If Mr. Annesley had not spoken to me as he did last night,—could never have so spoken to me,—I should have been a miserable girl, but my love for him would have been just as stern. I should have remained and thought of it, and have been unhappy through my whole life. But he has spoken, and I am exultant. That is what I mean by stern. All that is most important, at any rate to me."

"I am here now to tell you that it is impossible."

"Very well, mamma. Then things must go on, and we must bide our time."

"It is proper that I should tell you that he has disgraced himself."

"Never! I will not admit it. You do not know the circumstances," exclaimed Florence.

"It is most impertinent in you to pretend that you know them better than I do," said her mother, indignantly.

"The story was told to me by himself."

"Yes; and therefore told untruly."

"I grieve that you should think so of him, mamma; but I cannot help it. Where you have got your information I cannot tell. But that mine has been accurately told to me I feel certain."

"At any rate, my duty is to look after you and to keep you from harm. I can only do my duty to the best of my ability. Mr. Annesley is, to my thinking, a most objectionable young man, and he will, I believe, be in the hands of the police before long. Evidence will have to be given, in which your name will, unfortunately, be mentioned."

"Why my name?"

"It is not probable that he will keep it a secret, when cross-questioned, as to his having divulged the story to some one. He will declare that he has told it to you. When that time shall come it will be well that we should be out of the country. I propose to start from here on this day week."

"Uncle Magnus will not be able to have us then."

"We must loiter away our time on the road. I look upon it as quite imperative that we shall both be out of England within eight days' time of this."

"But where will you go?"

"Never mind. I do not know that I have as yet quite made up my mind. But you may understand that we shall start from Cheltenham this day week. Baker will go with us, and I shall leave the other two servants in charge of the house. I cannot tell you anything farther as yet,—except that I will never consent to your marriage with Mr. Henry Annesley. You had better know that for certain, and then there will be less cause for unhappiness between us." So saying, the angry ghost with the night-cap on stalked out of the room.

It need hardly be explained that Mrs. Mountjoy's information respecting the scene in London had come to her from Augustus Scarborough. When he told her that Annesley had been the last in London to see his brother Mountjoy, and had described the nature of the scene that had occurred between them, he had no doubt forgotten that he himself had subsequently seen his brother. In the story, as he had told it, there was no need to mention himself,—no necessity for such a character in making up the tragedy of that night. No doubt, according to his idea, the two had been alone together. Harry had struck the blow by which his brother had been injured, and had then left him in the street. Mountjoy had subsequently disappeared, and Harry had told to no one that such an encounter had taken place. This had been the meaning of Augustus Scarborough when he informed his aunt that Harry had been the last who had seen Mountjoy before his disappearance. To Mrs. Mountjoy the fact had been most injurious to Harry's character. Harry had wilfully kept the secret while all the world was at work looking for Mountjoy Scarborough; and, as far as Mrs. Mountjoy could understand, it might well be that Harry had struck the fatal blow that had sent her nephew to his long account. All the impossibilities in the case had not dawned upon her. It had not occurred to her that Mountjoy could not have been killed and his body made away with without some great effort, in the performance of which the "scamp" would hardly have risked his life or his character. But the scamp was certainly a scamp, even though he might not be a murderer, or he would have revealed the secret. In fact, Mrs. Mountjoy believed in the matter exactly what Augustus had intended, and, so believing, had resolved that her daughter should suffer any purgatory rather than become Harry's wife.

But her daughter made her resolutions exactly in the contrary direction. She in truth did know what had been done on that night, while her mother was in ignorance. The extent of her mother's ignorance she understood, but she did not at all know where her mother had got her information. She felt that Harry's secret was in hands other than he had intended, and that some one must have spoken of the scene. It occurred to Florence at the moment that this must have come from Mountjoy himself, whom she believed,—and rightly believed,—to have been the only second person present on the occasion. And if he had told it to any one, then must that "any one" know where and how he had disappeared. And the information must have been given to her mother solely with the view of damaging Harry's character, and of preventing Harry's marriage.

Thinking of all this, Florence felt that a premeditated and foul attempt,—for, as she turned it in her mind, the attempt seemed to be very foul,—was being made to injure Harry. A false accusation was brought against him, and was grounded on a misrepresentation of the truth in such a manner as to subvert it altogether to Harry's injury. It should have no effect upon her. To this determination she came at once, and declared to herself solemnly that she would be true to it. An attempt was made to undermine him in her estimation; but they who made it had not known her character. She was sure of herself now, within her own bosom, that she was bound in a peculiar way to be more than ordinarily true to Harry Annesley. In such an emergency she ought to do for Harry Annesley more than a girl in common circumstances would be justified in doing for her lover. Harry was maligned, ill-used, and slandered. Her mother had been induced to call him a scamp, and to give as her reason for doing so an account of a transaction which was altogether false, though she no doubt had believed it to be true.

As she thought of all this she resolved that it was her duty to write to her lover, and tell him the story as she had heard it. It might be most necessary that he should know the truth. She would write her letter and post it,—so that it should be altogether beyond her mother's control,—and then would tell her mother that she had written it. She at first thought that she would keep a copy of the letter and show it to her mother. But when it was written,—those first words intended for a lover's eyes which had ever been produced by her pen,—she found that she could not subject those very words to her mother's hard judgment.

Her letter was as follows:

DEAR HARRY,—You will be much surprised at receiving a letter from me so soon after our meeting last night. But I warn you that you must not take it amiss. I should not write now were it not that I think it may be for your interest that I should do so. I do not write to say a word about my love, of which I think you may be assured without any letter. I told mamma last night what had occurred between us, and she of course was very angry. You will understand that, knowing how anxious she has been on behalf of my cousin Mountjoy. She has always taken his part, and I think it does mamma great honor not to throw him over now that he is in trouble. I should never have thrown him over in his trouble, had I ever cared for him in that way. I tell you that fairly, Master Harry.

But mamma, in speaking against you, which she was bound to do in supporting poor Mountjoy, declared that you were the last person who had seen my cousin before his disappearance, and she knew that there had been some violent struggle between you. Indeed, she knew all the truth as to that night, except that the attack had been made by Mountjoy on you. She turned the story all round, declaring that you had attacked him,—which, as you perceive, gives a totally different appearance to the whole matter. Somebody has told her,—though who it may have been I cannot guess,—but somebody has been endeavoring to do you all the mischief he can in the matter, and has made mamma think evil of you. She says that after attacking him, and brutally ill-using him, you had left him in the street, and had subsequently denied all knowledge of having seen him. You will perceive that somebody has been at work inventing a story to do you a mischief, and I think it right that I should tell you.

But you must never believe that I shall believe anything to your discredit. It would be to my discredit now. I know that you are good, and true, and noble, and that you would not do anything so foul as this. It is because I know this that I have loved you, and shall always love you. Let mamma and others say what they will, you are now to me all the world. Oh, Harry, Harry, when I think of it, how serious it seems to me, and yet how joyful! I exult in you, and will do so, let them say what they may against you. You will be sure of that always. Will you not be sure of it?

But you must not write a line in answer, not even to give me your assurance. That must come when we shall meet at length,—say after a dozen years or so. I shall tell mamma of this letter, which circumstances seem to demand, and shall assure her that you will write no answer to it.

Oh, Harry, you will understand all that I might say of my feelings in regard to you.

Your own,   FLORENCE.

This letter, when she had written it and copied it fair and posted the copy in the pillar-box close by, she found that she could not in any way show absolutely to her mother. In spite of all her efforts it had become a love-letter. And what genuine love-letter can a girl show even to her mother? But she at once told her of what she had done. "Mamma, I have written a letter to Harry Annesley."

"You have?"

"Yes, mamma; I have thought it right to tell him what you had heard about that night."

"And you have done this without my permission,—without even telling me what you were going to do?"

"If I had asked you, you would have told me not."

"Of course I should have told you not. Good gracious! has it come to this, that you correspond with a young gentleman without my leave, and when you know that I would not have given it?"

"Mamma, in this instance it was necessary."

"Who was to judge of that?"

"If he is to be my husband—"

"But he is not to be your husband. You are never to speak to him again. You shall never be allowed to meet him; you shall be taken abroad, and there you shall remain, and he shall hear nothing about you. If he attempts to correspond with you—"

"He will not."

"How do you know?"

"I have told him not to write."

"Told him, indeed! Much he will mind such telling! I shall give your Uncle Magnus a full account of it all and ask for his advice. He is a man in a high position, and perhaps you may think fit to obey him, although you utterly refuse to be guided in any way by your mother." Then the conversation for the moment came to an end. But Florence, as she left her mother, assured herself that she could not promise any close obedience in any such matters to Sir Magnus.

CHAPTER XIV. THEY ARRIVE IN BRUSSELS

For some weeks after the party at Mrs. Armitage's house, and the subsequent explanations with her mother, Florence was made to suffer many things. First came the one week before they started, which was perhaps the worst of all. This was specially embittered by the fact that Mrs. Mountjoy absolutely refused to divulge her plans as they were made. There was still a fortnight before she could be received at Brussels, and as to that fortnight she would tell nothing.

Her knowledge of human nature probably went so far as to teach her that she could thus most torment her daughter. It was not that she wished to torment her in a revengeful spirit. She was quite sure within her own bosom that she did all in love. She was devoted to her daughter. But she was thwarted; and therefore told herself that she could best farther the girl's interests by tormenting her. It was not meditated revenge, but that revenge which springs up without any meditation, and is often therefore the most bitter. "I must bring her nose to the grindstone," was the manner in which she would have probably expressed her thoughts to herself. Consequently Florence's nose was brought to the grindstone, and the operation made her miserable. She would not, however, complain when she had discovered what her mother was doing. She asked such questions as appeared to be natural, and put up with replies which purposely withheld all information. "Mamma, have you not settled on what day we shall start?" "No, my dear." "Mamma, where are we going?" "I cannot tell you as yet; I am by no means sure myself." "I shall be glad to know, mamma, what I am to pack up for use on the journey." "Just the same as you would do on any journey." Then Florence held her tongue, and consoled herself with thinking of Harry Annesley.

At last the day came, and she knew that she was to be taken to Boulogne. Before this time she had received one letter from Harry, full of love, full of thanks,—just what a lover's letter ought to have been;—but yet she was disturbed by it. It had been delivered to herself in the usual way, and she might have concealed the receipt of it from her mother, because the servants in the house were all on her side. But this would not be in accordance with the conduct which she had arranged for herself, and she told her mother. "It is just an acknowledgment of mine to him. It was to have been expected, but I regret it."

"I do not ask to see it," said Mrs. Mountjoy, angrily.

"I could not show it you, mamma, though I think it right to tell you of it."

"I do not ask to see it, I tell you. I never wish to hear his name again from your tongue. But I knew how it would be;—of course. I cannot allow this kind of thing to go on. It must be prevented."

"It will not go on, mamma."

"But it has gone on. You tell me that he has already written. Do you think it proper that you should correspond with a young man of whom I do not approve?" Florence endeavored to reflect whether she did think it proper or not. She thought it quite proper that she should love Harry Annesley with all her heart, but was not quite sure as to the correspondence. "At any rate, you must understand," continued Mrs. Mountjoy, "that I will not permit it. All letters, while we are abroad, must be brought to me; and if any come from him they shall be sent back to him. I do not wish to open his letters, but you cannot be allowed to receive them. When we are at Brussels I shall consult your uncle upon the subject. I am very sorry, Florence, that there should be this cause of quarrel between us; but it is your doing."

"Oh, mamma, why should you be so hard?"

"I am hard, because I will not allow you to accept a young man who has, I believe, behaved very badly, and who has got nothing of his own."

"He is his uncle's heir."

"We know what that may come to. Mountjoy was his father's heir; and nothing could be entailed more strictly than Tretton. We know what entails have come to there. Mr. Prosper will find some way of escaping from it. Entails go for nothing now; and I hear that he thinks so badly of his nephew that he has already quarrelled with him. And he is quite a young man himself. I cannot think how you can be so foolish,—you, who declared that you are throwing your cousin over because he is no longer to have all his father's property."

"Oh, mamma, that is not true."

"Very well, my dear."

"I never allowed it to be said in my name that I was engaged to my cousin Mountjoy."

"Very well, I will never allow it to be said in my name that with my consent you are engaged to Mr. Henry Annesley."

Six or seven days after this they were settled together most uncomfortably in a hotel at Boulogne. Mrs. Mountjoy had gone there because there was no other retreat to which she could take her daughter, and because she had resolved to remove her from beyond the sphere of Harry Annesley's presence. She had at first thought of Ostend; but it had seemed to her that Ostend was within the kingdom reigned over by Sir Magnus and that there would be some impropriety in removing from thence to the capital in which Sir Magnus was reigning. It was as though you were to sojourn for three days at the park-gates before you were entertained at the mansion. Therefore they stayed at Boulogne, and Mrs. Mountjoy tried the bathing, cold as the water was with equinoctial gales, in order that there might be the appearance of a reason for her being at Boulogne. And for company's sake, in the hope of maintaining some fellowship with her mother, Florence bathed also. "Mamma, he has not written again," said Florence, coming up one day from the stand.

"I suppose that you are impatient."

"Why should there be a quarrel between us? I am not impatient. If you would only believe me, it would be so much more happy for both of us. You always used to believe me."

"That was before you knew Mr. Harry Annesley."

There was something in this very aggravating,—something specially intended to excite angry feelings. But Florence determined to forbear. "I think you may believe me, mamma. I am your own daughter, and I shall not deceive you. I do consider myself engaged to Mr. Annesley."

"You need not tell me that."

"But while I am living with you I will promise not to receive letters from him without your leave. If one should come I will bring it to you, unopened, so that you may deal with it as though it had been delivered to yourself. I care nothing about my uncle as to this affair. What he may say cannot affect me, but what you say does affect me very much. I will promise neither to write nor to hear from Mr. Annesley for three months. Will not that satisfy you?" Mrs. Mountjoy would not say that it did satisfy her; but she somewhat mitigated her treatment of her daughter till they arrived together at Sir Magnus's mansion.

They were shown through the great hall by three lackeys into an inner vestibule, where they encountered the great man himself. He was just then preparing to be put on to his horse, and Lady Mountjoy had already gone forth in her carriage for her daily airing, with the object, in truth, of avoiding the new-comers. "My dear Sarah," said Sir Magnus, "I hope I have the pleasure of seeing you and my niece very well. Let me see, your name is—"

"My name is Florence," said the young lady so interrogated.

"Ah yes; to be sure. I shall forget my own name soon. If any one was to call me Magnus without the 'Sir,' I shouldn't know whom they meant." Then he looked his niece in the face, and it occurred to him that Anderson might not improbably desire to flirt with her. Anderson was the riding attache, who always accompanied him on horseback, and of whom Lady Mountjoy had predicted that he would be sure to flirt with the minister's niece. At that moment Anderson himself came in, and some ceremony of introduction took place. Anderson was a fair-haired, good-looking young man, with that thorough look of self-satisfaction and conceit which attaches are much more wont to exhibit than to deserve. For the work of an attaché at Brussels is not of a nature to bring forth the highest order of intellect; but the occupations are of a nature to make a young man feel that he is not like other young men.

"I am so sorry that Lady Mountjoy has just gone out. She did not expect you till the later train. You have been staying at Boulogne. What on earth made you stay at Boulogne?"

"Bathing," said Mrs. Mountjoy, in a low voice.

"Ah, yes; I suppose so. Why did you not come to Ostend? There is better bathing there, and I could have done something for you. What! The horses ready, are they? I must go out and show myself, or otherwise they'll all think that I am dead. If I were absent from the boulevard at this time of day I should be put into the newspapers. Where is Mrs. Richards?" Then the two guests, with their own special Baker, were made over to the ministerial house-keeper, and Sir Magnus went forth upon his ride.

"She's a pretty girl, that niece of mine," said Sir Magnus.

"Uncommonly pretty," said the attaché.

"But I believe she is engaged to some one. I quite forget who; but I know there is some aspirant. Therefore you had better keep your toe in your pump, young man."

"I don't know that I shall keep my toe in my pump because there is another aspirant," said Anderson. "You rather whet my ardor, sir, to new exploits. In such circumstances one is inclined to think that the aspirant must look after himself. Not that I conceive for a moment that Miss Mountjoy should ever look after me."

When Mrs. Mountjoy came down to the drawing-room there seemed to be quite "a party" collected to enjoy the hospitality of Sir Magnus, but there were not, in truth, many more than the usual number at the board. There were Lady Mountjoy, and Miss Abbot, and Mr. Anderson, with Mr. Montgomery Arbuthnot, the two attaches. Mr. Montgomery Arbuthnot was especially proud of his name, but was otherwise rather a humble young man as an attaché, having as yet been only three months with Sir Magnus, and desirous of perfecting himself in Foreign Office manners under the tuition of Mr. Anderson. Mr. Blow, Secretary of Legation, was not there. He was a married man of austere manners, who, to tell the truth, looked down from a considerable height, as regarded Foreign Office knowledge, upon his chief.

It was Mr. Blow who did the "grinding" on behalf of the Belgian Legation, and who sometimes did not hesitate to let it be known that such was the fact. Neither he nor Mrs. Blow was popular at the Embassy; or it may, perhaps, be said with more truth that the Embassy was not popular with Mr. and Mrs. Blow. It may be stated, also, that there was a clerk attached to the establishment, Mr. Bunderdown, who had been there for some years, and who was good-naturedly regarded by the English inhabitants as a third attaché. Mr. Montgomery Arbuthnot did his best to let it be understood that this was a mistake. In the small affairs of the legation, which no doubt did not go beyond the legation, Mr. Bunderdown generally sided with Mr. Blow. Mr. Montgomery Arbuthnot was recognized as a second mounted attaché, though his attendance on the boulevard was not as constant as that of Mr. Anderson, in consequence, probably, of the fact that he had not a horse of his own. But there were others also present. There were Sir Thomas Tresham, with his wife, who had been sent over to inquire into the iron trade of Belgium. He was a learned free-trader who could not be got to agree with the old familiar views of Sir Magnus,—who thought that the more iron that was produced in Belgium the less would be forthcoming from England. But Sir Thomas knew better, and as Sir Magnus was quite unable to hold his own with the political economist, he gave him many dinners and was civil to his wife. Sir Thomas, no doubt, felt that in doing so Sir Magnus did all that could be expected from him. Lady Tresham was a quiet little woman, who could endure to be patronized by Lady Mountjoy without annoyance. And there was M. Grascour, from the Belgian Foreign Office, who spoke English so much better than the other gentlemen present that a stranger might have supposed him to be a school-master whose mission it was to instruct the English Embassy in their own language.

"Oh, Mrs Mountjoy, I am so ashamed of myself!" said Lady Mountjoy, as she waddled into the room two minutes after the guests had been assembled. She had a way of waddling that was quite her own, and which they who knew her best declared that she had adopted in lieu of other graces of manner. She puffed a little also, and did contrive to attract peculiar attention. "But I have to be in my carriage every day at the same hour. I don't know what would be thought of us if we were absent." Then she turned, with a puff and a waddle, to Miss Abbot. "Dear Lady Tresham was with us." Mrs. Mountjoy murmured something as to her satisfaction at not having delayed the carriage-party, and bethought herself how exactly similar had been the excuse made by Sir Magnus himself. Then Lady Mountjoy gave another little puff, and assured Florence that she hoped she would find Brussels sufficiently gay,—"not that we pretend at all to equal Paris."

"We live at Cheltenham," said Florence, "and that is not at all like Paris. Indeed, I never slept but two nights at Paris in my life."

"Then we shall do very well at Brussels." After this she waddled off again, and was stopped in her waddling by Sir Magnus, who sternly desired her to prepare for the august ceremony of going in to dinner. The one period of real importance at the English Embassy was, no doubt, the daily dinner-hour.

Florence found herself seated between Mr. Anderson, who had taken her in, and M. Grascour, who had performed the same ceremony for her ladyship. "I am sure you will like this little capital very much," said M. Grascour. "It is as much nicer than Paris as it is smaller and less pretentious." Florence could only assent. "You will soon be able to learn something of us; but in Paris you must be to the manner born, or half a lifetime will not suffice."

"We'll put you up to the time of day," said Mr. Anderson, who did not choose, as he said afterward, that this tidbit should be taken out of his mouth.

"I dare say that all that I shall want will come naturally without any putting up."

"You won't find it amiss to know a little of what's what. You have not got a riding-horse here?"

"Oh no," said Florence.

"I was going on to say that I can manage to secure one for you. Billibong has got an excellent horse that carried the Princess of Styria last year." Mr. Anderson was supposed to be peculiarly up to everything concerning horses.

"But I have not got a habit. That is a much more serious affair."

"Well, yes. Billibong does not keep habits: I wish he did. But we can manage that too. There does live a habit-maker in Brussels."

"Ladies' habits certainly are made in Brussels," said M. Grascour. "But if Miss Mountjoy does not choose to trust a Belgian tailor there is the railway open to her. An English habit can be sent."

"Dear Lady Centaur had one sent to her only last year, when she was staying here," said Lady Mountjoy across her neighbor, with two little puffs.

"I shall not at all want the habit," said Florence, "not having the horse, and indeed, never being accustomed to ride at all."

"Do tell me what it is that you do do," said Mr. Anderson, with a convenient whisper, when he found that M. Grascour had fallen into conversation with her ladyship. "Lawn-tennis?"

"I do play at lawn-tennis, though I am not wedded to it."

"Billiards? I know you play billiards."

"I never struck a ball in my life."

"Goodness gracious, how odd! Don't you ever amuse yourself at all? Are they so very devotional down at Cheltenham?"

"I suppose we are stupid. I don't know that I ever do especially amuse myself."

"We must teach you;—we really must teach you. I think I may boast of myself that I am a good instructor in that line. Will you promise to put yourself into my hands?"

"You will find me a most unpromising pupil."

"Not in the least. I will undertake that when you leave this you shall be *au fait* at everything. Leap frog is not too heavy for me and spillikins not too light. I am up to them all, from backgammon to a cotillon,—not but what I prefer the cotillon for my own taste."

"Or leap-frog, perhaps," suggested Florence.

"Well, yes; leap-frog used to be a good game at Gother School, and I don't see why we shouldn't have it back again. Ladies, of course, must have a costume on purpose. But I am fond of anything that requires a costume. Don't you like everything out of the common way? I do." Florence assured him that their tastes were wholly dissimilar, as she liked everything in the common way. "That's what I call an uncommonly pretty girl," he said afterward to M. Grascour, while Sir Magnus was talking to Sir Thomas. "What an eye!"

"Yes, indeed; she is very lovely."

"My word, you may say that! And such a turn of the shoulders! I don't say which are the best-looking, as a rule, English or Belgians, but there are very few of either to come up to her."

"Anderson, can you tell us how many tons of steel rails they turn out at Liège every week? Sir Thomas asks me, just as though it were the simplest question in the world."

"Forty million," said Anderson,—"more or less."

"Twenty thousand would, perhaps, be nearer the mark," said M. Grascour; "but I will send him the exact amount to-morrow."

CHAPTER XV. MR. ANDERSON'S LOVE

Lady Mountjoy had certainly prophesied the truth when she said that Mr. Anderson would devote himself to Florence. The first week in Brussels passed by quietly enough. A young man can hardly declare his passion within a week, and Mr. Anderson's ways in that particular were well known. A certain amount of license was usually given to him, both by Sir Magnus and Lady Mountjoy, and when he would become remarkable by the rapidity of his changes the only adverse criticism would come generally from Mr. Blow. "Another peerless Bird of Paradise," Mr. Blow would say. "If the birds were less numerous, Anderson might, perhaps, do something." But at the end of the week, on this occasion, even Sir Magnus perceived that Anderson was about to make himself peculiar.

"By George!" he said one morning, when Sir Magnus had just left the outer office, which he had entered with the object of giving some instruction as to the day's ride, "take her altogether, I never saw a girl so fit as Miss Mountjoy." There was something very remarkable in this speech, as, according to his usual habit of life, Anderson would certainly have called her Florence, whereas his present appellation showed an unwonted respect.

"What do you mean when you say that a young lady is fit?" said Mr. Blow.

"I mean that she is right all round, which is a great deal more than can be said of most of them."

"The divine Florence—" began Mr. Montgomery Arbuthnot, struggling to say something funny.

"Young man, you had better hold your tongue, and not talk of young ladies in that language."

"I do believe that he is going to fall in love," said Mr. Blow.

"I say that Miss Mountjoy is the fittest girl I have seen for many a day; and when a young puppy calls her the divine Florence, he does not know what he is about."

"Why didn't you blow Mr. Blow up when he called her a Bird of Paradise?" said Montgomery Arbuthnot. "Divine Florence is not half so disrespectful of a young lady as Bird of Paradise. Divine Florence means divine Florence, but Bird of Paradise is chaff."

"Mr. Blow, as a married man," said Anderson, "has a certain freedom allowed him. If he uses it in bad taste, the evil falls back upon his own head. Now, if you please, we'll change the conversation." From this it will be seen that Mr. Anderson had really fallen in love with Miss Mountjoy.

But though the week had passed in a harmless way to Sir Magnus and Lady Mountjoy,—in a harmless way to them as regarded their niece and their attaché,—a certain amount of annoyance had, no doubt, been felt by Florence herself. Though Mr. Anderson's expressions of admiration had been more subdued than usual, though he had endeavored to whisper his love rather than to talk it out loud, still the admiration had been both visible and audible, and especially so to Florence herself. It was nothing to Sir Magnus with whom his attaché flirted. Anderson was the younger son of a baronet who had a sickly elder brother, and some fortune of his own. If he chose to marry the girl, that would be well for her; and if not, it would be quite well that the young people should amuse themselves. He expected Anderson to help to put him on his horse, and to ride with him at the appointed hour. He, in return, gave Anderson his dinner and as much wine as he chose to drink. They were both satisfied with each other, and Sir Magnus did not choose to interfere with the young man's amusements. But Florence did not like being the subject of a young man's love-making, and complained to her mother.

Now, it had come to pass that not a word had been said as to Harry Annesley since the mother and daughter had reached Brussels. Mrs. Mountjoy had declared that she would consult her brother-in-law in that difficulty, but no such consultation had as yet taken place. Indeed, Florence would not have found her sojourn at Brussels to be unpleasant were it not for Mr. Anderson's unpalatable little whispers. She had taken them as jokes as long as she had been able to do so, but was now at last driven to perceive that other people would not do so. "Mamma," she said, "don't you think that that Mr. Anderson is an odious young man?"

"No, my dear, by no means. What is there odious about him? He is very lively; he is the second son of Sir Gregory Anderson, and has very comfortable means of his own."

"Oh, mamma, what does that signify?"

"Well, my dear, it does signify. In the first place, he is a gentleman, and in the next, has a right to make himself attentive to any young lady in your position. I don't say anything more. I am not particularly wedded to Mr. Anderson. If he were to come to me and ask for my permission to address you, I should simply refer him to yourself, by which I should mean to imply that if he could contrive to recommend himself to you I should not refuse my sanction."

Then the subject for that moment dropped, but Florence was astonished to find that her mother could talk about it, not only without reference to Harry Annesley, but also without an apparent thought of Mountjoy Scarborough; and it was distressing to her to think that her mother should pretend to feel that she, her own daughter, should be free to receive the advances of another suitor. As she reflected it came across her mind that Harry was so odious that her mother would have been willing to accept on her behalf any suitor who presented himself, even though her daughter, in accepting him, should have proved herself to be heartless. Any alternative would have been better to her mother than that choice to which Florence had determined to devote her whole life.

"Mamma," she said, going back to the subject on the next day, "if I am to stay here for three weeks longer—"

"Yes, my dear, you are to stay here for three weeks longer."

"Then somebody must say something to Mr. Anderson."

"I do not see who can say it but you yourself. As far as I can see, he has not misbehaved."

"I wish you would speak to my uncle."

"What am I to tell him?"

"That I am engaged."

"He would ask me to whom, and I cannot tell him. I should then be driven to put the whole case in his hands, and to ask his advice. You do not suppose that I am going to say that you are engaged to marry that odious young man? All the world knows how atrociously badly he has behaved to your own cousin. He left him lying for dead in the street by a blow from his own hand; and though from that day to this nothing has been heard of Mountjoy, nothing is known to the police of what may have been his fate;—even stranger, he may have perished under the usage which he received, yet Mr. Annesley has not thought it right to say a word of what had occurred. He has not dared even to tell an inspector of police the events of that night. And the young man was your own cousin, to whom you were known to have been promised for the last two years."

"No, no!" said Florence.

"I say that it was so. You were promised to your cousin, Mountjoy Scarborough."

"Not with my own consent."

"All your friends,—your natural friends,—knew that it was to be so. And now you expect me to take by the hand this young man who has almost been his murderer!"

"No, mamma, it is not true. You do not know the circumstances, and you assert things which are directly at variance with the truth."

"From whom do you get your information? From the young man himself. Is that likely to be true? What would Sir Magnus say as to that were I to tell him?"

"I do not know what he would say, but I do know what is the truth. And can you think it possible that I should now be willing to accept this foolish young man in order thus to put an end to my embarrassments?"

Then she left her mother's room, and, retreating to her own, sat for a couple of hours thinking, partly in anger and partly in grief, of the troubles of her situation. Her mother had now, in truth, frightened her as to Harry's position. She did begin to see what men might say of him, and the way in which they might speak of his silence, though she was resolved to be as true to him in her faith as ever. Some exertion of spirit would, indeed, be necessary. She was beginning to understand in what way the outside world might talk of Harry Annesley, of the man to whom she had given herself and her whole heart. Then her mother was right. And as she thought of it she began to justify her mother. It was natural that her mother should believe the story which had been told to her, let it have come from where it might. There was in her mind some suspicion of the truth. She acknowledged a great animosity to her cousin Augustus, and regarded him as one of the causes of her unhappiness. But she knew nothing of the real facts; she did not even suspect that Augustus had seen his brother after Harry had dealt with him, or that he was responsible for his brother's absence. But she knew that she disliked him, and in some way she connected his name with Harry's misfortune.

Of one thing she was certain: let them,—the Mountjoys, and Prospers, and the rest of the world,—think and say what they would of Harry, she would be true to him. She could understand that his character might be made to suffer, but it should not suffer in her estimation. Or rather, let it suffer ever so, that should not affect her love and her truth. She did not say this to herself. By saying it even to herself she would have committed some default of truth. She did not whisper it even to her own heart. But within her heart there was a feeling that, let Harry be right or wrong in what he had done, even let it be proved, to the satisfaction of all the world, that he had sinned grievously when he had left the man stunned and bleeding on the pavement,—for to such details her mother's story had gone,—still, to her he should be braver, more noble, more manly, more worthy of being loved, than was any other man. She, perceiving the difficulties that were in store for her, and looking forward to the misfortune under which Harry might be placed, declared to herself that he should at least have one friend who would be true to him.

"Miss Mountjoy, I have come to you with a message from your aunt." This was said, three or four days after the conversation between Florence and her mother, by

Mr. Anderson, who had contrived to follow the young lady into a small drawing-room after luncheon. What was the nature of the message it is not necessary for us to know. We may be sure that it had been manufactured by Mr. Anderson for the occasion. He had looked about and spied, and had discovered that Miss Mountjoy was alone in the little room. And in thus spying we consider him to have been perfectly justified. His business at the moment was that of making love, a business which is allowed to override all other considerations. Even the making an office copy of a report made by Mr. Blow for the signature of Sir Magnus might, according to our view of life, have been properly laid aside for such a purpose. When a young man has it in him to make love to a young lady, and is earnest in his intention, no duty, however paramount, should be held as a restraint. Such was Mr. Anderson's intention at the present moment; and therefore we think that he was justified in concocting a message from Lady Mountjoy. The business of love-making warrants any concoction to which the lover may resort. "But oh, Miss Mountjoy, I am so glad to have a moment in which I can find you alone!" It must be understood that the amorous young gentleman had not yet been acquainted with the young lady for quite a fortnight.

"I was just about to go up-stairs to my mother," said Florence, rising to leave the room.

"Oh, bother your mother! I beg her pardon and yours;—I really didn't mean it. There is such a lot of chaff going on in that outer room, that a fellow falls into the way of it whether he likes it or no."

"My mother won't mind it at all; but I really must go."

"Oh no. I am sure you can wait for five minutes. I don't want to keep you for more than five minutes. But it is so hard for a fellow to get an opportunity to say a few words."

"What words can you want to say to me, Mr. Anderson?" This she said with a look of great surprise, as though utterly unable to imagine what was to follow.

"Well, I did hope that you might have some idea of what my feelings are."

"Not in the least."

"Haven't you, now? I suppose I am bound to believe you, though I doubt whether I quite do. Pray excuse me for saying this, but it is best to be open." Florence felt that he ought to be excused for doubting her, as she did know very well what was coming. "I—I—Come, then; I love you! If I were to go on beating about the bush for twelve months I could only come to the same conclusion."

"Perhaps you might then have considered it better."

"Not in the least. Fancy considering such a thing as that for twelve months before you speak of it! I couldn't do it,—not for twelve days."

"So I perceive, Mr. Anderson."

"Well, isn't it best to speak the truth when you're quite sure of it? If I were to remain dumb for three months, how should I know but what some one else might come in the way?"

"But you can't expect that I should be so sudden?"

"That's just where it is. Of course I don't. And yet girls have to be sudden too."

"Have they?"

"They're expected to be ready with their answer as soon as they're asked. I don't say this by way of impertinence, but merely to show that I have some justification. Of course, if you like to say that you must take a week to think of it, I am prepared for that. Only let me tell my own story first."

"You shall tell your own story, Mr. Anderson; but I am afraid that it can be to no purpose."

"Don't say that,—pray, don't say that,—but do let me tell it." Then he paused; but, as she remained silent, after a moment he resumed the eloquence of his appeal. "By George! Miss Mountjoy, I have been so struck of a heap that I do not know whether I am standing on my head or my heels. You have knocked me so completely off my pins that I am not at all like the same person. Sir Magnus himself says that he never saw such a difference. I only say that to show that I am quite in earnest. Now I am not quite like a fellow that has no business to fall in love with a girl. I have four hundred a year besides my place in the Foreign Office. And then, of course, there are chances." In this he alluded to his brother's failing health, of which he could not explain the details to Miss Mountjoy on the present occasion. "I don't mean to say that this is very splendid, or that it is half what I should like to lay at your feet. But a competence is comfortable."

"Money has nothing to do with it, Mr. Anderson."

"What, then? Perhaps it is that you don't like a fellow. What girls generally do like is devotion, and, by George, you'd have that. The very ground that you tread upon is sweet to me. For beauty,—I don't know how it is, but to my taste there is no one I ever saw at all like you. You fit me—well, as though you were made for me. I know that another fellow might say it a deal better, but no one more truly. Miss Mountjoy, I love you with all my heart, and I want you to be my wife. Now you've got it!"

He had not pleaded his cause badly, and so Florence felt. That he had pleaded it hopelessly was a matter of course. But he had given rise to feelings of gentle regard rather than of anger. He had been honest, and had contrived to make her believe him. He did not come up to her ideal of what a lover should be, but he was nearer to it than Mountjoy Scarborough. He had touched her so closely that she determined at once to tell him the truth, thinking that she might best in this way put an end to his passion forever. "Mr. Anderson," she said, "though I have known it to be vain, I have thought it best to listen to you, because you asked it."

"I am sure I am awfully obliged to you."

"And I ought to thank you for the kind feeling you have expressed to me. Indeed, I do thank you. I believe every word you have said. It is better to show my confidence in your truth than to pretend to the humility of thinking you untrue."

"It is true; it is true,—every word of it."

"But I am engaged." Then it was sad to see the thorough change which came over the young man's face. "Of course a girl does not talk of her own little affairs to strangers, or I would let you have known this before, so as to have prevented it. But, in truth, I am engaged."

"Does Sir Magnus know it, or Lady Mountjoy?"

"I should think not."

"Does your mother?"

"Now you are taking advantage of my confidence, and pressing your questions too closely. But my mother does know of it. I will tell you more;—she does not approve of it. But it is fixed in Heaven itself. It may well be that I shall never be able to marry the gentleman to whom I allude, but most certainly I shall marry no one else. I have told you this because it seems to be necessary to your welfare, so that you may get over this passing feeling."

"It is no passing feeling," said Anderson, with some tragic grandeur.

"At any rate, you have now my story, and remember that it is trusted to you as a gentleman. I have told it you for a purpose." Then she walked out of the room, leaving the poor young man in temporary despair.

CHAPTER XVI. MR. AND MISS GREY

It was now the middle of October, and it may be said that from the time in which old Mr. Scarborough had declared his intention of showing that the elder of his sons had no right to the property, Mr. Grey, the lawyer, had been so occupied with the Scarborough affairs as to have had left him hardly a moment for other considerations.

He had a partner, who during these four months had, in fact, carried on the business. One difficulty had grown out of another till Mr. Grey's whole time had been occupied; and all his thoughts had been filled with Mr. Scarborough, which is a matter of much greater moment to a man than the loss of his time. The question of Mountjoy Scarborough's position had been first submitted to him in June. October had now been reached and Mr. Grey had been out of town only for a fortnight, during which fortnight he had been occupied entirely in unravelling the mystery. He had at first refused altogether to have anything to do with the unravelling, and had desired that some other lawyer might be employed. But it had gradually come to pass that he had entered heart and soul into the case, and, with many execrations on his own part against Mr. Scarborough, could find a real interest in nothing else. He had begun his investigations with a thorough wish to discover that Mountjoy Scarborough was, in truth, the heir. Though he had never loved the young man, and, as he went on with his investigations, became aware that the whole property would go to the creditors should he succeed in proving that Mountjoy was the heir, yet for the sake of abstract honesty he was most anxious that it should be so. And he could not bear to think that he and other lawyers had been taken in by the wily craft of such a man as the Squire of Tretton. It went thoroughly against the grain with him to have to acknowledge that the estate would become the property of Augustus. But it was so, and he did acknowledge it. It was proved to him that, in spite of all the evidence which he had hitherto seen in the matter, the squire had not married his wife until after the birth of his eldest son. He did acknowledge it, and he said bravely that it must be so. Then there came down upon him a crowd of enemies in the guise of baffled creditors, all of whom believed, or professed to believe, that he, Mr. Grey, was in league with the squire to rob them of their rights.

If it could be proved that Mountjoy had no claim to the property, then would it go nominally to Augustus, who according to their showing was also one of the confederates, and the property could thus, they said, be divided. Very shortly the squire would be dead, and then the confederates would get everything, to the utter exclusion of poor Mr. Tyrrwhit, and poor Mr. Samuel Hart, and all the other poor creditors, who would thus be denuded, defrauded, and robbed by a lawyer's trick. It was in this spirit that Mr. Grey was attacked by Mr. Tyrrwhit and the others; and Mr. Grey found it very hard to bear.

And then there was another matter which was also very grievous to him. If it were as he now stated,—if the squire had been guilty of this fraud,—to what punishment would he be subjected? Mountjoy was declared to have been innocent. Mr. Tyrrwhit, as he put the case to his own lawyers, laughed bitterly as he made this suggestion. And Augustus was, of course, innocent. Then there was renewed laughter. And Mr. Grey! Mr. Grey had, of course, been innocent. Then the laughter was very loud. Was it to be believed that anybody could be taken in by such a story as this? There was he, Mr. Tyrrwhit: he had ever been known as a sharp fellow; and Mr. Samuel Hart, who was now away on his travels, and the others;—they were all of them sharp fellows. Was it to be believed that such a set of gentlemen, so keenly alive to their own interest, should be made the victims of such a trick as this? Not if they knew it! Not if Mr. Tyrrwhit knew it!

It was in this shape that the matter reached Mr. Grey's ears; and then it was asked, if it were so, what would be the punishment to which they would be subjected who had defrauded Mr. Tyrrwhit of his just claim. Mr. Tyrrwhit, who on one occasion made his way into Mr, Grey's presence, wished to get an answer to that question from Mr. Grey. "The man is dying," said Mr. Grey, solemnly.

"Dying! He is not more likely to die than you are, from all I hear." At this time rumors of Mr. Scarborough's improved health had reached the creditors in London. Mr. Tyrrwhit had begun to believe that Mr. Scarborough's dangerous condition had been part of the hoax; that there had been no surgeon's knives, no terrible operations, no moment of almost certain death. "I don't believe he's been ill at all," said Mr. Tyrrwhit.

"I cannot help your belief," said Mr. Grey.

"But because a man doesn't die and recovers, is he on that account to be allowed to cheat people, as he has cheated me, with impunity?"

"I am not going to defend Mr. Scarborough; but he has not, in fact, cheated you."

"Who has? Come; do you mean to tell me that if this goes on I shall not have been defrauded of a hundred thousand pounds?"

"Did you ever see Mr. Scarborough on the matter?"

"No; it was not necessary."

"Or have you got his writing to any document? Have you anything to show that he knew what his son was doing when he borrowed money of you? Is it not perfectly clear that he knew nothing about it?"

"Of course he knew nothing about it then,—at that time. It was afterward that his fraud began. When he found that the estate was in jeopardy, then the falsehood was concocted."

"Ah, there, Mr. Tyrrwhit, I can only say, that I disagree with you. I must express my opinion that if you endeavor to recover your money on that plea you will be beaten. If you can prove fraud of that kind, no doubt you can punish those who have been guilty of it,—me among the number."

"I say nothing of that," said Mr. Tyrrwhit.

"But if you have been led into your present difficulty by an illegal attempt on the part of my client to prove an illegitimate son to have been legitimate, and then to have changed his mind for certain purposes, I do not see how you are to punish him. The act will have been attempted and not completed. And it will have been an act concerning his son and not concerning you."

"Not concerning me!" shrieked Mr. Tyrrwhit.

"Certainly not, legally. You are not in a position to prove that he knew that his son was borrowing money from you on the credit of the estate. As a fact he certainly did not know it."

"We shall see about that," said Mr. Tyrrwhit.

"Then you must see about it, but not with my aid. As a fact I am telling you all that I know about it. If I could I would prove Mountjoy Scarborough to be his father's heir to-morrow. Indeed, I am altogether on your side in the matter,—if you would believe it." Here Mr. Tyrrwhit again laughed. "But you will not believe it, and I do not ask you to do so. As it is we must be opposed to each other."

"Where is the young man?" asked Mr. Tyrrwhit.

"Ah, that is a question I am not bound to answer, even if I knew. It is a matter on which I say nothing. You have lent him money, at an exorbitant rate of interest."

"It is not true."

"At any rate it seems so to me; and it is out of the question that I should assist you in recovering it. You did it at your own peril, and not on my advice. Good-morning, Mr. Tyrrwhit." Then Mr. Tyrrwhit went his way, not without sundry threats as to the whole Scarborough family.

It was very hard upon Mr. Grey, because he certainly was an honest man and had taken up the matter simply with a view of learning the truth. It had been whispered to him within the last day or two that Mountjoy Scarborough had lately been seen alive, and gambling with reckless prodigality, at Monte Carlo. It had only been told to him as probably true, but he certainly believed it. But he knew nothing of the details of his disappearance, and had not been much surprised, as he had never believed that the young man had been murdered or had made away with himself. But he had heard before that of the quarrel in the street between him and Harry Annesley; and the story had been told to him so as to fall with great discredit on Harry Annesley's head.

According to that story Harry Annesley had struck his foe during the night and had left him for dead upon the pavement. Then Mountjoy Scarborough had been missing, and Harry Annesley had told no one of the quarrel. There had been some girl in question. So much and no more Mr. Grey had heard, and was, of course, inclined to think that Harry Annesley must have behaved very badly. But of the mode of Mountjoy's subsequent escape he had heard nothing.

Mr. Grey at this time was living down at Fulham, in a small, old-fashioned house which over-looked the river, and was called the Manor-house. He would have said that it was his custom to go home every day by an omnibus, but he did, in truth, almost always remain at his office so late as to make it necessary that he should return by a cab. He was a man fairly well to do in the world, as he had no one depending on him but one daughter,—no one, that is to say, whom he was obliged to support. But he had a married sister with a scapegrace husband and six daughters whom, in fact, he did support. Mrs. Carroll, with the kindest intentions in the world, had come and lived near him. She had taken a genteel house in Bolsover Terrace,—a genteel new house on the Fulham Road, about a quarter of a mile from her brother. Mr. Grey lived in the old Manor-house, a small, uncomfortable place, which had a nook of its own, close upon the water, and with a lovely little lawn. It was certainly most uncomfortable as a gentleman's residence, but no consideration would induce Mr. Grey to sell it. There were but two sitting-rooms in it, and one was for the most part uninhabited. The up-stairs drawing-room was furnished, but any one with half an eye could see that it was never used. A "stray" caller might be shown up there, but callers of that class were very uncommon in Mr. Grey's establishment.

With his own domestic arrangements Mr. Grey would have been quite contented, had it not been for Mrs. Carroll. It was now some years since he had declared that though Mr. Carroll,—or Captain Carroll, as he had then been called,—was an improvident, worthless, drunken Irishman, he would never see his sister want. The consequence was that Carroll had come with his wife and six daughters and taken a house close to him. There are such "whips and scorns" in the world to which a man shall be so subject as to have the whole tenor of his life changed by them. The hero bears them heroically, making no complaints to those around him. The common man shrinks, and squeals, and cringes, so that he is known to those around him as one especially persecuted. In this respect Mr. Grey was a grand hero. When he spoke to his friends of Mrs. Carroll his friends were taught to believe that his outside arrangements with his sister were perfectly comfortable. No doubt there did creep out among those who were most intimate with him a knowledge that Mr. Carroll,—for the captain had, in truth, never been more than a lieutenant, and had now long since sold out,—was impecunious, and a trouble rather than otherwise. But I doubt whether there was a single inhabitant of the neighborhood of Fulham who was aware that Mrs. Carroll and the Miss Carrolls cost Mr. Grey on an average above six hundred a year.

There was one in Mr. Grey's family to whom he was so attached that he would, to oblige her, have thrown over the whole Carroll family; but of this that one person would not hear. She hated the whole Carroll family with an almost unholy hatred, of which she herself was endeavoring to repent daily, but in vain. She could not do other than hate them, but she could do other than allow her father to withdraw his fostering protection; for this one person was Mr. Grey's only daughter and his one close domestic associate. Miss Dorothy Grey was known well to all the neighborhood, and was both feared and revered. As we shall have much to do with her in the telling of our story, it may be well to make her stand plainly before the reader's eyes.

In the first place, it must be understood that she was motherless, brotherless and sisterless. She had been Mr. Grey's only child, and her mother had been dead for fifteen or sixteen years. She was now about thirty years of age, but was generally regarded as ranging somewhere between forty and fifty. "If she isn't nearer fifty than forty I'll eat my old shoes," said a lady in the neighborhood to a gentleman. "I've known her these twenty years, and she's not altered in the least." As Dolly Grey had been only ten twenty years ago, the lady must have been wrong. But it is singular how a person's memory of things may be created out of their present appearances. Dorothy herself had apparently no desire to set right this erroneous opinion which the neighborhood entertained respecting her. She did not seem to care whether she was supposed to be thirty, or forty, or fifty. Of youth, as a means of getting lovers, she entertained a profound contempt. That no lover would ever come she was assured, and would not at all have known what to do with one had he come. The only man for whom she had ever felt the slightest regard was her father. For some women about she did entertain a passionless, well-regulated affection, but they were generally the poor, the afflicted, or the aged. It was, however, always necessary that the person so signalized should be submissive. Now, Mrs. Carroll, Mr. Grey's sister, had long since shown that she was not submissive enough, nor were the girls, the eldest of whom was a pert, ugly, well-grown minx, now about eighteen years old. The second sister, who was seventeen, was supposed to be a beauty, but which of the two was the more odious in the eyes of their cousin it would be impossible to say.

Miss Dorothy Grey was Dolly only to her father. Had any one else so ventured to call her she would have started up at once, the outraged aged female of fifty. Even her aunt, who was trouble enough to her, felt that it could not be so. Her uncle tried it once, and she declined to come into his presence for a month, letting it be fully understood that she had been insulted.

And yet she was not, according to my idea, by any means an ill-favored young woman. It is true that she wore spectacles; and, as she always desired to have her eyes about with her, she never put them off when out of bed. But how many German girls do the like, and are not accounted for that reason to be plain? She was tall and well-made, we may almost say robust. She had the full use of all her limbs, and was never ashamed of using them. I think she was wrong when she would be seen to wheel the barrow about the garden, and that her hands must have suffered in her attempts to live down the conventional absurdities of the world. It is true that she did wear gloves during her gardening, but she wore them only in obedience to her father's request. She had bright eyes, somewhat far apart, and well-made, wholesome, regular features. Her nose was large, and her mouth was large, but they were singularly intelligent, and full of humor when she was pleased in conversation. As to her hair, she was too indifferent to enable one to say that it was attractive; but it was smoothed twice a day, was very copious, and always very clean. Indeed, for cleanliness from head to foot she was a model. "She is very clean, but then it's second to nothing to her," had said a sarcastic old lady, who had meant to imply that Miss Dorothy Grey was not constant at church. But the sarcastic old lady had known nothing about it. Dorothy Grey never stayed away from morning church unless her presence was desired by her father, and for once or twice that she might do so she would take her father with her three or four times,—against the grain with him, it must be acknowledged.

But the most singular attribute of the lady's appearance has still to be mentioned. She always wore a slouch hat, which from motives of propriety she called her bonnet, which gave her a singular appearance, as though it had been put on to thatch her entirely from the weather. It was made generally of black straw, and was round, equal at all points of the circle, and was fastened with broad brown ribbons. It was supposed in the neighborhood to be completely weather-tight.

The unimaginative nature of Fulham did not allow the Fulham mind to gather in the fact that, at the same time, she might possess two or three such hats. But they were undoubtedly precisely similar, and she would wear them in London with exactly the same indifference as in the comparatively rural neighborhood of her own residence. She would, in truth, go up and down in the omnibus, and would do so alone, without the slightest regard to the opinion of any of her neighbors. The Carroll girls would laugh at her behind her back, but no Carroll girl had been seen ever to smile before her face, instigated to do so by their cousin's vagaries.

But I have not yet mentioned that attribute of Miss Grey's which is, perhaps, the most essential in her character. It is necessary, at any rate, that they should know it who wish to understand her nature. When it had once been brought home to her that duty required her to do this thing or the other, or to say this word or another, the thing would be done or the word said, let the result be what it might. Even to the displeasure of her father the word was said or the thing was done. Such a one was Dolly Grey.

CHAPTER XVII. MR. GREY DINES AT HOME

Mr. Grey returned home in a cab on the day of Mr. Tyrrwhit's visit, not in the happiest humor. Though he had got the best of Mr. Tyrrwhit in the conversation, still, the meeting, which had been protracted, had annoyed him. Mr. Tyrrwhit had made accusations against himself personally which he knew to be false, but which, having been covered up, and not expressed exactly, he had been unable to refute. A man shall tell you you are a thief and a scoundrel in such a manner as to make it impossible for you to take him by the throat. "You, of course, are not a thief and a scoundrel," he shall say to you, but shall say it in such a tone of voice as to make you understand that he conceives you to be both. We all know the parliamentary mode of giving an opponent the lie so as to make it impossible that the Speaker shall interfere.

Mr. Tyrrwhit had treated Mr. Grey in the same fashion; and as Mr. Grey was irritable, thin-skinned, and irascible, and as he would brood over things of which it was quite unnecessary that a lawyer should take any cognizance, he went back home an unhappy man. Indeed, the whole Scarborough affair had been from first to last a great trouble to him. The work which he was now performing could not, he imagined, be put into his bill. To that he was supremely indifferent; but his younger partner thought it a little hard that all the other work of the firm should be thrown on his shoulders during the period which naturally would have been his holidays, and he did make his feelings intelligible to Mr. Grey. Mr. Grey, who was essentially a just man, saw that his partner was right, and made offers, but he would not accede to the only proposition which his partner made. "Let him go and look for a lawyer elsewhere," said his partner. They both of them knew that Mr. Scarborough had been thoroughly dishonest, but he had been an old client. His father before him had been a client of Mr. Grey's father. It was not in accordance with Mr. Grey's theory to treat the old man after this fashion. And he had taken intense interest in the matter. He had, first of all, been quite sure that Mountjoy Scarborough was the heir; and though Mountjoy Scarborough was not at all to his taste, he had been prepared to fight for him. He had now assured himself, after most laborious inquiry, that Augustus Scarborough was the heir; and although, in the course of the business, he had come to hate the cautious, money-loving Augustus twice worse than the gambling spendthrift Mountjoy, still, in the cause of honesty and truth and justice, he fought for Augustus against the world at large, and against the band of creditors, till the world at large and the band of creditors began to think that he was leagued with Augustus,—so as to be one of those who would make large sums of money out of the irregularity of the affair. This made him cross, and put him into a very bad humor as he went back to Fulham.

One thing must be told of Mr. Grey which was very much to his discredit, and which, if generally known, would have caused his clients to think him to be unfit to be the recipient of their family secrets;—he told all the secrets to Dolly. He was a man who could not possibly be induced to leave his business behind him at his office. It made the chief subject of conversation when he was at home. He would even call Dolly into his bedroom late at night, bringing her out of bed for the occasion, to discuss with her some point of legal strategy,—of legal but still honest strategy,—which had just occurred to him. Maybe he had not quite seen his way as to the honesty, and wanted Dolly's opinion on the subject. Dolly would come in in her dressing-gown, and, sitting on his bed, would discuss the matter with him as advocate against the devil. Sometimes she would be convinced; more frequently she would hold her own. But the points which were discussed in that way, and the strength of argumentation which was used on either side, would have surprised the clients, and the partner, and the clerks, and the eloquent barrister who was occasionally employed to support this side or the other. The eloquent barrister, or it might be the client himself, startled sometimes at the amount of enthusiasm which Mr. Grey would throw into his argument, would little dream that the very words had come from the young lady in her dressing-gown. To tell the truth, Miss Grey thoroughly liked these discussions, whether held on the lawn, or in the dining-room arm-chairs, or during the silent hours of the night. They formed, indeed, the very salt of her life. She felt herself to be the Conscience of the firm. Her father was the Reason. And the partner, in her own phraseology, was the—Devil. For it must be understood that Dolly Grey had a spice of fun about her, of which her father had the full advantage. She would not have called her father's partner the "Devil" to any other ear but her father's. And that her father knew, understanding also the spirit in which the sobriquet had been applied. He did not think that his partner was worse than another man, nor did he think that his daughter so thought. The partner, whose name was Barry, was a man of average honesty, who would occasionally be surprised at the searching justness with which Mr. Grey would look into a matter after it had been already debated for a day or two in the office. But Mr. Barry, though he had the pleasure of Miss Grey's acquaintance, had no idea of the nature of the duties which she performed in the firm.

"I'm nearly broken-hearted about this abominable business," said Mr. Grey, as he went upstairs to his dressing room. The normal hour for dinner was half-past six. He had arrived on this occasion at half-past seven, and had paid a shilling extra to the cabman to drive him quick. The man, having a lame horse, had come very slowly, fidgeting Mr. Grey into additional temporary discomfort. He had got his additional shilling, and Mr. Grey had only additional discomfort. "I declare I think he is the wickedest old man the world ever produced." This he said as Dolly followed him upstairs; but Dolly, wiser than her father, would say nothing about the wicked old man in the servants' hearing.

In five minutes Mr. Grey came down "dressed,"—by the use of which word was implied the fact that he had shaken his neckcloth, washed his hands and face, and put on his slippers. It was understood in the household that, though half-past six was the hour named for dinner, half-past seven was a much more probable time. Mr. Grey pertinaciously refused to have it changed.

"*Stare super vias antiquas*," he had stoutly said when the proposition had been made to him; by which he had intended to imply that, as during the last twenty years he had been compelled to dine at half-past six instead of six, he did not mean to be driven any farther in the same direction. Consequently his cook was compelled to prepare his dinner in such a manner that it might be eaten at one hour or the other, as chance would have it.

The dinner passed without much conversation other than incidental to Mr. Grey's wants and comforts. His daughter knew that he had been at the office for eight hours, and knew also that he was not a young man. Every kind of little cosseting was, therefore, applied to him. There was a pheasant for dinner, and it was essentially necessary, in Dolly's opinion, that he should have first the wing, quite hot, and then the leg, also hot, and that the bread-sauce should be quite hot on the two occasions. For herself, if she had had an old crow for dinner it would have been the same thing. Tea and bread-and-butter were her luxuries, and her tea and bread-and-butter had been enjoyed three hours ago. "I declare I think that, after all, the leg is the better joint of the two."

"Then why don't you have the two legs?"

"There would be a savor of greediness in that, though I know that the leg will go down,—and I shouldn't then be able to draw the comparison. I like to have them both, and I like always to be able to assert my opinion that the leg is the better joint. Now, how about the apple-pudding? You said I should have an apple-pudding." From which it appeared that Mr. Grey was not superior to having the dinner discussed in his presence at the breakfast-table. The apple-pudding came, and was apparently enjoyed. A large portion of it was put between two plates. "That's for Mrs. Grimes," suggested Mr. Grey. "I am not quite sure that Mrs. Grimes is worthy of it." "If you knew what it was to be left without a shilling of your husband's wages you'd think yourself worthy." When the conversation about the pudding was over Mr. Grey ate his cheese, and then sat quite still in his arm-chair over the fire while the things were being taken away. "I declare I think he is the wickedest man the world has ever produced," said Mr. Grey as soon as the door was shut, thus showing by the repetition of the words he had before used that his mind had been intent on Mr. Scarborough rather than on the pheasant.

"Why don't you have done with them?"

"That's all very well; but you wouldn't have done with them if you had known them all your life."

"I wouldn't spend my time and energies in white-washing any rascal," said Dolly, with vigor.

"You don't know what you'd do. And a man isn't to be left in the lurch altogether because he's a rascal. Would you have a murderer hanged without some one to stand up for him?"

"Yes, I would," said Dolly, thoughtlessly.

"And he mightn't have been a murderer after all; or not legally so, which as far as the law goes is the same thing."

But this special question had been often discussed between them, and Mr. Grey and Dolly did not intend to be carried away by it on the present occasion. "I know all about that," she said; "but this isn't a case of life and death. The old man is only anxious to save his property, and throws upon you all the burden of doing it. He never agrees with you as to anything you say."

"As to legal points he does."

"But he keeps you always in hot water, and puts forward so much villany that I would have nothing farther to do with him. He has been so crafty that you hardly know now which is, in truth, the heir."

"Oh yes, I do," said the lawyer. "I know very well, and am very sorry that it should be so. And I cannot but feel for the rascal because the dishonest effort was made on behalf of his own son."

"Why was it necessary?" said Dolly, with sparks flying from her eye. "Throughout from the beginning he has been bad. Why was the woman not his wife?"

"Ah! why, indeed. But had his sin consisted only in that, I should not have dreamed of refusing my assistance as a family lawyer. All that would have gone for nothing then."

"When evil creeps in," said Dolly, sententiously, "you cannot put it right afterward."

"Never mind about that. We shall never get to the end if you go back to Adam and Eve."

"People don't go back often enough."

"Bother!" said Mr. Grey, finishing his second and last glass of port-wine. "Do keep yourself in some degree to the question in dispute. In advising an attorney of to-day as to how he is to treat a client you can't do any good by going back to Adam and Eve. Augustus is the heir, and I am bound to protect the property for him from these money-lending harpies. The moment the breath is out of the old man's body they will settle down upon it if we leave them an inch of ground on which to stand. Every detail of his marriage must be made as clear as daylight; and that must be done in the teeth of former false statements."

"As far as I can see, the money-lending harpies are the honestest lot of people concerned."

"The law is not on their side. They have got no right. The estate, as a fact, will belong to Augustus the moment his father dies. Mr. Scarborough endeavored to do what he could for him whom he regarded as his eldest son. It was very wicked. He was adding a second and a worse crime to the first. He was flying in the face of the laws of his country. But he was successful; and he threw dust into my eyes, because he wanted to save the property for the boy. And he endeavored to make it up to his second son by saving for him a second property. He was not selfish; and I cannot but feel for him."

"But you say he is the wickedest man the world ever produced."

"Because he boasts of it all, and cannot be got in any way to repent. He gives me my instructions as though from first to last he had been a highly honorable man, and only laughs at me when I object. And yet he must know that he may die any day. He only wishes to have this matter set straight so that he may die. I could forgive him altogether if he would but once say that he was sorry for what he'd done. But he has completely the air of the fine old head of a family who thinks he is to be put into marble the moment the breath is out of his body, and that he richly deserves the marble he is to be put into."

"That is a question between him and his God," said Dolly.

"He hasn't got a God. He believes only in his own reason,—and is content to do so, lying there on the very brink of eternity. He is quite content with himself, because he thinks that he has not been selfish. He cares nothing that he has robbed every one all round. He has no reverence for property and the laws which govern it. He was born only with the life-interest, and he has determined to treat it as though the fee-simple had belonged to him. It is his utter disregard for law, for what the law has decided, which makes me declare him to have been the wickedest man the world ever produced."

"It is his disregard for truth which makes you think so."

"He cares nothing for truth. He scorns it and laughs at it. And yet about the little things of the world he expects his word to be taken as certainly as that of any other gentleman."

"I would not take it."

"Yes, you would, and would be right too. If he would say he'd pay me a hundred pounds to-morrow, or a thousand, I would have his word as soon as any other man's bound. And yet he has utterly got the better of me, and made me believe that a marriage took place, when there was no marriage. I think I'll have a cup of tea."

"You won't go to sleep, papa?"

"Oh yes, I shall. When I've been so troubled as that I must have a cup of tea." Mr. Grey was often troubled, and as a consequence Dolly was called up for consultations in the middle of the night.

At about one o'clock there came the well-known knock at Dolly's door and the usual invitation. Would she come into her father's room for a few minutes? Then her father trotted back to his bed, and Dolly, of course, followed him as soon as she had clothed herself decently.

"Why didn't you tell me?"

"I thought I had made up my mind not to go; or I thought rather that I should be able to make up my mind not to go. But it is possible that down there I may have some effect for good."

"What does he want of you?"

"There is a long question about raising money with which Augustus desires to buy the silence of the creditors."

"Could he get the money?" asked Dolly.

"Yes, I think he could. The property at present is altogether unembarrassed. To give Mr. Scarborough his due, he has never put his name to a scrap of paper; nor has he had occasion to do so. The Tretton pottery people want more land, or rather more water, and a large sum of money will be forthcoming. But he doesn't see the necessity of giving Mr. Tyrrwhit a penny-piece, or certainly Mr. Hart. He would send them away howling without a scruple. Now, Augustus is anxious to settle with them, for some reason which I do not clearly understand. But he wishes to do so without any interference on his father's part. In fact, he and his father have very different ideas as to the property. The squire regards it as his, but Augustus thinks that any day may make it his own. In fact, they are on the very verge of quarrelling." Then, after a long debate, Dolly consented that her father should go down to Tretton, and act, if possible, the part of peace-maker.

CHAPTER XVIII. THE CARROLL FAMILY

"Aunt Carroll is coming to dinner to-day," said Dolly the next day, with a serious face.

"I know she is. Have a nice dinner for her. I don't think she ever has a nice dinner at home."

"And the three eldest girls are coming."

"Three!"

"You asked them yourself on Sunday."

"Very well. They said their papa would be away on business." It was understood that Mr. Carroll was never asked to the Manor-house.

"Business! There is a club he belongs to where he dines and gets drunk once a month. It's the only thing he does regularly."

"They must have their dinner, at any rate," said Mr. Grey. "I don't think they should suffer because he drinks." This had been a subject much discussed between them, but on the present occasion Miss Grey would not renew it. She despatched her father in a cab, the cab having been procured because he was supposed to be a quarter of an hour late, and then went to work to order her dinner.

It has been said that Miss Grey hated the Carrolls; but she hated the daughters worse than the mother, and of all the people she hated in the world she hated Amelia Carroll the worst. Amelia, the eldest, entertained an idea that she was more of a personage in the world's eyes than her cousin,—that she went to more parties, which certainly was true if she went to any,—that she wore finer clothes, which was also true, and that she had a lover, whereas Dolly Grey,—as she called her cousin behind her back,—had none. This lover had something to do with horses, and had only been heard of, had never been seen, at the Manor-house. Sophy was a good deal hated also, being a forward, flirting, tricky girl of seventeen, who had just left the school at which Uncle John had paid for her education. Georgina, the third, was still at school under similar circumstances, and was pardoned her egregious noisiness and romping propensities under the score of youth. She was sixteen, and was possessed of terrible vitality. "I am sure they take after their father altogether," Mr. Grey had once said when the three left the Manor-house together.

At half-past six punctually they came. Dolly heard a great clatter of four people leaving their clogs and cloaks in the hall, and would not move out of the unused drawing-room, in which for the moment she was seated. Betsey had to prepare the dinner-table down-stairs, and would have been sadly discomfited had she been driven to do it in the presence of three Carroll girls. For it must be understood that Betsey had no greater respect for the Carroll girls than her mistress. "Well, Aunt Carroll, how does the world use you?"

"Very badly. You haven't been up to see me for ten days."

"I haven't counted; but when I do come I don't often do any good. How are Minna, and Brenda, and Potsey?"

"Poor Potsey has got a nasty boil under her arm."

"It comes from eating too much toffy," said Georgina. "I told her it would."

"How very nasty you are!" said Miss Carroll. "Do leave the child and her ailments alone!"

"Poor papa isn't very well, either," said Sophy, who was supposed to be her father's pet.

"I hope his state of health will not debar him from dining with his friends to-night," said Miss Grey.

"You have always something ill-natured to say about papa," said Sophy.

"Nothing will ever keep him back when conviviality demands his presence." This came from his afflicted wife, who, in spite of all his misfortunes, would ever speak with some respect of her husband's employments. "He wasn't at all in a fit state to go to-night, but he had promised, and that was enough."

When they had waited three-quarters of an hour Amelia began to complain,—certainly not without reason. "I wonder why Uncle John always keeps us waiting in this way?"

"Papa has, unfortunately, something to do with his time, which is not altogether his own." There was not much in these words, but the tone in which they were uttered would have crushed any one more susceptible than Amelia Carroll. But at that moment the cab arrived, and Dolly went down to meet her father.

"Have they come?" he asked.

"Come," she answered, taking his gloves and comforter from him, and giving him a kiss as she did so. "That girl up-stairs is nearly famished."

"I won't be half a moment," said the repentant father, hastening up-stairs to go through his ordinary dressing arrangement.

"I wouldn't hurry for her," said Dolly; "but of course you'll hurry. You always do, don't you, papa?" Then they sat down to dinner.

"Well, girls, what is your news?"

"We were out to-day on the Brompton Road," said the eldest, "and there came up Prince Chitakov's drag with four roans."

"Prince Chitakov! I didn't know there was such a prince."

"Oh, dear, yes; with very stiff mustaches, turned up high at the corners, and pink cheeks, and a very sharp, nobby-looking hat, with a light-colored grey coat, and light gloves. You must know the prince."

"Upon my word, I never heard of him, my dear. What did the prince do?"

"He was tooling his own drag, and he had a lady with him on the box. I never saw anything more tasty than her dress,—dark red silk, with little fluffy fur ornaments all over it. I wonder who she was?"

"Mrs. Chitakov, probably," said the attorney.

"I don't think the prince is a married man," said Sophy.

"They never are, for the most part," said Amelia; "and she wouldn't be Mrs. Chitakov, Uncle John."

"Wouldn't she, now? What would she be? Can either of you tell me what the wife of a Prince of Chitakov would call herself?"

"Princess of Chitakov, of course," said Sophy. "It's the Princess of Wales."

"But it isn't the Princess of Christian, nor yet the Princess of Teck, nor the Princess of England. I don't see why the lady shouldn't be Mrs. Chitakov, if there is such a lady."

"Papa, don't bamboozle her," said his daughter.

"But," continued the attorney, "why shouldn't the lady have been his wife? Don't married ladies wear little fluffy fur ornaments?"

"I wish, John, you wouldn't talk to the girls in that strain," said their mother. "It really isn't becoming."

"To suggest that the lady was the gentleman's wife?"

"But I was going to say," continued Amelia, "that as the prince drove by he kissed his hand—he did, indeed. And Sophy and I were walking along as demurely as possible. I never was so knocked of a heap in all my life."

"He did," said Sophy. "It's the most impertinent thing I ever heard. If my father had seen it he'd have had the prince off the box of the coach in no time."

"Then, my dear," said the attorney, "I am very glad that your father did not see it." Poor Dolly, during this conversation about the prince, sat angry and silent, thinking to herself in despair of what extremes of vulgarity even a first cousin of her own could be guilty. That she should be sitting at table with a girl who could boast that a reprobate foreigner had kissed his hand to her from the box of a fashionable four-horsed coach! For it was in that light that Miss Grey regarded it. "And did you have any farther adventures besides this memorable encounter with the prince?"

"Nothing nearly so interesting," said Sophy.

"That was hardly to be expected," said the attorney. "Jane, you will have a glass of port-wine? Girls, you must have a glass of port-wine to support you after your disappointment with the prince."

"We were not disappointed in the least," said Amelia.

"Pray, pray, let the subject drop," said Dolly.

"That is because the prince did not kiss his hand to you," said Sophy. Then Miss Grey sunk again into silence, crushed beneath this last blow.

In the evening, when the dinner-things had been taken away, a matter of business came up, and took the place of the prince and his mustaches. Mrs. Carroll was most anxious to know whether her brother could "lend" her a small sum of twenty pounds. It came out in conversation that the small sum was needed to satisfy some imperious demand made upon Mr. Carroll by a tailor. "He must have clothes, you know," said the poor woman, wailing. "He doesn't have many, but he must have some." There had been other appeals on the same subject made not very long since, and, to tell the truth, Mr. Grey did require to have the subject argued, in fear of the subsequent remarks which would be made to him afterward by his daughter if he gave the money too easily. The loan had to be arranged in full conclave, as otherwise Mrs. Carroll would have found it difficult to obtain access to her brother's ear. But the one auditor whom she feared was her niece. On the present occasion Miss Grey simply took up her book to show that the subject was one which had no interest for her; but she did undoubtedly listen to all that was said on the subject. "There was never anything settled about poor Patrick's clothes," said Mrs. Carroll, in a half-whisper. She did not care how much her own children heard, and she knew how vain it was to attempt so to speak that Dolly should not hear.

"I dare say something ought to be done at some time," said Mr. Grey, who knew that he would be told, when the evening was over, that he would give away all his substance to that man if he were asked.

"Papa has not had a new pair of trousers this year," said Sophy.

"Except those green ones he wore at the races," said Georgina.

"Hold your tongue, miss!" said her mother. "That was a pair I made up for him and sent them to the man to get pressed."

"When the hundred a year was arranged for all our dresses," said Amelia, "not a word was said about papa. Of course, papa is a trouble."

"I don't see that he is more of a trouble than any one else," said Sophy. "Uncle John would not like not to have any clothes."

"No, I should not, my dear."

"And his own income is all given up to the house uses." Here Sophy touched imprudently on a sore subject. His "own" income consisted of what had been saved out of his wife's fortune, and was thus named as in opposition to the larger sum paid to Mrs. Carroll by Mr. Grey. There was one hundred and fifty pounds a year coming from settled property, which had been preserved by the lawyer's care, and which was regarded in the family as "papa's own."

It certainly is essential for respectability that something should be set apart from a man's income for his wearing apparel; and though the money was, perhaps, improperly so designated, Dolly would not have objected had she not thought that it had already gone to the race-course,—in company with the green trousers. She had her own means of obtaining information as to the Carroll family. It was very necessary that she should do so, if the family was to be kept on its legs at all. "I don't think any good can come from discussing what my uncle does with the money." This was Dolly's first speech. "If he is to have it, let him have it, but let him have as little as possible."

"I never heard anybody so cross as you always are to papa," said Sophy.

"Your cousin Dorothy is very fortunate," said Mrs. Carroll. "She does not know what it is to want for anything."

"She never spends anything—on herself," said her father. "It is Dolly's only fault that she won't."

"Because she has it all done for her," said Amelia.

Dolly had gone back to her book, and disdained to make any farther reply. Her father felt that quite enough had been said about it, and was prepared to give the twenty pounds, under the idea that he might be thought to have made a stout fight upon the subject. "He does want them very badly—for decency's sake," said the poor wife, thus winding up her plea. Then Mr. Grey got out his check-book and wrote the check for twenty pounds. But he made it payable, not to Mr. but to Mrs. Carroll.

"I suppose, papa, nothing can be done about Mr. Carroll." This was said by Dolly as soon as the family had withdrawn.

"In what way 'done,' my dear?"

"As to settling some farther sum for himself."

"He'd only spend it, my dear."

"That would be intended," said Dolly.

"And then he would come back just the same."

"But in that case he should have nothing more. Though they were to declare that he hadn't a pair of trousers in which to appear at a race-course, he shouldn't have it."

"My dear," said Mr. Grey, "you cannot get rid of the gnats of the world. They will buzz and sting and be a nuisance. Poor Jane suffers worse from this gnat than you or I. Put up with it; and understand in your own mind that when he comes for another twenty pounds he must have it. You needn't tell him, but so it must be."

"If I had my way," said Dolly, after ten minutes' silence, "I would punish him. He is an evil thing, and should be made to reap the proper reward. It is not that I wish to avoid my share of the world's burdens, but that justice should be done. I don't know which I hate the worst,—Uncle Carroll or Mr. Scarborough."

The next day was Sunday, and Dolly was very anxious before breakfast to induce her father to say that he would go to church with her; but he was inclined to be obstinate, and fell back upon his usual excuse, saying that there were Scarborough papers which it would be necessary that he should read before he started for Tretton on the following day.

"Papa, I think it would do you good if you came."

"Well, yes; I suppose it would. That is the intention; but somehow it fails with me sometimes."

"Do you think that you hate people when you go to church as much as when you don't?"

"I am not sure that I hate anybody very much."

"I do."

"That seems an argument for your going."

"But if you don't hate them it is because you won't take the trouble, and that again is not right. If you would come to church you would be better for it all round. You'd hate Uncle Carroll's idleness and abominable self-indulgence worse than you do."

"I don't love him, as it is, my dear."

"And I should hate him less. I felt last night as though I could rise from my bed and go and murder him."

"Then you certainly ought to go to church."

"And you had passed him off just as though he were a gnat from which you were to receive as little annoyance as possible, forgetting the influence he must have on those six unfortunate children. Don't you know that you gave her that twenty pounds simply to be rid of a disagreeable subject?"

"I should have given it ever so much sooner, only that you were looking at me."

"I know you would, you dear, sweet, kind-hearted, but most un-Christian, father. You must come to church, in order that some idea of what Christianity demands of you may make its way into your heart. It is not what the clergyman may say of you, but that your mind will get away for two hours from that other reptile and his concerns." Then Mr. Grey, with a loud, long sigh, allowed his boots, and his gloves, and his church-going hat, and his church-going umbrella to be brought to him. It was, in fact, his aversion to these articles that Dolly had to encounter.

It may be doubted whether the church services of that day did Mr. Grey much good; but they seemed to have had some effect upon his daughter, from the fact that in the afternoon she wrote a letter in kindly words to her aunt: "Papa is going to Tretton, and I will come up to you on Tuesday. I have got a frock which I will bring with me as a present for Potsey; and I will make her sew on the buttons for herself. Tell Minna I will lend her that book I spoke of. About those boots—I will go with Georgina to the boot-maker." But as to Amelia and Sophy she could not bring herself to say a good-natured word, so deep in her heart had sunk that sin of which they had been guilty with reference to Prince Chitakov.

On that night she had a long discussion with her father respecting the affairs of the Scarborough family. The discussion was held in the dining-room, and may, therefore, be supposed to have been premeditated. Those at night in Mr. Grey's own bedroom were generally the result of sudden thought. "I should lay down the law to him—" began Dolly.

"The law is the law," said her father.

"I don't mean the law in that sense. I should tell him firmly what I advised, and should then make him understand that if he did not follow my advice I must withdraw. If his son is willing to pay these money-lenders what sums they have actually advanced, and if by any effort on his part the money can be raised, let it be done. There seems to be some justice in repaying out of the property that which was lent to the property when by Mr. Scarborough's own doing the property was supposed to go into the eldest son's hands. Though the eldest son and the money-lenders be spendthrifts and profligates alike, there will in that be something of fairness. Go there prepared with your opinion. But if either father or son will not accept it, then depart, and shake the dust from your feet."

"You propose it all as though it were the easiest thing in the world."

"Easy or difficult. I would not discuss anything of which the justice may hereafter be disputed."

What was the result of the consultation on Mr. Grey's mind he did not declare, but he resolved to take his daughter's advice in all that she said to him.

CHAPTER XIX. MR. GREY GOES TO TRETTON

Mr. Grey went down to Tretton with a great bag of papers. In fact, though he told his daughter that he had to examine them all before he started, and had taken them to Fulham for that purpose, he had not looked at them. And, as another fact, the bag was not opened till he got home again. They had been read;—at any rate, what was necessary. He knew his subject. The old squire knew it well.

Mr. Grey was going down to Tretton, not to convey facts or to explain the law, but in order that he might take the side either of the father or of the son. Mr. Scarborough had sent for the lawyer to support his view of the case; and the son had consented to meet him in order that he might the more easily get the better of his father.

Mr. Grey had of late learned one thing which had before been dark to him,—had seen one phase of this complicated farrago of dishonesty which had not before been visible to him. Augustus suspected his father of some farther treachery. That he should be angry at having been debarred from his birthright so long,—debarred from the knowledge of his birthright,—was, Mr. Grey thought, natural. A great wrong had been, at least, intended; and that such a man should resent it was to have been expected. But of late Mr. Grey had discovered that it was not in that way that the son's mind worked. It was not anger but suspicion that he showed; and he used his father's former treatment of him as a justification for the condemnation implied in his thoughts. There is no knowing what an old man may do who has already acted as he had done. It was thus that he expressed himself both by his words and deeds, and did so openly in his father's presence, Mr. Grey had not seen them together, but knew from the letters of both of them that such was the case. Old Mr. Scarborough scorned his son's suspicions, and disregarded altogether any words that might be said as to his own past conduct. He was willing, or half willing, that Mountjoy's debts should be, not paid, but settled. But he was willing to do nothing toward such a step except in his own way. While the breath was in his body the property was his, and he chose to be treated as its only master. If Augustus desired to do anything by "post-obits," let him ruin himself after his own fashion. "It is not very likely that Augustus can raise money by post obits, circumstanced as the property is," he had written to Mr. Grey, with a conveyed sneer and chuckle as to the success of his own villany. It was as though he had declared that the money-lenders had been too well instructed as to what tricks Mr. Scarborough could play with his property to risk a second venture.

Augustus had, in truth, been awaiting his father's death with great impatience. It was unreasonable that a man should live who had acted in such a way and who had been so cut about by the doctors. His father's demise had, in truth, been promised to him, and to all the world. It was an understood thing, in all circles which knew anything, that old Mr. Scarborough could not live another month. It had been understood some time, and was understood at the present moment; and yet Mr. Scarborough went on living,—no doubt, as an invalid in the last stage of probable dissolution, but still with the full command of his intellect and mental powers for mischief. Augustus, suspecting him as he did, had begun to fear that he might live too long. His brother had disappeared, and he was the heir. If his father would die,—such had been his first thought,—he could settle with the creditors immediately, before any tidings should be heard of his brother. But tidings had come. His brother had been seen by Mr. Hart at Monte Carlo; and though Mr. Hart had not yet sent home the news to the other creditors, the news had been sent at once to Augustus Scarborough by his own paid attendant upon his brother. Of Mr. Hart's "little game" he did not yet know the particulars; but he was confident that there was some game.

Augustus by no means gave his mother credit for the disgraceful conduct imputed to her in the story as now told by her surviving husband. It was not that he believed in the honesty of his mother, whom he had never known, and for whose memory he cared little, but that he believed so fully in the dishonesty of his father. His father, when he had thoroughly understood that Mountjoy had enveloped the property in debt, so that nothing but a skeleton would remain when the bonds were paid, had set to work, and by the ingenuity of his brain had resolved to redeem, as far as the Scarboroughs were concerned, their estate from its unfortunate position.

It was so that Augustus believed; this was the theory existing in his mind. That his father should have been so clever, and Mr. Grey so blind, and even Mr. Hart and Mr. Tyrrwhit so easily hoodwinked, was remarkable. But so it was,—or might probably be so. He felt no assurance, but there was ever present to him the feeling of great danger. But the state of things as arranged by his father might be established by himself. If he could get these creditors to give up their bonds while his father's falsehood was still believed, it would be a great thing. He had learned by degrees how small a proportion of the money claimed had, in fact, been advanced to Mountjoy, and had resolved to confine himself to paying that. That might now probably be accepted with gratitude. The increasing value of the estate might bear that without being crushed. But it should be done at once, while Mountjoy was still absent and before Mr. Tyrrwhit at any rate knew that Mountjoy had not been killed. Then had happened that accidental meeting with Mr. Hart at

Monte Carlo. That idiot of a keeper of his had been unable to keep Mountjoy from the gambling-house. But Mr. Hart had as yet told nothing. Mr. Hart was playing some game of his own, in which he would assuredly be foiled. The strong hold which Augustus had was in the great infirmity of his father and in the blindness of Mr. Grey, but it would be settled. It ought to have been well that the thing should be settled already by his father's death. Augustus did feel strongly that the squire ought to complete his work by dying. Were the story, as now told by him, true, he ought certainly to die, so as to make speedy atonement for his wickedness. Were it false, then he ought to go quickly, so that the lie might be effectual. Every day that he continued to live would go far to endanger the discovery. Augustus felt that he must at once have the property in his own hands, so as to buy the creditors and obtain security.

Mr. Grey, who was not so blind as Augustus thought him, saw a great deal of this. Augustus suspected him as well as the squire. His mind went backward and forward on these suspicions. It was more probable that the squire should have contrived all this with the attorney's assistance than without it. The two, willing it together, might be very powerful. But then Mr. Grey would hardly dare to do it. His father knew that he was dying; but Mr. Grey had no such easy mode of immediate escape if detected. And his father was endowed with a courage as peculiar as it was great. He did not think that Mr. Grey was so brave a man as his father. And then he could trace the payment of no large sum to Mr. Grey,—such as would have been necessary as a bribe in such a case. Augustus suspected Mr. Grey, on and off. But Mr. Grey was sure that Augustus suspected his own father. Now, of one thing Mr. Grey was certain:—Augustus was, in truth, the rightful heir. The squire had at first contrived to blind him,—him, Mr. Grey,—partly by his own acuteness, partly through the carelessness of himself and those in his office, partly by the subornation of witnesses who seemed to have been actually prepared for such an event. But there could be no subsequent blinding. Mr. Grey had a well-earned reputation for professional acuteness and honesty. He knew there was no need for such suspicions as those now entertained by the young man; but he knew also that they existed, and he hated the young man for entertaining them.

When he arrived at Tretton Park he first of all saw Mr. Septimus Jones, with whom he was not acquainted. "Mr. Scarborough will be here directly. He is out somewhere about the stables," said Mr. Jones, in that tone of voice with which a guest at the house,—a guest for pleasure,—may address sometimes a guest who is a guest on business. In such a case the guest on pleasure cannot be a gentleman, and must suppose that the guest on business is not one either.

Mr. Grey, thinking that the Mr. Scarborough spoken of could not be the squire, put Mr. Jones right. "It is the elder Mr. Scarborough whom I wish to see. There is quite time enough. No doubt Miss Scarborough will be down presently."

"You are Mr. Grey, I believe?"

"That is my name."

"My friend, Augustus Scarborough, is particularly anxious to see you before you go to his father. The old man is in very failing health, you know."

"I am well acquainted with the state of Mr. Scarborough's health," said Mr. Grey, "and will leave it to himself to say when I shall see him. Perhaps to-morrow will be best." Then he rung the bell; but the servant entered the room at the same moment and summoned him up to the squire's chamber. Mr. Scarborough also wished to see Mr. Grey before his son, and had been on the alert to watch for his coming.

On the landing he met Miss Scarborough. "He does seem to keep up his strength," said the lady. "Mr. Merton is living in the house now, and watches him very closely." Mr. Merton was a resident young doctor, whom Sir William Brodrick had sent down to see that all medical appliances were at hand as the sick man might require them. Then Mr. Grey was shown in, and found the squire recumbent on a sofa, with a store of books within his reach, and reading apparatuses of all descriptions, and every appliance which the ingenuity of the skilful can prepare for the relief of the sick and wealthy.

"This is very kind of you, Mr. Grey," said the squire, speaking in a cheery voice. "I wanted you to come very much, but I hardly thought that you would take the trouble. Augustus is here, you know."

"So I have heard from that gentleman down-stairs."

"Mr. Jones? I have never had the pleasure of seeing Mr. Jones. What sort of a gentleman is Mr. Jones to look at?"

"Very much like other gentlemen."

"I dare say. He has done me the honor to stay a good deal at my house lately. Augustus never comes without him. He is *fidus Achates*, I take it, to Augustus. Augustus has never asked whether he can be received. Of course it does not matter. When a man is the eldest son, and, so to say, the only one, he is apt to take liberties with his father's house. I am so sorry that in my position I cannot do the honors and receive him properly. He is a very estimable and modest young man, I believe?" As Mr. Grey had not come down to Tretton either to be a spy on Mr. Jones or to answer questions concerning him, he held his tongue. "Well, Mr. Grey, what do you think about it;—eh?" This was a comprehensive question, but Mr. Grey well understood its purport. What did he, Mr. Grey, think of the condition to which the affairs of Tretton had been brought, and those of Mr. Scarborough himself and of his two sons? What did he think of Mountjoy, who had disappeared and was still absent? What did he think of Augustus, who was not showing his gratitude in the best way for all that had been done for him? And what did he think of the squire himself, who from his death-bed had so well contrived to have his own way in everything,—to do all manner of illegal things without paying any of the penalties to which illegality is generally subject? And having asked the question he paused for an answer.

Mr. Grey had had no personal interview with the squire since the time at which it had been declared that Mountjoy was not the heir. Then some very severe words had been spoken. Mr. Grey had first sworn that he did not believe a word of what was said to him, and had refused to deal with the matter at all. If carried out Mr. Scarborough must take it to some other lawyer's office. There had, since that, been a correspondence as to much of which Mr. Scarborough had been forced to employ an amanuensis. Gradually Mr. Grey had assented, in the first instance on behalf of Mountjoy, and then on behalf of Augustus. But he had done so in the expectation that he should never again see the squire in this world. He, too, had been assured that the man would die, and had felt that it would be better that the management of things should then be in honest hands, such as his own, and in the hands of those who understood them, than be confided to those who did not not understand them, and who might probably not be honest.

But the squire had not died, and here he was again at Tretton as the squire's guest. "I think," said Mr. Grey. "that the less said about a good deal of it the better."

"That, of course, is sweeping condemnation, which, however, I expect. Let that be all as though it had been expressed. You don't understand the inner man which rules me,—how it has struggled to free itself from conventionalities. Nor do I quite understand how your inner man has succumbed to them and encouraged them."

"I have encouraged an obedience to the laws of my country. Men generally find it safer to do so."

"Exactly, and men like to be safe. Perhaps a condition of danger has had its attractions for me. It is very stupid, but perhaps it is so. But let that go. The rope has been round my own neck and not round that of others. Perhaps I have thought of late that if danger should come I could run away from it all, by the help of the surgeon. They have become so skilful now that a man has no chance in that way. But what do you think of Mountjoy and Augustus?"

"I think that Mountjoy has been very ill-used."

"But I endeavored to do the best I could for him."

"And that Augustus has been worse used."

"But he, at any rate, has been put right quite in time. Had he been brought up as the eldest son he might have done as Mountjoy did." Then there came a little gleam of satisfaction across the squire's face as he felt the sufficiency of his answer. "But they are neither of them pleased."

"You cannot please men by going wrong, even in their own behalf."

"I'm not so sure of that. Were you to say that we cannot please men ever by doing right on their behalf you would perhaps be nearer the mark. Where do you think that Mountjoy is?" A rumor, had reached Mr. Grey that Mountjoy had been seen at Monte Carlo, but it had been only a rumor. The same had, in truth, reached Mr. Scarborough, but he chose to keep his rumor to himself. Indeed, more than a rumor had reached him.

"I think that he will turn up safely," said the lawyer. "I think that if it were made worth his while he would turn up at once."

"Is it not better that he should be away?" Mr. Grey shrugged his shoulders. "What's the good of his coming back into a nest of hornets? I have always thought that he did very well to disappear. Where is he to live if he came back? Should he come here?"

"Not with his gambling debts unpaid at the club."

"That might have been settled. Though, indeed, his gambling was as a tub that has no bottom to it. There has been nothing for it but to throw him over altogether. And yet how very much the better he has been of the two! Poor Mountjoy!"

"Poor Mountjoy!"

"You see, if I hadn't disinherited him I should have had to go on paying for him till the whole estate would have been squandered even during my lifetime."

"You speak as though the law had given you the power of disinheriting him."

"So it did."

"But not the power of giving him the inheritance."

"I took that upon myself. There I was stronger than the law. Now I simply and humbly ask the law to come and help me. And the upshot is that Augustus takes upon himself to lecture me and to feel aggrieved. He is not angry with me for what I did about Mountjoy, but is quarrelling with me because I do not die. I have no idea of dying just to please him. I think it important that I should live just at present."

"But will you let him have the money to pay these creditors?"

"That is what I want to speak about. If I can see the list of the sums to be paid, and if you can assure yourself that by paying them I shall get back all the post-obit bonds which Mountjoy has given, and that the money can be at once raised upon a joint mortgage, to be executed by me and Augustus, I will do it. But the first thing must be to know the amount. I will join Augustus in nothing without your consent. He wants to assume the power himself. In fact, the one thing he desires is that I shall go. As long as I remain he shall do nothing except by my co-operation. I will see you and him to-morrow, and now you may go and eat your dinner. I cannot tell you how much obliged I am to you for coming." And then Mr. Grey left the room, went to his chamber, and in process of time made his way into the drawing-room.

CHAPTER XX. MR. GREY'S OPINION OF THE SCARBOROUGH FAMILY

Had Augustus been really anxious to see Mr. Grey before Mr. Grey went to his father, he would probably have managed to do so. He did not always tell Mr. Jones everything. "So the fellow has hurried up to the governor the moment he came into the house," he said.

"He's with him now."

"Of course he is. Never mind. I'll be even with him in the long-run." Then he greeted the lawyer with a mock courtesy as soon as he saw him. "I hope your journey has done you no harm, Mr. Grey."

"Not in the least."

"It's very kind of you, I am sure, to look after our poor concerns with so much interest. Jones, don't you think it is time they gave us some dinner? Mr. Grey, I'm sure, must want his dinner."

"All in good time," said the lawyer.

"You shall have your dinner, Mr. Grey. It is the least we can do for you." Mr. Grey felt that in every sound of his voice there was an insult, and took special notice of every tone, and booked them all down in his memory. After dinner he asked some unimportant question with reference to the meeting that was to take place in the morning, and was at once rebuked. "I do not know that we need trouble our friend here with our private concerns," he said.

"Not in the least," said Mr. Grey. "You have already been talking about them in my presence and in his. It is necessary that I should have a list of the creditors before I can advise your father."

"I don't see it; but, however, that is for you to judge. Indeed, I do not know on what points my father wants your advice. A lawyer generally furnishes such a list." Then Mr. Grey took up a book, and was soon left alone by the younger men.

In the morning he walked out in the park, so as to have free time for thought. Not a word farther had been said between him and Augustus touching their affairs. At breakfast Augustus discussed with his friend the state of the odds respecting some race and then the characters of certain ladies. No subjects could have been less interesting to Mr. Grey, as Augustus was aware. They breakfasted at ten, and twelve had been named for the meeting. Mr. Grey had an hour or an hour and a half for his walk, in which he could again turn over in his mind all these matters of which his thoughts had been full for now many a day.

Of two or three facts he was certain. Augustus was the legitimate heir of his father. Of that he had seen ample documentary evidence. The word of no Scarborough should go for anything with him;—but of that fact he was assured. Whether the squire knew aught of Mountjoy he did not feel sure, but that Augustus did he was quite certain. Who was paying the bills for the scapegrace during his travels he could not say, but he thought it probable that Augustus was finding the money. He, Mountjoy, was kept away, so as to be out of the creditors' way.

He thought, therefore, that Augustus was doing this, so that he might the more easily buy up the debts. But why should Augustus go to the expense of buying up the debts, seeing that the money must ultimately come out of his own pocket? Because,—so Mr. Grey thought,—Augustus would not trust his own father. The creditors, if they could get hold of Mountjoy when his father was dead, and when the bonds would all become payable, might possibly so unravel the facts as to make it apparent that, after all, the property was Mountjoy's. This was not Mr. Grey's idea, but was Mr. Grey's idea of the calculation which Augustus was making for his own government. According to Mr. Grey's reading of all the facts of the case, such were the suspicions which Augustus entertained in the matter. Otherwise, why should he be anxious to take a step which would redound only to the advantage of the creditors? He was quite certain that no money would be paid, at any rate, by Augustus, solely with the view of honestly settling their claims.

But there was another subject which troubled his mind excessively as he walked across the park. Why should he soil his hands, or, at any rate, trouble his conscience, with an affair so unclean, so perplexed, and so troublesome? Why was he there at Tretton at all, to be insulted by a young blackguard such as he believed Augustus Scarborough to be? Augustus Scarborough, he knew, suspected him. But he, in return, suspected Augustus Scarborough. The creditors suspected him. Mountjoy suspected him. The squire did not suspect him, but he suspected the squire. He never could again feel himself to be on comfortable terms of trusting legal friendship with a man who had played such a prank in reference to his marriage as this man had performed. Why, then, should he still be concerned in a matter so distasteful to him? Why should he not wipe his hands of it all and retreat? There was no act of parliament compelling him to meddle with the dirt.

Such were his thoughts. But yet he knew that he was compelled. He did feel himself bound to look after interests which he had taken in hand now for many years. It had been his duty,—or the duty of some one belonging to him,—to see into the deceit by which an attempt had been made to rob Augustus Scarborough of his patrimony. It had been his duty, for a while, to protect Mountjoy, and the creditors who had lent their money to Mountjoy, from what he had believed to be a flagitious attempt. Then, as soon as he felt that the flagitious attempt had been made previously, in Mountjoy's favor, it became his duty to protect Augustus, in spite of the strong personal dislike which from the first he had conceived for that young man.

And then he doubtless had been attracted by the singularity of all that had been done in the affair, and of all that was likely to be done. He had said to himself that the matter should be made straight, and that he would make it straight. Therefore, during his walk in the park, he resolved that he must persevere.

At twelve o'clock he was ready to be taken up to the sick man's room. When he entered it, under the custody of Miss Scarborough, he found that Augustus was there. The squire was sitting up, with his feet supported, and was apparently in a good humor. "Well, Mr. Grey," he said, "have you settled this matter with Augustus?"

"I have settled nothing."

"He has not spoken to me about it at all," said Augustus.

"I told him I wanted a list of the creditors. He said that it was my duty to supply it. That was the extent of our conversation."

"Which he thought it expedient to have in the presence of my friend, Mr. Jones. Mr. Jones is very well in his way, but he is not acquainted with all my affairs."

"Your son, Mr. Scarborough, has made no tender to me of any information."

"Nor, sir, has Mr. Grey sought for any information from me." During this little dialogue Mr. Scarborough turned his face, with a smile, from one to the other, without a word.

"If Mr. Grey has anything to suggest in the way of advice, let him suggest it," said Augustus.

"Now, Mr. Grey," said the squire, with the same smile.

"Till I get farther information," said Mr. Grey, "I can only limit myself to giving the advice which I offered to you yesterday."

"Perhaps you will repeat it, so that he may hear it," said the squire.

"If you get a list of those to whom your son Mountjoy owes money, and an assurance that the moneys named in that list have been from time to time lent by them to him,—the actual amount, I mean,—then I think that if you and your son Augustus shall together choose to pay those amounts, you will make the best reparation in your power for the injury you have no doubt done in having contrived that it should be understood that Mountjoy was legitimate."

"You need not discuss," said the squire, "any injuries that I have done. I have done a great many, no doubt."

"But," continued the lawyer, "before any such payment is made, close inquiries should be instituted as to the amounts of money which have absolutely passed."

"We should certainly be taken in," said the squire. "I have great admiration for Mr. Samuel Hart. I do believe that it would be found impossible to extract the truth from Mr. Samuel Hart. If Mr. Samuel Hart does not make money yet out of poor Mountjoy I shall be surprised."

"The truth may be ascertained," said Mr. Grey. "You should get some accountant to examine the checks."

"When I remember how easy it was to deceive some really clever men as to the evidence of my marriage—" began Mr. Scarborough. So the squire began, but then stopped himself, with a shrug of his shoulders. Among the really clever men who had been easily deceived Mr. Grey was, if not actually first in importance, foremost, at any rate, in name.

"The truth may be ascertained," Mr. Grey repeated, almost with a scowl of anger upon his brow.

"Well, yes; I suppose it may. It will be difficult, in opposition to Mr. Samuel Hart."

"You must satisfy yourselves, at any rate. These men will know that they have no other hope of getting a shilling."

"It is a little hard to make them believe anything," said the squire. "They fancy, you know, that if they could get a hold of Mountjoy, so as to have him in their hands when the breath is out of my body and the bonds are really due, that then it may be made to turn out that he is really the heir."

"We know that it is not so," said Mr. Grey. At this Augustus smiled blandly.

"We know. But it is what we can make Mr. Samuel Hart know. In truth, Mr. Samuel Hart never allows himself to know anything,—except the amount of money which he may have at his banker's. And it will be difficult to convince Mr. Tyrrwhit. Mr. Tyrrwhit is assured that all of us,—you and I, and Mountjoy and Augustus,—are in a conspiracy to cheat him and the others."

"I don't wonder at it," said Mr. Grey.

"Perhaps not," continued the squire; "the circumstances, no doubt, are suspicious. But he will have to find out his mistake. Augustus is very anxious to pay these poor men their money. It is a noble feeling on the part of Augustus; you must admit that, Mr. Grey." The irony with which this was said was evident in the squire's face and voice. Augustus only quietly laughed. The attorney sat as firm as death. He was not going to argue with such a statement or to laugh at such a joke. "I suppose it will come to over a hundred thousand pounds."

"Eighty thousand, I should think," said Augustus. "The bonds amount to a great deal more than that—twice that."

"It is for him to judge," said the squire, "whether he is bound by his honor to pay so large a sum to men whom I do not suppose he loves very well."

"The estate can bear it," said Augustus.

"Yes, the estate can bear it," said the attorney. "They should be paid what they have expended. That is my idea. Your son thinks that their silence will be worth the money."

"What makes you say that?" demanded Augustus.

"Just my own opinion."

"I look upon it as an insult."

"Would you be kind enough to explain to us what is your reason for wishing to do this thing?" asked Mr. Grey.

"No, sir; I decline to give any reason. But those which you ascribe to me are insulting."

"Will you deny them?"

"I will not assent to anything,—coming from you,—nor will I deny anything. It is altogether out of your place as an attorney to ascribe motives to your clients. Can you raise the money, so that it shall be forthcoming at once? That is the question."

"On your father's authority, backed by your signature, I imagine that I can do so. But I will not answer as a certainty. The best thing would be to sell a portion of the property. If you and your father will join, and Mountjoy also with you, it may be done."

"What has Mountjoy got to do with it?" asked the father.

"You had better have Mountjoy also. There may be some doubt as to the title. People will think so after the tricks that have been played." This was said by the lawyer; but the squire only laughed. He always showed some enjoyment of the fun which arose from the effects of his own scheming. The legal world, with its entails, had endeavored to dispose of his property, but he had shown the legal world that it was not an easy task to dispose of anything in which he was concerned.

"How will you get hold of Mountjoy?" asked Augustus. Then the two older men only looked at each other. Both of them believed that Augustus knew more about his brother than any one else. "I think you had better send to Mr. Annesley and ask him."

"What does Annesley know about him?" asked the squire.

"He was the last person who saw him, at any rate, in London."

"Are you sure of that?" said Mr. Grey.

"I think I may say that I am. I think, at any rate, that I know that there was a violent quarrel between them in the streets,—a quarrel in which the two men proceeded to blows,—and that Annesley struck him in such a way as to leave him for dead upon the pavement. Then the young man walked away, and Mountjoy has not been heard of, or, at least, has not been seen since. That a man should have struck such a blow, and then, on the spur of the moment, thinking of his own safety, should have left his opponent, I can understand. I should not like to be accused of such treatment myself, but I can understand it. I cannot understand that the man should have been missing altogether, and that then he should have held his tongue."

"How do you know all this?" asked the attorney.

"It is sufficient that I do know it."

"I don't believe a word of it," said the squire.

"Coming from you, of course I must put up with any contradiction," said Augustus. "I should not bear it from any one else," and he looked at the attorney.

"One has a right to ask for your authority," said his father.

"I cannot give it. A lady is concerned whose name I shall not mention. But it is of less importance, as his own friends are acquainted with the nature of his conduct. Indeed, it seems odd to see you two gentlemen so ignorant as to the matter which has been a subject of common conversation in most circles. His uncle means to cut him out from the property."

"Can he too deal with entails?" said the squire.

"He is still in middle life, and he can marry. That is what he intended to do, so much is he disgusted with his nephew. He has already stopped the young man's allowance, and swears that he shall not have a shilling of his money if he can help it. The police for some time were in great doubt whether they would not arrest him. I think I am justified in saying that he is a thorough reprobate."

"You are not at all justified," said the father.

"I can only express my opinion, and am glad to say that the world agrees with me."

"It is sickening, absolutely sickening," said the squire, turning to the attorney. "You would not believe, now—"

But he stopped himself. "What would not Mr. Grey believe?" asked the son.

"There is no one one knows better than you that after the row in the street,—when Mountjoy was, I believe, the aggressor,—he was again seen by another person. I hate such deceit and scheming." Here Augustus smiled. "What are you sniggering there at, you blockhead?"

"Your hatred, sir, at deceit and scheming. The truth is that when a man plays a game well, he does not like to find that he has any equal. Heaven forbid that I should say that there is rivalry here. You, sir, are so pre-eminently the first that no one can touch you." Then he laughed long,—a low, bitter, inaudible laugh,—during which Mr. Grey sat silent.

"This comes well from you!" said the father.

"Well, sir, you would try your hand upon me. I have passed over all that you have done on my behalf. But when you come to abuse me I cannot quite take your words as calmly as though there had been—no, shall I say, antecedents? Now about this money. Are we to pay it?"

"I don't care one straw about the money. What is it to me? I don't owe these creditors anything."

"Nor do I."

"Let them rest, then, and do the worst they can. But upon the whole, Mr. Grey," he added, after a pause, "I think we had better pay them. They have endeavored to be insolent to me, and I have therefore ignored their claim. I have told them to do their worst. If my son here will agree with you in raising the money, and if Mountjoy,—as he, too, is necessary,—will do so, I too will do what is required of me. If eighty thousand pounds will settle it all, there ought not to be any difficulty. You can inquire what the real amount would be. If they choose to hold to their bonds, nothing will come of it;—that's all."

"Very well, Mr. Scarborough. Then I shall know how to proceed. I understand that Mr. Scarborough, junior, is an assenting party?" Mr. Scarborough, junior, signified his assent by nodding his head.

"That will do, then, for I think that I have a little exhausted myself." Then he turned round upon his couch, as though he intended to slumber. Mr. Grey left the room, and Augustus followed him, but not a word was spoken between them. Mr. Grey had an early dinner and went up to London by an evening train. What became of Augustus he did not inquire, but simply asked for his dinner and for a conveyance to the train. These were forthcoming, and he returned that night to Fulham.

"Well?" said Dolly, as soon as she had got him his slippers and made him his tea.

"I wish with all my heart I had never seen any one of the name of Scarborough!"

"That is of course;—but what have you done?"

"The father has been a great knave. He has set the laws of his country at defiance, and should be punished most severely. And Mountjoy Scarborough has proved himself to be unfit to have any money in his hands. A man so reckless is little better than a lunatic. But compared with Augustus they are both estimable, amiable men. The father has ideas of philanthropy, and Mountjoy is simply mad. But Augustus is as dishonest as either of them, and is odious also all round." Then at length he explained all that he had learned, and all that he had advised, and at last went to bed combating Dolly's idea that the Scarboroughs ought now to be thrown over altogether.

CHAPTER XXI. MR. SCARBOROUGH'S THOUGHTS OF HIMSELF

When Mr. Scarborough was left alone he did not go to sleep, as he had pretended, but lay there for an hour, thinking of his position and indulging to the full the feelings of anger which he now entertained toward his second son. He had never, in truth, loved Augustus. Augustus was very like his father in his capacity for organizing deceit, for plotting, and so contriving that his own will should be in opposition to the wills of all those around him. But they were thoroughly unlike in the object to be attained. Mr. Scarborough was not a selfish man. Augustus was selfish and nothing else. Mr. Scarborough hated the law,—because it was the law and endeavored to put a restraint upon him and others. Augustus liked the law,—unless when in particular points it interfered with his own actions. Mr. Scarborough thought that he could do better than the law. Augustus wished to do worse. Mr. Scarborough never blushed at what he himself attempted, unless he failed, which was not often the case. But he was constantly driven to blush for his son. Augustus blushed for nothing and for nobody. When Mr. Scarborough had declared to the attorney that just praise was due to Augustus for the nobility of the sacrifice he was making, Augustus had understood his father accurately and determined to be revenged, not because of the expression of his father's thoughts, but because he had so expressed himself before the attorney. Mr. Scarborough also thought that he was entitled to his revenge.

When he had been left alone for an hour he rung the bell, which was close at his side, and called for Mr. Merton. "Where is Mr. Grey?"

"I think he has ordered the wagonette to take him to the station."

"And where is Augustus?"

"I do not know."

"And Mr. Jones? I suppose they have not gone to the station. Just feel my pulse, Merton. I am afraid I am very weak." Mr. Merton felt his pulse and shook his head. "There isn't a pulse, so to speak."

"Oh yes; but it is irregular. If you will exert yourself so violently—"

"That is all very well; but a man has to exert himself sometimes, let the penalty be what it may. When do you think that Sir William will have to come again?" Sir

William, when he came, would come with his knife, and his advent was always to be feared.

"It depends very much on yourself, Mr. Scarborough. I don't think he can come very often, but you can make the distances long or short. You should attend to no business."

"That is absolute rubbish."

"Nevertheless, it is my duty to say so. Whatever arrangements may be required, they should be made by others. Of course, if you do as you have done this morning, I can suggest some little relief. I can give you tonics and increase the amount; but I cannot resist the evil which you yourself do yourself."

"I understand all about it."

"You will kill yourself if you go on."

"I don't mean to go on any farther,—not as I have done to-day; but as to giving up business, that is rubbish. I have got my property to manage, and I mean to manage it myself as long as I live. Unfortunately, there have been accidents which make the management a little rough at times. I have had one of the rough moments to-day, but they shall not be repeated. I give you my word for that. But do not talk to me about giving up my business. Now I'll take your tonics, and then would you have the kindness to ask my sister to come to me?"

Miss Scarborough, who was always in waiting on her brother, was at once in the room. "Martha," he said, "where is Augustus?"

"I think he has gone out."

"And where is Mr. Septimus Jones?"

"He is with him, John. The two are always together."

"You would not mind giving my compliments to Mr. Jones, and telling him that his bedroom is wanted?"

"His bedroom wanted! There are lots of bedrooms, and nobody to occupy them."

"It's a hint that I want him to go; he'd understand that."

"Would it not be better to tell Augustus?" asked the lady, doubting much her power to carry out the instructions given to her.

"He would tell Augustus. It is not, you see, any objection I have to Mr. Jones. I have not the pleasure of his acquaintance. He is a most agreeable young man, I'm sure; but I do not care to entertain an agreeable young man without having a word to say on the subject. Augustus does not think it worth his while even to speak to me about him. Of course, when I am gone, in a month or so,—perhaps a week or two,—he can do as he pleases."

"Don't, John!"

"But it is so. While I live I am master at least of this house. I cannot see Mr. Jones, and I do not wish to have another quarrel with Augustus. Mr. Merton says that every time I get angry it gives Sir William another chance with the knife. I thought that perhaps you could do it." Then Miss Scarborough promised that she would do it, and, having her brother's health very much at heart, she did do it. Augustus stood smiling while the message was, in fact, conveyed to him, but he made no answer. When the lady had done he bobbed his head to signify that he acknowledged the receipt of it, and the lady retired.

"I have got my walking-papers," he said to Septimus Jones ten minutes afterward.

"I don't know what you mean."

"Don't you? Then you must be very thick-headed. My father has sent me word that you are to be turned out. Of course he means it for me. He does not wish to give me the power of saying that he sent me away from the house,—me, whom he has so long endeavored to rob,—me, to whom he owes so much for taking no steps to punish his fraud. And he knows that I can take none, because he is on his death-bed."

"But you couldn't, could you, if he were—were anywhere else?"

"Couldn't I? That's all you know about it. Understand, however, that I shall start to-morrow morning, and unless you like to remain here on a visit to him, you had better go with me." Mr. Jones signified his compliance with the hint, and so Miss Scarborough had done her work.

Mr. Scarborough, when thus left alone, spent his time chiefly in thinking of the condition of his sons. His eldest son, Mountjoy, who had ever been his favorite, whom as a little boy he had spoiled by every means in his power, was a ruined man. His debts had all been paid, except the money due to the money-lenders. But he was not the less a ruined man. Where he was at this moment his father did not know. All the world knew the injustice of which he had been guilty on his boy's behalf, and all the world knew the failure of the endeavor. And now he had made a great and a successful effort to give back to his legitimate heir all the property. But in return the second son only desired his death, and almost told him so to his face. He had been proud of Augustus as a lad, but he had never loved him as he had loved Mountjoy. Now he knew that he and Augustus must henceforward be enemies. Never for a moment did he think of giving up his power over the estate as long as the estate should still be his. Though it should be but for a month, though it should be but for a week, he would hold his own. Such was the nature of the man, and when he swallowed Mr. Merton's tonics he did so more with the idea of keeping the property out of his son's hands than of preserving his own life. According to his view, he had done very much for Augustus, and this was the return which he received!

And in truth he had done much for Augustus. For years past it had been his object to leave to his second son as much as would come to his first. He had continued to put money by for him, instead of spending his income on himself.

Of this Mr. Grey had known much, but had said nothing when he was speaking those severe words which Mr. Scarborough had always contrived to receive with laughter. But he had felt their injustice, though he had himself ridiculed the idea of law. There had been the two sons, both born from the same mother, and he had willed that they should be both rich men, living among the foremost of their fellow men, and the circumstances of the property would have helped him. The income from year to year went on increasing.

The water-mills of Tretton and the town of Tretton had grown and been expanded within his domain, and the management of the sales in Mr. Grey's hands had been judicious. The revenues were double now what they had been when Mr. Scarborough first inherited it. It was all, no doubt, entailed, but for twenty years he had enjoyed the power of accumulating a sum of money for his second son's sake,—or would have enjoyed it, had not the accumulation been taken from him to pay Mountjoy's debts. It was in vain that he attempted to make Mountjoy responsible for the money. Mountjoy's debts, and irregularities, and gambling went on, till Mr. Scarborough found himself bound to dethrone the illegitimate son, and to place the legitimate in his proper position.

In doing the deed he had not suffered much, though the circumstances which had led to the doing of it had been full of pain. There had been an actual pleasure to him in thus showing himself to be superior to the conventionalities of the world. There was Augustus still ready to occupy the position to which he had in truth been born. And at the moment Mountjoy had gone—he knew not where. There had been gambling debts which, coming as they did after many others, he had refused to pay. He himself was dying at the moment, as he thought. It would be better for him to take up with Augustus. Mountjoy he must leave to his fate. For such a son, so reckless, so incurable, so hopeless, it was impossible that anything farther should be done. He would at least enjoy the power of leaving those wretched creditors without their money. There would be some triumph, some consolation, in that. So he had done, and now his heir turned against him!

It was very bitter to him, as he lay thinking of it all. He was a man who was from his constitution and heart capable of making great sacrifices for those he loved. He had a most thorough contempt for the character of an honest man. He did not believe in honesty, but only in mock honesty. And yet he would speak of an honest man with admiration, meaning something altogether different from the honesty of which men ordinarily spoke. The usual honesty of the world was with him all pretence, or, if not, assumed for the sake of the character it would achieve. Mr. Grey he knew to be honest; Mr. Grey's word he knew to be true; but he fancied that Mr. Grey had adopted this absurd mode of living with the view of cheating his neighbors by appearing to be better than others. All virtue and all vice were comprised by him in the words "good-nature" and "ill-nature." All church-going propensities,—and these propensities in his estimate extended very widely,—he scorned from the very bottom of his heart. That one set of words should be deemed more wicked than another, as in regard to swearing, was to him a sign either of hypocrisy, of idolatry, or of feminine weakness of intellect. To women he allowed the privilege of being, in regard to thought, only something better than dogs. When his sister Martha shuddered at some exclamation from his mouth, he would say to himself simply that she was a woman, not an idiot or a hypocrite. Of women, old and young, he had been very fond, and in his manner to them very tender; but when a woman rose to a way of thinking akin to his own, she was no longer a woman to his senses. Against such a one his taste revolted. She sunk to the level of a man contaminated by petticoats. And law was hardly less absurd to him than religion. It consisted of a perplexed entanglement of rules got together so that the few might live in comfort at the expense of the many.

Robbery, if you could get to the bottom of it, was bad, as was all violence; but taxation was robbery, rent was robbery, prices fixed according to the desire of the seller and not in obedience to justice, were robbery. "Then you are the greatest of robbers," his friends would say to him. He would admit it, allowing that in such a state of society he was not prepared to go out and live naked in the streets if he could help it. But he delighted to get the better of the law, and triumphed in his own iniquity, as has been seen by his conduct in reference to his sons.

In this way he lived, and was kind to many people, having a generous and an open hand. But he was a man who could hate with a bitter hatred, and he hated most those suspected by him of mean or dirty conduct. Mr. Grey, who constantly told him to his face that he was a rascal, he did not hate at all. Thinking Mr. Grey to be in some respects idiotic, he respected him, and almost loved him. He thoroughly believed Mr. Grey, thinking him to be an ass for telling so much truth unnecessarily. And he had loved his son Mountjoy in spite of all his iniquities, and had fostered him till it was impossible to foster him any longer. Then he had endeavored to love Augustus, and did not in the least love him the less because his son told him frequently of the wicked things he had done. He did not object to be told of his wickedness even by his son. But Augustus suspected him of other things than those of which he accused him, and attempted to be sharp with him and to get the better of him at his own game. And his son laughed at him and scorned him, and regarded him as one who was troublesome only for a time, and who need not be treated with much attention, because he was there only for a time. Therefore he hated Augustus. But Augustus was his heir, and he knew that he must die soon.

But for how long could he live? And what could he yet do before he died? A braver man than Mr. Scarborough never lived,—that is, one who less feared to die. Whether that is true courage may be a question, but it was his, in conjunction with courage of another description. He did not fear to die, nor did he fear to live. But what he did fear was to fail before he died. Not to go out with the conviction that he was vanishing amid the glory of success, was to him to be wretched at his last moment, and to be wretched at his last moment, or to anticipate that he should be so, was to him,—even so near his last hours,—the acme of misery. How much of life was left to him, so that he might recover something of success? Or was any moment left to him?

He could not sleep, so he rung his bell, and again sent for Mr. Merton. "I have taken what you told me."

"So best," said Mr. Merton. For he did not always feel assured that this strange patient would take what had been ordered.

"And I have tried to sleep."

"That will come after a while. You would not naturally sleep just after the tonic."

"And I have been thinking of what you said about business. There is one thing I must do, and then I can remain quiet for a fortnight, unless I should be called upon to disturb my rest by dying."

"We will hope not."

"That may go as it pleases," said the sick man. "I want you now to write a letter for me to Mr. Grey." Mr. Merton had undertaken to perform the duties of secretary as well as doctor, and had thought in this way to obtain some authority over his patient for the patient's own good; but he had found already that no authority had come to him. He now sat down at the table close to the bedside, and prepared to write in accordance with Mr. Scarborough's dictation. "I think that Grey,—the lawyer, you know,—is a good man."

"The world, as far as I hear it, says that he is honest."

"I don't care a straw what the world says. The world says that I am dishonest, but I am not." Merton could only shrug his shoulders. "I don't say that because I want you to change your opinion. I don't care what you think. But I tell you a fact. I doubt whether Grey is so absolutely honest as I am, but, as things go, he is a good man."

"Certainly."

"But the world, I suppose, says that my son Augustus is honest?"

"Well, yes; I should suppose so."

"If you have looked into him and have seen the contrary, I respect your intelligence."

"I did not mean anything particular."

"I dare say not, and if so, I mean nothing particular as to your intelligence. He, at any rate, is a scoundrel. Mountjoy—you know Mountjoy?"

"Never saw him in my life."

"I don't think he is a scoundrel,—not all round. He has gambled when he has not had money to pay. That is bad. And he has promised when he wanted money, and broken his word as soon as he had got it, which is bad also. And he has thought himself to be a fine fellow because he has been intimate with lords and dukes, which is very bad. He has never cared whether he paid his tailor. I do not mean that he has merely got into debt, which a young man such as he cannot help; but he has not cared whether his breeches were his or another man's. That too is bad. Though he has been passionately fond of women, it has only been for himself, not for the women, which is very bad. There is an immense deal to be altered before he can go to heaven."

"I hope the change may come before it is too late," said Merton.

"These changes don't come very suddenly, you know. But there is some chance for Mountjoy. I don't think that there is any for Augustus." Here he paused, but Merton did not feel disposed to make any remark. "You don't happen to know a young man of the name of Annesley,—Harry Annesley?"

"I have heard his name from your son."

"From Augustus? Then you didn't hear any good of him, I'm sure. You have heard all the row about poor Mountjoy's disappearance?"

"I heard that he did disappear."

"After a quarrel with that Annesley?"

"After some quarrel. I did not notice the name at the time."

"Harry Annesley was the name. Now, Augustus says that Harry Annesley was the last person who saw Mountjoy before his disappearance,—he last who knew him. He implies thereby that Annesley was the conscious or unconscious cause of his disappearance."

"Well, yes."

"Certainly it is so. And as it has been thought by the police, and by other fools, that Mountjoy was murdered,—that his disappearance was occasioned by his death, either by murder or suicide, it follows that Annesley must have had something to do with it. That is the inference, is it not?"

"I should suppose so," said Merton.

"That is manifestly the inference which Augustus draws. To hear him speak to me about it you would suppose that he suspected Annesley of having killed Mountjoy."

"Not that, I hope."

"Something of the sort. He has intended it to be believed that Annesley, for his own purposes, has caused Mountjoy to be made away with. He has endeavored to fill the police with that idea. A policeman, generally, is the biggest fool that London, or England, or the world produces, and has been selected on that account. Therefore the police have a beautifully mysterious but altogether ignorant suspicion as to Annesley. That is the doing of Augustus, for some purpose of his own. Now, let me tell you that Augustus saw Mountjoy after Annesley had seen him, that he knows this to be the case, and that it was Augustus, who contrived Mountjoy's disappearance. Now what do you think of Augustus?" This was a question which Merton did not find it very easy to answer. But Mr. Scarborough waited for a reply. "Eh?" he exclaimed.

"I had rather not give an opinion on a point so raised."

"You may. Of course you understand that I intend to assert that Augustus is the greatest blackguard you ever knew. If you have anything to say in his favor you can say it."

"Only that you may be mistaken. Living down here, you may not know the truth."

"Just that. But I do know the truth. Augustus is very clever; but there are others as clever as he is. He can pay, but then so can I. That he should want to get Mountjoy out of the way is intelligible. Mountjoy has become disreputable, and had better be out of the way. But why persistently endeavor to throw the blame upon young Annesley? That surprises me;—only I do not care much about it. I hear now for the first time that he has ruined young Annesley, and that does appear to be very horrible. But why does he want to pay eighty thousand pounds to these creditors? That I should wish to do so,—out of a property which must in a very short time become his,—would be intelligible. I may be supposed to have some affection for Mountjoy, and, after all, am not called upon to pay the money out of my own pocket. Do you understand it?"

"Not in the least," said Merton, who did not, indeed, very much care about it.

"Nor do I;—only this, that if he could pay these men and deprive them of all power of obtaining farther payment, let who would have the property, they at any rate would be quiet. Augustus is now my eldest son. Perhaps he thinks he might not remain so. If I were out of the way, and these creditors were paid, he thinks that poor Mountjoy wouldn't have a chance. He shall pay this eighty thousand pounds. Mountjoy hasn't a chance as it is; but Augustus shall pay the penalty."

Then he threw himself back on the bed, and Mr. Merton begged him to spare himself the trouble of the letter for the present. But in a few minutes he was again on his elbow and took some farther medicine. "I'm a great ass," he said, "to help Augustus in playing his game. If I were to go off at once he would be the happiest fellow left alive. But come, let us begin." Then he dictated the letter as follows:

DEAR MR. GREY,—

I have been thinking much of what passed between us the other day. Augustus seems to be in a great hurry as to paying the creditors, and I do not see why he should not be gratified, as the money may now be forthcoming. I presume that the sales, which will be completed before Christmas, will nearly enable us to stop their mouths. I can understand that Mountjoy should be induced to join with me and Augustus, so that in disposing of so large a sum of money the authority of all may be given, both of myself and of the heir, and also of him who a short time since was supposed to be the heir. I think that you may possibly find Mountjoy's address by applying to Augustus, who is always clever in such matters.

But you will have to be certain that you obtain all the bonds. If you can get Tyrrwhit to help you you will be able to be sure of doing so. The matter to him is one of vital importance, as his sum is so much the largest. Of course he will open his mouth very wide; but when he finds that he can get his principal and nothing more, I think that he will help you. I am afraid that I must ask you to put yourself in correspondence with Augustus. That he is an insolent scoundrel I will admit; but we cannot very well complete this affair without him. I fancy that he now feels it to be his interest to get it all done before I die, as the men will be clamorous with their bonds as soon as the breath is out of my body.—

Yours sincerely,   JOHN SCARBOROUGH.

"That will do," he said, when the letter was finished. But when Mr. Merton turned to leave the room Mr. Scarborough detained him. "Upon the whole, I am not dissatisfied with my life," he said.

"I don't know that you have occasion," rejoined Mr. Merton. In this he absolutely lied, for, according to his thinking, there was very much in the affairs of Mr. Scarborough's life which ought to have induced regret. He knew the whole story of the birth of the elder son, of the subsequent marriage, of Mr. Scarborough's fraudulent deceit which had lasted so many years, and of his later return to the truth, so as to save the property, and to give back to the younger son all of which for so many years he, his father, had attempted to rob him.

All London had talked of the affair, and all London had declared that so wicked and dishonest an old gentleman had never lived. And now he had returned to the truth simply with the view of cheating the creditors and keeping the estate in the family. He was manifestly an old gentleman who ought to be, above all others, dissatisfied with his own life; but Mr. Merton, when the assertion was made to him, knew not what other answer to make.

"I really do not think I have, nor do I know one to whom heaven with all its bliss will be more readily accorded. What have I done for myself?"

"I don't quite know what you have done all your life."

"I was born a rich man, and then I married,—not rich as I am now, but with ample means for marrying."

"After Mr. Mountjoy's birth," said Merton, who could not pretend to be ignorant of the circumstance.

"Well, yes. I have my own ideas about marriage and that kind of thing, which are, perhaps, at variance with yours." Whereupon Merton bowed. "I had the best wife in the world, who entirely coincided with me in all that I did. I lived entirely abroad, and made most liberal allowances to all the agricultural tenants. I rebuilt all the cottages;—go and look at them. I let any man shoot his own game till Mountjoy came up in the world and took the shooting into his own hands. When the people at the pottery began to build I assisted them in every way in the world. I offered to keep a school at my own expense, solely on the understanding that what they call Dissenters should be allowed to come there. The parson spread abroad a rumor that I was an atheist, and consequently the School was kept for the Dissenters only. The School-board has come and made that all right, though the parson goes on with his rumor. If he understood me as well as I understand him, he would know that he is more of an atheist than I am. I gave my boys the best education, spending on them more than double what is done by men with twice my means. My tastes were all simple, and were not specially vicious. I do not know that I have ever made any one unhappy. Then the estate became richer, but Mountjoy grew more and more expensive. I began to find that with all my economies the estate could not keep pace with him, so as to allow me to put by anything for Augustus. Then I had to bethink myself what I had to do to save the estate from those rascals."

"You took peculiar steps."

"I am a man who does take peculiar steps. Another would have turned his face to the wall in my state of health, and have allowed two dirty Jews such as Tyrrwhit and Samuel Hart to have revelled in the wealth of Tretton. I am not going to allow them to revel. Tyrrwhit knows me, and Hart will have to know me. They could not keep their hands to themselves till the breath was out of my body. Now I am about to see that each shall have his own shortly, and the estate will still be kept in the family."

"For Mr. Augustus Scarborough?"

"Yes, alas, yes! But that is not my doing. I do not know that I have cause to be dissatisfied with myself, but I cannot but own that I am unhappy. But I wished you to understand that though a man may break the law, he need not therefore be accounted bad, and though he may have views of his own as to religious matters, he need not be an atheist. I have made efforts on behalf of others, in which I have allowed no outward circumstances to control me. Now I think I do feel sleepy."

CHAPTER XXII. HARRY ANNESLEY IS SUMMONED HOME

"Just now I am triumphant," Harry Annesley had said to his hostess as he left Mrs. Armitage's house in the Paragon, at Cheltenham. He was absolutely triumphant, throwing his hat up into the air in the abandonment of his joy. For he was not a man to have conceived so well of his own parts as to have flattered himself that the girl must certainly be his.

There are at present a number of young men about who think that few girls are worth the winning, but that any girl is to be had, not by asking,—which would be troublesome,—but simply by looking at her. You can see the feeling in their faces. They are for the most part small in stature, well made little men, who are aware that they have something to be proud of, wearing close-packed, shining little hats, by which they seem to add more than a cubit to their stature; men endowed with certain gifts of personal—dignity I may perhaps call it, though the word rises somewhat too high. They look as though they would be able to say a clever thing; but their spoken thoughts seldom rise above a small, acrid sharpness. They respect no one; above all, not their elders. To such a one his horse comes first, if he have a horse; then a dog; and then a stick; and after that the mistress of his affections. But their fault is not altogether of their own making. It is the girls themselves who spoil them and endure their inanity, because of that assumed look of superiority which to the eyes of the outside world would be a little offensive were it not a little foolish. But they do not marry often. Whether it be that the girls know better at last, or that they themselves do not see sufficiently clearly their future dinners, who can say? They are for the most part younger brothers, and perhaps have discovered the best way of getting out of the world whatever scraps the world can afford them. Harry Annesley's faults were altogether of another kind. In regard to this young woman, the Florence whom he had loved, he had been over-modest. Now his feeling of glory was altogether redundant. Having been told by Florence that she was devoted to him, he walked with his head among the heavens. The first instinct with such a young man as those of whom I have spoken teaches him, the moment he has committed himself, to begin to consider how he can get out of the scrape. It is not much of a scrape, for when an older man comes this way, a man verging toward baldness, with a good professional income, our little friend is forgotten and he is passed by without a word. But Harry had now a conviction,—on that one special night,—that he never would be forgotten and never would forget. He was filled at once with an unwonted pride. All the world was now at his feet, and all the stars were open to him. He had begun to have a glimmering of what it was that Augustus Scarborough intended to do; but the intentions of Augustus Scarborough were now of no moment to him. He was clothed in a panoply of armor which would be true against all weapons. At any rate, on that night and during the next day this feeling remained the same with him.

Then he received a summons from his mother at Buston. His mother pressed him to come at once down to the parsonage. "Your uncle has been with your father, and has said terrible things about you. As you know, my brother is not very strong-minded, and I should not care so much for what he says were it not that so much is in his hands. I cannot understand what it is all about, but your father says that he does nothing but threaten. He talks of putting the entail on one side. Entails used to be fixed things, I thought; but since what old Mr. Scarborough did nobody seems to regard them now. But even suppose the entail does remain, what are you to do about the income? Your father thinks you had better come down and have a little talk about the matter."

This was the first blow received since the moment of his exaltation. Harry knew very well that the entail was fixed, and could not be put aside by Mr. Prosper, though Mr. Scarborough might have succeeded with his entail; but yet he was aware that his present income was chiefly dependent on his uncle's good-will. To be reduced to live on his fellowship would be very dreadful. And that income, such as it was, depended entirely on his celibacy. And he had, too, as he was well aware, engendered habits of idleness during the last two years. The mind of a young man so circumstanced turns always first to the Bar, and then to literature. At the Bar he did not think that there could be any opening for him. In the first place, it was late to begin; and then he was humble enough to believe of himself that he had none of the peculiar gifts necessary for a judge or for an advocate. Perhaps the knowledge that six or seven years of preliminary labor would be necessary was somewhat of a deterrent.

The rewards of literature might be achieved immediately. Such was his idea. But he had another idea,—perhaps as erroneous,—that this career would not become a gentleman who intended to be Squire of Buston. He had seen two or three men, decidedly Bohemian in their modes of life, to whom he did not wish to assimilate himself. There was Quaverdale, whom he had known intimately at St. John's, and who was on the Press. Quaverdale had quarrelled absolutely with his father, who was also a clergyman, and having been thrown altogether on his own resources, had come out as a writer for *The Coming Hour*. He made his five or six hundred a year in a rattling, loose, uncertain sort of fashion, and was,—so thought Harry Annesley,—the dirtiest man of his acquaintance. He did not believe in the six hundred a year, or Quaverdale would certainly have changed his shirt more frequently, and would sometimes have had a new pair of trousers. He was very amusing, very happy, very thoughtless, and as a rule altogether impecunious. Annesley had never known him without the means of getting a good dinner, but those means did not rise to the purchase of a new hat. Putting Quaverdale before him as an example, Annesley could not bring himself to choose literature as a profession. Thinking of all this when he received his mother's letter, he assured himself that Florence would not like professional literature.

He wrote to say that he would be down at Buston in five days' time. It does not become a son who is a fellow of a college and the heir to a property to obey his parents too quickly. But he gave up the intermediate days to thinking over the condition which bound him to his uncle, and to discussing his prospects with Quaverdale, who, as usual, was remaining in town doing the editor's work for *The Coming Hour*. "If he interfered with me I should tell him to go to bed," said Quaverdale. The allusion was, of course, made to Mr. Prosper.

"I am not on those sort of terms with him."

"I should make my own terms, and then let him do his worst. What can he do? If he means to withdraw his beggarly two hundred and fifty pounds, of course he'll do it."

"I suppose I do owe him something, in the way of respect."

"Not if he threatens you in regard to money. What does it come to? That you are to cringe at his heels for a beggarly allowance which he has been pleased to bestow upon you without your asking. 'Very well, my dear fellow,' I should say to him, 'you can stop it the moment you please. For certain objects of your own,—that your heir might live in the world after a certain fashion,—you have bestowed it. It has been mine since I was a child. If you can reconcile it to your conscience to discontinue it, do so.' You would find that he would have to think twice about it."

"He will stop it, and what am I to do then? Can I get an opening on any of these papers?" Quaverdale whistled,—a mode of receiving the overture which was not pleasing to Annesley. "I don't suppose that anything so very super-human in the way of intellect is required." Annesley had got a fellowship, whereas Quaverdale had done nothing at the university.

"Couldn't you make a pair of shoes? Shoemakers do get good wages."

"What do you mean? A fellow never can get you to be serious for two minutes together.

"I never was more serious in my life."

"That I am to make shoes?"

"No, I don't quite think that. I don't suppose you can make them. You'd have first to learn the trade and show that you were an adept."

"And I must show that I am an adept before I can write for *The Coming Hour*." There was a tone of sarcasm in this which was not lost on Quaverdale.

"Certainly you must; and that you are a better adept than I who have got the place, or some other unfortunate who will have to be put out of his berth. *The Coming Hour* only requires a certain number. Of course there are many newspapers in London, and many magazines, and much literary work going. You may get your share of it, but you have got to begin by shoving some incompetent fellow out. And in order to be able to begin you must learn the trade."

"How did you begin?"

"Just in that way. While you were roaming about London like a fine gentleman I began by earning twenty-four shillings a week."

"Can I earn twenty-four shillings a week?"

"You won't because you have already got your fellowship. You had a knack at writing Greek iambics, and therefore got a fellowship. I picked up at the same time the way of stringing English together. I also soon learned the way to be hungry. I'm not hungry now very often, but I've been through it. My belief is that you wouldn't get along with my editor."

"That's your idea of being independent."

"Certainly it is. I do his work, and take his pay, and obey his orders. If you think you can do the same, come and try. There's not room here, but there is, no doubt, room elsewhere. There's the trade to be learned, like any other trade; but my belief is that even then you could not do it. We don't want Greek iambics."

Harry turned away disgusted. Quaverdale was like the rest of the world, and thought that a peculiar talent and a peculiar tact were needed for his own business. Harry believed that he was as able to write a leading article, at any rate, as Quaverdale, and that the Greek iambics would not stand in his way. But he conceived it to be probable that his habits of cleanliness might do so, and gave up the idea for the present. He thought that his friend should have welcomed him with an open hand into the realms of literature; and, perhaps, it was the case that Quaverdale attributed too much weight to the knack of turning readable paragraphs on any subject at any moment's notice.

But what should he do down at Buston? There were three persons there with whom he would have to contend,—his father, his mother, and his uncle. With his father he had always been on good terms, but had still been subject to a certain amount of gentle sarcasm. He had got his fellowship and his allowance, and so had been lifted above his father's authority. His father thoroughly despised his brother-in-law, and looked down upon him as an absolute ass. But he was reticent, only dropping a word here and there, out of deference, perhaps, to his wife, and from a feeling lest his son might be deficient in wise courtesy, if he were encouraged to laugh at his benefactor. He had said a word or two as to a profession when Harry left Cambridge, but the word or two had come to nothing. In those days the uncle had altogether ridiculed the idea, and the mother, fond of her son, the fellow and the heir, had altogether opposed the notion. The rector himself was an idle, good-looking, self-indulgent man,—a man who read a little and understood what he read, and thought a little and understood what he thought, but who took no trouble about anything. To go through the world comfortably with a rather large family and a rather small income was the extent of his ambition. In regard to his eldest son he had begun well. Harry had been educated free, and had got a fellowship. He had never cost his father a shilling. And now the eldest of two grown-up daughters was engaged to be married to the son of a brewer living in the little town of Buntingford. This also was a piece of good-luck which the rector accepted with a thankful heart. There was another grown-up girl, also pretty, and then a third girl not grown up and the two boys who were at present at school at Royston. Thus burdened, the Rev. Mr. Annesley went through the world with as jaunty a step as was possible, making but little of his troubles, but anxious to make as much as he could of his advantages. Of these, the position of Harry was the brightest, if only Harry would be careful to guard it. It was quite out of the question that he should find an income for Harry if the squire stopped the two hundred and fifty pounds per annum which he at present allowed him.

Then there was Harry's mother, who had already very frequently discounted the good things which were to fall to Harry's lot. She was a dear, good, motherly woman, all whose geese were certainly counted to be swans. And of all swans Harry was the whitest; whereas, in purity of plumage, Mary, the eldest daughter, who had won the affections of the young Buntingford brewer, was the next. That Harry's allowance should be stopped would be almost as great a misfortune as though Mr. Thoroughbung were to break his neck out hunting with the Puckeridge hounds,—an amusement which, after the manner of brewers, he was much in the habit of following. Mrs. Annesley had lived at Buston all her life, having been born at the Hall. She was an excellent mother of a family, and a good clergyman's wife, being in both respects more painstaking and assiduous than her husband. But she did maintain something of respect for her brother, though in her inmost heart she knew that he was a fool. But to have been born Squire of Buston was something, and to have reached the age of fifty unmarried, so as to leave the position of heir open to her own son, was more. To such a one a great deal was due; but of that deal Harry was but little disposed to pay any part. He must be talked to, and very seriously talked to, and if possible saved from the sin of offending his easily-offended uncle. A terrible idea had been suggested to her lately by her husband. The entail might be made altogether inoperative by the marriage of her brother. It was a fearful notion, but one which if it entered into her brother's head might possibly be carried out. No one before had ever dreamed of anything so dangerous to the Annesley interests, and Mrs. Annesley now felt that by due submission on the part of the heir it might be avoided.

But the squire himself was the foe whom Harry most feared. He quite understood that he would be required to be submissive, and, even if he were willing, he did not know how to act the part. There was much now that he would endure for the sake of Florence. If Mr. Prosper demanded that after dinner he should hear a sermon, he would sit and hear it out. It would be a bore, but might be endured on behalf of the girl whom he loved. But he much feared that the cause of his uncle's displeasure was deeper than that. A rumor had reached him that his uncle had declared his conduct to Mountjoy Scarborough to have been abominable. He had heard no words spoken by his uncle, but threats had reached him through his mother, and also through his uncle's man of business. He certainly would go down to Buston, and carry himself toward his uncle with what outward signs of respect would be possible. But if his uncle accused him, he could not but tell his uncle that he knew nothing of the matter of which he was talking. Not for all Buston could he admit that he had done anything mean or ignoble. Florence, he was quite sure, would not desire it. Florence would not be Florence were she to desire it. He thought that he could trace the hands,—or rather the tongues,—through which the calumny had made its way down to the Hall. He would at once go to the Hall, and tell his uncle all the facts. He would describe the gross ill-usage to which he had been subjected. No doubt he had left the man sprawling upon the pavement, but there had been no sign that the man had been dangerously hurt; and when two days afterward the man had vanished, it was clear that he could not have vanished without legs. Had he taken himself off,—as was probable,—then why need Harry trouble himself as to his vanishing? If some one else had helped him in escaping,—as was also probable,—why had not that some one come and told the circumstances when all the inquiries were being made? Why should he have been expected to speak of the circumstances of such an encounter, which could not have been told but to Captain Scarborough's infinite disgrace? And he could not have told of it without naming Florence Mountjoy.

His uncle, when he heard the truth, must acknowledge that he had not behaved badly. And yet Harry, as he turned it all in his mind was uneasy as to his own conduct. He could not quite acquit himself in that he had kept secret all the facts of that midnight encounter in the face of the inquiries which had been made, in that he had falsely assured Augustus Scarborough of his ignorance. And yet he knew that on no consideration would he acknowledge himself to have been wrong.

CHAPTER XXIII. THE RUMORS AS TO MR. PROSPER

It was still October when Harry Annesley went down to Buston, and the Mountjoys had just reached Brussels. Mr. Grey had made his visit to Tretton and had returned to London. Harry went home on an understanding,—on the part of his mother, at any rate,—that he should remain there till Christmas. But he felt himself very averse to so long a sojourn. If the Hall and park were open to him he might endure it. He would take down two or three stiff books which he certainly would never read, and would shoot a few pheasants, and possibly ride one of his future brother-in-law's horses with the hounds. But he feared that there was to be a quarrel by which he would be debarred from the Hall and the park; and he knew, too, that it would not be well for him to shoot and hunt when his income should have been cut off. It would be necessary that some great step should be taken at once; but then it would be necessary, also, that Florence should agree to that step. He had a modest lodging in London, but before he started he prepared himself for what must occur by giving notice. "I don't say as yet that I shall give them up; but I might as well let you know that it's possible." This he said to Mrs. Brown, who kept the lodgings, and who received this intimation as a Mrs. Brown is sure to do. But where should he betake himself when his home at Mrs. Brown's had been lost? He would, he thought, find it quite impossible to live in absolute idleness at the rectory. Then in an unhappy frame of mind he went down by the train to Stevenage, and was there met by the rectory pony-carriage.

He saw it all in his mother's eye the moment she embraced him. There was some terrible trouble in the wind, and what could it be but his uncle? "Well, mother, what is it?"

"Oh, Harry, there is such a sad affair up at the Hall!"

"Is my uncle dead?"

"Dead! No!"

"Then why do you look so sad?—

   "'Even such a man, so faint, so spiritless,
   So dull, so dead in look, so woe-begone,
   Drew Priam's curtain in the dead of night.'"

"Oh Harry do not laugh. Your uncle says such dreadful things!"

"I don't care much what he says. The question is—what does he mean to do?"

"He declares that he will cut you off altogether."

"That is sooner said than done."

"That is all very well, Harry; but he can do it. Oh, Harry! But come and sit down and talk to me. I told your father to be out, so that I might have you alone; and the dear girls are gone into Buntingford."

"Ah, like them! Thoroughbung will have enough of them."

"He is our only happiness now."

"Poor Thoroughbung! I pity him if he has to do happiness for the whole household."

"Joshua is a most excellent young man. Where we should be without him I do not know." The flourishing young brewer was named Joshua, and had been known to Harry for some years, though never as yet known as a brother-in-law.

"I am sure he is; particularly as he has chosen Molly to be his wife. He is just the young man who ought to have a wife."

"Of course he ought."

"Because he can keep a family. But now about my uncle. He is to perform this ceremony of cutting me off. Will he turn out to have had a wife and family in former ages? I have no doubt old Scarborough could manage it, but I don't give my uncle credit for so much cleverness."

"But in future ages—" said the unhappy mother, shaking her head and rubbing her eyes.

"You mean that he is going to have a family?"

"It is all in the hands of Providence," said the parson's wife.

"Yes; that is true. He is not too old yet to be a second Priam, and have his curtains drawn the other way. That's his little game, is it?"

"There's a sort of rumor about, that it is possible."

"And who is the lady?"

"You may be sure there will be no lack of a lady if he sets his mind upon it. I was turning it over in my mind, and I thought of Matilda Thoroughbung."

"Joshua's aunt!"

"Well; she is Joshua's aunt, no doubt. I did just whisper the idea to Joshua, and he says that she is fool enough for anything. She has twenty-five thousand pounds of her own, but she lives all by herself."

"I know where she lives,—just out of Buntingford, as you go to Royston. But she's not alone. Is Uncle Prosper to marry Miss Tickle also?" Miss Tickle was an estimable lady living as companion to Miss Thoroughbung.

"I don't know how they may manage; but it has to be thought of, Harry. We only know that your uncle has been twice to Buntingford."

"The lady is fifty, at any rate."

"The lady is barely forty. She gives out that she is thirty-six. And he could settle a jointure on her which would leave the property not worth having."

"What can I do?"

"Yes, indeed, my dear; what can you do?"

"Why is he going to upset all the arrangements of my life, and his life, after such a fashion as this?"

"That's just what your father says."

"I suppose he can do it. The law will allow him. But the injustice would be monstrous. I did not ask him to take me by the hand when I was a boy and lead me into this special walk of life. It has been his own doing. How will he look me in the face and tell me that he is going to marry a wife? I shall look him in the face and tell him of my wife."

"But is that settled?"

"Yes, mother; it is settled. Wish me joy for having won the finest lady that ever walked the earth." His mother blessed him,—but said nothing about the finest lady,—who at that moment she believed to be the future bride of Mr. Joshua Thoroughbung. "And when I shall tell my uncle that it is so, what will he say to me? Will he have the face then to tell me that I am to be cut out of Buston? I doubt whether he will have the courage."

"He has thought of that, Harry."

"How thought of it, mother?"

"He has given orders that he is not to see you."

"Not to see me!"

"So he declares. He has written a long letter to your father, in which he says that he would be spared the agony of an interview."

"What! is it all done, then?"

"Your father got the letter yesterday. It must have taken my poor brother a week to write it."

"And he tells the whole plan,—Matilda Thoroughbung, and the future family?"

"No, he does not say anything about Miss Thoroughbung He says that he must make other arrangements about the property."

"He can't make other arrangements; that is, not until the boy is born. It may be a long time first, you know."

"But the jointure?"

"What does Molly say about it?"

"Molly is mad about it and so is Joshua. Joshua talks about it just as though he were one of us, and he says that the old people at Buntingford would not hear of it." The old people spoken of were the father and mother of Joshua, and the half-brother of Miss Matilda Thoroughbung. "But what can they do?"

"They can do nothing. If Miss Matilda likes Uncle Prosper—"

"Likes, my dear! How young you are! Of course she would like a country house to live in, and the park, and the county society. And she would like somebody to live with besides Miss Tickle."

"My uncle, for instance."

"Yes, your uncle."

"If I had my choice, mother, I should prefer Miss Tickle."

"Because you are a silly boy. But what are you to do now?"

"In this long letter which he has written to my father does he give no reason?"

"Your father will show you the letter. Of course he gives reasons. He says that you have done something which you ought not to have done—about that wretched Mountjoy Scarborough."

"What does he know about it?—the idiot!"

"Oh, Harry!"

"Well, mother, what better can I say of him? He has taken me as a child and fashioned my life for me; has said that this property should be mine, and has put an income into my hand as though I were an eldest son; has repeatedly declared, when his voice was more potent than mine, that I should follow no profession. He has bound himself to me, telling all the world that I was his heir. And now he casts me out because he has heard some cock-and-bull story, of the truth of which he knows nothing. What better can I say of him than call him an idiot? He must be that or else a heartless knave. And he says that he does not mean to see me,—me with whose life he has thus been empowered to interfere, so as to blast it if not to bless it, and intends to turn me adrift as he might do a dog that did not suit him! And because he knows that he cannot answer me he declares that he will not see me."

"It is very hard, Harry."

"Therefore I call him an idiot in preference to calling him a knave. But I am not going to be dropped out of the running in that way, just in deference to his will. I shall see him. Unless they lock him up in his bedroom I shall compel him to see me."

"What good would that do, Harry? That would only set him more against you."

"You don't know his weakness."

"Oh yes, I do; he is very weak."

"He will not see me, because he will have to yield when he hears what I have to say for myself. He knows that, and would therefore fain keep away from me. Why should he be stirred to this animosity against me?"

"Why indeed?"

"Because there is some one who wishes to injure me more strong than he is, and who has got hold of him. Some one has lied behind my back."

"Who has done this?"

"Ah, that is the question. But I know who has done it, though I will not name him just now. This enemy of mine, knowing him to be weak,—knowing him to be an idiot, has got hold of him and persuaded him. He believes the story which is told to him, and then feels happy in shaking off an incubus. No doubt I have not been very soft with him,—nor, indeed, hard. I have kept out of his way, and he is willing to resent it; but he is afraid to face me and tell me that it is so. Here are the girls come back from Buntingford. Molly, you blooming young bride, I wish you joy of your brewer."

"He's none the worse on that account, Master Harry," said the eldest sister.

"All the better,—very much the better. Where would you be if he was not a brewer? But I congratulate you with all my heart, old girl. I have known him ever so long, and he is one of the best fellows I do know."

"Thank you, Harry," and she kissed him.

"I wish Fanny and Kate may even do so well."

"All in good time," said Fanny.

"I mean to have a banker—all to myself," said Kate.

"I wish you may have half as good a man for your husband," said Harry.

"And I am to tell you," continued Molly, who was now in high good-humor, "that there will be always one of his horses for you to ride as long as you remain at home. It is not every brother-in-law that would do as much as that for you."

"Nor yet every uncle," said Kate, shaking her head, from which Harry could see that this quarrel with his uncle had been freely discussed in the family circle.

"Uncles are very different," said the mother; "uncles can't be expected to do everything as though they were in love."

"Fancy Uncle Peter in love!" said Kate. Mr. Prosper was called Uncle Peter by the girls, though always in a sort of joke. Then the other two girls shook their heads very gravely, from which Harry learned that the question respecting the choice of Miss Matilda Thoroughbung as a mistress for the Hall had been discussed also before them.

"I am not going to marry all the family," said Molly.

"Not Miss Matilda, for instance," said her brother, laughing.

"No, especially not Matilda. Joshua is quite as angry about his aunt as anybody here can be. You'll find that he is more of an Annesley than a Thoroughbung."

"My dear," said the mother, "your husband will, as a matter of course, think most of his own family. And so ought you to do of his family, which will be yours. A married woman should always think most of her husband's family." In this way the mother told her daughter of her future duties; but behind the mother's back Kate made a grimace, for the benefit of her sister Fanny, showing thereby her conviction that in a matter of blood,—what she called being a gentleman,—a Thoroughbung could not approach an Annesley.

"Mamma does not know it as yet," Molly said afterward in privacy to her brother, "but you may take it for granted that Uncle Peter has been into Buntingford and has made an offer to Aunt Matilda. I could tell it at once, because she looked so sharp at me to-day. And Joshua says that he is sure it is so by the airs she gives herself."

"You think she'll have him?"

"Have him! Of course she'll have him. Why shouldn't she? A wretched old maid living with a companion like that would have any one."

"She has got a lot of money."

"She'll take care of her money, let her alone for that.

"And she'll have his house to live in. And there'll be a jointure. Of course, if there were to be children—"

"Oh, bother!"

"Well, perhaps there will not. But it will be just as bad. We don't mean even to visit them; we think it so very wicked. And we shall tell them a bit of our mind as soon as the thing has been publicly declared."

CHAPTER XXIV. HARRY ANNESLEY'S MISERY

The conversation which took place that evening between Harry and his father was more serious in its language, though not more important in its purpose. "This is bad news, Harry," said the rector.

"Yes, indeed, sir.'"

"Your uncle, no doubt, can do as he pleases."

"You mean as to the income he has allowed me?"

"As to the income! As to the property itself. It is bad waiting for dead men's shoes."

"And yet it is what everybody does in this world. No one can say that I have been at all in a hurry to step into my uncle's shoes. It was he that first told you that he should never marry, and as the property had been entailed on me, he undertook to bring me up as his son."

"So he did."

"Not a doubt about it, sir. But I had nothing to say to it. As far as I understand, he has been allowing me two hundred and fifty pounds a year for the last dozen years."

"Ever since you went to the Charter-house."

"At that time I could not be expected to have a word to say to it. And it has gone on ever since."

"Yes, it has gone on ever since."

"And when I was leaving Cambridge he required that I should not go into a profession."

"Not exactly that, Harry."

"It was so that I understood it. He did not wish his heir to be burdened with a profession. He said so to me himself."

"Yes, just when he was in his pride because you had got your fellowship. But there was a contract understood, if not made."

"What contract?" asked Harry, with an air of surprise.

"That you should be to him as a son."

"I never undertook it. I wouldn't have done it at the price,—or for any price. I never felt for him the respect or the love that were due to a father. I did feel both of them, to the full, for my own father. They are a sort of a thing which we cannot transfer."

"They may be shared, Harry," said the rector, who was flattered.

"No, sir; in this instance that was not possible."

"You might have sat by while he read a sermon to his sister and nieces. You understood his vanity, and you wounded it, knowing what you were doing. I don't mean to blame you, but it was a misfortune. Now we must look it in the face and see what must be done. Your mother has told you that he has written to me. There is his letter. You will see that he writes with a fixed purpose." Then he handed to Harry a letter written on a large sheet of paper, the reading of which would be so long that Harry seated himself for the operation.

The letter need not here be repeated at length. It was written with involved sentences, but in very decided language. It said nothing of Harry's want of duty, or not attending to the sermons, or of other deficiencies of a like nature, but based his resolution in regard to stopping the income on his nephew's misconduct,—as it appeared to him,—in a certain particular case. And unfortunately,—though Harry was prepared to deny that his conduct on that occasion had been subject to censure,—he could not contradict any of the facts on which Mr. Prosper had founded his opinion. The story was told in reference to Mountjoy Scarborough, but not the whole story. "I understand that there was a row in the streets late at night, at the end of which young Mr. Scarborough was left as dead under the railings." "Left for dead!" exclaimed Harry. "Who says that he was left for dead? I did not think him to be dead."

"You had better read it to the end," said his father, and Harry read it. The letter went on to describe how Mountjoy Scarborough was missed from his usual haunts, how search was made by the police, how the newspapers were filled with the strange incident, and how Harry had told nothing of what had occurred. "But beyond this," the letter went on to say, "he positively denied, in conversation with the gentleman's brother, that he had anything to do with the gentleman on the night in question. If this be so, he absolutely lied. A man who would lie on such an occasion, knowing himself to have been guilty of having beaten the man in such a way as to have probably caused his death,—for he had left him for dead under the railings in a London street and in the midnight hour,—and would positively assert to the gentleman's brother that he had not seen the gentleman on the night in question, when he had every reason to believe that he had killed him,—a deed which might or might not be murder,—is not fit to be recognized as my heir."

There were other sentences equally long and equally complicated, in all of which Mr. Prosper strove to tell the story with tragic effect, but all of which had reference to the same transaction. He said nothing as to the ultimate destination of the property, nor of his own proposed marriage. Should he have a son, that son would, of course, have the property. Should there be no son, Harry must have it, even though his conduct might have been ever so abominable. To prevent this outrage on society, his marriage,—with its ordinary results,—would be the only step. Of that he need say nothing. But the two hundred and fifty pounds would not be paid after the Christmas quarter, and he must decline for the future the honor of receiving Mr. Henry Annesley at the Hall.

Harry, when he had read it all, began to storm with anger. The man, as he truly observed, had grossly insulted him. Mr. Prosper had called him a liar and had hinted that he was a murderer. "You can do nothing to him," his father said. "He is your uncle, and you have eaten his bread."

"I can't call him out and fight him."

"You must let it alone."

"I can make my way into the house and see him."

"I don't think you can do that. You will find it difficult to get beyond the front-door, and I would advise you to abandon all such ideas. What can you say to him?"

"It is false!"

"What is false? Though in essence it is false, in words it is true. You did deny that you had seen him."

"I forget what passed. Augustus Scarborough endeavored to pump me about his brother, and I did not choose to be pumped. As far as I can ascertain now, it is he that is the liar. He saw his brother after the affair with me."

"Has he denied it?"

"Practically he denies it by asking me the question. He asked me with the ostensible object of finding out what had become of his brother when he himself knew what had become of him."

"But you can't prove it. He positively says that you did deny having seen him on the night in question, I am not speaking of Augustus Scarborough, but of your uncle. What he says is true, and you had better leave him alone. Take other steps for driving the real truth into his brain."

"What steps can be taken with such a fool?"

"Write your own account of the transaction, so that he shall read it. Let your mother have it. I suppose he will see your mother."

"And so beg his favor."

"You need beg for nothing. Or if the marriage comes off—"

"You have heard of the marriage, sir?"

"Yes; I have heard of the marriage. I believe that he contemplates it. Put your statement of what did occur, and of your motives, into the hands of the lady's friends. He will be sure to read it."

"What good will that do?"

"No good, but that of making him ashamed of himself. You have got to read the world a little more deeply than you have hitherto done. He thinks that he is quarrelling with you about the affair in London, but it is in truth because you have declined to hear him read the sermons after having taken his money."

"Then it is he that is the liar rather than I."

"I, who am a moderate man, would say that neither is a liar. You did not choose to be pumped, as you call it, and therefore spoke as you did. According to the world's ways that was fair enough. He, who is sore at the little respect you have paid him, takes any ground of offence rather than that. Being sore at heart, he believes anything. This young Scarborough in some way gets hold of him, and makes him accept this cock-and-bull story. If you had sat there punctual all those Sunday evenings, do you think he would have believed it then?"

"And I have got to pay such a penalty as this?" The rector could only shrug his shoulders. He was not disposed to scold his son. It was not the custom of the house that Harry should be scolded. He was a fellow of his college and the heir to Buston, and was therefore considered to be out of the way of scolding. But the rector felt that his son had made his bed and must now lie on it, and Harry was aware that this was his father's feeling.

For two or three days he wandered about the country very down in the mouth. The natural state of ovation in which the girls existed was in itself an injury to him. How could he join them in their ovation, he who had suffered so much? It seemed to be heartless that they should smile and rejoice when he,—the head of the family, as he had been taught to consider himself,—was being so cruelly ill-used. For a day or two he hated Thoroughbung, though Thoroughbung was all that was kind to him. He congratulated him with cold congratulations, and afterward kept out of his way. "Remember, Harry, that up to Christmas you can always have one of the nags. There's Belladonna and Orange Peel. I think you'd find the mare a little the faster, though perhaps the horse is the bigger jumper." "Oh, thank you!" said Harry, and passed on. Now, Thoroughbung was fond of his horses, and liked to have them talked about, and he knew that Harry Annesley was treating him badly. But he was a good-humored fellow, and he bore it without complaint. He did not even say a cross word to Molly. Molly, however, was not so patient. "You might be a little more gracious when he's doing the best he can for you. It is not every one who will lend you a horse to hunt for two months." Harry shook his head, and wandered away miserable through the fields, and would not in these days even set his foot upon the soil of the park. "He was not going to intrude any farther," he said to the rector. "You can come to church, at any rate," his father said, "for he certainly will not be there while you are at the parsonage." Oh yes, Harry would go to the church. "I have yet to understand that Mr. Prosper is owner of the church, and the path there from the rectory is, at any rate, open to the public;" for at Buston the church stands on one corner of the park.

This went on for two or three days, during which nothing farther was said by the family as to Harry's woes. A letter was sent off to Mrs. Brown, telling her that the lodgings would not be required any longer, and anxious ideas began to crowd themselves on Harry's mind as to his future residence. He thought that he must go back to Cambridge and take his rooms at St. John's and look for college work. Two fatal years, years of idleness and gayety, had been passed, but still he thought that it might be possible. What else was there open for him? And then, as he roamed about the fields, his mind naturally ran away to the girl he loved. How would he dare again to look Florence in the face? It was not only the two hundred and fifty pounds per annum that was gone: that would have been a small income on which to marry. And he had never taken the girl's own money into account. He had rather chosen to look forward to the position as squire of Buston, and to take it for granted that it would not be very long before he was called upon to fill the position. He had said not a word to Florence about money, but it was thus that he had regarded the matter. Now the existing squire was going to marry, and the matter could not so be regarded any longer. He saw half a dozen little Prospers occupying half a dozen little cradles, and a whole suite of nurseries established at the Hall. The name of Prosper would be fixed at Buston, putting it altogether beyond his reach.

In such circumstances would it not be reasonable that Florence should expect him to authorize her to break their engagement? What was he now but the penniless son of a poor clergyman, with nothing on which to depend but a miserable stipend, which must cease were he to marry? He knew that he ought to give her back her troth; and yet, as he thought of doing so, he was indignant with her. Was love to come to this? Was her regard for him to be counted as nothing? What right had he to expect that she should be different from any other girl?

Then he was more miserable than ever, as he told himself that such would undoubtedly be her conduct. As he walked across the fields, heavy with the mud of a wet October day, there came down a storm of rain which wet him through. Who does not know the sort of sensation which falls upon a man when he feels that even the elements have turned against him,—how he buttons up his coat and bids the clouds open themselves upon his devoted bosom?

> "Blow, winds, and crack your cheeks! rage, blow,
> You cataracts and hurricanes!"

It is thus that a man is apt to address the soft rains of heaven when he is becoming wet through in such a frame of mind; and on the present occasion Harry likened himself to Leer. It was to him as though the steeples were to be drenched and the cocks drowned when he found himself wet through. In this condition he went back to the house, and so bitter to him were the misfortunes of the world that he would hardly condescend to speak while enduring them. But when he had entered the drawing-room his mother greeted him with a letter. It had come by the day mail, and his mother looked into his face piteously as she gave it to him. The letter was from Brussels, and she could guess from whom it had come. It might be a sweetly soft love-letter; but then it might be neither sweet nor soft, in the condition of things in which Harry was now placed. He took it and looked at it, but did not dare to open it on the spur of the moment. Without a word he went up to his room, and then tore it asunder. No doubt, he said to himself, it would allude to his miserable stipend and penniless condition. The letter ran as follows:

Dearest Harry,—

I think it right to write to you, though mamma does not approve of it. I have told her, however, that in the present circumstances I am bound to do so, and that I should implore you not to answer. Though I must write, there must be no correspondence between us. Rumors have been received here very detrimental to your character." Harry gnashed his teeth as he read this. "Stories are told about your meeting with Captain Scarborough in London, which I know to be only in part true. Mamma says that because of them I ought to give up my engagement, and my uncle, Sir Magnus, has taken upon himself to advise me to do so. I have told them both that that which is said of you is in part untrue; but whether it be true or whether it be false, I will never give up my engagement unless you ask me to do so. They tell me that as regards your pecuniary prospects you are ruined. I say that you cannot be ruined as long as you have my income. It will not be much, but it will, I should think, be enough.

And now you can do as you please. You may be quite sure that I shall be true to you, through ill report and good report. Nothing that mamma can say to me will change me, and certainly nothing from Sir Magnus.

And now there need not be a word from you, if you mean to be true to me. Indeed, I have promised that there shall be no word, and I expect you to keep my promise for me. If you wish to be free of me, then you must write and say so.

But you won't wish it, and therefore I am yours, always, always, always your own
FLORENCE.

Harry read the letter standing up in the middle of the room, and in half a minute he had torn off his wet coat and kicked one of his wet boots to the farther corner of the room. Then there was a knock at the door, and his mother entered, "Tell me, Harry, what she says."

He rushed up to his mother, all damp and half-shod as he was, and seized her in his arms. "Oh, mother, mother!"

"What is it, dear?"

"Read that, and tell me whether there ever was a finer human being!" Mrs. Annesley did read it, and thought that her own daughter Molly was just as fine a creature. Florence was simply doing what any girl of spirit would do. But she saw that her son was as jubilant now as he had been downcast, and she was quite willing to partake of his comfort. "Not write a word to her! Ha, ha! I think I see myself at it!"

"But she seems to be in earnest there."

"In earnest! And so am I in earnest. Would it be possible that a fellow should hold his hand and not write? Yes, my girl; I think that I must write a line. I wonder what she would say if I were not to write?"

"I think she means that you should be silent."

"She has taken a very odd way of assuming it. I am to keep her promise for her,—my darling, my angel, my life! But I cannot do that one thing. Oh, mother, mother, if you knew how happy I am! What the mischief does it all signify,—Uncle Prosper, Miss Thoroughbung, and the rest of it,—with a girl like that?"

CHAPTER XXV. HARRY AND HIS UNCLE

Harry was kissed all round by the girls, and was congratulated warmly on the heavenly excellence of his mistress. They could afford to be generous if he would be good-natured. "Of course you must write to her," said Molly, when he came down-stairs with dry clothes.

"I should think so, mother."

"Only she does seem to be so much in earnest about it," said Mrs. Annesley.

"I think she would rather get just a line to say that he is in earnest too," said Fanny.

"Why should not she like a love-letter as much as any one else?" said Kate, who had her own ideas. "Of course she has to tell him about her mamma, but what need he care for that? Of course mamma thinks that Joshua need not write to Molly, but Molly won't mind."

"I don't think anything of the kind, miss."

"And besides, Joshua lives in the next parish," said Fanny, "and has a horse to ride over on if he has anything to say."

"At any rate, I shall write," said Harry, "even at the risk of making her angry." And he did write as follows:

> "Buston,
> October, 188—.

"My Own Dear Girl,—It is impossible that I should not send one line in answer. Put yourself in my place, and consult your own feelings. Think that you have a letter so full of love, so noble, so true, so certain to fill you with joy, and then say whether you would let it pass without a word of acknowledgment. It would be absolutely impossible. It is not very probable that I should ask you to break your engagement, which in the midst of my troubles is the only consolation I have. But when a man has a rock to stand upon like that, he does not want anything else. As long as a man has the one person necessary to his happiness to believe in him, he can put up with the ill opinion of all the others. You are to me so much that you outweigh all the world.

"I did not choose to have my secret pumped out of me by Augustus Scarborough. I can tell you the whole truth now. Mountjoy Scarborough had told me that he regarded you as affianced to him, and required me to say that I would—drop you. You know now how probable that was. He was drunk on the occasion,—had made himself purposely drunk, so as to get over all scruples,—and attacked me with his stick. Then came a scrimmage, in which he was upset. A sober man has always the best of it." I am afraid that Harry put in that little word sober for a purpose. The opportunity of declaring that he was sober was too good too be lost. "I went away and left him, certainly not dead, nor apparently much hurt. But if I told all this to Augustus Scarborough, your name must have come out. Now I should not mind. Now I might tell the truth about you,—with great pride, if occasion required it. But I couldn't do it then. What would the world have said to two men fighting in the streets about a girl, neither of whom had a right to fight about her? That was the reason why I told an untruth,—because I did not choose to fall into the trap which Augustus Scarborough had laid for me.

"If your mother will understand it all, I do not think she will object to me on that score. If she does quarrel with me, she will only be fighting the Scarborough game, in which I am bound to oppose her. I am afraid the fact is that she prefers the Scarborough game,—not because of my sins, but from auld lang syne.

"But Augustus has got hold of my Uncle Prosper, and has done me a terrible injury. My uncle is a weak man, and has been predisposed against me from other circumstances. He thinks that I have neglected him, and is willing to believe anything against me. He has stopped my income,—two hundred and fifty pounds a year,—and is going to revenge himself on me by marrying a wife. It is too absurd, and the proposed wife is aunt of the man whom my sister is going to marry. It makes such a heap of confusion. Of course, if he becomes the father of a family I shall be nowhere. Had I not better take to some profession? Only what shall I take to? It is almost too late for the Bar. I must see you and talk over it all.

"You have commanded me not to write, and now there is a long letter! It is as well to be hung for a sheep as a lamb. But when a man's character is at stake he feels that he must plead for it. You won't be angry with me because I have not done all that you told me? It was absolutely necessary that I should tell you that I did not mean to ask you to break your engagement, and one word has led to all the others. There shall be only one other, which means more than all the rest:—that I am yours, dearest, with all my heart,   HARRY ANNESLEY."

"There," he said to himself, as he put the letter into the envelope, "she may think it too long, but I am sure she would not have been pleased had I not written at all."

That afternoon Joshua was at the rectory, having just trotted over after business hours at the brewery because of some special word which had to be whispered to

Molly, and Harry put himself in his way as he went out to get on his horse in the stable-yard. "Joshua," he said, "I know that I owe you an apology."

"What for?"

"You have been awfully good to me about the horses, and I have been very ungracious."

"Not at all."

"But I have. The truth is, I have been made thoroughly miserable by circumstances, and, when that occurs, a man cannot pick himself up all at once. It isn't my uncle that has made me wretched. That is a kind of thing that a man has to put up with, and I think that I can bear it as well as another. But an attack has been made upon me which has wounded me."

"I know all about it."

"I don't mind telling you, as you and Molly are going to hit it off together. There is a girl I love, and they have tried to interfere with her."

"They haven't succeeded?"

"No, by George! And now I'm as right as a trivet. When it came across me that she might have—might have yielded, you know,—it was as though all had been over. I ought not to have suspected her."

"But she's all right?"

"Indeed she is. I think you'll like her when you see her some day. If you don't, you have the most extraordinary taste I ever knew a man to possess. How about the horse?"

"I have four, you know."

"What a grand thing it is to be a brewer!"

"And there are two of them will carry you. The other two are not quite up to your weight."

"You haven't been out yet?"

"Well, no;—not exactly out. The governor is the best fellow in the world, but he draws the line at cub-hunting. He says the business should be the business till November. Upon my word, I think he's right."

"And how many days a week after that?"

"Well, three regular. I do get an odd day with the Essex sometimes, and the governor winks."

"The governor hunts himself as often as you."

"Oh dear no; three a week does for the governor, and he is beginning to like frosty weather, and to hear with pleasure that one of the old horses isn't as fit as he should be. He's what they call training off. Good-bye, old fellow. Mind you come out on the 7th of November."

But Harry, though he had been made happy by the letter from Florence, had still a great many troubles on his mind. His first trouble was the having to do something in reference to his uncle. It did not appear to him to be proper to accept his uncle's decision in regard to his income, without, at any rate, attempting to see Mr. Prosper. It would be as though he had taken what was done as a matter of course,—as though his uncle could stop the income without leaving him any ground of complaint. Of the intended marriage,—if it were intended,—he would say nothing. His uncle had never promised him in so many words not to marry, and there would be, he thought, something ignoble in his asking his uncle not to do that which he intended to do himself without even consulting his uncle about it. As he turned it all over in his mind he began to ask himself why his uncle should be asked to do anything for him, whereas he had never done anything for his uncle. He had been told that he was the heir, not to the uncle, but to Buston, and had gradually been taught to look upon Buston as his right,—as though he had a certain defeasible property in the acres. He now began to perceive that there was no such thing. A tacit contract had been made on his behalf, and he had declined to accept his share of the contract. But he had been debarred from following any profession by his uncle's promised allowance. He did not think that he could complain to his uncle about the proposed marriage; but he did think that he could ask a question or two as to the income.

Without saying a word to any of his own family he walked across the park, and presented himself at the front-door of Buston Hall. In doing so he would not go upon the grass. He had told his father that he would not enter the park, and therefore kept himself to the road. And he had dressed himself with some little care, as a man does when he feels that he is going forth on some mission of importance. Had he intended to call on old Mr. Thoroughbung there would have been no such care. And he rung at the front-door, instead of entering the house by any of the numerous side inlets with which he was well acquainted. The butler understood the ring, and put on his company-coat when he answered the bell.

"Is my uncle at home, Matthew?" he said.

"Mr. Prosper, Mr. Harry? Well, no; I can't say that he just is;" and the old man groaned, and wheezed, and looked unhappy.

"He is not often out at this time." Matthew groaned again, and wheezed more deeply, and looked unhappier. "I suppose you mean to say that he has given orders that I am not to be admitted?" To this the butler made no answer, but only looked woefully into the young man's face. "What is the meaning of it all, Matthew?"

"Oh, Mr. Harry, you shouldn't ask me, as is merely a servant."

Harry felt the truth of this rebuke, but was not going to put up with it.

"That's all my eye, Matthew; you know all about it as well as any one. It is so. He does not want to see me."

"I don't think he does, Mr. Harry."

"And why not? You know the whole of my family story as well as my father does, or my uncle. Why does he shut his doors against me, and send me word that he does not want to see me?"

"Well Mr. Harry, I'm not just able to say why he does it,—and you the heir. But if I was asked I should make answer that it has come along of them sermons." Then Matthew looked very serious, and bathed his head.

"I suppose so."

"That was it, Mr. Harry. We, none of us, were very fond of the sermons."

"I dare say not."

"We in the kitchen. But we was bound to have them, or we should have lost our places."

"And now I must lose my place." The butler said nothing, but his face assented. "A little hard, isn't it, Matthew? But I wish to say a few words to my uncle,—not to express any regret about the sermons, but to ask what it is that he intends to do." Here Matthew shook his head very slowly. "He has given positive orders that I shall not be admitted?"

"It must be over my dead body, Mr. Harry," and he stood in the way with the door in his hand, as though intending to sacrifice himself should he be called upon to do so by the nature of the circumstances. Harry, however, did not put him to the test; but bidding him good-bye with some little joke as to his fidelity, made his way back to the parsonage.

That night before he went to bed he wrote a letter to his uncle, as to which he said not a word to either his father, or mother, or sisters. He thought that the letter was a good letter, and would have been proud to show it; but he feared that either his father or mother would advise him not to send it, and he was ashamed to read it to Molly. He therefore sent the letter across the park the next morning by the gardener.

The letter was as follows:

My Dear Uncle,—

My father has shown me your letter to him, and, of course, I feel it incumbent on me to take some notice of it. Not wishing to trouble you with a letter I called this morning, but I was told by Matthew that you would not see me. As you have expressed yourself to my father very severely as to my conduct, I am sure you will agree with me that I ought not to let the matter pass by without making my own defence.

You say that there was a row in the streets between Mountjoy Scarborough and myself in which he was 'left for dead.' When I left him I did not think he had been much hurt, nor have I had reason to think so since. He had attacked me, and I had simply defended myself. He had come upon me by surprise; and, when I had shaken him off, I went away. Then in a day or two he had disappeared. Had he been killed, or much hurt, the world would have heard of it: but the world simply heard that he had disappeared, which could hardly have been the case had he been much hurt.

Then you say that I denied, in conversation with Augustus Scarborough, that I had seen his brother on the night in question. I did deny it. Augustus Scarborough, who was evidently well acquainted with the whole transaction, and who had, I believe, assisted his brother in disappearing, wished to learn from me what I had done, and to hide what he had done. He wished to saddle me with the disgrace of his brother's departure, and I did not choose to fall into his trap. At the moment of his asking me he knew that his brother was safe. I think that the word 'lie,' as used by you, is very severe for such an occurrence. A man is not generally held to be bound to tell everything respecting himself to the first person that shall ask him. If you will ask any man who knows the world,—my father, for instance,—I think you will be told that such conduct was not faulty.

But it is at any rate necessary that I should ask you what you intend to do in reference to my future life. I am told that you intend to stop the income which I have hitherto received. Will this be considerate on your part? (In his first copy of the letter Harry had asked whether it would be "fair," and had then changed the word for one that was milder.) When I took my degree you yourself said that it would not be necessary that I should go into any profession, because you would allow me an income, and would then provide for me, I took your advice in opposition to my father's, because it seemed then that I was to depend on you rather than on him. You cannot deny that I shall have been treated hardly if I now be turned loose upon the world.

I shall be happy to come and see you if you shall wish it, so as to save you the trouble of writing to me.

Your affectionate nephew,   HENRY ANNESLEY.

Harry might have been sure that his uncle would not see him,—probably was sure when he added the last paragraph. Mr. Prosper enjoyed greatly two things,—the mysticism of being invisible and the opportunity of writing a letter. Mr. Prosper had not a large correspondence, but it was laborious, and, as he thought, effective. He believed that he did know how to write a letter, and he went about it with a will. It was not probable that he would make himself common by seeing his nephew on such an occasion, or that he would omit the opportunity of spending an entire morning with pen and ink. The result was very short, but, to his idea, it was satisfactory.

"SIR," he began. He considered this matter very deeply; but as the entire future of his own life was concerned in it he felt that it became him to be both grave and severe.

I have received your letter and have read it with attention. I observe that you admit that you told Mr. Augustus Scarborough a deliberate untruth. This is what the plain-speaking world, when it wishes to be understood as using the unadorned English language, which is always the language which I prefer myself, calls a lie—A LIE! I do not choose that this humble property shall fall at my death into the hands of A LIAR. Therefore I shall take steps to prevent it,—which may or may not be successful.

As such steps, whatever may be their result, are to be taken, the income,—intended to prepare you for another alternative, which may possibly not now be forthcoming,—will naturally now be no longer allowed.—I am, sir, your obedient servant,   PETER PROSPER.

The first effect of the letter was to produce laughter at the rectory. Harry could not but show it to his father, and in an hour or two it became known to his mother and sister, and, under an oath of secrecy, to Joshua Thoroughbung. It could not be matter of laughter when the future hopes of Miss Matilda Thoroughbung were taken into consideration. "I declare I don't know what you are all laughing about," said Kate, "except that Uncle Peter does use such comical phrases." But Mrs. Annesley, though the most good-hearted woman in the world, was almost angry. "I don't know what you all see to laugh at in it. Peter has in his hands the power of making or marring Harry's future."

"But he hasn't," said Harry.

"Or he mayn't have," said the rector.

"It's all in the hands of the Almighty," said Mrs. Annesley, who felt herself bound to retire from the room and to take her daughter with her.

But, when they were alone, both the father and his son were very angry. "I have done with him forever," said Harry. "Let come what may, I will never see him or speak to him again. A 'lie,' and 'liar!' He has written those words in that way so as to salve his own conscience for the injustice he is doing. He knows that I am not a liar. He cannot understand what a liar means, or he would know that he is one himself."

"A man seldom has such knowledge as that."

"Is it not so when he stigmatizes me in this way merely as an excuse to himself? He wants to be rid of me,—probably because I did not sit and hear him read the sermons. Let that pass. I may have been wrong in that, and he may be justified; but because of that he cannot believe really that I have been a liar,—a liar in such a determined way as to make me unfit to be his heir."

"He is a fool, Harry! That is the worst of him."

"I don't think it is the worst."

"You cannot have worse. It is dreadful to have to depend on a fool,—to have to trust to a man who cannot tell wrong from right. Your uncle intends to be a good man. If it were brought home to him that he were doing a wrong he would not do it. He would not rob; he would not steal; he must not commit murder, and the rest of it. But he is a fool, and he does not know when he is doing these things."

"I will wash my hands of him."

"Yes; and he will wash his hands of you. You do not know him as I do. He has taken it into his silly head that you are the chief of sinners because you said what was not true to that man, who seems really to be the sinner, and nothing will eradicate the idea. He will go and marry that woman because he thinks that in that way he can best carry his purpose, and then he will repent at leisure. I used to tell you that you had better listen to the sermons."

"And now I must pay for it!"

"Well, my boy, it is no good crying for spilt milk. As I was saying just now, there is nothing worse than a fool."

CHAPTER XXVI. MARMADUKE LODGE

On the 7th of next month two things occurred, each of great importance. Hunting commenced in the Puckeridge country, and Harry with that famous mare Belladonna was there. And Squire Prosper was driven in his carriage into Buntingford, and made his offer with all due formality to Miss Thoroughbung. The whole household, including Matthew, and the cook, and the coachman, and the boy, and the two house-maids, knew what he was going to do. It would be difficult to say how they knew, because he was a man who never told anything. He was the last man in England who, on such a matter, would have made a confidant of his butler. He never spoke to a servant about matters unconnected with their service. He considered that to do so would be altogether against his dignity. Nevertheless when he ordered his carriage, which he did not do very frequently at this time of the year, when the horses were wanted on the farm,—and of which he gave twenty-four hours' notice to all the persons concerned,—and when early in the morning he ordered that his Sunday suit should be prepared for wearing, and when his aspect grew more and more serious as the hour drew nigh, it was well understood by them all that he was going to make the offer that day.

He was both proud and fearful as to the thing to be done,—proud that he, the Squire of Buston, should be called on to take so important a step; proud by anticipation of his feelings as he would return home a jolly thriving wooer,—and yet a little fearful lest he might not succeed. Were he to fail the failure would be horrible to him. He knew that every man and woman about the place would know all about it. Among the secrets of the family there was a story, never now mentioned, of his having done the same thing, once before. He was then a young man, about twenty-five, and he had come forth to lay himself and Buston at the feet of a baronet's daughter who lived some twenty-five miles off. She was very beautiful, and was said to have a fitting dower, but he had come back, and had shut himself up in the house for a week afterward. To no human ears had he ever since spoken of his interview with Miss Courteney. The doings of that day had been wrapped in impenetrable darkness. But all Buston and the neighboring parishes had known that Miss Courteney had refused him. Since that day he had never gone forth again on such a mission.

There were those who said of him that his love had been so deep and enduring that he had never got the better of it. Miss Courteney had been married to a much grander lover, and had been taken off to splendid circles. But he had never mentioned her name. That story of his abiding love was throughly believed by his sister, who used to tell it of him to his credit when at the rectory the rector would declare him to be a fool. But the rector used to say that he was dumb from pride, or that he could not bear to have it known that he had failed at anything. At any rate, he had never again attempted love, and had formally declared to his sister that, as he did not intend to marry, Harry should be regarded as his son. Then at last had come the fellowship, and he had been proud of his heir, thinking that in some way he had won the fellowship himself, as he had paid the bills. But now all was altered, and he was to go forth to his wooing again.

There had been a rumor about the country that he was already accepted; but such was not the case. He had fluttered about Buntingford, thinking of it: but he had never put the question. To his thinking it would not have been becoming to do so without some ceremony. Buston was not to be made away during the turnings of a quadrille or as a part of an ordinary conversation. It was not probable,—nay, it was impossible,—that he should mention the subject to any one; but still he must visibly prepare for it, and I think that he was aware that the world around him knew what he was about.

And the Thoroughbung's knew, and Miss Matilda Thoroughbung knew well. All Buntingford knew. In those old days in which he had sought the hand of the baronet's daughter, the baronet's daughter, and the baronet's wife, and the baronet himself, had known what was coming, though Mr. Prosper thought that the secret dwelt alone in his own bosom. Nor did he dream now that Harry and Harry's father, and Harry's mother and sisters, had all laughed at the conspicuous gravity of his threat. It was the general feeling on the subject which made the rumor current that the deed had been done. But when he came down-stairs with one new gray kid-glove on, and the other dangling in his hand, nothing had been done.

"Drive to Buntingford," said the squire.

"Yes, sir," said Matthew, the door of the carriage in his hand.

"To Marmaduke Lodge."

"Yes, sir." Then Matthew told the coachman, who had heard the instructions very plainly, and knew them before he had heard them. The squire threw himself back in the carriage, and applied himself to wondering how he should do the deed. He had, in truth, barely studied the words,—but not, finally, the manner of delivering them. With his bare hand up to his eyes so that he might hold the glove unsoiled in the other, he devoted his intellect to the task; nor did he withdraw his hand till the carriage turned in at the gate. The drive up to the door of Marmaduke Lodge was very short, and he had barely time to arrange his waistcoat and his whiskers before the carriage stood still. He was soon told that Miss Thoroughbung was at home, and within a moment he found himself absolutely standing on the carpet in her presence.

Report had dealt unkindly with Miss Thoroughbung in the matter of her age. Report always does deal unkindly with unmarried young women who have ceased to be girls. There is an idea that they will wish to make themselves out to be younger than they are, and therefore report always makes them older. She had been called forty-five, and even fifty. Her exact age at this moment was forty-two, and as Mr. Prosper was only fifty there was no discrepancy in the marriage. He would have been young-looking for his age, but for an air of ancient dandyism which had grown upon him. He was somewhat dry, too, and skinny, with high cheekbones and large dull eyes. But he was clean, and grave, and orderly,—a man promising well to a lady on the lookout for a husband. Miss Thoroughbung was fat, fair, and forty to the letter, and she had a just measure of her own good looks, of which she was not unconscious. But she was specially conscious of twenty-five thousand pounds, the possession of which had hitherto stood in the way of her search after a husband. It was said commonly about Buntingford that she looked too high, seeing that she was only a Thoroughbung and had no more than twenty-five thousand pounds.

But Miss Tickle was in the room, and might have been said to be in the way, were it not that a little temporary relief was felt by Mr. Prosper to be a comfort. Miss Tickle was at any rate twenty years older than Miss Thoroughbung, and was of all slaves at the same time the humblest and the most irritating. She never asked for anything, but was always painting the picture of her own deserts. "I hope I have the pleasure of seeing Miss Tickle quite well," said the squire, as soon as he had paid his first compliments to the lady of his love.

"Thank you, Mr. Prosper, pretty well. My anxiety is all for Matilda." Matilda had been Matilda to her since she had been a little girl, and Miss Tickle was not going now to drop the advantage which the old intimacy gave her.

"I trust there is no cause for it."

"Well, I'm not so sure. She coughed a little last night, and would not eat her supper. We always do have a little supper. A despatched crab it was; and when she would not eat it I knew there was something wrong."

"Nonsense! what a fuss you make. Well, Mr. Prosper, have you seen your nephew yet?"

"No, Miss Thoroughbung; nor do I intend to see him. The young man has disgraced himself."

"Dear, dear; how sad!"

"Young men do disgrace themselves, I fear, very often," said Miss Tickle.

"We won't talk about it, if you please, because it is a family affair."

"Oh no," said Miss Thoroughbung.

"At least, not as yet. It may be;—but never mind, I would not wish to be premature in anything."

"I am always telling Matilda so. She is so impulsive. But as you may have matters of business, Mr. Prosper, on which to speak to Miss Thoroughbung, I will retire."

"It is very thoughtful on your part, Miss Tickle."

Then Miss Tickle retired; from which it may be surmised that the probable circumstances of the interview had been already discussed between the ladies. Mr. Prosper drew a long breath, and sighed audibly, as soon as he was alone with the object of his affections. He wondered whether men were ever bright and jolly in such circumstances. He sighed again, and then he began: "Miss Thoroughbung!"

"Mr. Prosper!"

All the prepared words had flown from his memory. He could not even bethink himself how he ought to begin. And, unfortunately, so much must depend upon manner! But the property was unembarrassed, and Miss Thoroughbung thought it probable that she might be allowed to do what she would with her own money. She had turned it all over to the right and to the left, and she was quite minded to accept him. With this view she had told Miss Tickle to leave the room, and she now felt that she was bound to give the gentleman what help might be in her power. "Oh, Miss Thoroughbung!" he said.

"Mr. Prosper, you and I are such good friends, that—that—that—"

"Yes, indeed. You can have no more true friend than I am,—not even Miss Tickle."

"Oh, bother Miss Tickle! Miss Tickle is very well."

"Exactly so. Miss Tickle is very well; a most estimable person."

"We'll leave her alone just at present."

"Yes, certainly. We had better leave her alone in our present conversation. Not but what I have a strong regard for her." Mr. Prosper had surely not thought of the opening he might be giving as to a future career for Miss Tickle by such an assertion.

"So have I, for the matter of that, but we'll drop her just now." Then she paused, but he paused also. "You have come over to Buntingford to-day probably in order that you might congratulate them at the brewery on the marriage with one of your family." Then Mr. Prosper frowned, but she did not care for his frowning. "It will not be a bad match for the young lady, as Joshua is fairly steady, and the brewery is worth money."

"I could have wished him a better brother-in-law," said the lover, who was taken away from the consideration of his love by the allusion to the Annesleys. He had thought of all that, and in the dearth of fitting objects of affection had resolved to endure the drawback of the connection. But it had for a while weighed very seriously with him, so that had the twenty-five thousand pounds been twenty thousand pounds, he might have taken himself to Miss Puffle, who lived near Saffron Walden and who would own Snickham Manor when her father died. The property was said to be involved, and Miss Puffle was certainly forty-eight. As an heir was the great desideratum, he had resolved that Matilda Thoroughbung should be the lady, in spite of the evils attending the new connection. He did feel that in throwing over Harry he would have to abandon all the Annesleys, and to draw a line between himself with Miss Thoroughbung and the whole family of the Thoroughbungs generally.

"You mustn't be too bitter against poor Molly," said Miss Thoroughbung.

Mr. Prosper did not like to be called bitter, and, in spite of the importance of the occasion, could not but show that he did not like it. "I don't think that we need talk about it."

"Oh dear no. Kate and Miss Tickle need neither of them be talked about." Mr. Prosper disliked all familiarity, and especially that of being laughed at, but Miss Thoroughbung did laugh. So he drew himself up, and dangled his glove more slowly than before. "Then you were not going on to congratulate them at the brewery?"

"Certainly not."

"I did not know."

"My purpose carries me no farther than Marmaduke Lodge. I have no desire to see any one to-day besides Miss Thoroughbung."

"That is a compliment."

Then his memory suddenly brought back to him one of his composed sentences. "In beholding Miss Thoroughbung I behold her on whom I hope I may depend for all the future happiness of my life." He did feel that it had come in the right place. It had been intended to be said immediately after her acceptance of him. But it did very well where it was. It expressed, as he assured himself, the feelings of his heart, and must draw from her some declaration of hers.

"Goodness gracious me, Mr. Prosper!"

This sort of coyness was to have been expected, and he therefore continued with another portion of his prepared words, which now came glibly enough to him. But it was a previous portion. It was all the same to Miss Thoroughbung, as it declared plainly the gentleman's intention. "If I can induce you to listen to me favorably, I shall say of myself that I am the happiest gentleman in Hertfordshire."

"Oh, Mr. Prosper!"

"My purpose is to lay at your feet my hand, my heart, and the lands of Buston." Here he was again going backward, but it did not much matter now in what sequence the words were said. The offer had been thoroughly completed and was thoroughly understood.

"A lady, Mr. Prosper, has to think of these things," said Miss Thoroughbung.

"Of course I would not wish to hurry you prematurely to any declaration of your affections."

"But there are other considerations, Mr. Prosper. You know about my property?"

"Nothing particularly. It has not been a matter of consideration with me." This he said with some slight air of offence. He was a gentleman, whereas Miss Thoroughbung was hardly a lady. Matter of consideration her money of course had been. How should he not consider it? But he was aware that he ought not to rush on that subject, but should leave it to the arrangement of lawyers, expressing his own views through her own lawyer. To her it was the thing of most importance, and she had no feelings which induced her to be silent on a matter so near to her. She rushed.

"But it has to be considered, Mr. Prosper. It is all my own, and comes to very nearly one thousand a year. I think it is nine hundred and seventy-two pounds six shillings and eightpence. Of course, when there is so much money it would have to be tied up somehow." Mr. Prosper was undoubtedly disgusted, and if he could have receded at this moment would have transferred his affections to Miss Puffle. "Of course you understand that."

She had not accepted him as yet, nor said a word of her regard for him. All that went, it seemed, as a matter of no importance whatever. He had been standing for the last few minutes, and now he remained standing and looking at her. They were both silent, so that he was obliged to speak. "I understand that between a lady and gentleman so circumstanced there should be a settlement."

"Just so."

"I also have some property," said Mr. Prosper, with a touch of pride in his tone.

"Of course you have. Goodness gracious me! Why else would you come? You have got Buston, which I suppose is two thousand a year. At any rate it has that name. But it isn't your own."

"Not my own?"

"Well, no. You couldn't leave it to your widow, so that she might give it to any one she pleased when you were gone." Here the gentleman frowned very darkly, and thought that after all Miss Puffle would be the woman for him. "All that has to be considered, and it makes Buston not exactly your own. If I were to have a daughter she wouldn't have it."

"No, not a daughter," said Mr. Prosper, still wondering at the thorough knowledge of the business in hand displayed by the lady.

"Oh, if it were to be a son, that would be all right, and then my money would go to the younger children, divided equally between the boys and girls." Mr. Prosper shook his head as he found himself suddenly provided with so plentiful and thriving a family. "That, I suppose, would be the way of the settlement, together with a certain income out of Buston set apart for my use. It ought to be considered that I should have to provide a house to live in. This belongs to my brother, and I pay him forty pounds a year for it. It should be something better than this."

"My dear Miss Thoroughbung, the lawyer would do all that." There did come upon him an idea that she, with her aptitude for business, would not be altogether a bad helpmate.

"The lawyers are very well; but in a transaction of this kind there is nothing like the principals understanding each other. Young women are always robbed when their money is left altogether to the gentlemen."

"Robbed!"

"Don't suppose I mean you, Mr. Prosper; and the robbery I mean is not considered disgraceful at all. The gentlemen I mean are the fathers and the brothers, and the uncles and the lawyers. And they intend to do right after the custom of their fathers and uncles. But woman's rights are coming up."

"I hate woman's rights."

"Nevertheless they are coming up. A young woman doesn't get taken in as she used to do. I don't mean any offence, you know." This was said in reply to Mr. Prosper's repeated frown. "Since woman's rights have come up a young woman is better able to fight her own battle."

Mr. Prosper was willing to admit that Miss Thoroughbung was fair, but she was fat also, and at least forty. There was hardly need that she should refer so often to her own unprotected youth. "I should like to have the spending of my own income, Mr. Prosper;—that's a fact."

"Oh, indeed!"

"Yes, I should. I shouldn't care to have to go to my husband if I wanted to buy a pair of stockings."

"An allowance, I should say."

"And that should be my own income."

"Nothing to go to the house?"

"Oh yes. There might be certain things which I might agree to pay for. A pair of ponies I should like."

"I always keep a carriage and a pair of horses."

"But the ponies would be my lookout. I shouldn't mind paying for my own maid, and the champagne, and my clothes, of course, and the fish-monger's bill. There would be Miss Tickle, too. You said you would like Miss Tickle. I should have to pay for her. That would be about enough, I think."

Mr. Prosper was thoroughly disgusted; but when he left Marmaduke Lodge he had not said a word as to withdrawing from his offer. She declared that she would put her terms into writing and give them to her lawyer, who would communicate with Mr. Grey.

Mr. Prosper was surprised to find that she knew the name of his lawyer, who was in truth our old friend. And then, while he was still hesitating, she astounded,—nay, shocked him by her mode of ending the conference. She got up and, throwing her arms round his neck, kissed him most affectionately. After that there was no retreating for Mr. Prosper,—no immediate mode of retreat, at all events. He could only back out of the room, and get into his carriage, and be carried home as quickly as possible.

CHAPTER XXVII. THE PROPOSAL

It had never happened to him before. The first thought that came upon Mr. Prosper, when he got into his carriage, was that it had never occurred to him before. He did not reflect that he had not put himself in the way of it: but now the strangeness of the sensation overwhelmed him. He inquired of himself whether it was pleasant, but he found himself compelled to answer the question with a negative. It should have come from him, but not yet; not yet, probably, for some weeks. But it had been done, and by the doing of it she had sealed him utterly as her own. There was no getting out of it now. He did feel that he ought not to attempt to get out of it after what had taken place. He was not sure but that the lady had planned it all with that purpose; but he was sure that a strong foundation had been laid for a breach of promise case if he were to attempt to escape. What might not a jury do against him, giving damages out of the acres of Buston Hall? And then Miss Thoroughbung would go over to the other Thoroughbungs and to the Annesleys, and his condition would become intolerable. In some moments, as he was driven home, he was not sure but that it had all been got up as a plot against him by the Annesleys.

When he got out of his carriage Matthew knew that things had gone badly with his master; but he could not conjecture in what way. The matter had been fully debated in the kitchen, and it had been there decided that Miss Thoroughbung was certainly to be brought home as the future mistress of Buston. The step to be taken by their master was not popular in the Buston kitchen. It had been there considered that Master Harry was to be the future master, and, by some perversity of intellect, they had all thought that this would occur soon. Matthew was much older than the squire, who was hardly to be called a sickly man, and yet Matthew had made up his mind that Mr. Harry was to reign over him as Squire of Buston. When, therefore, the tidings came that Miss Thoroughbung was to brought to Buston as the mistress, there had been some slight symptoms of rebellion. "They didn't want any 'Tilda Thoroughbung there." They had their own idea of a lady and a gentleman, which, as in all such cases, was perfectly correct. They knew the squire to be a fool, but they believed him to be a gentleman. They heard that Miss Thoroughbung was a clever woman, but they did not believe her to be a lady. Matthew had said a few words to the cook as to a public-house at Stevenage. She had told him not to be an old fool, and that he would lose his money, but she had thought of the public-house. There had been a mutinous feeling. Matthew helped his master out of the carriage, and then came a revulsion. That "froth of a beer-barrel," as Matthew had dared to call her, had absolutely refused his master.

Mr. Prosper went into the house very meditative, and sad at heart. It was a matter almost of regret to him that it had not been as Matthew supposed. But he was caught and bound, and must make the best of it. He thought of all the particulars of her proposed mode of living, and recapitulated them to himself. A pair of ponies, her own maid, champagne, the fish-monger's bill, and Miss Tickle. Miss Puffle would certainly not have required such expensive luxuries. Champagne and the fish would require company for their final consumption.

The ponies assumed a tone of being quite opposed to that which he had contemplated. He questioned with himself whether he would like Miss Tickle as a perpetual inmate. He had, in sheer civility, expressed a liking for Miss Tickle, but what need could there be to a married woman of a Miss Tickle? And then he thought of the education of the five or six children which she had almost promised him! He had suggested to himself simply an heir,—just one heir,—so that the nefarious Harry might be cut out. He already saw that he would not be enriched to the extent of a shilling by the lady's income. Then there would be all the trouble and the disgrace of a separate purse. He felt that there would be disgrace in having the fish and champagne, which were consumed in his own house,—paid for by his wife without reference to him. What if the lady had a partiality for champagne? He knew nothing about it, and would know nothing about it, except when he saw it in her heightened color. Despatched crabs for supper! He always went to bed at ten, and had a tumbler of barley-water brought to him,—a glass of barley-water with just a squeeze of lemon-juice.

He saw ruin before him. No doubt she was a good manager, but she would be a good manager for herself. Would it not be better for him to stand the action for breach of promise, and betake himself to Miss Puffle? But Miss Puffle was fifty, and there could be no doubt that the lady ought to be younger than the gentleman. He was much distressed in mind. If he broke off with Miss Thoroughbung, ought he to do so at once, before she had had time to put the matter into the hands of the lawyer? And on what plea should he do it? Before he went to bed that night he did draw out a portion of a letter, which, however, was never sent:

"MY DEAR MISS THOROUGHBUNG,—

"In the views which we both promulgated this morning I fear that there was some essential misunderstanding as to the mode of life which had occurred to both of us. You, as was so natural at your age, and with your charms, have not been slow to anticipate a coming period of uncheckered delights. Your allusion to a pony-carriage, and other incidental allusions,"—he did not think it well to mention more particularly the fish and the champagne,—"have made clear the sort of future life which you have pictured to yourself. Heaven forbid that I should take upon myself to find fault with anything so pleasant and so innocent! But my prospects of life are different, and in seeking the honor of an alliance with you I was looking for a quiet companion in my declining years, and it might be also to a mother to a possible future son. When you honored me with an unmistakable sign of your affection, on my going, I was just about to explain all this. You must excuse me if my mouth was then stopped by the mutual ardor of our feeling. I was about to say—" But he had found it difficult to explain what he had been about to say, and on the next morning, when the time for writing had come, he heard news which detained him for the day, and then the opportunity was gone.

On the following morning, when Matthew appeared at his bedside with his cup of tea at nine o'clock, tidings were brought him. He took in the *Buntingford Gazette*, which came twice a week, and as Matthew laid it, opened and unread, in its accustomed place, he gave the information, which he had no doubt gotten from the paper. "You haven't heard it, sir, I suppose, as yet?"

"Heard what?"

"About Miss Puffle."

"What about Miss Puffle? I haven't heard a word. What about Miss Puffle?" He had been thinking that moment of Miss Puffle,—of how she would be superior to Miss Thoroughbung in many ways,—so that he sat up in his bed, holding the untasted tea in his hand.

"She's gone off with young Farmer Tazlehurst."

"Miss Puffle gone off, and with her father's tenant's son!"

"Yes indeed, sir. She and her father have been quarrelling for the last ten years, and now she's off. She was always riding and roistering about the country with them dogs and them men; and now she's gone."

"Oh heavens!" exclaimed the squire, thinking of his own escape.

"Yes, indeed, sir. There's no knowing what any one of them is up to. Unless they gets married afore they're thirty, or thirty-five at most, they're most sure to get such ideas into their head as no one can mostly approve." This had been intended by Matthew as a word of caution to his master, but had really the opposite effect. He resolved at the moment that the latter should not be said of Miss Thoroughbung.

And he turned Matthew out of the room with a flea in his ear. "How dare you speak in that way of your betters? Mr. Puffle, the lady's father, has for many years been my friend. I am not saying anything of the lady, nor saying that she has done right. Of course, down-stairs, in the servants' hall, you can say what you please; but up here, in my presence, you should not speak in such language of a lady behind whose chair you may be called upon to wait."

"Very well, sir; I won't no more," said Matthew, retiring with mock humility. But he had shot his bolt, and he supposed successfully. He did not know what had taken place between his master and Miss Thoroughbung; but he did think that his speech might assist in preventing a repetition of the offer.

Miss Puffle gone off with the tenant's son! The news made matrimony doubly dangerous to him, and yet robbed him of the chief reason by which he was to have been driven to send her a letter. He could not, at any rate, now fall back upon Miss Puffle. And he thought that nothing would have induced Miss Thoroughbung to go off with one of the carters from the brewery. Whatever faults she might have, they did not lie in that direction. Champagne and ponies were, as faults, less deleterious.

Miss Puffle gone off with young Tazlehurst,—a lady of fifty, with a young man of twenty-five! and she the reputed heiress of Snickham Manor! It was a comfort to him as he remembered that Snickham Manor had been bought no longer ago than by the father of the present owner. The Prospers been at Buston ever since the time of George the First. You cannot make a silk purse out of a sow's ear. He had been ever assuring himself of that fact, which was now more of a fact than ever. And fifty years old! It was quite shocking. With a steady middle-aged man like himself, and with the approval of her family, marriage might have been thought of. But this harum-scarum young tenant's son, who was in no respect a gentleman, whose only thought was of galloping over hedges and ditches, such an idea showed a state of mind which—well, absolutely disgusted him. Mr. Prosper, because he had grown old himself, could not endure to think that others, at his age, should retain a smack of their youth. There are ladies besides Miss Puffle who like to ride across the country with a young man before them, or perhaps following, and never think much of their fifty years.

But the news certainly brought to him a great change of feelings, so that the letter to which he had devoted the preceding afternoon was put back into the letter-case, and was never finished. And his mind immediately recurred to Miss Thoroughbung, and he bethought himself that the objection which he felt was, perhaps, in part frivolous. At any rate, she was a better woman than Miss Puffle. She certainly would run after no farmer's son. Though she she might be fond of champagne, it was, he thought, chiefly for other people. Though she was ambitious of ponies, the ambition might be checked. At any rate, she could pay for her own ponies, whereas Mr. Puffle was a very hale old man of seventy. Puffle, he told himself, had married young, and might live for the next ten years, or twenty. To Mr. Prosper, whose imagination did not fly far afield, the world afforded at present but two ladies. These were Miss Puffle and Miss Thoroughbung, and as Miss

Puffle had fallen out of the running, there seemed to be a walk-over for Miss Thoroughbung.

He did think, during the two or three days which passed without any farther step on his part,—he did think how it might be were he to remain unmarried. As regarded his own comfort, he was greatly tempted. Life would remain so easy to him! But then duty demanded of him that he should marry, and he was a man who, in honest, sober talk, thought much of his duty. He was absurdly credulous, and as obstinate as a mule. But he did wish to do what was right. He had been convinced that Harry Annesley was a false knave, and had been made to swear an oath that Harry should not be his heir. Harry had been draped in the blackest colors, and to each daub of black something darker had been added by his uncle's memory of those neglected sermons. It was now his first duty in life to beget an heir, and for that purpose a wife must be had.

Putting aside the ponies and the champagne,—and the despatched crab, the sound of which, as coming to him from Miss Tickle's mouth, was uglier than the other sounds,—he still thought that Miss Thoroughbung would answer his purpose. From her side there would not be making of a silk purse; but then "the boy" would be his boy as well as hers, and would probably take more after the father. He passed much of these days with the "Peerage" in his hand, and satisfied himself that the best blood had been maintained frequently by second-rate marriages. Health was a great thing. Health in the mother was everything. Who could be more healthy than Miss Thoroughbung? Then he thought of that warm embrace. Perhaps, after all, it was right that she should embrace him after what he had said to her.

Three days only had passed by, and he was still thinking what ought to be his next step, when there came to him a letter from Messrs. Soames & Simpson, attorneys in Buntingford. He had heard of Messrs. Soames & Simpson, had been familiar with their names for the last twenty years, but had never dreamed that his own private affairs should become a matter of consultation in their office. Messrs. Grey & Barry, of Lincoln's Inn, were his lawyers, who were quite gentlemen. He knew nothing against Messrs. Soames & Simpson, but he thought that their work consisted generally in the recovery of local debts. Messrs. Soames & Simpson now wrote to him with full details as to his future life. Their client Miss Thoroughbung, had communicated to them his offer of marriage. They were acquainted with all the lady's circumstances, and she had asked them for their advice. They had proposed to her that the use of her own income should be by deed left to herself. Some proportion of it should go into the house, and might be made matter of agreement. They suggested that an annuity of a thousand pounds a year, in shape of dower, should be secured to their client in the event of her outliving Mr. Prosper. The estate should, of course, be settled on the eldest child. The mother's property should be equally divided among the other children. Buston Hall should be the residence of the widow till the eldest son should be twenty-four, after which Mr. Prosper would no doubt feel that their client would have to provide a home for herself. Messrs. Soames & Simpson did not think that there was anything in this to which Mr. Prosper would object, and if this were so, they would immediately prepare the settlement. "That woman didn't say against it, after all," said Matthew to himself as he gave the letter from the lawyers to his master.

The letter made Mr. Prosper very angry. It did, in truth, contain nothing more than a repetition of the very terms which the lady had herself suggested; but coming to him through these local lawyers it was doubly distasteful. What was he to do? He felt it to be out of the question to accede at once. Indeed, he had a strong repugnance to putting himself into communication with the Buntingford lawyers. Had the matter been other than it was, he would have gone to the rector for advice. The rector generally advised him.

But that was out of the question now. He had seen his sister once since his visit to Buntingford, but had said nothing to her about it. Indeed, he had been anything but communicative, so that Mrs. Annesley had been forced to leave him with a feeling almost of offense. There was no help to be had in that quarter, and he could only write to Mr. Grey, and ask that gentleman to assist him in his difficulties.

He did write to Mr. Grey, begging for his immediate attention. "There is that fool Prosper going to marry a brewer's daughter down at Buntingford," said Mr. Grey to his daughter.

"He's sixty years old."

"No, my love. He looks it, but he's only fifty. A man at fifty is supposed to be young enough to marry. There's a nephew who has been brought up as his heir; that's the hard part of it. And the nephew is mixed up in some way with the Scarboroughs."

"Is it he who is to marry that young lady?"

"I think it is. And now there's some devil's play going on. I've got nothing to do with it."

"But you will have."

"Not a turn. Mr. Prosper can marry if he likes it. They have sent him most abominable proposals as to the lady's money; and as to her jointure, I must stop that if I can, though I suppose he is not such a fool as to give way."

"Is he soft?"

"Well, not exactly. He likes his own money. But he's a gentleman, and wants nothing but what is or ought to be his own."

"There are but few like that now."

"It's true of him. But then he does not know what is his own, or what ought to be. He's almost the biggest fool I have ever known, and will do an injustice to that boy simply from ignorance." Then he drafted his letter to Mr. Prosper, and gave it to Dolly to read. "That's what I shall propose. The clerk can put it into proper language. He must offer less than he means to give."

"Is that honest, father?"

"It's honest on my part, knowing the people with whom I have to deal. If I were to lay down the strict minimum which he should grant, he would add other things which would cause him to act not in accordance with my advice. I have to make allowance for his folly,—a sort of windage, which is not dishonest. Had he referred her lawyers to me I could have been as hard and honest as you please." All which did not quite satisfy Dolly's strict ideas of integrity.

But the terms proposed were that the lady's means should be divided so that one-half should go to herself for her own personal expenses, and the other half to her husband for the use of the house; that the lady should put up with a jointure of two hundred and fifty pounds, which ought to suffice when joined to her own property, and that the settlement among the children should be as recommended by Messrs. Soames & Simpson.

"And if there are not any children, papa?"

"Then each will receive his or her own property."

"Because it may be so."

"Certainly, my dear; very probably."

CHAPTER XXVIII. MR. HARKAWAY

When the first Monday in November came Harry was still living at the rectory. Indeed, what other home had he in which to live? Other friends had become shy of him besides his uncle. He had been accustomed to receive many invitations. Young men who are the heirs to properties, and are supposed to be rich because they are idle, do get themselves asked about here and there, and think a great deal of themselves in consequence. "There's young Jones. He is fairly good-looking, but hasn't a word to say for himself. He will do to pair off with Miss Smith, who'll talk for a dozen. He can't hit a hay-stack, but he's none the worse for that. We haven't got too many pheasants. He'll be sure to come when you ask him,—and he'll be sure to go."

So Jones is asked, and considers himself to be the most popular man in London. I will not say that Harry's invitations had been of exactly that description; but he too had considered himself to be popular, and now greatly felt the withdrawal of such marks of friendship. He had received one "put off"—from the Ingoldsbys of Kent. Early in June he had promised to be there in November. The youngest Miss Ingoldsby was very pretty, and he, no doubt, had been gracious. She knew that he had meant nothing,—could have meant nothing. But he might come to mean something, and had been most pressingly asked. In September there came a letter to him to say that the room intended for him at Ingoldsby had been burnt down. Mrs. Ingoldsby was so extremely sorry, and so were the "girls!" Harry could trace it all up. The Ingoldsbys knew the Greens, and Mrs. Green was Sister to Septimus Jones, who was absolutely the slave,—the slave, as Harry said, repeating the word to himself with emphasis,—of Augustus Scarborough. He was very unhappy, not that he cared in the least for any Miss Ingoldsby, but that he began to be conscious that he was to be dropped.

He was to be taken up, on the other hand, by Joshua Thoroughbung. Alas! alas! though he smiled and resolved to accept his brother-in-law with a good heart, this did not in the least salve the wound. His own county was to him less than other counties, and his own neighborhood less than other neighborhoods. Buntingford was full of Thoroughbungs, the best people in the world, but not quite up to what he believed to be his mark. Mr. Prosper himself was the stupidest ass! At Welwyn people smelled of the City. At Stevenage the parsons' set began. Baldock was a *caput mortuum* of dulness. Royston was alive only on market-days. Of his own father's house, and even of his mother and sisters, he entertained ideas that savored a little of depreciation. But, to redeem him from this fault,—a fault which would have led to the absolute ruin of his character had it not been redeemed and at last cured,—there was a consciousness of his own vanity and weakness. "My father is worth a dozen of them, and my mother and sisters two dozen," he would say of the Ingoldsbys when he went to bed in the room that was to be burnt down in preparation for his exile. And he believed it. They were honest; they were unselfish; they were unpretending. His sister Molly was not above owning that her young brewer was all the world to her; a fine, honest, bouncing girl, who said her prayers with a meaning, thanked the Lord for giving her Joshua, and laughed so loud that you could hear her out of the rectory garden half across the park. Harry knew that they were good,—did in his heart know that where the parsons begin the good things were likely to begin also.

He was in this state of mind, the hand of good pulling one way and the devil's pride the other, when young Thoroughbung called for him one morning to carry him on to Cumberlow Green. Cumberlow Green was a popular meet in that county, where meets have not much to make them popular except the good-humor of those who form the hunt. It is not a county either pleasant or easy to ride over, and a Puckeridge fox is surely the most ill-mannered of foxes. But the Puckeridge men are gracious to strangers, and fairly so among themselves. It is more than can be said of Leicestershire, where sportsmen ride in brilliant boots and breeches, but with their noses turned supernaturally into the air. "Come along; we've four miles to do, and twenty minutes to do it in. Halloo, Molly, how d'ye do? Come up on to the step and give us a kiss."

"Go away!" said Molly, rushing back into the house. "Did you ever hear anything like his impudence?"

"Why shouldn't you?" said Kate. "All the world knows it." Then the gig, with the two sportsmen, was driven on. "Don't you think he looks handsome in his pink coat?" whispered Molly, afterward, to her elder sister. "Only think; I have never seen him in a red coat since he was my own. Last April, when the hunting was over, he hadn't spoken out; and this is the first day he has worn pink this year."

Harry, when he reached the meet, looked about him to watch how he was received. There are not many more painful things in life than when an honest, gallant young fellow has to look about him in such a frame of mind. It might have been worse had he deserved to be dropped, some one will say. Not at all. A different condition of mind exists then, and a struggle is made to overcome the judgment of men which is not in itself painful. It is part of the natural battle of life, which does not hurt one at all,—unless, indeed, the man hate himself for that which has brought upon him the hatred of others. Repentance is always an agony,—and should be so.

Without the agony there can be no repentance. But even then it is hardly so sharp as that feeling of injustice which accompanies the unmeaning look, and dumb faces, and pretended indifference of those who have condemned.

When Harry descended from the gig he found himself close to old Mr. Harkaway, the master of the hounds. Mr. Harkaway was a gentleman who had been master of these hounds for more than forty years, and had given as much satisfaction as the county could produce. His hounds, which were his hobby, were perfect. His horses were good enough for the Hertfordshire lanes and Hertfordshire hedges. His object was not so much to run a fox as to kill him in obedience to certain rules of the game. Ever so many hinderances have been created to bar the killing a fox,—as for instance that you shouldn't knock him on the head with a brick-bat,—all of which had to Mr. Harkaway the force of a religion. The laws of hunting are so many that most men who hunt cannot know them all. But no law had ever been written, or had become a law by the strength of tradition, which he did not know.

To break them was to him treason. When a young man broke them he pitied the young man's ignorance, and endeavored to instruct him after some rough fashion. When an old man broke them, he regarded him as a fool who should stay at home, or as a traitor who should be dealt with as such. And with such men he could deal very hardly. Forty years of reigning had taught him to believe himself to be omnipotent, and he was so in his own hunt. He was a man who had never much affected social habits. The company of one or two brother sportsmen to drink a glass of port-wine with him and then to go early to bed, was the most of it. He had a small library, but not a book ever came off the shelf unless it referred to farriers or the *res venatica*. He was unmarried. The time which other men gave to their wives and families he bestowed upon his hounds. To his stables he never went, looking on a horse as a necessary adjunct to hunting,—expensive, disagreeable, and prone to get you into danger. When anyone flattered him about his horse he would only grunt, and turn his head on one side. No one in these latter years had seen him jump any fence. But yet he was always with his hounds, and when any one said a kind word as to their doings, that he would take as a compliment. It was they who were there to do the work of the day, which horses and men could only look at. He was a sincere, honest, taciturn, and withal, affectionate man, who could on an occasion be very angry with those who offended him. He knew well what he could do, and never attempted that which was beyond his power. "How are you, Mr. Harkaway?" said Harry.

"How are you, Mr. Annesley? how are you?" said the master, with all the grace of which he was capable. But Harry caught a tone in his voice which he thought implied displeasure. And Mr. Harkaway had in truth heard the story,—how Harry had been discarded at Buston because he had knocked the man down in the streets at night-time and had then gone away. After that Mr. Harkaway toddled off, and Harry sat and frowned with embittered heart.

"Well, Malt-and-hops, and how are you?" This came from a fast young banker who lived in the neighborhood, and who thus intended to show his familiarity with the brewer; but when he saw Annesley, he turned round and rode away. "Scaly trick that fellow played the other day. He knocked a fellow down, and, when he thought that he was dead, he lied about it like old boots." All of which made itself intelligible to Harry. He told himself that he had always hated that banker.

"Why do you let such a fellow as that call you Malt-and-hops?" he said to Joshua.

"What,—young Florin? He's a very good fellow, and doesn't mean anything."

"A vulgar cad, I should say."

Then he rode on in silence till he was addressed by an old gentleman of the county who had known his father for the last thirty years. The old gentleman had had nothing about him to recommend him either to Harry's hatred or love till he spoke; and after that Harry hated him. "How d'you do, Mr. Annesley?" said the old gentleman, and then rode on. Harry knew that the old man had condemned him as the others had done, or he would never have called him Mr. Annesley. He felt that he was "blown upon" in his own county, as well as by the Ingoldsbys down in Kent.

They had but a moderate day's sport, going a considerable distance in search of it, till an incident arose which gave quite an interest to the field generally, and nearly brought Joshua Thoroughbung into a scrape. They were drawing a covert which was undoubtedly the property of their own hunt,—or rather just going to draw it,—when all of a sudden they became aware that every hound in the pack was hunting. Mr. Harkaway at once sprung from his usual cold, apathetic manner into full action. But they who knew him well could see that it was not the excitement of joy. He was in an instant full of life, but it was not the life of successful enterprise. He was perturbed and unhappy, and his huntsman, Dillon,—a silent, cunning, not very popular man, who would obey his master in everything,—began to move about rapidly, and to be at his wit's end. The younger men prepared themselves for a run,—one of those sudden, short, decisive spurts which come at the spur of the moment, and on which a man, if he is not quite awake to the demands of the moment, is very apt to be left behind. But the old stagers had their eyes on Mr. Harkaway, and knew that there was something amiss.

Then there appeared another field of hunters, first one man leading them, then others following, and after them the first ruck and then the crowd. It was apparent to all who knew anything that two packs had joined. These were the Hitchiners, as the rival sportsmen would call them, and this was the Hitchin Hunt, with Mr.

Fairlawn, their master. Mr. Fairlawn was also an old man, popular, no doubt, in his own country, but by no means beloved by Mr. Harkaway. Mr. Harkaway used to declare how Fairlawn had behaved very badly about certain common coverts about thirty years ago, when the matter had to be referred to a committee of masters. No one in these modern days knew aught of the quarrel, or cared. The men of the two hunts were very good friends, unless they met under the joint eyes of the two masters, and then they were supposed to be bound to hate each other. Now the two packs were mixed together, and there was only one fox between them.

The fox did not trouble them long. He could hardly have saved himself from one pack, but very soon escaped from the fangs of the two. Each hound knew that his neighbor hound was a stranger, and, in scrutinizing the singularity of the occurrence, lost all the power of hunting. In ten minutes there were nearly forty couples of hounds running hither and thither, with two huntsmen and four whips swearing at them with strange voices, and two old gentlemen giving orders each in opposition to the other. Then each pack was got together, almost on the same ground, and it was necessary that something should be done. Mr. Harkaway waited to see whether Mr. Fairlawn would ride away quickly to his own country. He would not have spoken to Mr. Fairlawn if he could have helped it. Mr. Fairlawn was some miles away from his country. He must have given up the day for lost had he simply gone away. But there was another covert a mile off, and he thought that one of his hounds had "shown a line,"—or said that he thought so.

Now, it is well known that you may follow a hunted fox through whatever country he may take you to, if only your hounds are hunting him continuously. And one hound for that purpose is as good as thirty, and if a hound can only "show a line" he is held to be hunting. Mr. Fairlawn was quite sure that one of his hounds had been showing a line, and had been whipped off it by one of Mr. Harkaway's men. The man swore that he had only been collecting his own hounds. On this plea Mr. Fairlawn demanded to take his whole pack into Greasegate Wood,—the very covert that Mr. Harkaway had been about to draw. "I'm d—d if you do!" said Mr. Harkaway, standing, whip in hand, in the middle of the road, so as to prevent the enemy's huntsman passing by with his hounds. It was afterward declared that Mr. Harkaway had not been heard to curse and swear for the last fifteen years. "I'm d—d if I don't!" said Mr. Fairlawn, riding up to him. Mr. Harkaway was ten years the older man, and looked as though he had much less of fighting power. But no one saw him quail or give an inch. Those who watched his face declared that his lips were white with rage and quivered with passion.

To tell the words which passed between them after that would require Homer's pathos and Homer's imagination. The two old men scowled and scolded at each other, and, had Mr. Fairlawn attempted to pass, Mr. Harkaway would certainly have struck him with his whip. And behind their master a crowd of the Puckeridge men collected themselves,—foremost among whom was Joshua Thoroughbung. "Take 'em round to the covert by Winnipeg Lane," said Mr. Fairlawn to his huntsman. The man prepared to take his pack round by Winnipeg Lane, which would have added a mile to the distance. But the huntsman, when he had got a little to the left, was soon seen scurrying across the country in the direction of the covert, with a dozen others at his heels, and the hounds following him. But old Mr. Harkaway had seen it too, and having possession of the road, galloped along it at such a pace that no one could pass him.

All the field declared that they had regarded it as impossible that their master should move so fast. And Dillon, and the whips, and Thoroughbung, and Harry Annesley, with half a dozen others, kept pace with him. They would not sit there and see their master outmanoeuvred by any lack of readiness on their part. They got to the covert first, and there, with their whips drawn, were ready to receive the second pack. Then one hound went in without an order; but for their own hounds they did not care. They might find a fox and go after him, and nobody would follow them. The business here at the covert-side was more important and more attractive.

Then it was that Mr. Thoroughbung nearly fell into danger. As to the other hounds,—Mr. Fairlawn's hounds,—doing any harm in the covert, or doing any good for themselves or their owners, that was out of the question. The rival pack was already there, with their noses up in the air, and thinking of anything but a fox; and this other pack,—the Hitchiners,—were just as wild. But it was the object of Mr. Fairlawn's body-guard to say that they had drawn the covert in the teeth of Mr. Harkaway, and to achieve this one of the whips thought that he could ride through the Puckeridge men, taking a couple of hounds with him. That would suffice for triumph.

But to prevent such triumph on the part of the enemy Joshua Thoroughbung was prepared to sacrifice himself. He rode right at the whip, with his own whip raised, and would undoubtedly have ridden over him had not the whip tried to turn his horse sharp round, stumbled and fallen in the struggle, and had not Thoroughbung, with his horse, fallen over him.

It will be the case that a slight danger or injury in one direction will often stop a course of action calculated to create greater dangers and worse injuries. So it was in this case. When Dick, the Hitchin whip, went down, and Thoroughbung, with his horse, was over him,—two men and two horses struggling together on the ground,—all desire to carry on the fight was over.

The huntsman came up, and at last Mr. Fairlawn also, and considered it to be their duty to pick up Dick, whose breath was knocked out of him by the weight of Joshua Thoroughbung, and the Puckeridge side felt it to be necessary to give their aid to the valiant brewer. There was then no more attempt to draw the covert. Each general in gloomy silence took off his forces, and each afterward deemed that the victory was his. Dick swore, when brought to himself, that one of his hounds had gone in, whereas Squire 'Arkaway "had swore most 'orrid oaths that no 'Itchiner 'ound should ever live to put his nose in. One of 'is 'ounds 'ad, and Squire 'Arkaway would have to be—" Well, Dick declared that he would not say what would happen to Mr. Harkaway.

CHAPTER XXIX. RIDING HOME

The two old gentlemen rode away, each in his own direction, in gloomy silence. Not a word was said by either of them, even to one of his own followers. It was nearly twenty miles to Mr. Harkaway's house, and along the entire twenty miles he rode silent. "He's in an awful passion," said Thoroughbung; "he can't speak from anger." But, to tell the truth, Mr. Harkaway was ashamed of himself. He was an old gentleman, between seventy and eighty, who was supposed to go out for his amusement, and had allowed himself to be betrayed into most unseemly language. What though the hound had not "shown a line?" Was it necessary that he, at his time of life, should fight on the road for the maintenance of a trifling right of sport. But yet there came upon him from time to time a sense of the deep injury done to him. That man Fairlawn, that blackguard, that creature of all others the farthest removed from a gentleman, had declared that in his, Mr. Harkaway's teeth, he would draw his, Mr. Harkaway's covert! Then he would urge on his old horse, and gnash his teeth; and then, again, he would be ashamed. "*Tantœne animis cœlestibus irœ?*"

But Thoroughbung rode home high in spirits, very proud, and conscious of having done good work. He was always anxious to stand well with the hunt generally, and was aware that he had now distinguished himself. Harry Annesley was on one side of him, and on the other rode Mr. Florin, the banker. "He's an abominable liar!" said Thoroughbung, "a wicked, wretched liar!" He was alluding to the Hitchiner's whip, whom in his wrath he had nearly sent to another world. "He says that one of his hounds got into the covert, but I was there and saw it all. Not a nose was over the little bank which runs between the field and the covert."

"You must have seen a hound if he had been there," said the banker.

"I was as cool as a cucumber, and could count the hounds he had with him. There were three of them. A big black-spotted bitch was leading, the one that I nearly fell upon. When the man went down the hound stopped, not knowing what was expected of him. How should he? The man would have been in the covert, but, by George! I managed to stop him."

"What did you mean to do to him when you rode at him so furiously?" asked Harry.

"Not let him get in there. That was my resolute purpose. I suppose I should have knocked him off his horse with my whip."

"But suppose he had knocked you off your horse?" suggested the banker.

"There is no knowing how that might have been. I never calculated those chances. When a man wants to do a thing like that he generally does it."

"And you did it?" said Harry.

"Yes; I think I did. I dare say his bones are sore. I know mine are. But I don't care for that in the least. When this day comes to be talked about, as I dare say it will be for many a long year, no one will be able to say that the Hitchiners got into that covert." Thoroughbung, with the genuine modesty of an Englishman, would not say that he had achieved by his own prowess all this glory for the Puckeridge Hunt, but he felt it down to the very end of his nails.

Had he not been there that whip would have got into the wood, and a very different tale would then have been told in those coming years to which his mind was running away with happy thoughts. He had ridden the aggressors down; he had stopped the first intrusive hound. But though he continued to talk of the subject, he did not boast in so many words that he had done it. His "*veni, vidi, vici,*" was confined to his own bosom.

As they rode home together there came to be a little crowd of men round Thoroughbung, giving him the praises that were his due. But one by one they fell off from Annesley's side of the road. He soon felt that no one addressed a word to him. He was, probably, too prone to encourage them in this. It was he that fell away, and courted loneliness, and then in his heart accused them. There was do doubt something of truth in his accusations; but another man, less sensitive, might have lived it down. He did more than meet their coldness half-way, and then complained to himself of the bitterness of the world. "They are like the beasts of the field," he said, "who when another beast has been wounded, turn upon him and rend him to death." His future brother-in-law, the best natured fellow that ever was born, rode on thoughtless, and left Harry alone for three or four miles, while he received the pleasant plaudits of his companions. In Joshua's heart was that tale of the whip's discomfiture. He did not see that Molly's brother was alone as soon as he would have done but for his own glory. "He is the same as the others," said Harry to himself. "Because that man has told a falsehood of me, and has had the wit to surround it with circumstances, he thinks it becomes him to ride away and cut me." Then he asked himself some foolish questions as to himself and as to Joshua Thoroughbung, which he did not answer as he should have done, had he remembered that he was then riding Thoroughbung's horse, and that his sister was to become Thoroughbung's wife.

After half an hour of triumphant ovation, Joshua remembered his brother-in-law, and did fall back so as to pick him up. "What's the matter, Harry? Why don't you come on and join us?"

"I'm sick of hearing of that infernal squabble."

"Well; as to a squabble, Mr. Harkaway behaved quite right. If a hunt is to be kept up, the right of entering coverts must be preserved for the hunt they belong to. There was no line shown. You must remember that there isn't a doubt about that. The hounds were all astray when we joined them. It's a great question whether they brought their fox into that first covert. There are they who think that Bodkin was just riding across the Puckeridge country in search of a fox." Bodkin was Mr. Fairlawn's huntsman. "If you admit that kind of thing, where will you be? As a hunting country, just nowhere. Then as a sportsman, where are you? It is necessary to put down such gross fraud. My own impression is that Mr. Fairlawn should be turned out from being master. I own I feel very strongly about it. But then I always have been fond of hunting."

"Just so," said Harry, sulkily, who was not in the least interested as to the matter on which Joshua was so eloquent.

Then Mr. Proctor rode by, the gentleman who in the early part of the day disgusted Harry by calling him "mister." "Now, Mr. Proctor," continued Joshua, "I appeal to you whether Mr. Harkaway was not quite right? If you won't stick up for your rights in a hunting county—" But Mr. Proctor rode on, wishing them good-night, very discourteously declining to hear the remainder of the brewer's arguments. "He's in a hurry, I suppose," said Joshua.

"You'd better follow him. You'll find that he'll listen to you then."

"I don't want him to listen to me particularly."

"I thought you did." Then for half an hour the two men rode on in silence.

"What's the matter with you Harry?" said Joshua. "I can see there's something up that riles you. I know you're a fellow of your college, and have other things to think of besides the vagaries of a fox."

"The fellow of a college!" said Harry, who, had he been in a good-humor, would have thought much more of being along with a lot of fox-hunters than of any college honors.

"Well, yes; I suppose it is a great thing to be a fellow of a college. I never could have been one if I had mugged forever."

"My being a fellow of a college won't do me much good. Did you see that old man Proctor go by just now?"

"Oh yes; he never likes to be out after a certain hour."

"And did you see Florin, and Mr. Harkaway, and a lot of others? You yourself have been going on ahead for the last hour without speaking to me."

"How do you mean without speaking to you?" said Joshua, turning sharp round.

Then Harry Annesley reflected that he was doing an injustice to his future brother-in-law.

"Perhaps I have done you wrong," he said.

"You have."

"I beg your pardon. I believe you are as honest and true a fellow as there is in Hertfordshire, but for those others—"

"You think it's about Mountjoy Scarborough, then?" asked Joshua.

"I do. That infernal fool, Peter Prosper, has chosen to publish to the world that he has dropped me because of something that he has heard of that occurrence. A wretched lie has been told with a purpose by Mountjoy Scarborough's brother, and my uncle has taken it into his wise head to believe it. The truth is, I have not been as respectful to him as he thinks I ought, and now he resents my neglect in this fashion. He is going to marry your aunt in order that he may have a lot of children, and cut me out. In order to justify himself, he has told these lies about me, and you see the consequence;—not a man in the county is willing to speak to me."

"I really think a great deal of it's fancy."

"You go and ask Mr. Harkaway. He's honest, and he'll tell you. Ask this new cousin of yours, Mr. Prosper."

"I don't know that they are going to make a match of it, after all."

"Ask my own father. Only think of it,—that a puling, puking idiot like that, from a mere freak, should be able to do a man such a mischief! He can rob me of my income, which he himself has brought me up to expect. That he can do by a stroke of his pen. He can threaten to have sons like Priam. All that is within his own bosom. But to justify himself to the world at large, he picks up a scandalous story from a man like Augustus Scarborough, and immediately not a man in the county will speak to me. I say that that is enough to break a man's heart,—not the injury done which a man should bear, but the injustice of the doing. Who wants his beggarly allowance! He can do as he likes about his own money. I shall never ask him for his money. But that he should tell such a lie as this about the county is more than a man can endure."

"What was it that did happen?" asked Joshua.

"The man met me in the street when he was drunk, and he struck at me and was insolent. Of course I knocked him down. Who wouldn't have done the same? Then his brother found him somewhere, or got hold of him, and sent him out of the country, and says that I had held my tongue when I left him in the street. Of course I held my tongue. What was Mountjoy to me? Then Augustus has asked me sly questions, and accuses me of lying because I did not choose to tell him everything. It all comes out of that."

Here they had reached the rectory, and Harry, after seeing that the horses were properly supplied with gruel, took himself and his ill-humor up-stairs to his own chamber. But Joshua had a word or two to say to one of the inmates of the rectory.

He felt that it would be improper to ride his horse home without giving time to the animal to drink his gruel, and therefore made his way into the little breakfast-parlor, where Molly had a cup of tea and buttered toast ready for him. He of course told her first of the grand occurrence of the day,—how the two packs of hounds had mixed themselves together, how violently the two masters had fallen out and had nearly flogged each other, how Mr. Harkaway had sworn horribly,—who had never been heard to swear before,—how a final attempt had been made to seize a second covert, and how, at last, it had come to pass that he had distinguished himself. "Do you mean to say that you absolutely rode over the unfortunate man?" asked Molly.

"I did. Not that the man had the worst of it,—or very much the worse. There we were both down, and the two horses, all in a heap together."

"Oh, Joshua, suppose you had been kicked!"

"In that case I should have been—kicked."

"But a kick from an infuriated horse!"

"There wasn't much infuriation about him. The man had ridden all that out of the beast."

"You are sure to laugh at me, Joshua, because I think what terrible things might have happened to you. Why do you go putting yourself so forward in every danger, now that you have got somebody else to depend upon you and to care for you? It's very, very wrong."

"Somebody had to do it, Molly. It was most important, in the interests of hunting generally, that those hounds should not have been allowed to get into that covert. I don't think that outsiders ever understand how essential it is to maintain your rights. It isn't as though it were an individual. The whole county may depend upon it."

"Why shouldn't it be some man who hasn't got a young woman to look after?" said Molly, half laughing and half crying.

"It's the man who first gets there who ought to do it," said Joshua. "A man can't stop to remember whether he has got a young woman or not."

"I don't think you ever want to remember." Then that little quarrel was brought to the usual end with the usual blandishments, and Joshua went on to discuss with her that other source of trouble, her brother's fall. "Harry is awfully cut up," said the brewer.

"You mean these affairs about his uncle?"

"Yes. It isn't only the money he feels, or the property, but people look askew at him. You ought all of you to be very kind to him."

"I am sure we are."

"There is something in it to vex him. That stupid old fool, your uncle—I beg your pardon, you know, for speaking of him in that way—"

"He is a stupid old fool."

"Is behaving very badly. I don't know whether he shouldn't be treated as I did that fellow up at the covert."

"Ride over him?"

"Something of that kind. Of course Harry is sore about it, and when a man is sore he frets at a thing like that more than he ought to do. As for that aunt of mine at Buntingford, there seems to be some hitch in it. I should have said she'd have married the Old Gentleman had he asked her."

"Don't talk like that, Joshua."

"But there is some screw loose. Simpson came up to my father about it yesterday, and the governor let enough of the cat out of the bag to make me know that the thing is not going as straight as she wishes."

"He has offered, then?"

"I am sure he has asked her."

"And your aunt will accept him?" asked Molly.

"There's probably some difference about money. It's all done with the intention of injuring poor Harry. If he were my own brother I could not be more unhappy about him. And as to Aunt Matilda, she's a fool. There are two fools together. If they choose to marry we can't hinder them. But there is some screw loose, and if the two young lovers don't know their own minds things may come right at last." Then, with some farther blandishments, the prosperous brewer walked away.

CHAPTER XXX. PERSECUTION

In the mean time Florence Mountjoy was not passing her time pleasantly at Brussels. Various troubles there attended her. All her friends around her were opposed to her marriage with Harry Annesley. Harry Annesley had become a very unsavory word in the mouths of Sir Magnus and the British Embassy generally. Mrs. Mountjoy told her grief to her brother-in-law, who thoroughly took her part, as did also, very strongly, Lady Mountjoy. It got to be generally understood that Harry was a *mauvais sujet*. Such was the name that was attached to him, and the belief so conveyed was thoroughly entertained by them all. Sir Magnus had written to friends in London, and the friends in London bore out the reports that were so conveyed. The story of the midnight quarrel was told in a manner very prejudicial to poor Harry, and both Sir Magnus and his wife saw the necessity of preserving their niece from anything so evil as such a marriage. But Florence was very firm, and was considered to be very obstinate. To her mother she was obstinate but affectionate To Sir Magnus she was obstinate and in some degree respectful. But to Lady Mountjoy she was neither affectionate nor respectful. She took a great dislike to Lady Mountjoy, who endeavored to domineer; and who, by the assistance of the two others, was in fact tyrannical. It was her opinion that the girl should be compelled to abandon the man, and Mrs. Mountjoy found herself constrained to follow this advice. She did love her daughter, who was her only child. The main interest of her life was centred in her daughter. Her only remaining ambition rested on her daughter's marriage. She had long revelled in the anticipation of being the mother-in-law of the owner of Tretton Park. She had been very proud of her daughter's beauty.

Then had come the first blow, when Harry Annesley had come to Montpelier Place and had been welcomed by Florence. Mrs. Mountjoy had seen it all long before Florence had been aware of it. And the first coming of Harry had been long before the absolute disgrace of Captain Scarborough,—at any rate, before the tidings of that disgrace had reached Cheltenham. Mrs. Mountjoy had been still able to dream of Tretton Park, after the Jews had got their fingers on it,—even after the Jews had been forced to relinquish their hold. It can hardly be said that up to this very time Mrs. Mountjoy had lost all hope in her nephew, thinking that as the property had been entailed some portion of it must ultimately belong to him. She had heard that Augustus was to have it, and her desires had vacillated between the two. Then Harry had positively declared himself, and Augustus had given her to understand how wretched, how mean, how wicked had been Harry's conduct. And he fully explained to her that Harry would be penniless. She had indeed been aware that Buston,—quite a trifling thing compared to Tretton,—was to belong to him. But entails were nothing nowadays. It was part of the radical abomination to which England was being subjected. Not even Buston was now to belong to Harry Annesley. The small income which he had received from his uncle was stopped. He was reduced to live upon his fellowship,—which would be stopped also if he married. She even despised him because he was the fellow of a college;—she had looked for a husband for her daughter so much higher than any college could produce. It was not from any lack of motherly love that she was opposed to Florence, or from any innate cruelty that she handed her daughter over to the tender mercies of Lady Mountjoy.

And since she had been at Brussels there had come up farther hopes. Another mode had shown itself of escaping Harry Annesley, who was of all catastrophes the most dreaded and hated. Mr. Anderson, the second secretary of legation,—he whose business it was to ride about the boulevard with Sir Magnus,—had now declared himself in form. "Never saw a fellow so bowled over," Sir Magnus had declared, by which he had intended to signify that Mr. Anderson was now truly in love. "I've seen him spooney a dozen times," Sir Magnus had said, confidentially, to his sister-in-law, "but he has never gone to this length. He has asked a lot of girls to have him, but he has always been off it again before the week was over. He has written to his mother now."

And Mr. Anderson showed his love by very unmistakable signs. Sir Magnus too, and Lady Mountjoy, were evidently on the same side as Mr. Anderson. Sir Magnus thought there was no longer any good in waiting for his nephew, the captain, and of that other nephew, Augustus, he did not entertain any very high idea. Sir Magnus had corresponded lately with Augustus, and was certainly not on his side. But he so painted Mr. Anderson's prospects in life, as did also Lady Mountjoy, as to make it appear that if Florence could put up with young Anderson she would do very well with herself.

"He's sure to be a baronet some of these days, you know," said Sir Magnus.

"I don't think that would go very far with Florence," said her mother.

"But it ought. Look about in the world and you'll see that it does go a long way. He'd be the fifth baronet."

"But his elder brother is alive."

"The queerest fellow you ever saw in your born days, and his life is not worth a year's purchase. He's got some infernal disease,—nostalgia, or what 'd'ye call it?

—which never leaves him a moment's peace, and then he drinks nothing but milk. Sure to go off;—cock sure."

"I shouldn't like Florence to count upon that."

"And then Hugh Anderson, the fellow here, is very well off as it is. He has four hundred pounds here, and another five hundred pounds of his own. Florence has, or will have, four hundred pounds of her own. I should call them deuced rich. I should, indeed, as beginners. She could have her pair of ponies here, and what more would she want?"

These arguments did go very far with Mrs. Mountjoy, the farther because in her estimation Sir Magnus was a great man. He was the greatest Englishman, at any rate, in Brussels, and where should she go for advice but to an Englishman? And she did not know that Sir Magnus had succeeded in borrowing a considerable sum of money from his second secretary of legation.

"Leave her to me for a little;—just leave her to me," said Lady Mountjoy.

"I would not say anything hard to her," said the mother, pleading for her naughty child.

"Not too hard, but she must be made to understand. You see there have been misfortunes. As to Mountjoy Scarborough, he's past hoping for."

"You think so?"

"Altogether. When a man has disappeared there's an end of him. There was Lord Baltiboy's younger son disappeared, and he turned out to be a Zouave corporal in a French regiment. They did get him out, of course, but then he went preaching in America. You may take it for granted, that when a man has absolutely vanished from the clubs, he'll never be any good again as a marrying man."

"But there's his brother, who, they say, is to have the property."

"A very cold-blooded sort of young man, who doesn't care a straw for his own family." He had received very sternly the overtures for a loan from Sir Magnus. "And he, as I understand, has never declared himself in Florence's favor. You can't count upon Augustus Scarborough."

"Not just count upon him."

"Whereas there's young Anderson, who is the most gentleman-like young man I know, all ready. It will have been such a turn of luck your coming here and catching him up."

"I don't know that it can be called a turn of luck. Florence has a very nice fortune of her own—"

"And she wants to give it to this penniless reprobate. It is just one of those cases in which you must deal roundly with a girl. She has to be frightened, and that's about the truth of it."

After this, Lady Mountjoy did succeed in getting Florence alone with herself into her morning-room. When her mother told her that her aunt wished to see her, she answered first that she had no special wish to see her aunt. Her mother declared that in her aunt's house she was bound to go when her aunt sent for her. To this Florence demurred. She was, she thought, her aunt's guest, but by no means at her aunt's disposal. But at last she obeyed her mother. She had resolved that she would obey her mother in all things but one, and therefore she went one morning to her aunt's chamber.

But as she went she was, on the first instance, caught by her uncle, and taken by him into a little private sanctum behind his official room. "My dear," he said, "just come in here for two minutes."

"I am on my way up to my aunt."

"I know it, my dear. Lady Mountjoy has been talking it all over with me. Upon my word you can't do anything better than take young Anderson."

"I can't do that, Uncle Magnus."

"Why not? There's poor Mountjoy Scarborough, he has gone astray."

"There is no question of my cousin."

"And Augustus is no better."

"There is no question of Augustus either."

"As to that other chap, he isn't any good;—he isn't indeed."

"You mean Mr. Annesley?"

"Yes; Harry Annesley, as you call him. He hasn't got a shilling to bless himself with, or wouldn't have if he was to marry you."

"But I have got something."

"Not enough for both of you, I'm afraid. That uncle of his has disinherited him."

"His uncle can't disinherit him."

"He's quite young enough to marry and have a family, and then Annesley will be disinherited. He has stopped his allowance, anyway, and you mustn't think of him. He did something uncommonly unhandsome the other day, though I don't quite know what."

"He did nothing unhandsome, Uncle Magnus."

"Of course a young lady will stand up for her lover, but you will really have to drop him. I'm not a hard sort of man, but this was something that the world will not stand. When he thought the man had been murdered he didn't say anything about it for fear they should tax him with it. And then he swore he had never seen him. It was something of that sort."

"He never feared that any one would suspect him."

"And now young Anderson has proposed. I should not have spoken else, but it's my duty to tell you about young Anderson. He's a gentleman all round."

"So is Mr. Annesley."

"And Anderson has got into no trouble at all. He does his duty here uncommonly well. I never had less trouble with any young fellow than I have had with him. No licking him into shape,—or next to none,—and he has a very nice private income. You together would have plenty, and could live here till you had settled on apartments. A pair of ponies would be just the thing for you to drive about and support the British interests. You think of it, my dear, and you'll find that I'm right." Then Florence escaped from that room and went up to receive the much more severe lecture which she was to have from her aunt.

"Come in, my dear," said Lady Mountjoy, in her most austere voice. She had a voice which could assume austerity when she knew her power to be in the ascendant. As Florence entered the room Miss Abbott left it by a door on the other side. "Take that chair, Florence. I want to have a few minutes' conversation with you." Then Florence sat down. "When a young lady is thinking of being married, a great many things have to be taken into consideration." This seemed to be so much a matter of fact that Florence did not feel it necessary to make any reply. "Of course I am aware you are thinking of being married."

"Oh yes," said Florence.

"But to whom?"

"To Harry Annesley," said Florence, intending to imply that all the world knew that.

"I hope not; I hope not. Indeed, I may say that it is quite out of the question. In the first place, he is a beggar."

"He has begged from none," said Florence.

"He is what the world calls a beggar, when a young man without a penny thinks of being married."

"I'm not a beggar, and what I've got will be his."

"My dear, you're talking about what you don't understand. A young lady cannot give her money away in that manner; it will not be allowed. Neither your mother, nor Sir Magnus, nor will I permit it." Here Florence restrained herself, but drew herself up in her chair as though prepared to speak out her mind if she should be driven. Lady Mountjoy would not permit it! She thought that she would feel herself quite able to tell Lady Mountjoy that she had neither power nor influence in the matter, but she determined to be silent a little longer. "In the first place, a gentleman who is a gentleman never attempts to marry a lady for her money."

"But when a lady has the money she can express herself much more clearly than she could otherwise."

"I don't quite understand what you mean by that, my dear."

"When Mr. Annesley proposed to me he was the acknowledged heir to his uncle's property."

"A trumpery affair at the best of it."

"It would have sufficed for me. Then I accepted him."

"That goes for nothing from a lady. Of course your acceptance was contingent on circumstances."

"It was so;—on my regard. Having accepted him, and as my regard remains just as warm as ever, I certainly shall not go back because of anything his uncle may do. I only say this to explain that he was quite justified in his offer. It was not for my small fortune that he came to me."

"I'm not so sure of that."

"But if my money can be of any use to him, he's quite welcome to it. Sir Magnus spoke to me about a pair of ponies. I'd rather have him than a pair of ponies."

"I'm coming to that just now. Here is Mr. Anderson."

"Oh yes; he's here."

There was certainly a touch of impatience in the tone in which this was uttered. It was as though she had said that Mr. Anderson had so contrived that she could have no doubt whatever about his continued presence. Mr. Anderson had made himself so conspicuous as to be visible to her constantly. Lady Mountjoy, who intended at present to sing Mr. Anderson's praises, felt this to be impertinent.

"I don't know what you mean by that. Mr. Anderson has behaved himself quite like a gentleman, and you ought to be very proud of any token you may receive of his regard and affection."

"But I'm not bound to return to it."

"You are bound to think of it when those who are responsible for your actions tell you to do so."

"Mamma, you mean?"

"I mean your uncle, Sir Magnus Mountjoy." She did not quite dare to say that she had meant herself. "I suppose you will admit that Sir Magnus is a competent judge of young men's characters?"

"He may be a judge of Mr. Anderson, because Mr. Anderson is his clerk."

There was something of an intention to depreciate in the word "clerk." Florence had not thought much of Mr. Anderson's worth, nor, as far as she had seen them, of the duties generally performed at the British Embassy. She was ignorant of the peculiar little niceties and intricacies which required the residence at Brussels of a gentleman with all the tact possessed by Sir Magnus. She did not know that while the mere international work of the office might be safely intrusted to Mr. Blow and Mr. Bunderdown, all those little niceties, that smiling and that frowning, that taking off of hats and only half taking them off, that genial, easy manner, and that stiff hauteur, formed the peculiar branch of Sir Magnus himself,—and, under Sir Magnus, of Mr. Anderson. She did not understand that even to that pair of ponies which was promised to her were to be attached certain important functions, which she was to control as the deputy of the great man's deputy And now she had called the great man's deputy a clerk!

"Mr. Anderson is no such thing," said Lady Mountjoy.

"His young man, then,—or private secretary;—only somebody else is that."

"You are very impertinent and very ungrateful. Mr. Anderson is second secretary of legation. There is no officer attached to our establishment of more importance. I believe you say it on purpose to anger me. And then you compare this gentleman to Mr. Annesley, a man to whom no one will speak."

"I will speak to him." Had Harry heard her say that, he ought to have been a happy man in spite of his trouble.

"You! What good can you do him?" Florence nodded her head, almost imperceptibly, but still there was a nod, signifying more than she could possibly say. She thought that she could do him a world of good if she were near him, and some good, too, though she were far away. If she were with him she could hang on to his arm,—or perhaps at some future time round his neck,—and tell him that she would be true to him though all others might turn away. And she could be just as true where she was, though she could not comfort him by telling him so with her own words. Then it was that she resolved upon writing that letter. He should already have what little comfort she might administer in his absence. "Now, listen to me, Florence. He is a thorough reprobate."

"I will not hear him so called. He is no reprobate."

"He has behaved in such a way that all England is crying out about him. He has done that which will never allow any gentleman to speak to him again."

"Then there will be more need that a lady should do so. But it is not true."

"You put your knowledge of character against that of Sir Magnus."

"Sir Magnus does not know the gentleman; I do. What's the good of talking of it, aunt? Harry Annesley has my word, and nothing on earth shall induce me to go back from it. Even were he what you say I would be true to him."

"You would?"

"Certainly I would. I could not willingly begin to love a man whom I knew to be base; but when I had loved him I would not turn because of his baseness;—I couldn't do it. It would be a great—a terrible misfortune; but it would have to be borne. But here—I know all the story to which you allude."

"I know it too."

"I am quite sure that the baseness has not been on his part. In defence of my name he has been silent. He might have spoken out, if he had known all the truth then. I was as much his own then as I am now. One of these days I suppose I shall be more so."

"You mean to marry him, then?"

"Most certainly I do, or I will never be married; and as he is poor now, and I must have my own money when I am twenty-four, I suppose I shall have to wait till then."

"Will your mother's word go for nothing with you?"

"Poor mamma! I do believe that mamma is very unhappy, because she makes me unhappy. What may take place between me and mamma I am not bound, I think, to tell you. We shall be away soon, and I shall be left to mamma alone."

And mamma would be left alone to her daughter, Lady Mountjoy thought. The visit must be prolonged so that at last Mr. Anderson might be enabled to prevail.

The visit had been originally intended for a month, but was now prolonged indefinitely. After that conversation between Lady Mountjoy and her niece two or three things happened, all bearing upon our story. Florence at once wrote her letter. If things were going badly in England with Harry Annesley, Harry should at any rate have the comfort of knowing what were her feelings,—if there might be comfort to him in that. "Perhaps, after all, he won't mind what I may say," she thought to herself; but only pretended to think it, and at once flatly contradicted her own "perhaps." Then she told him most emphatically not to reply. It was very important that she should write. He was to receive her letter, and there must be an end of it. She was quite sure that he would understand her. He would not subject her to the trouble of having to tell her own people that she was maintaining a correspondence, for it would amount to that. But still when the time came for the answer she had counted it up to the hour. And when Sir Magnus sent for her and handed to her the letter,—having discussed that question with her mother,—she fully expected it, and felt properly grateful to her uncle. She wanted a little comfort, too, and when she had read the letter she knew that she had received it.

There had been a few words spoken between the two elder ladies after the interview between Florence and Lady Mountjoy. "She is a most self-willed young woman," said Lady Mountjoy.

"Of course she loves her lover," said Mrs. Mountjoy, desirous of making some excuse for her own daughter. The girl was very troublesome, but not the less her daughter. "I don't know any of them that don't who are worth anything."

"If you regard it in that light, Sarah, she'll get the better of you. If she marries him she will be lost; that is the way you have got to look at it. It is her future happiness you must think of—and respectability. She is a headstrong young woman, and has to be treated accordingly."

"What would you do?"

"I would be very severe."

"But what am I to do? I can't beat her; I can't lock her up in her room."

"Then you mean to give it up?"

"No, I don't. You shouldn't be so cross to me," said poor Mrs. Mountjoy. When it had reached this the two ladies had become intimate. "I don't mean to give it up at all; but what am I to do?"

"Remain here for the next month, and—and worry her; let Mr. Anderson have his chance with her. When she finds that everything will smile with her if she accepts him, and that her life will be made a burden to her if she still sticks to her Harry Annesley, she'll come round, if she be like other girls. Of course a girl can't be made to marry a man, but there are ways and means." By this Lady Mountjoy meant that the utmost cruelty should be used which would be compatible with a good breakfast, dinner, and bedroom. Now, Mrs. Mountjoy knew herself to be incapable of this, and knew also, or thought that she knew, that it would not be efficacious.

"You stay here,—up to Christmas, if you like it," said Sir Magnus to his sister-in-law. "She can't but see Anderson every day, and that goes a long way. She, of course, puts on a resolute air as well as she can. They all know how to do that. Do you be resolute in return. The deuce is in it if we can't have our way with her among us. When you talk of ill usage nobody wants you to put her in chains. There are different ways of killing a cat. You get friends to write to you from England about young Annesley, and I'll do the same. The truth, of course, I mean."

"Nothing can be worse than the truth," said Mrs. Mountjoy, shaking her head, sorrowfully.

"Just so," said Sir Magnus, who was not at all sorrowful to hear so bad an account of the favored suitor. "Then we'll read her the letters. She can't help hearing them. Just the true facts, you know. That's fair; nobody can call that cruel. And then, when she breaks down and comes to our call, we'll all be as soft as mother's milk to her. I shall see her going about the boulevards with a pair of ponies yet." Mrs. Mountjoy felt that when Sir Magnus spoke of Florence coming to his call he did not know her daughter. But she had nothing better to do than to obey Sir Magnus. Therefore she resolved to stay at Brussels another period of six weeks and told Florence that she had so resolved. Just at present Brussels and Cheltenham would be all the same to Florence.

"It will be a dreadful bore having them so long," said poor Lady Mountjoy, piteously, to her husband. For in the presence of Sir Magnus she was by no means the valiant woman that she was with some of her friends.

"You find everything a bore. What's the trouble?"

"What am I to do with them?"

"Take 'em about in the carriage. Lord bless my soul! what have you got a carriage for?"

"Then, with Miss Abbott, there's never room for any one else."

"Leave Miss Abbott at home, then. What's the good of talking to me about Miss Abbott? I suppose it doesn't matter to you whom my brother's daughter marries?" Lady Mountjoy did not think that it did matter much; but she declared that she had already evinced the most tender solicitude. "Then stick to it. The girl doesn't want to go out every day. Leave her alone, where Anderson can get at her."

"He's always out riding with you."

"No, he's not; not always. And leave Miss Abbott at home. Then there'll be room for two others. Don't make difficulties. Anderson will expect that I shall do something for him, of course."

"Because of the money," said Lady Mountjoy, whispering.

"And I've got to do something for her too." Now, there was a spice of honesty about Sir Magnus. He knew that as he could not at once pay back these sums, he was bound to make it up in some other way. The debts would be left the same. But that would remain with Providence.

Then came Harry's letter, and there was a deep consultation. It was known to have come from Harry by the Buntingford post-mark. Mrs. Mountjoy proposed to consult Lady Mountjoy; but to that Sir Magnus would not agree. "She'd take her skin off her if she could, now that she's angered," said the lady's husband, who no doubt knew the lady well. "Of course she'll learn that the letter has been written, and then she'll throw it in our teeth. She wouldn't believe that it had gone astray in coming here. We should give her a sort of a whip-hand over us." So it was decided that Florence should have her letter.

CHAPTER XXXI. FLORENCE'S REQUEST

Thus it was arranged that Florence should be left in Mr. Anderson's way. Mr. Anderson, as Sir Magnus had said, was not always out riding. There were moments in which even he was off duty. And Sir Magnus contrived to ride a little earlier than usual so that he should get back while the carriage was still out on its rounds. Lady Mountjoy certainly did her duty, taking Mrs. Mountjoy with her daily, and generally Miss Abbott, so that Florence was, as it were, left to the mercies of Mr. Anderson. She could, of course, shut herself up in her bedroom, but things had not as yet become so bad as that. Mr. Anderson had not made himself terrible to her. She did not, in truth, fear Mr. Anderson at all, who was courteous in his manner and complimentary in his language, and she came at this time to the conclusion that if Mr. Anderson continued his pursuit of her she would tell him the exact truth of the case. As a gentleman, and as a young man, she thought that he would sympathize with her. The one enemy whom she did dread was Lady Mountjoy. She too had felt that her aunt could "take her skin off her," as Sir Magnus had said. She had not heard the words, but she knew that it was so, and her dislike to Lady Mountjoy was in proportion. It cannot be said that she was afraid. She did not intend to leave her skin in her aunt's hands. For every inch of skin taken she resolved to have an inch in return. She was not acquainted with the expressive mode of language which Sir Magnus had adopted, but she was prepared for all such attacks. For Sir Magnus himself, since he had given up the letter to her, she did feel some regard.

Behind the British minister's house, which, though entitled to no such name, was generally called the Embassy, there was a large garden, which, though not much used by Sir Magnus or Lady Mountjoy, was regarded as a valuable adjunct to the establishment. Here Florence betook herself for exercise, and here Mr. Anderson, having put off the muddy marks of his riding, found her one afternoon. It must be understood that no young man was ever more in earnest than Mr. Anderson. He, too, looking through the glass which had been prepared for him by Sir Magnus, thought that he saw in the not very far distant future a Mrs. Hugh Anderson driving a pair of gray ponies along the boulevard and he was much pleased with the sight. It reached to the top of his ambition. Florence was to his eyes really the sort of a girl whom a man in his position ought to marry. A secretary of legation in a small foreign capital cannot do with a dowdy wife, as may a clerk, for instance, in the Foreign Office. A secretary of legation,—the second secretary, he told himself,—was bound, if he married at all, to have a pretty and *distinguée* wife. He knew all about the intricacies which had fallen in a peculiar way into his own hand. Mr. Blow might have married a South Sea Islander, and would have been none the worse as regarded his official duties. Mr. Blow did not want the services of a wife in discovering and reporting all the secrets of the Belgium iron trade. There was no intricacy in that, no nicety. There was much of what, in his lighter moments, Mr. Anderson called "sweat." He did not pretend to much capacity for such duties; but in his own peculiar walk he thought that he was great. But it was very fatiguing, and he was sure that a wife was necessary to him. There were little niceties which none but a wife could perform. He had a great esteem for Sir Magnus. Sir Magnus was well thought of by all the court, and by the foreign minister at Brussels. But Lady Mountjoy was really of no use. The beginning and the end of it all with her was to show herself in a carriage. It was incumbent upon him, Anderson, to marry.

He was loving enough, and very susceptible. He was too susceptible, and he knew his own fault, and he was always on guard against it,—as behooved a young man with such duties as his. He was always falling in love, and then using his diplomatic skill in avoiding the consequences. He had found out that though one girl had looked so well under waxlight she did not endure the wear and tear of the day. Another could not be always graceful, or, though she could talk well enough during a waltz, she had nothing to say for herself at three o'clock in the morning. And he was driven to calculate that he would be wrong to marry a girl without a shilling. "It is a kind of thing that a man cannot afford to do unless he's sure of his position," he had said on such an occasion to Montgomery Arbuthnot, alluding especially to his brother's state of health. When Mr. Anderson spoke of not being sure of his position he was always considered to allude to his brother's health. In this way he had nearly got his little boat on to the rocks more than once, and had given some trouble to Sir Magnus. But now he was quite sure. "It's all there all round," he had said to Arbuthnot more than once. Arbuthnot said that it was there—"all round, all round." Waxlight and daylight made no difference to her. She was always graceful. "Nobody with an eye in his head can doubt that," said Anderson. "I should think not, by Jove!" replied Arbuthnot. "And for talking,—you never catch her out; never." "I never did, certainly," said Arbuthnot, who, as third secretary, was obedient and kind-hearted. "And then look at her money. Of course a fellow wants something to help him on. My position is so uncertain that I cannot do without it." "Of course not." "Now, with some girls it's so deuced hard to find out. You hear that a girl has got money, but when the time comes it depends on the life of a father who doesn't think of dying;—damme, doesn't think of it."

"Those fellows never do," said Arbuthnot. "But here, you see, I know all about it. When she's twenty-four,—only twenty-four,—she'll have ten thousand pounds of her own. I hate a mercenary fellow." "Oh yes; that's beastly." "Nobody can say that of me. Circumstanced as I am, I want something to help to keep the pot boiling. She has got it,—quite as much as I want,—quite, and I know all about it without the slightest doubt in the world." For the small loan of fifteen hundred pounds Sir Magnus paid the full value of the interest and deficient security. "Sir Magnus tells me that if I'll only stick to her I shall be sure to win. There's some fellow in England has just touched her heart,—just touched it, you know." "I understand," said Arbuthnot, looking very wise. "He is not a fellow of very much account," said Anderson; "one of those handsome fellows without conduct and without courage." "I've known lots of 'em," said Arbuthnot. "His name is Annesley," said Anderson. "I never saw him in my life, but that's what Sir Magnus says. He has done something awfully disreputable. I don't quite understand what it is, but it's something which ought to make him unfit to be her husband. Nobody knows the world better than Sir Magnus, and he says that it is so." "Nobody does know the world better than Sir Magnus," said Arbuthnot. And so that conversation was brought to an end.

One day soon after this he caught her walking in the garden. Her mother and Miss Abbot were still out with Lady Mountjoy in the carriage, and Sir Magnus had retired after the fatigue of his ride to sleep for half an hour before dinner. "All alone, Miss Mountjoy?" he said.

"Yes, alone, Mr. Anderson. I'm never in better company."

"So I think; but then if I were here you wouldn't be all alone, would you?"

"Not if you were with me."

"That's what I mean. But yet two people may be alone, as regards the world at large. Mayn't they?"

"I don't understand the nicety of language well enough to say. We used to have a question among us when we were children whether a wild beast could howl in an empty cavern. It's the same sort of thing."

"Why shouldn't he?"

"Because the cavern would not be empty if the wild beast were in it. Did you ever see a girl bang an egg against a wall in a stocking, and then look awfully surprised because she had smashed it?"

"I don't understand the joke."

"She had been told she couldn't break an egg in an empty stocking. Then she was made to look in, and there was the broken egg for her pains. I don't know what made me tell you that story."

"It's a very good story. I'll get Miss Abbott to do it to-night. She believes everything."

"And everybody? Then she's a happy woman."

"I wish you'd believe everybody."

"So I do;—nearly everybody. There are some inveterate liars whom nobody can believe."

"I hope I am not regarded as one."

"You? certainly not. If anybody were to speak of you as such behind your back no one would take your part more loyally than I. But nobody would."

"That's something, at any rate. Then you do believe that I love you?"

"I believe that you think so."

"And that I don't know my own heart?"

"That's very common, Mr. Anderson. I wasn't quite sure of my own heart twelve months ago, but I know it now." He felt that his hopes ran very low when this was said. She had never before spoken to him of his rival, nor had he to her. He knew, or fancied that he knew, that "her heart had been touched," as he had said to Arbuthnot. But the "touch" must have been very deep if she felt herself constrained to speak to him on the subject. It had been his desire to pass over Mr. Annesley, and never to hear the name mentioned between them. "You were speaking of your own heart."

"Well I was, no doubt. It is a silly thing to talk of, I dare say."

"I'm going to tell you of my heart, and I hope you won't think it silly. I do so because I believe you to be a gentleman, and a man of honor." He blushed at the words and the tone in which they were spoken, but his heart fell still lower. "Mr. Anderson, I am engaged." Here she paused a moment, but he had nothing to say. "I am engaged to marry a gentleman whom I love with all my heart, and all my strength, and all my body. I love him so that nothing can ever separate me from him, or, at least, from the thoughts of him. As regards all the interests of life, I feel as though I were already his wife. If I ever marry any man I swear to you that it will be him." Then Mr. Anderson felt that all hope had utterly departed from him. She had said that she believed him to be a man of truth. He certainly believed her to be a true-speaking woman. He asked himself, and he found it to be quite impossible to doubt her word on this subject. "Now I will go on and tell you my troubles. My mother disapproves of the man. Sir Magnus has taken upon himself to disapprove, and Lady Mountjoy disapproves especially. I don't care two straws about Sir Magnus and Lady Mountjoy. As to Lady Mountjoy, it is simply an impertinence on her part, interfering with me." There was something in her face as she said this which made Mr. Anderson feel that if he could only succeed in having her and the pair of ponies he would be a prouder man than the ambassador at Paris. But he knew that it was hopeless. "As to my mother, that is indeed a sorrow. She has been to me the dearest mother, putting her only hopes of happiness in me. No mother was ever more devoted to a child, and of all children I should be the most ungrateful were I to turn against her. But from my early years she has wished me to marry a man whom I could not bring myself to love. You have heard of Captain Scarborough?"

"The man who disappeared?"

"He was and is my first cousin."

"He is in some way connected with Sir Magnus."

"Through mamma. Mamma is aunt to Captain Scarborough, and she married the brother of Sir Magnus. Well, he has disappeared and been disinherited. I cannot explain all about it, for I don't understand it; but he has come to great trouble. It was not on that account that I would not marry him. It was partly because I did not like him, and partly because of Harry Annesley. I will tell you everything because I want you to know my story. But my mother has disliked Mr. Annesley, because she has thought that he has interfered with my cousin."

"I understand all that."

"And she has been taught to think that Mr. Annesley has behaved very badly. I cannot quite explain it, because there is a brother of Captain Scarborough who has interfered. I never loved Captain Scarborough, but that man I hate. He has spread those stories. Captain Scarborough has disappeared, but before he went he thought it well to revenge himself on Mr. Annesley. He attacked him in the street late at night, and endeavored to beat him."

"But why?"

"Why indeed. That such a trumpery cause as a girl's love should operate with such a man!"

"I can understand it; oh yes,—I can understand it."

"I believe he was tipsy, and he had been gambling, and had lost all his money—more than all his money. He was a ruined man, and reckless and wretched. I can forgive him, and so does Harry. But in the struggle Harry got the best of it, and left him there in the street. No weapons had been used, except that Captain Scarborough had a stick. There was no reason to suppose him hurt, nor was he much hurt. He had behaved very badly, and Harry left him. Had he gone for a policeman he could only have given him in charge. The man was not hurt, and seems to have walked away."

"The papers were full of it."

"Yes, the papers were full of it, because he was missing. I don't know yet what became of him, but I have my suspicions."

"They say that he has been seen at Monaco."

"Very likely. But I have nothing to do with that. Though he was my cousin, I am touched nearer in another place. Young Mr. Scarborough, who, I suspect, knows all about his brother, took upon himself to cross-question Mr. Annesley. Mr. Annesley did not care to tell anything of that struggle in the streets, and denied that he had seen him. In truth, he did not want to have my name mentioned. My belief is that Augustus Scarborough knew exactly what had taken place when he asked the question. It was he who really was false. But he is now the heir to Tretton and a great man in his way, and in order to injure Harry Annesley he has spread abroad the story which they all tell here."

"But why?"

"He does;—that is all I know. But I will not be a hypocrite. He chose to wish that I should not marry Harry Annesley. I cannot tell you farther than that. But he has persuaded mamma, and has told every one. He shall never persuade me."

"Everybody seems to believe him," said Mr. Anderson, not as intending to say that he believed him now, but that he had done so.

"Of course they do. He has simply ruined Harry. He too has been disinherited now. I don't know how they do these things, but it has been done. His uncle has been turned against him, and his whole income has been taken from him. But they will never persuade me. Nor, if they did, would I be untrue to him. It is a grand thing for a girl to have a perfect faith in the man she has to marry, as I have—as I have. I know my man, and will as soon disbelieve in Heaven as in him. But were he what they say he is, he would still have to become my husband. I should be broken-hearted, but I should still be true. Thank God, though,—thank God,—he has done nothing and will do nothing to make me ashamed of him. Now you know my story."

"Yes; now I know it." The tears came very near the poor man's eyes as he answered.

"And what will you do for me?"

"What shall I do?"

"Yes; what will you do? I have told you all my story, believing you to be a fine-tempered gentleman. You have entertained a fancy which has been encouraged by Sir Magnus. Will you promise me not to speak to me of it again? Will you relieve me of so much of my trouble? Will you;—will you?" Then, when he turned away, she followed him, and put both her hands upon his arm. "Will you do that little thing for me?"

"A little thing!"

"Is it not a little thing,—when I am so bound to that other man that nothing can move me? Whether it be little or whether it be much, will you not do it?" She still held him by the arm, but his face was turned from her so that she could not see it. The tears, absolute tears, were running down his cheeks. What did it behoove him as a man to do? Was he to believe her vows now and grant her request, and was she then to give herself to some third person and forget Harry Annesley altogether? How would it be with him then? A faint heart never won a fair lady. All is fair in love and war. You cannot catch cherries by holding your mouth open. A great amount of wisdom such as this came to him at the spur of the moment. But there was her hand upon his arm, and he could not elude her request. "Will you not do it for me?" she asked again.

"I will," he said, still keeping his face turned away.

"I knew it;—I knew you would. You are high-minded and honest, and cannot be cruel to a poor girl. And if in time to come, when I am Harry Annesley's wife, we shall chance to meet each other,—as we will,—he shall thank you."

"I shall not want that. What will his thanks do for me? You do not think that I shall be silent to oblige him?" Then he walked forth from out of the garden, and she had never seen his tears. But she knew well that he was weeping, and she sympathized with him.